Jimmy Starlight and the Galactic Crystal

Book 1: Travel to Planet Atlantis.

A. W. van Rest

For Desiree

A big thanks to Gail Lord for editing the manuscript, to Lane Stone, Tom
Mangelsdorf, and Conchita Espino for reviewing it and making numerous suggestions
for improving its structure and flow, and to Nasim Maclay for giving it a first read.
And a special thanks to my wife Soraya for being fully supportive of my writing and
serving as my in-depth sounding board for the story line.

Table of Contents.

Prologue

Planet Atlantis' Sacred Book of History prophesizes a boy of Atlantean and Earthen descent will lead Atlanteans to victory over their archenemy, the VARS, in the first quarter of the 21st century. It also predicts he will recover a Galactic Crystal lost for thousands of years and use it to overcome this enemy, and his victory will transform Planet Earth and bring it universal peace and harmony. After this transformation, the boy will lead the people from Atlantis and Earth jointly into the new frontier in the far reaches of the universe.

Captain Antonius Starlight slowly paced back and forth in front of his communications console, looking at several of the two dozen small screens flickering live views of various places on Earth. He was worried, but he tried not to show it.

"Please bring up and steady Screen Seven," he asked one of the console operators, whose faces showed increasing concern.

"Okay, Captain," the operator responded, reconfiguring the communications system so it projected the image on Screen Seven as a large hologram floating above the communications console. This gave Captain Starlight a better view of Apollo Square, the main square in downtown Atlantis, the Captain's home town.

Atlantis was a city of over half a million people, sprawled out over a large island in the warm waters of the Atlantic Ocean's equatorial region on Earth, about 240,000 miles from where Captain Starlight was at the time—in the Command Post of Moon Base Osiris, located in what astronomers now refer to as the Sinus Medii region of the Moon. As part of their exploration of the universe, the Atlanteans had established two space ports in outer space—Moon Base Osiris and Star Base Orion on Mars.

Normally, Captain Starlight, the Commander of the Moon Base, thoroughly enjoyed looking at a live picture of Apollo Square; he loved seeing the daily "hustle and bustle" of all the people, vehicles, and goings-on within its confines. It reminded him of the happy times when, as a student at the Aquarius Academy, a preparatory school for Atlantis' Technical Institute, he passed by this square with its beautiful fountains twice a day during the six years he attended the

Academy. This day, however, the sight of Apollo Square made him sad. Since his beloved Atlantis had become engaged in a do-or-die struggle for its very existence with the VARS—a group of ruthless Space Invaders from across the Milky Way Galaxy—the square was empty and forlorn. The Captain worried about the wellbeing of his parents and younger siblings living in Atlantis. Everyone else in his Command Post worried equally about family and friends and stayed glued to the console screens showing various locations in the City where their loved ones had come under siege. They also agonized about the fate of Atlantis for another reason: if the aliens defeated the City, they would surely attack their Moon Base next.

"They've started firing lasers again, Captain," Lieutenant Strongfield, his second in command, reported. Standing next to him, her voice sounded somber as she pointed to one of the screens where they could see the flashes from the powerful laser beams fired at Atlantis by three alien spaceships.

"Yes, but it looks like the shield will hold its own," Captain Starlight noted, referring to the energy shield the Atlanteans had erected over Atlantis to protect themselves from the aliens. The shield deflected the lasers fired at the City into the surrounding waters of the Atlantic Ocean and instantly vaporized all other incoming projectiles sent to penetrate and destroy it.

"Let's hope it will continue to do so," the Lieutenant said, her voice breaking.

"I feel totally confident it will continue to hold and the City will be safe," Captain Starlight said forcefully to mitigate the concerns of his countrymen.

What he did not see on his screens, however, was the huge tsunami forming in the mid-Atlantic, as a result of the constant barrage of deflected Varsian laser beams hitting Mother Earth; and this tsunami was about to push a hundred-foot wall of water onto the shores of the unsuspecting City of Atlantis.

Chapter 2: VARS on Planet Earth

Looking for a new place to nest, the VARS discovered Earth a few months before their devastating attack on Atlantis—and they have lived amongst the human race ever since. They hailed from Varsius, a planet located on the far side of the Milky Way Galaxy. Since their early days on Earth, the VARS constantly meddled in its world affairs; unfortunately, true to their war mongering nature, these angry, coldhearted beings encouraged discord and strife, and focused their efforts on instilling hatred, distrust, and selfishness in the people they came in contact with.

For decades, prior to coming to Earth, the VARS fought amongst themselves—just like humans do all over the world. This resulted in the destruction of large parts of Varsius due to biological, radioactive and other environmental contamination. Their use of weapons of mass destruction to settle internal disputes left in its wake smoking, unlivable rubble. As living conditions on Varsius deteriorated, the VARS faced the distinct possibility of having to migrate to another planet, soon. In preparation for this, they searched their own star system for planets with atmospheres and climates similar to those of Varsius, but could not find any. The VARS then started to explore the Milky Way Galaxy's spiral arms, looking for habitable zones where planets akin to Varsius might reside.

One day, as part of this search, they decided to send Starship Trastic, their most advanced spaceship, capable of traveling at the speed of light, on an exploratory mission to the Orion spiral arm of their galaxy. Like other Varsian spaceships, Trastic, operated by a crew of three hundred under the command of a warlord, was immense—the size of three football fields. Built to fight Varsian enemies, rather than peacefully explore the universe, this Starship carried lethal laser weaponry powerful enough to destroy a whole city in a few seconds.

"Set course for Alpha section in Ra quadrant," barked Crokh, the commander of Trastic, as the ship departed the military base near Qyal, the capital city of Varsius.

"Yes, Commander," the ship's pilot replied, loud but respectful. "Setting course for Alpha section, Ra quadrant."

Shortly after the pilot verbally entered the coordinates for this section into the flight computer, Trastic sped towards its destination—an empty, remote area in space, about five million miles from Planet Varsius—and arrived there in a matter of seconds. The commander of Trastic headed to this area so he could open a vortex. Opening such a whirling tunnel in outer space would allow travel across the galaxy to their destination in seconds, instead of the years or even centuries it would take to go there at the speed of light, without passing through such a tunnel.

In the past, vortexes had collapsed on Varsius, and the resulting shockwave caused extensive collateral damage and severely injured many Varsian civilians. Since that time, all ship commanders received instructions to open these space tunnels only in outer space, preferably in Alpha Section, which all but eliminated the potential for collateral damage.

"Enable vortex to the Braq System," Crokh barked, this time at his Science Officer.

"Yes, Commander," the Science Officer responded, also loud and respectful.

The Braq System the Commander referred to was the Varsian name for the Orion Spiral Arm of the Milky Way Galaxy, which contains the solar system that Earth orbits in. Using the quantum space processor onboard Trastic, it took

6

the Science Officer only seconds to create the vortex, starting at the exact location of the spacecraft in Alpha section and connecting to the Orion Spiral Arm.

"Vortex enabled," the Science Officer noted.

"Is it stable enough for us to pass through?" Crokh asked brusquely, wanting some assurance, as they whizzed through it, the vortex would not collapse, trapping them for the rest of their lives.

"Our quantum processor indicates stability, Commander," the Science Officer replied.

"Prepare to enter vortex," Crokh shouted over the intercom system. This command gave heads-up to crewmembers to immediately secure all loose materials and strap themselves in their seats to keep from getting hurt by the sudden weightlessness aboard the spaceship upon entering the space tunnel.

Five minutes later, he barked at the pilot again, "Engage all magnetic motor systems and transfer-speed ahead."

As soon as the pilot implemented the order, the ship zoomed through the vortex at instantaneous transfer-speed; arriving seconds later in the Orion Arm—exactly where was not immediately clear.

"Navigator, identify the nearest star," Crokh ordered, as the ship stabilized. "I want to know where we are."

"Yes, Commander," the navigator replied loudly.

Using the ship's telescopes, it didn't take him long to identify the nearest star as Earth's Sun and conclude the ship had arrived exactly 500,000 miles from Planet Neptune. For the next few days, the crew of Trastic explored Neptune and the other outer planets and their moons, finding none of them capable of supporting their life form; then they chanced upon Planet Earth.

Over thousands of years, the VARS had evolved into human-like beings—on average six feet tall with light-brownish, scaly skin over most of their body. They were bipedal; had a brain, eyes, ears, lungs, and a nose; and, like humans, needed to breathe oxygen to keep all those organs functioning. After penetrating Earth's atmosphere, Trastic's crew took air samples and outside temperature readings and quickly determined the planet, with its oxygen-rich atmosphere and benign climate, suitable to support their life form.

"Bring the ship close to the surface and scour the land," Crokh snapped at the pilot, wanting to find a safe landing spot.

"Yes, Commander," the pilot responded, letting the huge ship glide silently across Earth's seas, plains, and mountain ranges.

Earth really appealed to Crokh as a potential new home for the VARS, because of its pristine environment and unpolluted air, which reminded him of his own planet years ago. Having found a spot to his liking, Crokh barked more orders at his crew to start landing procedures and maintain a watchful eye on their surroundings—with laser weapons ready to fire at anything that moved. He soon found out, however, in the area where they landed, a large island in the middle of the Pacific Ocean, their powerful weapons would not be needed.

"Prepare for exploration," Crokh ordered after the ship touched down in the island's coastal area.

A short time later, a dozen or so crewmembers, armed with deadly ray guns, walked down a small ramp extending from the side of the ship. They planned to walk to a nearby small fishing village to take a look at the human beings living there. As the last member of this scouting party came

8

down the ramp, the leader of the group hastily dispatched a message to the spaceship.

"Commander, we have visitors."

The island the VARS had landed on, sparsely populated, with no real civilization, had formed from ancient lava spills of a now inactive inland volcano. Its rocky, volcanic bottom had kept the islanders from developing agricultural lands and engaging in any meaningful animal husbandry. They directed their efforts mainly to building, using, and maintaining their fishing fleets. The majority of the island's people lived in small villages along the coast— simple hardworking fishermen using small sail-boats and rowing vessels to eke out a living from the sea. Seeing the large Varsian spacecraft descend from the skies made the islanders think the gods had come to earth; and, after the spaceship landed, they quickly ran up to pay their respects.

"Welcome, O'Lords, to our humble village," the village leader proclaimed, dropping to his knees in front of the spaceship, at the head of a large group of villagers who did the same.

After uttering those words, he reverently bent over until his forehead touched the ground before him, with all the other villagers following suit.

Crokh stood in the entrance to his spacecraft, not understanding a word of what the village leader had said. Surprised at seeing human beings looking very much like himself, he told his second in command standing beside him, "Give them food and wine, and for *now*, treat them well."

Even though he did not understand their verbal communication, he completely understood their venerating body language and their amazement at having seen the huge spacecraft descend silently from the air and land on their island. He knew, right then, they felt like the chosen people to whom the gods had just revealed themselves.

After receiving food and wine, the villagers got up off their knees and excitedly touched the gods, hoping their awesome power would somehow rub off on them. "Thank you, Lords," the village leader said with heartfelt deference after accepting their treats. "Thank you for coming to our island and feeding us; we feel honored to have you visit us."

Again, not understanding the man's words, Crokh just growled in Varsian, "Okay, okay, have some more food." Then, to his second in command, "Take a dozen men and lead these people back to their village. And find out what kind of weapons they have."

The VARS soon realized technological and scientific progress, and the development of sophisticated weaponry that comes with such progress, had largely bypassed this island. These peaceful, island people had no need for weaponry; a simple club and hammer had always sufficed. They had never seen energy-powered devices—not until the VARS landed on their island. Judging it a safe place to undertake further exploration, the VARS decided to build their first Earth Base on the island. After they built it, many of them migrated from Varsius to Earth, bringing with them their hoard of senseless values.

This marked the start of their brutal campaign to colonize our Planet.

Not too long ago, one mid-afternoon in late fall, two young watermen, the brothers Mike and Dave, sat in their small motorboat dutifully fishing the Chesapeake Bay for striped bass, locally known as rockfish. They took fishing seriously because their livelihood depended on it. The air over the Bay was clear and crisp and, at 50 degrees, cooler than the water temperature. The two brothers didn't mind the cool weather, because they were dressed warmly in comfortable, insulated coveralls, and loved being outside on the water in the clean, fresh air. And just like all the other locals living along the Maryland and Virginia shores of this 200 mile estuary, they considered the Chesapeake Bay the most beautiful place in the world.

"We're *sooo* lucky to make a living from what we like to do best—fishing on this gorgeous Bay," the younger brother, Dave, said, standing up in the boat with his arms held out wide, looking up at the clear blue skies. He loved the Chesapeake because of the stunning sunrises and sunsets that color the skies over the Bay at day's beginning and day's end, and for the incredibly beautiful vistas afforded by its tranquil back bays and marshes—home to herons, ospreys, bald eagles, and many other feathered friends.

"Couldn't agree more," Mike said, "much better than fishing those cold, cold waters off the coast of Alaska, like we used to. But I sure hope the stripers have made their way up from the ocean and start biting pretty soon."

"Yeah, so do I," Dave said, sitting back down in his bench chair. "They should have had plenty of time to finish their journey by now."

He was referring to the rockfish's travel up and down the Chesapeake Bay. During the winter months, they patrol the waters off the Atlantic coasts of Virginia and North Carolina; but in the spring, most of them enter the Chesapeake and travel 200 miles to the Bay's northern tip to ready themselves for their spawning runs up the Susquehanna River. After spawning in the upper reaches of the river, adult rockfish swim downstream and, having navigated their way to the ocean, join the summer migration going north along the New England coast. In the fall, they again return in large numbers to the Chesapeake Bay, when the ocean's water temperature drops below that of the Bay.

Since early morning, the brothers had bait-fished locally in their favorite spots but had very little to show for it. Wanting some more action, they decided to try their luck at trolling for rockfish with live bait. They started their run in the eastern part of the Bay, in the vicinity of the historic little town of St. Michaels, and within an hour or so reached the wide-open waters of the Chesapeake. About a mile and a half away from Maryland's Eastern Shore, a thirty-six foot Endeavour sailboat, making its way from St. Michaels, was on course to cross right in front of them, with its mainsail full and its colorful spinnaker rounded in front. Slowing their boat down to allow the Endeavour the right-of-way, they watched it pass by and admired the ship's long, sleek lines. The boy at the wheel, wearing an orange lifejacket, waved at them while the man and woman sitting upwind on one of the cockpit benches kept a close eye on things. Shortly after that, the brothers' uneventful day dramatically changed.

Having waved back to the boy, Dave all of a sudden jumped up, rocking the small boat from side to side. Pointing south, he grabbed his binoculars and scrutinized a flock of birds swirling around in circles while hovering close to the water, about a quarter of a mile from their craft. Through his binoculars, he could see large herring gulls frequently swoop down to the water and pick off small fish from the surface, after which they would flutter their wings feverishly as they scrambled back up in the air.

"Blitzers," he yelled out. "Hundreds of 'em."

He referred to blitzing rockfish, herding a large school of small fish to the surface so they could munch on them for dinner—much to the delight of the gulls, who also loved to munch on them.

"Quick, let me look," his older brother demanded, excited about the prospect of filling up their coolers.

Having seen the diving birds and the frenzied little fish flickering in the waters beneath them, he was about to put his binoculars down when he noticed in the distance a large black speedboat coming from the direction of the Eastern Shore, heading straight for the area where the birds swirled.

"Oops, we may have company," he said, laying the binoculars down on the nearest bench and grabbing the wheel. "Why don't you get the fishing poles with the top-water plugs ready," he suggested to his brother, as he pushed the accelerator handle forward and aimed the boat at the blitzers—just knowing their luck had turned.

It didn't take but a few minutes for them to reach the area where they intended to cast their lures among the breaking fish. Having killed the boat's engine so as not to scare away the big rockfish, they had just positioned themselves to start casting when the black speedboat ran at full speed through their casting area.

"What in the world!" Dave said angrily, when the black boat's wake rocked their fishing boat so fiercely, he had to grab the wheel to keep his balance. "What's he trying to do to us?"

"He'll chase away our fish!" Mike shouted, also furious. "I can't believe he would do this!"

On the Chesapeake, as in all other bodies of water, fishermen consider it very bad boating etiquette to run your motorboat through waters where anglers have cast their lines or are about to do so. The two brothers, livid over what had just happened, stared in disbelief at the black boat that kept right on going—right in the direction of the Endeavour. Then, they got the shock of their lives. It ran smack-dab into the sailboat, hitting it mid-ship, setting off a huge explosion that blew both boats out of the water in ten thousand pieces.

"Oh my," was all Dave could say, bewildered by what he had witnessed.

"Did you see that guy jump from the black boat just before it hit?" Mike asked his brother, also having a hard time fully grasping what just happened, and visibly shaken.

"Yes, I did," he answered, "and I can see him swimming around over there."

They both watched as the man was hoisted out of the water by another man in a second black boat that arrived out of nowhere shortly after the explosion reverberated through the air. After taking the man onboard, the second boat quickly sped off, with a huge plume of water shooting upward from beneath its stern.

Both brothers were even harder pressed to believe what they saw next. Suddenly, an aircraft appeared on the scene, hovering just above the floating debris in the water. It looked like a helicopter, except it didn't have the traditional rotating blades to keep it in the air; nor a stabilizing rotor on its tail section. All of a sudden, two persons—with what looked like jetpacks on their backs—jetted out of the top of the craft and started to glide horizontally over the water. Within seconds, they reached down and picked up two limp

14

bodies from the water and took them inside the craft. One person quickly returned and picked up a third limp body, which they also brought inside. Seconds later, the aircraft instantly disappeared from view.

"I can't believe what just happened over there," Mike said to his brother, taking off his fishing cap. He scratched his head and slumped down in his captain's chair, not knowing what to think about the scene he had just witnessed.

"Me neither," Dave agreed, just as stunned as his brother. "What was that, a super stealth plane or something?"

"Yeah, probably one of those top-secret jobbies just developed by the military; I don't know what else it could be, do you?"

"No idea," Dave said, also slumping down in the boat's rear bench seat. "But I think you're right—about it being top secret and all—'cause I've never seen one like it before."

When the Coast Guard arrived a short while later to investigate the explosion, heard over a large area of the Bay, they found the two men still sitting slumped down in their boat—still thunderstruck by what happened. After the brothers disclosed they had seen people with jetpacks on their backs take the bodies of the sailboat's three occupants onboard a strange-looking aircraft that shortly thereafter disappeared in thin air, the investigators quickly dismissed what they had to say. The Coast Guard's official report on the investigation, made public a few days afterwards, mentioned a bagful of empty beer cans found in the fishing boat's forward storage compartment, insinuating that when the accident occurred, the two brothers were most likely impaired from a combination of drugs and too much alcohol. And it went on to say, what exactly happened that day to the people onboard the Endeavour remains a mystery and continues to be under investigation.

After the pilots of the mysterious plane pulled the three occupants of the Endeavour out of the Chesapeake Bay, they delivered their lifeless bodies within five minutes to a hospital about sixty miles or so from the scene of the attempted assassination. When they were leaving the hospital's emergency room, the two pilots exchanged a few words while making their way back to the plane.

"My God, I certainly didn't expect this to happen to the boy," one of them remarked. "I hope Wander World can save him."

"Yes, I hope so, too," the other said. "I'm glad we got him and his parents to the hospital quickly."

"I wish they had called for assistance sooner. We might have kept this from happening to our future Leader."

"You're right."

"I'm sure they were VARS—those men in the speedboats."

"Yes, without a doubt."

The next day, the hospital's director and an attending physician discussed the plight of the boy and his parents in the director's office.

"Even though he's still in a coma, the boy seems to be responding to treatment in Wander World," the physician said. "Thank goodness he wore a lifejacket."

"What about his parents?" the director asked.

"They're also in a coma, barely alive, and they're not doing so well. As you probably know, they had no lifejackets on."

"What are their chances of making it through?"

"I don't want to venture any guesses at this time, but Wander World is their only chance—no matter how slim."

"Were you able to scan their memories?"

"No, just the boy's; using his scan we traced their whereabouts from the moment they left their cabin on the South River early in the day to the time of the explosion. We learned they were blindsided by a sneak attack; didn't see it coming."

"Let's hope for the best. Please keep me advised of their conditions."

"I'll let you know the minute I know more."

Just as the physician got ready to excuse himself, the director had another question for him. "By the way, since the boy seems to be responding to your treatment, do you see any medical reasons why we shouldn't utilize his recovery time to upload into his memory some of the information he'll need to function as our next Leader?"

The physician replied without hesitation, "Medically, I can't think of any reason not to; but as you know, we normally discuss any uploading procedure with the subject before initiation."

"Yes, that's what we normally do; but there is nothing normal about this situation. In this case, if we want to keep him alive and get him ready to fulfill the Prophecy, we don't have the luxury of following our normal procedures. The VARS know who he is and where he lives; and as we just learned, they'll do anything to keep him from realizing his destiny."

"I couldn't agree with you more; these are desperate times, requiring desperate measures. I suspect you've already given this quite a bid of thought; just let me know what sort of information upload you have in mind, and I'll see what I can do to get it done in a timely manner."

"Thanks, I greatly appreciate your willingness to cooperate," the director said. "And, yes, I spent most of last night thinking about our young protégé and what it's going to take for him to be strong and motivated enough to become the next Leader of our people; and how to achieve this without the assistance of his parents, who may not survive their ordeal."

"So, what did you come up with?"

"Well, first, he needs to understand the special relationship that exists between Planet Atlantis and Planet Earth; then he needs to come to grips with our ongoing struggle with the VARS and prepare himself to put an end to this mess. I think it's best to start him on his way by uploading into his memory some pertinent information about the Peacemaker and the ancient City of Atlantis, and the travel of our forefathers to the New Planet after the destruction of their City—do you agree?"

"Yes, that makes sense. Do you have anyone who can collect the info for us?"

"I'll do it myself; as a matter of fact, I've already put together a short write-up on the Peacemaker and our forefathers' use of their energy crystals. If you have the time, I can share it with you right now."

"Okay, that would be great; I do have a little time before my next hospital rounds."

The director, sitting behind his desk, took his MedPro out of his pocket and turned it on by running his finger diagonally across its screen. This small device not only served as his cell phone, but also as his medical analyzer and miniature word processor. After he laid it on his desk, he touched the screen again, causing it to be projected in the air as a small hologram. While it hovered just above his MedPro, he put both hands on the hologram's surface area and enlarged its size by spreading his fingers and moving his hands further apart. He then tapped the screen twice, and a laptop-size laser keyboard projected from the device onto his desk. Using the keyboard, he retrieved the document containing his write-up from storage on his processor's hard drive, and displayed it in the hologram above his desk.

"Here you have it," the director said. "Can you read the first page from where you're sitting? Is the character size large enough?"

Because the MedPro projected the hologram's text in a manner that allowed people a direct view of it from anywhere in the room, the physician, sitting directly across from the director, could look at the document straight-on, just like the director did.

"Yes, I have no problem seeing it," the physician responded as he leaned back in his chair and started to read the text the director slowly scrolled through.

***

The physician read that *Five thousand years ago an ancient metropolis by the name of Atlantis existed on Planet Earth. It stretched out over a large tropical island in the Atlantic Ocean—an island covered with rain forests outlining mountains that rose high up in the air like a jagged eyebrow. A population of almost a million people adorned their city with elegant fountains, ornate buildings, and beautiful parks. In its day, the City of Atlantis was the most powerful city in the world. It obtained much of its wealth from trade and commerce with the rest of the ancient world, but the City's real strength derived from the Atlanteans' use of their natural resources, especially their energy crystals. Mined from the island's rare quartz deposits, located in hot caves deep underground, these crystals, which were only deployed domestically, could not be found anywhere else on Earth. When exposed to sunlight, these specially cut gems amplified and completely absorbed the sun's energy, and then stored it in their core for future use. The density of this stored energy in individual crystals could reach extremely high levels; and when properly aligned with each other, their combined energy density could reach astronomically high levels—high enough to enable the Atlanteans to suspend gravity in the crystals' immediate vicinity and, more importantly, access the elemental forces of the universe's energy field. This ability gave them unlimited energy to power their homes, cars, industries, ships, and spacecraft. And almost miraculously, the energy from these crystals could also be used to treat health problems, rejuvenate their bodies, and speed up mind development—all without any adverse side effects.*

Most of their crystals, slightly elongated in shape, could easily fit in the palm of your hand, except for one extremely brilliant crystal with the shape and size of a basketball. Nobody really knew for sure where this large crystal actually came from; but according to Atlantean legend, it was one of the Galactic Crystals put on Earth by the Celestial Forces of the universe. These Beings, legend had it, delivered their crystals to various planets within our galaxy to keep them from being destroyed by malevolent forces in the universe. The Atlanteans' Galactic Crystal provided more power than all of their other crystals combined, and by studying the structure of this crystal, they had discovered the Sacred Geometry they used to cut their smaller crystals. The power of this Galactic Crystal, which the Atlanteans called the Peacemaker, was so awesome, that in order to ensure its peaceful utilization, only the Supreme Council of Atlantis—the City's highest governing body— could authorize its use. They had mandated its installation atop a tower on a small plateau on the highest mountain on the island, from where it could beam its energy waves, day and night, across the whole city and its surrounding areas, including its harbor, coastal waters, and air space. A small group of Atlanteans who reported directly to the Council operated and safeguarded the Peacemaker; and it could only be reached by Atlantis' antigravity aircraft landing vertically on the plateau's tiny airstrip. While mainly used for peaceful purposes, the crystals could also serve as lethal weapons and instruments of war; but Atlantis, a peaceful nation, had seldom used them for this purpose. And its most powerful weapon, the Peacemaker, which could emit a particle beam instantly vaporizing any object, even at very large distances, had never been used in the history of the City to settle a conflict. Actually, few people outside of Atlantis even knew it existed. In times of conflict, the crystals could quickly power up a defensive energy shield, erected over the city as a

21

*safeguard from any type of enemy attack. Such a shield,
consisting of invisible energy waves forming an energy
umbrella over the city, could destroy or deflect anything
coming in contact with it. Needless to say, these crystals
served as mighty deterrents to anyone on Earth
contemplating aggression towards Atlantis; but as it turned
out, they did not deter the VARS.*

In his write-up, the director also explained why the
Atlanteans established a small base on the Moon, which they
called Moon Base Osiris.

They established this base, he wrote, *a few years after
an exploratory mission to the Moon revealed the existence of
large underground quartz deposits. After the Atlanteans
discovered they could utilize these deposits to fabricate
crystals just like the ones in Atlantis, they set up their mining
and manufacturing facilities on the Moon. While the
Atlanteans used many of these crystals to provide energy for
their buildings and equipment on the Moon Base, they
shipped the majority of them to Atlantis. Over half of the
hundred or so Atlanteans living on the base worked in the
quartz mine; most of the others serviced the space-shuttle to
Earth and maintained its landing and takeoff facilities on the
Moon. Since the Moon has no protective and breathable
atmosphere, and damaging meteors pelt it on a daily basis, a
large dome made of glass stronger than steel covered the
whole base; and sections of the dome could open and close
to accommodate weekly shuttle landings and take-offs. Work
on the Moon was demanding, and all the Atlanteans working
there had gone through a rigorous qualifying process that
evaluated their physical and technical skills—and all had
undergone astronaut training.*

The last thing the director talked about in his document pertained to the Atlantean base on Mars.

A year after they completed Moon Base Osiris, he wrote, *the Atlanteans sent several probes to this planet; and after analyzing the data these probes sent back to Earth, they decided to build another base there. Their scientists concluded that, even though Mars' environment was not very hospitable to earthlings and, like the Moon, was lacking an atmosphere, the existence of consumable water in the surface soil of the planet made it a potential steppingstone for further exploration of their solar system. They also believed by using their crystals, Atlantis would someday be able to construct an artificial atmosphere on Mars—allowing for the growth of the same lush vegetation as found on Earth. A few years later, the Atlanteans built, at their Space Travel Complex in Atlantis, three large spaceships and take-off and landing facilities for travel to Mars. That same year, their first expedition to the Red Planet was launched; and not long thereafter, full-scale operations commenced on the construction of Marsian Star Base Orion—and the Atlantean colonization of Mars was underway. At the same time, the take-off and landing facilities at Moon Base Osiris were upgraded to accommodate travel of these large spaceships between Mars and the Moon.*

***

It came as no surprise to the physician that the ancient-Atlanteans' usage of their energy crystals pretty much described their modern-day usage too.

"This is all very useful information," he told the director when he finished reading the document. "After I impart this information to the boy's memory later today, he will be the wiser for it when serving as our next Leader. I can only hope he will locate our lost Peacemaker someday soon and put it to good use."

"I appreciate you saying that," the director said. "I'll email additional info in a Wander World virtual-reality video for you to upload early tomorrow morning, so the boy can experience firsthand some of the events that led up to the destruction of the City of Atlantis and the establishment of a new Atlantean civilization on our Planet. This will allow him to understand more clearly the origins of our feud with the VARS and how they caused the demise of Atlantis on Earth."

"Great, I'll be looking for it."

"Okay, and thanks again for your cooperation."

"You're welcome," the physician said before walking out of the director's office.

Chapter 5: The New Planet

Early the next morning the physician sat down at his desk in his hospital office, feeling very contented with himself. The evening before, using his quantum computer, he had successfully uploaded the director's short write-up into the young boy's memory; and he looked forward to providing the youngster with additional information to help him carry out the Prophecy and lead the Atlanteans to victory over the VARS. Having turned on his MedPro to check his email messages, he quickly located the one sent by the director. In that email, the director mentioned he included as an attachment the Wander World virtual-reality video he talked about the day before, and explained how it detailed several events in the life of Antonius Starlight. A one-time captain and astronaut in the City of Atlantis' military, Starlight became the first Leader of Planet Atlantis. He also mentioned, the narrated video's content was verbatim from information in the Atlantean Book of History, and the director suggested the physician take a look at the video to see if he might want to add or change anything before uploading it into the young boy's memory.

The physician did not hesitate to follow the director's advice, for he always enjoyed watching Wander World videos, especially those based on the Book of History—an indisputable source containing all of Atlantis' history dating back to the City's very beginnings. The Atlanteans had retrieved the historical information in this Book from the universe's energy field, where the collective memory of everything that had happened in Atlantis—and the rest of the cosmos—is stored. The physician also had another reason for watching the video from beginning to end. Whenever asked to upload information into someone's memory, he always made it a point, before doing so, to thoroughly acquaint himself with all of the selected materials; in this case, he wanted to make sure he would not cause any stress or emotional issues for the boy.

Having walked over to his medical cabinet, he retrieved a small virtual-reality visor from one of the shelves. This device, needed to watch Wander World videos, looked exactly like an oversized pair of sun glasses with very thick temples on the side. It was a very sophisticated total-immersion video player, driven by a miniature quantum computer built into a temple tip. It displayed videos on two built-in miniature 3-D screens—one in front of each eye— and with the help of a series of laminated sensors covering the visor's temples, its quantum computer could signal the brain and read its waves. This ability allowed a person watching a Wander World virtual-reality video to not only hear and see its content, but to also experience the thoughts, emotions, feelings, and all other sensory perceptions of the video's characters.

Like the director the day before, the physician used his MedPro to project a laser keyboard onto his desk. He first used his keyboard to remotely connect the visor to his MedPro's processor, and subsequently to open the email's attachment and download the Wander World video into the hard drive of his visor's quantum computer. After sitting back down in his desk chair and slipping the visor on, he started the video by touching a key on his laser keyboard. He then tilted his chair back, ready to experience it.

***

The first things the physician saw on his visor's 3-D screens were the title of the Wander World virtual reality video he was watching and the name of its first part.

Planet Atlantis—A New Beginning

Part One: Discovery of the New Planet.

He then proceeded to experience the video while listening attentively to the pleasant voices narrating it and bringing to life its story about the fate of Atlantis—a tale, at times heartbreaking, but altogether quite inspirational— which sent him some five thousand years back in time.

Many years ago, the physician heard the narrator say, *prior to having joined the Atlantean military, Antonius Starlight lived with his parents and younger siblings, Marcius and Clarissa, in a villa on the north coast of Atlantis. At the time, his father, James Starlight, was the Leader of the Atlantean Supreme Council, an important position in this powerful city.*

"Son, are you ready to go?" James asked one morning, worried his son would be late for school. "It's almost eight."

"Yes, Dad, I'll just be another minute," Antonius responded, putting his interactive reader and various other electronic gadgets together in his backpack.

"I'll bring the FlyAway in front," his father said. "Don't forget to bring your lunch and thank your mother for the nice birthday cake she made for you."

"Okay, Dad, I'll make sure to do that," Antonius said politely.

The FlyAway his father intended to bring around was a cigar-shaped, four-person vehicle—two seats upfront and two in the back—which could be either driven or flown around the island. Equipped with a completely silent anti-gravity engine powered by a few crystals, Antonius could drive it just like a car on the streets of the local neighborhoods and in the downtown area of Atlantis, or take it straight up in the air and fly it like a small plane through the island's air corridors to his destination. Containing air conditioning, stereo, and a host of technical gadgets, including GPS-based control and communication devices, it was the fastest and most convenient form of transportation in Atlantis.

When Antonius went to the kitchen to pick up the lunch his mother had prepared for him, his father went to the garage to fetch the FlyAway. As he parked it a little while later in the driveway in front of their villa, James felt a little nervous. That day his son turned seventeen, which meant Antonius had reached the legal age to operate a FlyAway by himself. It also meant he would take it to school by himself for the first time. He had driven and flown it for the past year with his dad in the passenger seat but never by himself. James considered his son fully capable of handling the vehicle—after all, he had personally trained him—but to see him leave in the FlyAway all by himself was going to be a little nerve-wracking for him.

"Thanks again, Mom, for the awesome birthday cake," Antonius told his mother after he kissed her goodbye on both cheeks. "And the icing and sprinkles, and all the other stuff on it, delicious."

"You're welcome," she said, giving him a big hug. "And, please, be careful where you set the FlyAway down when you get to school."

"Yes, Mom, I will," he assured her, grabbing his sandwich bag from the kitchen counter. He gave her a short wave and a "Bye, I love you," before hustling out of the kitchen and heading for the front door.

When he walked out of the house, his father opened the FlyAway's driver-side door and motioned for him to get into the driver's seat. Having hugged his dad and gotten into the craft, Antonius deposited his backpack on the passenger seat and strapped on his safety harness. He then switched on his vehicle's control system and, by talking into the steering wheel's built-in microphone, told the control system his destination.

"Bye, Dad, thanks for bringing it up front. I'll see you at dinner this evening."

"You're welcome, Son. Be careful where you set her down."

"Yes, Dad, Mom already reminded me," Antonius said, smiling.

He grabbed a hold of the steering wheel with both hands, pushed the gravity-release button on the right side, and pulled the steering column slowly towards himself. He then waved goodbye to his dad as the vehicle slowly levitated upward. When it reached control-level height, about one hundred feet above the ground, the island's traffic-monitoring system took over—controlling its direction, speed and altitude. James Starlight took a deep breath and silently wished his son a safe journey, as the FlyAway accelerated in the direction of downtown Atlantis. Then he went back into the garage to ready his other FlyAway, which he planned to fly to work in an hour or so.

Upon graduation from the Aquarius Academy, young Antonius Starlight enrolled in a five-year technical training

29

program at the Atlantis Technical Institute, where he studied physical sciences and developed an interest in understanding the forces that shaped the universe. Having graduated at the top of his class at the Institute, he decided to study Astronomy for another three years at the Atlantis Observatory—the place where he headed in his FlyAway that morning.

After taking off from their villa, he first passed over a large stretch of Atlantis' northern coast, dotted with small fishing villages. He could see the many small fishing boats that brought home the fresh catch every day from the crystal clear waters surrounding the island—waters that teamed with fish of every kind and size. Soon, the air corridor he flew in took him around the northern mountains, reaching high into the sky, and over the rainforest at the base of those mountains. He strained to make out some of the large animals dwelling there—elephants, tigers, buffalos, and boars—but the dense tree canopy kept them hidden. As he flew over these unspoiled wonders of nature, it hit him that he was actually flying all by himself for the first time. He felt immensely grateful and proud his parents trusted him enough to let him do this on his seventeenth birthday, and it made him feel like he was ready to take on whatever life put in front of him.

He had just started to soar over the large fertile plain stretching from the rain forest to Atlantis' urban area covering the southern half of the island, when the "little voice" spoke to him for the first time.

"Nice view, huh," it said very softly.

Not entirely sure if he heard something or not, Antonius continued to look below at the hundreds of little homesteads spread out across the plain providing Atlanteans with most of their daily fresh-food supply. All around he could see cattle, pigs, and chickens, and the vegetable and grain crops Atlantis' warm climate readied for harvest twice a year.

"Please, go see Professor Brightman, as soon as you get to the observatory," the little voice said a little louder.

"Why should I go...?" The words stuck in Antonius' throat.

Realizing he heard an actual voice, he quickly looked around and shot a glance in his rearview mirror to see if anything or anyone had concealed itself in the back of his vehicle; but he didn't notice anything alarming. *Dad's playing a joke on me again,* he thought, smiling, and then wondering what device emitted the voice.

Reading his mind, the little voice said, "Antonius, no one played a joke on you, so please take my advice seriously."

Not ruling out the possibility someone had used a device in his vehicle to trick him, Antonius said falteringly, "Who are you...? And where are you...?"

"I'm Tooku, and I'm sitting right next to you—but you can't see me," the voice said.

"What's a Tooku," Antonius said curiously, feeling a little uncomfortable to have an invisible something sitting next to him. "And why are you giving me advice...when I can't even see you?"

"Tooku is my name, and I'm your Celestial Guardian," the voice said calmly. "And I'm supposed to give you advice; just like I do with your father."

When the little voice mentioned giving advice to his father, it instantly got Antonius' full attention.

"Uh...yes...Dad told me about you guys. You're one of those other-dimensional spirits...right?"

"That's right. I'm from another dimension, and that's why you can't see me. But I'm not just one of those spirits; I'm your Guardian—your Celestial Guardian."

"So, what's the difference, and why do I need your advice anyway?"

"As your Guardian, I will advise you how to best reach your destiny. Like your father, you are destined to become a great leader of your people someday. And, in case you don't know it, leaders need advice on how to become great leaders and, then, even more advice on how to stay that way."

"Me...a great leader—no way," Antonius said amusingly.

"You will be!"

"So, how do I know you're really my Celestial Guardian and not some spirit who is just kidding me? Dad says there are bad spirits that sometimes do that."

"Just go see the professor, right away; you'll find out if I'm kidding you or not."

"Why Professor Brightman?"

"You'll see."

"But what do I say to him?"

"Tell him you want to work on his latest project."

"But I don't even know him."

The voice didn't answer.

"And what project is this anyway?"

The voice didn't answer again, so Antonius decided to let it be.

The whole time Antonius flew high-up in the air, the island's traffic monitoring system controlled his vehicle and in forty-five minutes guided him safely to his flight destination—the airspace above the set-down area for the

32

Atlantis Observatory in downtown Atlantis. He enjoyed looking down from high above on the center of town; it afforded him a scenic view of Atlantis' Central Park. This beautifully designed space, filled with exotic tropical plants and beds of colorful flowers, was the starting point of four tree-lined boulevards—built with polished granite cobblestones—that meandered seemingly forever throughout the City and around other beautiful parks and elegant monuments.

Air traffic had been light until Antonius approached the downtown area, where the number of vehicles flying in his vicinity increased from a few to hundreds, flying in all different directions all around him. He could see many of them darting in and out of the spaces between the downtown buildings, most of which were very tall, futuristic-looking structures—obelisk-shaped skyscrapers, elegant-looking space towers, and other high-rise buildings, including pyramid-shaped ones and cylindrical ones like the observatory. Several of the skyscrapers, connected to each other by sky bridges, reached twice as high into the sky as those of Earth's current cities. Some of the tallest ones had several smaller obelisk-shaped towers attached to their central tower, encircling their contours like long helixes. The space towers, which varied in height from a few hundred feet to half the reach of the skyscrapers, looked like covered, long-stemmed champagne glasses; and Antonius saw many flying vehicles landing and taking off from their flat roofs.

Since all the vehicles were controlled by the same traffic monitoring system that guided his craft, they avoided him as his FlyAway slowed down and came to a halt at his flight destination. Antonius could see the set-down area below him on the screen of his positioning system on the dashboard of his FlyAway. He slowly lowered it to the ground by holding his steering wheel with both hands and gently pushing the steering column away from his body. After landing the craft in the set-down area, he carefully drove it to the observatory's large parking lot, parking in his assigned space.

As he walked into the observatory, Antonius debated when to go see Professor Brightman—before or after class. The information screen, which listed the professor not only as an instructor but also as the director of the observatory's research program, indicated Prof. B was on the third floor. Since the little voice had twice urged Antonius to see the professor right away, he decided to be late for his first class and headed up the stairs to the professor's office.

"Come in," said Professor Brightman, in response to the knock on his office door. Seeing Antonius' smiley face, he beamed him a smile in return. "And what can I do for you, young man?"

Feeling rather uncomfortable about approaching someone regarding a project he didn't know anything about, Antonius hesitated before answering.

"I'm…interested in working on your latest project," he said, echoing the words of the little voice.

"And what latest project might that be?" the professor asked, as a frown appeared on his face.

Antonius was stumped by this question, but not for long. He knew, as director of the observatory's research program, the professor had primary oversight over the observatory's powerful telescopes. As a result of his class work, Antonius also knew these telescopes could peek deep into space and provide clear images of the solar system's planets and other astronomical objects far away in the Milky Way Galaxy. He therefore assumed—with very smart

34

conjecture—the project had something to do with the use of these telescopes to study an outer-space phenomenon; and he based his answer on this assumption.

"The one that's going to use our observatory's telescopes to study…uh, uh…something in space," Antonius bluffed with a straight face, holding his fingers crossed behind his back.

The frown on the professor's face deepened. "And just how do you happen to know about our latest project?" he wanted to know. "It's still confidential; we just presented the project's proposal to the Supreme Council last week."

I'm dead, Antonius thought, but he continued his bluff—though reluctantly.

"I don't…really know a great deal about it, but I would like to get involved with it…if that's possible?"

"Well, I'm sorry the word got out prematurely," the professor sighed. "We wanted to learn more about the New Planet before we let the rest of the world know about it."

"I'm sorry, too," Antonius said reluctantly, not knowing what planet the professor referred to.

"So, what's your name anyway?" the professor asked.

"Antonius Starlight."

The professor's frown disappeared at the mention of this name.

"Are you related to James Starlight—the Leader of our Council?"

"Yes, he's my father."

"Well—I'll be," the professor blurted out. "Now I know how you heard about the project; from your dad…right?"

"Uh…uh…uh," was all Antonius could muster, as he started to feel very uncomfortable about his bluff.

"Oh, don't worry," the professor said, grinning, "James sent you to the right person. He and I used to be class mates at the Aquarius Academy many years ago."

Now Antonius felt embarrassed for his bluff. The professor thought his father had told him about the project and advised him to get involved with it—but nothing could be further from the truth. Blaming all this confusion on the little voice, Antonius vowed silently, "The next time I hear that little voice, I'm going to give it a real piece of my mind."

Wanting to set the record straight and let the professor know his father had nothing to do with him showing up at his doorstep, he said quietly, "Professor, my father did not ask me to come here, and I actually don't know anything about..."

Before Antonius had a chance to finish what he wanted to say, the professor cut him off, saying, "No need to further explain, my boy. Like I said before, don't worry. You have come to the right person."

"But I really don't know what the project is about," Antonius said, grimacing.

"Well, let me give you some of the details then."

Antonius listened patiently as the professor told him that using their telescopes, the scientists at the observatory had discovered about a year ago an unknown planet in the solar system. Like the other eight planets, it orbited around the Sun; but unlike these planets, it was only visible through their telescopes for one day each month. The rest of the time, the scientists could not detect any signs of the planet's existence. What they were able to do, however, after observing it during twelve monthly appearances over the past year, was to establish the planet's trajectory around the Sun and determine its location in relation to Earth. Using the observatory's strongest telescope, which could spot an

36

astronomical object several galaxies away, they made two interesting observations: this newly discovered planet always moved around the Sun at the same orbital speed - and in the same orbit - as Earth, at a distance of about 93 million miles from the Sun; and this planet always trailed Earth in its orbit by about 100 million miles. Determined to know more about the makeup of this mostly invisible planet and curious to find out if it supported any life forms, the scientists wanted to send probes to photograph its environment and sample its atmosphere. They also hoped, eventually, to land probes on the surface, allowing them to make chemical and other analyses of its soil.

"And the project proposal we sent to the Council," the professor said, "requests funding to send these probes to the New Planet."

"Wow... that sounds like the kind of project I would love to get involved in," Antonius exclaimed, looking hopefully at the professor.

"I think that could be arranged," the professor said, with a twinkle in his eyes, "if we are, indeed, lucky enough to get the money to make it happen."

As it turned out, the professor did get the money for his project. He built and launched several new probes, and Antonius got what amounted to a paid assistantship to help with the project. During his first day on the job, Professor Brightman, a kind and patient man, took the time to show him how to operate the telescopes they used to conduct their research. Antonius could not believe his eyes when, with the professor at his side, he saw colorful images of the solar system displayed in a hologram in front of him, as they were captured by the observatory's most powerful telescopes. He had never seen the Sun, the Moon, and the planets so close up, and in such detail. It really surprised him the professor let him adjust the telescopes, so he could gaze deep into the Milky Way Galaxy and see images of exploding stars, quasars, pulsars, nebulas, and many different constellations.

"Professor, do you think there is life out there in the universe?" Antonius asked, fascinated by what he saw.

"Based on the number of stars in the universe, it would certainly not surprise me if that were the case," the professor responded.

He explained each of the galaxies displayed in front them contained over three hundred billion stars, and the universe might contained as many as five hundred billion galaxies.

Having quickly done the math in his head, Antonius said, "So there might be over one hundred and fifty sextillion stars in the universe, is that right?"

"That's right," the professor said, looking at him approvingly. "And with so many stars lighting up our universe, the odds are pretty good one or two of them resemble our Sun and serve as the life-blood of a planet teeming with life—just like Planet Earth. It wouldn't surprise me at all to discover such a planet exists in our own galaxy. In fact, I believe, in the not too distant future, we will find and communicate with other life forms; if not on this planet, then the next."

Little did Antonius know that before the decade ended, the professor's words would come to pass when the VARS came to town.

Professor Brightman could not believe his eyes when, shortly after he launched the first probe, the New Planet suddenly became visible and remained that way until the probe's work finished; after which it disappeared again. It *really surprised him when this happened every time he launched another probe; and neither the professor, nor any of the other scientists on his staff, had a good explanation for why this happened.*

As part of his assignment with the project, Antonius assisted the team of scientists with the collection and processing of the information the probes relayed back to Earth during their flybys and landings on the New Planet. By carefully studying the videos, pictures, and other flyby information, he quickly concluded the New Planet closely resembled Earth in terms of its atmosphere, climate, and vegetation. He also learned, although small varieties of animals lived on land and swam in the oceans, it did not appear to support any sentient life forms. So, Antonius was not surprised when Professor Brightman and other scientists at the observatory began entertaining the notion that Atlanteans might someday travel to the New Planet and establish a settlement there—just like they did on the Moon and on Mars. They understood, while father away, the presence of an atmosphere and a moderate climate would make logistics much simpler and more doable.

One day, while marveling at the latest images of the New Planet, still wondering why no humans inhabited this very Earth-like place, Antonius hit upon a novel idea to explain why the New Planet lit up every time a probe took off to inspect its premises. It might be, he thought, the planet actually gave the Atlanteans a helping hand in carrying out their exploratory work, while sending them at the same time an invitation to come and visit.

At the time, he didn't talk to any of his co-workers about this idea; he suspected they would most likely consider any notion about a planet extending a helping hand, along with an invitation to come and visit, to be, at best, naïve and, at worst, totally ludicrous. As it turned out, not communicating this notion was a good idea, because for some unknown reason the New Planet, all of a sudden, stopped revealing itself. The professor sent new probes to several locations in the solar system where he expected to see it based on the planet's known trajectory, but he found nothing but empty space. Having lost the subject of his research, he put the project on hold; and a few months later, he shut it down altogether.

Antonius was sorry when the project terminated, regretful that travel to the New Planet would not happen any time soon. He had fond memories of the days and nights he spent working on it. Because of his involvement with the project, the urge to know more about the universe had awakened within him, and he had started to dream about traveling into space. He saw himself exploring the Moon, Mars, and the other planets, and eventually visiting other star systems in the Milky Way Galaxy, and beyond. He did not know his participation in the project would someday help save the Atlantean race from total oblivion.

Upon graduation from the Atlantis Observatory with a degree in Astronomy, Antonius nurtured his dream while on an obligatory three year stint in the Atlantean military. After finishing basic training, he made good use of an opportunity to participate in a pilot training program; and when he completed it, he received a commission as Lieutenant in the Atlantean Defense Force. Having demonstrated his aviation skills for several years, he applied and was accepted for astronaut training. After qualifying for his astronaut insignia, he finally realized his dream of traveling into space when, at the young age of twenty-five, the Military High

Command of Atlantis appointed him Commander of Moon Base Osiris, with the rank of Captain.

Not long thereafter, the first Varsian spaceship arrived on Earth. This marked the beginning of a turbulent era—one that witnessed the unraveling of the mostly peaceful coexistence of the planet's inhabitants.

Part Two: Destruction of a City.

After building their first base on Earth, the VARS traveled to other parts of the world. Most of the people they came into contact with also treated them as gods and showered them with veneration. They quickly determined that, compared to them, earthlings were rather primitive, with Atlanteans the exception.

The VARS viewed Atlantis as a major obstacle to their plans to subjugate and colonize Earth. They knew conquering and ruling this City would not be easy, not by any means. They, therefore, preferred to make a deal with the Atlanteans, one that would allow them to quickly take over the rest of the world. A few months after they first landed on Planet Earth, Commander Crokh traveled to Atlantis to see if he could strike such an agreement.

"Set course for Atlantis," Crokh instructed his spaceship's pilot, as Trastic took off from the Varsian Earth Base and headed for the big island.

"Yes, Commander," the pilot responded, entering the coordinates for Atlantis into the ship's computer.

It took the spaceship only a few seconds to get to Atlantean airspace, and when they arrived there, Crokh instructed the pilot not to enter. He knew Atlantis had an air traffic control system in operation and was not the kind of place where one landed a spaceship unannounced.

41

"Get Atlantis' permission to land," he then instructed his Communications Officer while the ship circled Atlantean airspace.

Since coming to Earth, the VARS—using sophisticated computer software—had quickly developed the ability to communicate with earthlings in their native tongues, and the officer transmitted a message in the Atlanteans' language.

"Atlantis, this is spaceship Trastic requesting permission to land," the Communications Officer radioed Atlantis' air traffic control system. To Crokh's big surprise, the Atlanteans denied his request for landing.

While the rest of the world looked up to the VARS as gods, the Atlanteans viewed them not with veneration but with suspicion and deep concern over their intentions in coming to their planet. Atlanteans had noticed the number of VARS running around on Earth seemed to increase month after month, and the aliens had started to build two more Earth Bases in strategic locations around the world. To them, rightly so, it appeared the VARS intended to take over the world; and the Atlanteans were not about to let a Varsian spaceship with awesome destructive capabilities land on their island. And so the Atlanteans told them, if they wanted to visit Atlantis, it would be on their terms. The VARS could send a delegation to the City in one of the small shuttle craft onboard their spacecraft.

"Tell them I demand our spacecraft be allowed to land immediately," a furious Crokh yelled at his Communications Officer upon learning of the Atlantean response to his request—feeling severely slighted by this turn of events.

"Yes, sir, right away," the officer responded, not wanting to further arouse his Commander, who manifested typical Varsian impatience.

Understandably, the Atlanteans gave them the same response: "Permission to land a small shuttle craft only."

"Tell 'em if they continue to ignore our demands, there will be dire consequences," Crokh said hotly, breathing fire. "And remind them, we can deploy lasers powerful enough to destroy their island."

His all-or-nothing, no-compromise attitude was characteristic of the Varsian conflicts on their own planet— conflicts that quickly led to destructive warring among the VARS themselves.

Again the Atlanteans returned the same response: "Permission to land a small shuttle craft only."

This time, Crokh decided the time for dialogue had reached its limits and instructed his Weapons Officer to fire a destructive laser beam at the largest building in the City.

"Let's teach them a lesson," he crowed, as Trastic's large laser gun sent a particle beam speeding towards its target.

Expecting an instant implosion of the building, Crokh got another big surprise when nothing happened. When it became apparent the VARS might become belligerent, the Atlanteans had quickly erected an energy shield over their city, protecting them from harm by the spaceship's destructive weapons. After the shield repelled several additional laser beam attacks, Crokh decided to send a delegation to Atlantis in one of his small shuttle craft; but to save face, he sent along with them a list of his demands regarding Atlantis' surrender to Varsian authorities.

The demands he put forth shocked the Atlantean Supreme Council, and they quickly and totally rejected every one of them. Never in the history of Atlantis had anyone ever had the folly to ask the Atlanteans to give up self-rule, and disclose all technical and scientific information regarding

43

their energy shield and the use of their crystals. The Council quickly sent the Varsian delegation packing back to their ship, after which Crokh dispatched another message threatening total annihilation of the City if the Atlanteans disregarded a final opportunity to meet his demands—an opportunity the Council left dangling.

Upon return to his island base, Crokh reported his unsuccessful attempt to strike a deal with Atlantis to his superior on Varsius.

"I expect the City to fight us for control of Earth," he communicated to him.

"And I expect you to resolve this issue promptly," his superior responded.

"In order to do that, I need two more ships," Crokh advised.

He explained, based on the calculations of his Science Officer, the combined firepower of three spaceships should easily penetrate Atlantis' energy shield and quickly wipe the City from the face of the Earth.

"We'll send the ships, and for your sake I hope you're correct," his superior responded menacingly.

"Just one other thing," Crokh said. "I have become aware of Atlantean bases on the Moon and Mars and would like to destroy both of them."

"Good idea," his superior responded, "I'll plan to send one of our ships to Earth by way of Mars and the other by way of the Moon—good target practice for them."

Captain Starlight had watched the goings-on between Atlantis and the VARS on the screens of his communications console in his Command Post on Moon Base Osiris. Convinced the VARS intended to destroy his beautiful City, he had racked his brain for options to keep Atlantis out of harm's way. He soon realized he had no real options; he was on the Moon, far away from Earth, with no real weapons to deter Varsian aggression against his City—and, for that matter, against his Moon Base too. And having no weapons to protect his base bothered Captain Starlight immensely.

"I'm afraid it's just a matter of time before the VARS will attempt to destroy both our Moon Base and Star Base Orion," he told lieutenant Strongfield, as they sat in his office, shortly after Crokh's unsuccessful laser attacks against Atlantis.

"If you feel so sure about that, why not ask your superiors in Atlantis for permission to build an energy shield for our base," she suggested. "We can use the crystals we normally ship to Earth."

"I actually intend to do just that," Captain Starlight confided in her.

Not wasting any further time, he used the communications equipment in his office to send a message to the Military High Command in Atlantis requesting permission to build the shield because of his serious concerns about potential Varsian laser attacks on his Moon Base. To his surprise, they denied his request. When he appealed their decision, they turned him down again, and also informed him the Supreme Council had drafted a peace proposal they intended to deliver to the VARS the next day. They believed once these aliens grasped they could never penetrate Atlantis' energy shield they would cease their aggression and accept Atlantis' peace proposal; and they might eventually become Atlantis' partners in further exploration of the universe.

The Captain reacted to this supposition with total disbelief; in his mind, Varsian cooperation with Atlantis appeared about as likely as grapes growing outdoors on the Moon—a highly unlikely event in his opinion. The fact the VARS had not hesitated to unleash a laser attack against Atlantis demonstrated their ruthlessness and intention to strike at anything Atlantean, including Atlantis' bases in Space.

"How totally naïve the Council is," the Lieutenant exclaimed when the Captain told her about the High Command's response. "What can we do now?"

"Unfortunately, not much," Captain Starlight replied. "We've been instructed to stand by for further orders and for now suspend our shuttle flights."

Later that evening, preparing for bed, he fretted over the fact the Council did not seem to grasp the VARS' plan. They seemed unaware the VARS would not rest until they had removed Atlantis as an obstacle to world domination—either by having total control over the City or totally destroying it. He also obsessed over the fact that, with their ability to travel at the speed of light, Varsian spaceships coming from Earth could reach his Moon Base in seconds and, in less than a second, blast it to smithereens. For a moment, he considered building the energy shield anyway, even though the High Command had ordered him not to; but then his military training took over, and he quickly put the idea out of his mind. Shortly thereafter, he heard the little voice again, the one that had advised him many years ago to go and see Professor Brightman at the Atlantis Observatory.

"Go ahead and build the energy shield," the little voice said gently.

"Oh, no, Tooku…not you again," Captain Starlight exclaimed jokingly.

He affectionately remembered the little voice urging him to become involved with the project studying the makeup of the newly discovered planet. Working on that project had not only been a nice source of pocket money for him during his days at the observatory but, more importantly, it had inspired him to make space exploration his career.

"Please build the shield—you need to start building it tomorrow morning," Tooku said, sounding rather urgent.

"But they told me not to build it," Captain Starlight said. "And where have you been, anyway?"

"I advised your father. And you didn't need me till now."

Antonius knew the little voice had given sound advice to his father on several occasions.

"And...why do I need you now?" he asked.

"Because you will soon lead your people."

That caught the Captain completely off guard. Even though he was very proud of his dad, he had no desire to follow in his footsteps and become a member of the Supreme Council, let alone its Leader. Besides, he thought, I'm too far away from home to do any leading any time soon.

"And... how can I lead my people?" he asked, "I'm on the Moon!"

"You'll see. Just build the shield."

"And...why should I go against my orders and build it?"

"Because they will attack your base and destroy everything in it, including the two ships from Mars. It makes perfect strategic sense for them to do so."

When the VARS first launched their laser attack against Atlantis, two of the large Atlantean spaceships on their way from Mars to Earth diverted to the Moon Base. The High Command instructed Captain Starlight to keep them there until they could safely resume their flights back to Earth without Varsian interference. In view of a likely

47

Varsian assault on his base, Captain Starlight understood the importance of keeping these ships protected—not having them would severely restrict travel to and from Mars.

"And by the way, Tooku," Antonius said, "why didn't you advise my father to let us build the shield?"

"I did advise him that."

"So, why didn't he follow your advice?"

"He did follow my advice and recommended you should be allowed to build a shield to protect your Moon Base. But unfortunately, the rest of the Council overrode his advice."

"Well, I'm glad to know that," Antonius said, feeling relieved his father was on his side, but also chilled by the shortsightedness of the rest of the Council.

And so, due to the prompting of the little voice and the knowledge his dad felt the same about building the shield, he started to seriously contemplate erecting it. After thinking all night about the consequences—both positive and negative— of going against the orders of his superiors, he decided he had to do what best protected the safety of the people under his command. And the next morning, he asked the Lieutenant and a small group of trusted compatriots to quietly and quickly configure the crystals to power an energy shield for the defense of Moon Base Osiris and the two ships from Mars.

The energy shield became operational within twenty-four hours, and Captain Starlight started to feel much better about the safety of his base. However, what peace of mind the installation of the shield brought him quickly dissipated when his Command Post intercepted a frantic message from the Commander of Star Base Orion on Mars to Atlantis' Military High Command:

Under attack from a large spaceship – stop
Unable to defend ourselves – stop
Much damage from lasers – stop
Understand help will come too late – stop
God save us – stop
Give our love to our families – stop

When he looked at the screen on his communications console that showed a live view of the Star Base on Mars, Captain Starlight observed a large Varsian spaceship firing its weapons at the Base. Then the screen went blank, which meant the Star Base and all its communications gear had been destroyed.

After putting his Moon Base on full alert for an enemy attack, Captain Starlight received an urgent message from his superiors in Atlantis notifying him of the destruction on Mars and directing him to utilize the crystals to make an energy shield for his base. At the very moment he received this message, another Varsian spaceship opened fire on the Moon Base; and to his great relief, the energy shield worked to perfection and successfully deflected the Varsian laser bursts directed against it. Antonius felt even more vindicated when the Varsian commander of the spaceship realized his weapons could not penetrate the shield and decided to break off the attack on the Moon and continue on his journey to Earth to join the other two Varsian spaceships in their fight against Atlantis. He intended to come back and deal with the Moon Base after helping defeat the City.

When the other two Varsian spacecraft arrived on Earth, an ecstatic Commander Crokh boasted to his crew,

"Now we'll teach the Atlanteans a lesson from which they'll never recover."

His plan, previously conveyed to the commanders of the other ships, had two simple steps: line up the three spaceships side by side in the air above Atlantis; and then, at his command, fire their laser guns simultaneously at precisely the same spot on the energy shield. According to the calculations of his Science Officer, the combined firepower of the three spaceships would overwhelm and penetrate the shield.

"Three, two, one—fire now," Crokh ordered, as the three ships hovered above Atlantis.

While the spaceships unleashed their lasers simultaneously at the City, the Science Officer held his fingers crossed, hoping his advice to his commander would bear fruit and destroy the shield. He knew if it didn't, it would be his life on the line, not just his job.

Unfortunately for him and the other VARS, it turned out he had underestimated the effectiveness and strength of Atlantis' energy shield; and the Varsian lasers did not penetrate it, even after several attempts. Frustrated, the three commanders sent laser burst after laser burst hurling towards Atlantis; to no avail—the shield held.

In the meantime, a debate took place within the ranks of the Supreme Council of Atlantis as to whether or not the Peacemaker should be used to shoot down the three attacking spaceships. Several voices called for their destruction; but many more Council members, including Antonius' father—a peace-loving individual—objected, because it meant perhaps a thousand VARS would go to their early graves.

Nobody, including the VARS, could have foreseen the tragedy that happened next. Having been deflected into the ocean by the energy shield, the constant, day-long barrage of Varsian laser beams hitting the Earth suddenly caused a devastating earthquake in the waters off Atlantis' coast—followed by an even-more devastating underwater landslide. The quake resulted in the formation of a powerful tsunami, unnoticed until it hit Atlantis with a hundred-foot wall of water. As the unstoppable mass wrought destruction on the City, the Atlanteans used the Peacemaker, which in the end could not keep the peace, to obliterate the three Varsian spaceships. Within minutes after the tsunami devastated the City, the underwater landslide slowly pulled all of Atlantis beneath the surging waters of the Atlantic Ocean—erasing all evidence of the existence of the most magnificent civilization the world has ever known.

Part Three: Escape from the Moon.

Watching with horror on their faces as the destruction of their homeland unfolded on the screens of their communications console in the Atlantean Command Post on the Moon, Captain Starlight and his countrymen could not believe what they witnessed. Stricken with grief over the near certain demise of his family in the Atlantic Ocean's waters, the Captain retreated to his private office and closed the door, isolating himself from his countrymen's cries of desperation.

"Take the big ships to the New Planet," the little voice said gently, after Antonius sank himself with a deep sigh into his office's recliner, totally bewildered by what had just unfolded on Earth.

51

Getting no response, Tooku repeated, "Take the big ships to the New Planet."

Captain Starlight heard it the first time, but he was still too dazed to manage a response. After the little voice repeated its suggestion for a third time, the Captain started to pull himself together.

"Tooku...is that you?"

"Yes, it's me, Antonius."

"What planet...are you talking about?"

"The New Planet you saw at the observatory through the telescopes and in the fly-by pictures. Take the two big ships from Mars and go to the New Planet, with all your people onboard."

"We can't do that," Captain Starlight said, now feeling a little more clear-headed.

"And why not?" Tooku inquired.

"Because the planet has disappeared...gone."

"No, it hasn't gone anywhere; you just can't see it right now."

"What...? How can that be?"

"It's still there, but in another dimension."

"You mean... just like you live in another dimension?"

"That's right, like me, except I live in a dimension that is different from the one in which the New Planet resides."

"But if it resides in another dimension, then how could we have seen it?"

"Because it wanted you to see it and crossed over from another dimension to let you do so."

"Please, get serious. Why would it want to do that?"

"It wanted to let you know you could come and live there."

As soon as Tooku said that, Antonius recalled the novel thought he had many years ago while helping

52

Professor Brightman with the New Planet. At the time, he had an idea akin to what Tooku just told him. He had surmised the New Planet lit up every time the Atlanteans launched a probe in its direction to extend them an invitation to visit there.

"So, why does it want Atlanteans to live there?"

"As a sister planet of Earth, it needs to have humans living on it. And the New Planet knows Atlanteans will not endanger it or destroy its environment."

While he contemplated Tooku's advice to travel to the New Planet, Captain Starlight suddenly realized the implication of what the little voice had just revealed to him.

"If what you say about the New Planet is true, it must be alive."

"You're right—it is alive."

"And how can this be?"

"Many planets in other dimensions can make their presence known to attract visitors to their habitats."

"And how do we know it's safe for us to live there?"

"Because it has prepared itself for you for many years and made its environment just like that of Earth—a safe place for you to live in. The planet wanted Atlanteans to know this when it revealed itself to you many years ago."

All this gave Captain Starlight much to ponder. What Tooku said made sense to him, but he realized he needed a few more answers before he could make a recommendation to his people about traveling to another planet.

"So, how can we find this New Planet?" he asked Tooku.

"That can't be too difficult for you, Captain. You already know its orbit—the same as that of Earth—and it always resides in this orbit about 100 or so million miles from your planet. Using your spaceship's computer, you

53

shouldn't have much difficulty preparing a flight plan that will get you there; and the planet will show itself to you as soon as you take off."

"What assurances do we have; it stopped showing itself the last time we tried to find it."

Tooku explained that when the VARS started to actively explore the Milky Way Galaxy for a new home, the New Planet did not want to show itself on a regular basis and risk discovery by these very destructive beings.

"But now the time is right for you to go there and if, for whatever reason, it does not show itself when you depart the Moon, you can always turn around and come back."

In spite of this explanation, Captain Starlight still felt uncomfortable about the notion of taking his people on a dangerous trip to an invisible planet in another dimension. In particular, he worried about their inability to quickly leave the New Planet if things didn't work out.

"Even if we landed there safely," he said to Tooku, "we can't quickly return here without having the proper takeoff facilities and equipment over there."

"No need to return here; there won't be much left to return to."

"We'll still have our Moon Base to return to."

"Yes, but not for long—the VARS will come with other ships and destroy it."

"But we have an energy shield."

"Yes, you have a shield but no extensive food supplies. And if you venture out to Earth for more supplies, you'll have to open the shield; and then they will zap you—both your ship and your base will be gone."

I can't argue with that, the Captain thought, they will eventually destroy our base. But even with this realization,

Antonius still could not commit to traveling to the New Planet.

"My people will want to go to Earth and look for possible survivors and the remains of their loved ones."

"They will not find any survivors; and if your people go to Earth, the VARS will hunt them down and kill them."

"But even if their families have perished, they—like me—will still want to go back to Earth and fight against the VARS, regardless of the outcome."

"Better to go to the New Planet and save yourselves to fight another day—when the odds for success have improved."

Again, Captain Starlight found himself agreeing with Tooku's logic, but he also knew that logic flees in the face of anger. Once his people dealt with their grief over the loss of their loved ones, anger—not logic—would rule the day; and they would insist on returning to Earth and taking up arms against the VARS, no matter what.

"I can make it so that all of your loved ones are safe and in hiding around the world, with friends and people sympathetic to their plight," Tooku proclaimed all of a sudden.

"You can do what?"

Tooku repeated it.

"Please, don't play with the sorrow of my people," the Captain said, not believing what he just heard, and feeling aggravated.

"I'm honestly not trying to do that," Tooku replied.

"So, then how can you save our loved ones?" the Captain asked skeptically. "I thought you said before, there were no survivors."

"As your Celestial Guardian, I can change that. I can make it so that there are survivors—your loved ones."

55

"You can change what already happened? How is that possible?"

"In my dimension, the past, present, and future all happen at the same time. I can shape and change your present to determine your future; and your past will immediately realign itself with whatever your present becomes. And I can do the same for all of your people."

"So, what you are saying is that if I and my people get on our two big ships and head for the New Planet, you can make it so that our loved ones are alive and protected—somewhere on Earth."

"Yes, that's right."

"And can you also make it so that at a later time we can be reunited with them?"

"Yes, I can."

That revelation blew Captain Starlight's mind, and he had, at first, a hard time believing it. But then he thought of a very good reason to trust what the little voice had told him; it had forewarned him of the Varsian attack on his base and—thank goodness—advised him to raise the protective shield. So, once again, Captain Starlight decided to follow the little voice's recommendation and take his people to the New Planet. But before he could actually do this, he had some convincing to do. First of all, he had to convince his people not to return to Earth at this time. Then, he had to convince them going to the New Planet, without the ability to return to the Moon or Earth any time soon, was the right thing to do. And finally, he had to convince them their loved ones had survived and would reunite with them at a later time—exactly when, he didn't know. This last round of convincing would require a big leap of faith, and he needed some good advice from his Celestial Guardian on how to get them to take it.

"Tooku, how can I convince my people their families have survived and will join them at a later time?"

"Dreams," Tooku said. "I will give them all the same dream. Tell them they will dream tonight about their loved ones having survived; and in their dreams, their loved ones will urge them to go to the New Planet and build a new Atlantis, so they can be reunited there when the time is right."

During a meeting held later that day, Captain Starlight, using many of the same words and arguments Tooku had used on him earlier, urged his people to prepare themselves for the trip to the New Planet; and later that night, he dreamt about his family being safe and sound with a tribe of Hapua Indians in North America. In his dream, his father explained to him how the Tsunami Early Warning System of Atlantis had alerted him and many other Atlanteans to the rising waters; and how he had immediately put his family in their FlyAway and flown high up in the air—escaping the destruction inflicted upon their island. After many hours of flying westward, they touched down in a beautiful land, full of primitive people who thought they were gods and treated them well. His father also urged him to lead his people to the New Planet and build a new Atlantis, where he, his mother, and his two sisters would soon see him again.

To their amazement, just as Captain Starlight had predicted during the meeting the day before, all of his people had similar dreams about their loved ones escaping in their FlyAways from the sinking island and reaching distant lands in different parts of the world. Like him, they dreamt their families were alive and their loved ones urged them to journey to the New Planet, where they would join them at a later time.

The next day, having reached unanimous agreement to evacuate the Moon and not return to Earth, Captain Starlight and his small band of one hundred or so Atlanteans blasted off from Moon Base Osiris in two large spaceships, making their way to the New Planet. After a three-month journey, they landed there safely and began laying the foundation of an even more magnificent civilization than the one they lost on Earth. They named the New Planet "Atlantis" and built their capital city, Poseidon, with the help of the crystals brought with them from the Moon. They also covered this new city with an energy shield to keep it forever safe from Varsian aggression—or so they hoped?

Within two decades after their arrival on Planet Atlantis, the Atlanteans had figured out how to bend the space-time continuum around their planet—again through the use of their magnificent crystals. This enabled them to create a space portal directly connecting Atlantis to Earth. Using this portal, which they kept well-hidden from the VARS, they traveled to Earth in seconds—without having to worry about the VARS' powerful spacecraft patrolling the skies—to secretly conduct a worldwide search for their loved ones. Having located most of them within a few years, the Atlanteans established an underground network to transport these relatives from hideaways around the world to the space portal, from where they traveled to Planet Atlantis—just as Tooku had said. In many cases, their family members had intermarried with local tribes that had offered them safe-haven; and, in those instances, their spouses and offspring—numbering over a thousand—also journeyed to Atlantis.

After all the families had been reunited on Planet Atlantis, the Atlanteans instituted the same form of government that had served the City of Atlantis so well, prior *to its destruction; and they elected Captain Starlight the first Leader of their new Supreme Council. While searching for their loved ones on Earth, the Atlanteans had tried unsuccessfully to also locate the Peacemaker, last used to destroy the Varsian spaceships, shortly before the City of Atlantis slid beneath the waters of the Atlantic Ocean. The resting place of this Galactic Crystal remains a mystery to this day.*

***

When the video ended and the physician removed the visor from his face, he took a deep breath and let out a big "whew," astounded by what he had witnessed. He had experienced exactly what Antonius Starlight experienced five thousand years ago—he had felt what the young man felt and sensed what he sensed, including his skepticism when Tooku told him he could change events that already took place. He had ridden the same emotional rollercoaster the Captain went on when his homeland disappeared from the earth, and he experienced Antonius' anguish when he thought his whole family had perished in the raging waters of the Atlantic Ocean. Recalling the director told him in his email that he extracted the video story verbatim from the Book of History, a recording of actual events occurring on Earth, the physician realized by watching the video he had actually travelled several thousand years back in time and, in a real sense, become Antonius Starlight. This fascinated him so much he hoped to watch the video again someday soon. He knew after uploading it into the young boy's memory, he too, upon awakening, would be able to recall all of these remarkable experiences, and actually become one of his forefathers— Antonius Starlight. He would meet that important and intriguing creature from another dimension—Tooku—who made it a habit of creeping up on Atlanteans to advise them on becoming great Leaders. The physician fervently hoped the boy had his own Celestial Guardian.

It didn't take the physician very long to make up his mind to go ahead and safely upload the video into the youngster's memory, and he didn't waste any time getting himself ready to do so. When he entered the room where the boy still lay in a coma, his MedPro vibrated twice, alerting him an email just arrived in his mailbox. Noticing it came from the director, he quickly opened it and was taken by surprise by what it asked him to do—upload into the boy's memory ten attached Wander World virtual-reality training videos that would make him proficient in flying all of Atlantis' antigravity aircraft.

Chapter 6: Dreams

To most people, and certainly to himself, Jimmy Starlight
came across as an average twelve-year old kid. He looked
average: blue eyes, nicely trimmed blond hair, about five feet
tall, and weighing around 110 pounds. He did well in school,
where he participated in some advanced courses in the sixth
grade; and like any other average kid his age, he had many
diverse interests: bicycle riding, violin playing, soccer,
horseback riding, and karate, to name a few. He lived in an
average second-level condominium with his grandmother,
Eloise, and his dog, Sparkles; in an average neighborhood,
called Belle View; in a nice town in Northern Virginia,
called Alexandria. And, like most average twelve-year olds,
he had a best friend—his was called David Whitefeather.
Things, however, are often not what they appear to be, and
Jimmy would soon realize he was not so average after all.

Jimmy loved living in Belle View. It bordered on a
beautiful park along the Potomac River, where on weekends
and holidays, he, his grandmother, and his uncle, John,
would often go picnicking; and where he and his uncle would
go fishing once in a while. He loved riding his bicycle on the
bike path running along the tree-lined parkway that cut
through his neighborhood. The ten-mile bike path let him
live out his "Tour de France" fantasy. He would race his
bicycle as fast as he could, for as long as he could; and then,
with his arms raised in celebration, imagine crossing the
finish line of this famous bicycle race in Paris—in the yellow
jersey, of course, and ahead of all the other competitors. He
also liked Belle View because it was located within walking

distance of Alexandria's historic district: Old Town Alexandria.

Within eyesight of Washington, D.C., Old Town has an abundance of eighteenth- and nineteenth-century architecture and many historic attractions relating to famous Americans, such as George Washington, Thomas Jefferson, George Mason, and Robert E. Lee. To be frank, Jimmy liked Old Town not so much for its roster of historic sites as for its ghost tours and ice cream parlors. He'd gone on several of Old Town's ghost tours and loved listening to stories about scary ghosts wandering around in its old buildings and graveyards. He also enjoyed hearing about the Town's legends and unsolved mysteries, as told in eerie voices by the eighteenth-century-costumed guides who led these nightly lantern tours. And on weekends, it had become a tradition for his grandmother to take him for dinner in one of Old Town's many restaurants and afterwards—this being the major reason why he liked this town so much—for dessert in one of its many ice cream parlors.

Jimmy had faced adversity early-on in his life; his mother and father had both perished in an accident seven years ago. Since then, Eloise, his grandmother on his mother's side, had raised him with the help of Uncle John, his late father's cousin. Judging by Jimmy's pleasant demeanor and outgoing personality, they had been quite successful in helping him handle and eventually overcome the terrible shock to his young life resulting from the sudden loss of both his parents. While he often thought about them and still missed them very much, especially when he saw other kids playing with their parents, Jimmy had stopped grieving and was determined to get on with his life. He actually didn't know much about the mishap that killed them, except that, as his uncle told him, they had perished in a boating accident. But he did know beyond a shadow of a doubt, they constantly looked down on him from heaven, and he always made sure he did things to make them proud of him. He worked very hard at being as good a student as he possibly could be and managed to make the honor roll every year since he started school. His scholastic achievements made him proud, and he genuinely looked forward to going to school every morning.

One winter night, a few seasons ago, Jimmy had a very strange dream. It differed from all the dreams he'd ever had before; and when he woke up the next morning, he could hardly wait to tell his grandmother about it. After a quick shower, he hastily dressed himself and shortly thereafter sat down at the breakfast table in their small dining room while his grandmother was still in the kitchen, pulling together his favorite breakfast: some fruit, yogurt, a glass of orange juice, a soft-boiled egg, and toast.

"Grandma, I've got to tell you about *the* most unbelievable dream I *ever* had," he told her excitedly, as she put his meal on the table. "You are *so* not going to believe this!"

"Great, but please eat your breakfast first," she pleaded. "You don't want to be late for school."

Jimmy was so keyed up that, in spite of her plea, he told her about his dream halfway through his breakfast.

"In my dream," he said, with a mouthful of yogurt, "I flew high-up in the sky on the back of a beautiful deer."

"What kind of a deer?"

"One without antlers."

"You mean a doe—*a female deer,*" Eloise said, jokingly rendering her version of some of the lyrics about a doe in the "Do-Re-Mi" song on her favorite "Sound of Music" disk.

63

"Yes, a female deer, with large brown eyes and very soft skin," Jimmy said, chuckling about her vocal rendition. "And down below, I saw a desert-like place where they had started to build a huge pyramid. It looked about halfway completed and next to it stood a large sphinx."

"A pyramid with a sphinx, how interesting," Eloise said, motioning him to finish eating his egg and toast.

Jimmy knew from school that pyramids served as tombs for ancient Egyptian kings; and last year, his history teacher had played a video in class showing a pyramid from both the inside and outside. The video's narrator stated it took over 20,000 slave laborers thirty years to build the Great Pyramid at Giza, in Egypt, some 4500 years ago. The narrator also said that in the construction of the walls of the Great Pyramid, these laborers used ropes and pulleys to lift over two million blocks of stone in place, each weighing on average five thousand pounds—and some of these blocks actually weighed as much as eighteen thousand pounds.

"You won't believe this, Grandma," Jimmy continued, "but in my dream, they didn't use ropes and pulleys to raise the large blocks of stone onto the walls of the pyramid; only some small airplanes."

He explained these small planes resembled little helicopters but didn't have any engines or rotating blades. It actually looked as if they used some kind of a magnet to pick up the huge stones and move them about like toy building blocks.

"I also saw a large hole in the ground not too far from where they built the pyramid," Jimmy said. "And in it, I could see people cutting large stones from its rocky bottom, using lasers like the ones in the Star Wars movies."

"Something like a quarry?" Eloise asked, while pointing to the fruit she wanted him to start eating.

"Yes, something like that."

Jimmy also explained, other small rotor-less aircraft raised these newly cut stones very slowly from the quarry—again without the use of ropes or cables—and deposited them in a field next to it. There he saw hundreds of these stones sitting on the ground side-by-side in long rows, neatly arranged by size. Other similar aircraft picked up some of the stones and transported them from the quarry grounds to the pyramid's construction site—again without any visible lifting tools or equipment. Once at the site, the aircraft slowed down and, heeding the hand signals of workers on the ground, carefully deposited the stones in their specified locations on top of the unfinished walls of the pyramid.

"Some of the people on the ground gave instructions to the small planes by talking into what looked like walkie-talkies, like the ones I have in my room," Jimmy said. "And all of them wore clothing just like the ancient Egyptians in the video I saw in school. It was weird!"

"Your dream has so many things happening in it," Eloise said, trying to picture all the details of what he described for her. "How can you remember it all?"

"I dunno," Jimmy said. "But there's more. In my dream, only about twenty or so people worked on that pyramid—not twenty thousand slave laborers, like the school video told us. And one person, draped in a long white robe, stood next to the Sphinx, like a statue, without ever moving."

He told her this bearded, dignified-looking man held in his hands what looked like a huge sparkling ball—about the size of a basketball—which emitted streaks of bright white light and was surrounded by a white halo.

After recalling almost all of the details of his dream, Jimmy felt rather proud of it. "What do you think it all means, Grandma?" he asked, looking at her questioningly.

At first, she just pensively shook her head as she tried to comprehend everything he just told her. Then, looking at him with a gentle expression on her face, she responded softly, "That was really a very, very interesting and mysterious dream, but I really couldn't tell you what it all means." This was followed by, "Hmm, what do you think about it?"

"I don't have a clue either," Jimmy said.

A short while later, he finished drinking his orange juice, took the lunch she had prepared for him from the refrigerator, got his book bag from his room, pecked a kiss on his grandmother's cheek, and scooted off to school.

"Hello, anyone home?" Uncle John said softly later that evening, opening the front door to Jimmy's condominium unit.

He had let himself into the building and the unit itself, using his own set of keys; and the only one to greet him at the door was Sparkles, the Golden Retriever he had given Jimmy as a puppy five years ago for his seventh birthday. Neither Jimmy nor his grandmother heard John announce himself. Jimmy sat at his desk in his room intensely focused on his homework, and Eloise attended to her dishwashing chores in the kitchen, where the running water drowned out most other noises. Seeing John, Sparkles excitedly jumped up against him, wanting to lick his face. When he pushed her back down laughing, she ran into the kitchen to announce his presence to Eloise. Not having gotten her attention immediately, she ran into Jimmy's room, and then back out again, barking loudly to let him know his uncle had arrived.

"Uncle John," Jimmy let out when he finally came out of his room to see why Sparkles was making such a ruckus. She almost knocked him down jumping up against him and

trying to lick his face. Having embraced his uncle, Jimmy
hugged Sparkles too, burying his face in her soft lustrous
gold coat. He had fallen in love with her the moment he laid
eyes on her, and they had quickly become inseparable.
Indoors, she would quietly sit next to him while he sat on the
sofa in their living-room, reading the books on his Kindle, or
lie peacefully next to him on his bed when he'd gone to
sleep. Outdoors, she would tirelessly go after the gadgets and
widgets Jimmy threw for her to fetch, like a stick, a tennis
ball, or his Frisbee.

"Grandma, Uncle John is here," Jimmy called out to
Eloise.

When she saw John, Eloise's eyes lit up with joy. She
loved him as a son and wouldn't know what to do without
him. She could not conceive of being able to raise Jimmy
without his help and constant attention to the boy's needs.

John had just passed his early forties and lived by
himself in a small townhouse about a ten-minute walk from
Jimmy's house. Like his grandmother, Jimmy loved him
dearly and respected him as if he was his father. While he
didn't know exactly what kind of work his uncle did for a
living, he suspected it had something to do with the
government. John always drove into Washington, D.C., early
in the morning and often worked till late at night; and one of
Jimmy's teachers had told him that most of the people
commuting to the nation's capital either directly or indirectly
worked for the federal government. In spite of his busy job,
John had taken it upon himself to serve as a father figure in
Jimmy's life. To make sure Jimmy and his grandmother had
everything under control, he'd always either stop by their
condominium right after work—as he did that evening—or
call on the days he could not. He had also taken a personal
interest in the quality of his young cousin's education and

67

become a member of his school's Parent Teacher Association when Jimmy started elementary school; this year he served as the PTA's president. John knew the more he kept Jimmy involved in constructive activities, the more he'd stay away from the non-productive ones that could lure a boy into trouble. So, whenever possible, he'd accompany Jimmy— usually with Eloise in tow—to after-school events, such as parents-day picnics, book fairs, concerts, and the like; and he could always be counted on to help him with his school science projects. On weekends, he'd often take Jimmy to the local library to work on his homework assignments or, since he loved to read, just to check out some new books or load others on his Kindle. John also made it a point to set aside time to take Jimmy outdoors, so he could do some horseback riding and participate in sports like soccer and tennis; or just get some fresh air out in the countryside while giving his grandma Eloise some much needed downtime for herself. John was always fun to be around; and because of his upbeat disposition and happy-go-lucky attitude, both Jimmy and Eloise always loved it when he came to visit.

"I'm so glad you stopped by this evening," Eloise said, as she kissed him on both cheeks. "Jimmy and I baked a pie, just in case you came."

"It's your favorite, Uncle John—pecan pie," Jimmy piped in. "And we also have your favorite tea to go with it."

"I just can't believe how much you guys spoil me," John replied gracefully, when Eloise served him the pie with his green tea. Having tasted it, he proclaimed, "Nobody makes better pie than the two of you!"

Jimmy's face beamed and Eloise felt rather proud of her cooking skills. While they all happily munched on the pecan pie, Jimmy told his uncle about his dream. Hoping for a good explanation, he asked, "What do you think it means, Uncle John?"

John's initial response was not much different from that of Eloise.

"Sounds like a fascinating dream," he said, "but who knows what it means or why you had it." Noticing disappointment registering on Jimmy's face, he slowly added, "But…from what you've told me…it sounds like in your dream the ancient Egyptians got some help in building their pyramids from some folks with little helicopters—rather than having to use hordes of slaves to do the job. And it also sounds like these little helicopters had some sort of antigravity device powering 'em, allowing 'em to fly without rotating blades or propellers. This, of course, also explains why they could easily lift and transport those large stones used to build that pyramid."

Noticing Jimmy's face perk up, he continued, "And, perhaps, the large sparkling ball you saw in your dream was really a large crystal, emitting some kind of a particle beam that made the antigravity devices in these little planes work."

Talk about the use of antigravity devices and particle-beam emitting crystals really peaked Jimmy's interest, and he paid close attention to what John had to say. He had read about gravity in one of the science books Uncle John had picked out for him in the library. The book said gravity is one of the four fundamental forces in the universe and the reason why everything on Earth has weight, and stays right here on the edge of the planet instead of flying off into space. He also read the Sun's gravity keeps Earth and the other planets in their orbits around this star, and Earth's gravity keeps the Moon in its orbit around the planet.

Never having heard about antigravity, Jimmy asked, "So, what are these antigravity devices anyway—the ones you mentioned—and where can I get one?"

"These devices belong to a group of space-age technologies that allow you to suspend gravity," John responded. "You can't buy them just yet, but in the not-too-distant future you will be able to. We'll need them and other advanced technologies when we travel to other planets and, eventually, to other solar systems; and our scientists work hard to make them a reality."

"So, how can they make airplanes fly?" Jimmy asked, curiously.

"Antigravity technology makes them weightless, allowing 'em to float in the air like a blimp—just as in your dream," John replied.

Jimmy quickly grasped that by utilizing antigravity devices, the little air planes could also easily lift and move the large stones around, since these devices would also have rendered them weightless.

Before going home that evening, John promised him that one day he would show him how these antigravity devices and other space-age technologies might work. When he had left, Jimmy couldn't help but wonder why his uncle seemed to know so much about these kinds of things, and why he appeared quite confident they would be available in the not-too-distant future. He had noticed John said we would need them *when* we travel to the other planets, not *if* we travel there; and he appeared to be quite certain we would someday travel to other star systems, too.

Having said goodnight to his grandma before going to bed, Jimmy confided just how excited he felt about what John had said about his dream, and he couldn't wait to hear a lot more about all the anti-gravity stuff he'd talked about.

After John walked out of Jimmy's condominium building that evening, he noticed a black van parked across the street. He had earlier seen the same van parked in the same spot just before he entered Jimmy's building. At that time, he couldn't glance inside it because the bright sunlight reflected of the car's deeply tinted glass. But this time as he strolled by the van, enough of the yellowish stream of light, emanating from a bright streetlamp lodged on a pole just above the van, filtered through its windows for him to vaguely discern two dark figures sitting in the front seats. When he turned around to ask about their reason for sitting there all evening long, the black van, all of a sudden, started up and slowly drove away.

"VARS," John murmured angrily, watching the van disappear around the corner.

He took his cell phone out of his jacket pocket and placed a call to a school in western Virginia—the Piedmont International Academy. When an operator picked up, he identified himself and asked to speak to the director; shortly thereafter, the woman in charge of the school got on the line.

"I just wanted you to know I discovered two of their operatives spying on him," John told her.

He explained a black van with darkened windows and two people in it had parked for several hours in front of Jimmy's building. The director immediately understood what he meant by *operatives*—VARS or henchmen working for them.

"How could they have found out where he lives?" she asked.

"I don't know. I hope there isn't a leak."

"Please keep a very close eye on him, and let me know if you need additional manpower. No need to tell you how high the stakes are."

"Okay, I'll do that."

"Thank you for letting me know about this."

"You're welcome, and I should also tell you Jimmy had a dream last night—about what sounded like the Peacemaker."

"What sort of a dream?" she asked.

"It had to do with the Great Pyramid and the Sphinx in Egypt. From what he told me, it sounded like they used the Peacemaker to power antigravity vehicles aiding in the pyramid's construction."

"That's very interesting; it may have something to do with the Prophecy. What do you think?"

"Yes, that's what I wondered about."

"I will ask our Atlantean friends in Egypt if anyone has heard any rumors about the Peacemaker or any of our other crystals possibly ending up there."

"That sounds like a good idea."

"Thanks again for calling," the director said, before hanging up.

After talking with the director, John carefully stepped behind some of the tall bushes growing in front of Jimmy's building. He stood there for well over an hour, keeping a close eye on his surroundings to see if the occupants of the black van were up to anything else. As he walked home, he again wondered how the VARS could have known about Jimmy. He found it hard to believe they had an informant inside his organization. *Atlanteans would never betray their own and work for the enemy, especially the VARS,* he thought. But he had an eerie feeling the VARS were well-informed about Jimmy's destiny and getting ready to interfere in it. He felt somewhat relieved that Eloise and Jimmy had Sparkles in the house to keep an eye on them when he was not around.

A month or so after his first strange dream, Jimmy had another one, just as perplexing to him as the first. It involved the same solemn stranger decked out in a white robe, standing silently next to the Sphinx. As in his first dream, the man held with both hands what Jimmy now thought of as a huge crystal emitting streaks of bright white light. Unlike that dream, however, the stranger didn't just stand there with the crystal in his hands, but he actually handed it to him. After he took it, carefully cradling it with both arms, Jimmy felt its power; and a most pleasant feeling permeated his body. Holding the crystal made him feel weightless, like floating in the air. Then, "poof," the man and his crystal instantly disappeared, and he found himself standing in a little room surrounded by four stone walls. The room smelled musky, and he could see a small entranceway providing access to it from what looked like a long narrow tunnel. Then he saw the crystal again, this time sitting on a large pedestal in the middle of the room, still emitting its bright light, with the white halo surrounding it. He walked over to the pedestal, aching to hold the crystal again, to once more experience the beautiful, peaceful feeling it brought him before. Then, when he was about to touch it, it vanished—and he woke up.

Because of his two very mysterious dreams involving the big crystal, Jimmy Starlight suspected he was not a typical twelve-year old after all. His suspicion would increase drastically after his little world began to turn upside down.

After he had his second dream, Jimmy couldn't stop thinking about it for the longest time; and as with the first one, he constantly wondered what it meant and why he had it. When his uncle dropped by at the end of the week to play some chess, Jimmy told him about his dream, and asked if he had ever seen such a large crystal. His conversation with the director of the Piedmont International Academy about the Peacemaker came to John's mind; and for a split second, he considered telling Jimmy about it. But he discarded the thought because he didn't want to divulge anything about Jimmy's prophesized role in the Atlanteans' struggle with the VARS, without thoroughly preparing him for it.

"No, I've never seen that kind of a crystal," John told him, "but that doesn't mean there might not be one stashed away somewhere on this earth."

Wanting to steer Jimmy's train of thought away from his dream, John offered to take him and his friend David on a one-day skiing trip the following weekend in the nearby mountains of western Virginia. Jimmy gladly accepted his invitation, and for the rest of the day his mind was on skiing. Having never skied before, he had lots of questions for John about ski equipment, resorts, lifts, and slopes; and he couldn't wait to ask David if he would be able to go.

Early the next morning, the ringer of the intercom system to the outside door of the building buzzed inside Jimmy's condominium unit. He had just finished dressing in his bedroom; and after running into the hallway to respond to this piercing sound, he quickly pushed the "communicate" button on the intercom. Wondering who would stop by this early in the day, he took a deep breath before speaking into the system's built-in microphone.

"Hello, who is it?"

An excited voice on the other end responded.

"Jimmy, it's me, David. We're going for doughnuts and hot chocolate at Bennant's—wanna come?"

Bennant's referred to the bakery located in the shopping center about a fifteen minute walk from Jimmy's house. David, who lived in a high-rise condominium just around the corner from him intended to walk over to Bennant's with his family for breakfast; and he wanted to know if Jimmy would like to tag along—he didn't have to ask twice.

"Oh, yeah, for sure!" Jimmy replied. "Hold on, let me ask Grandma."

After an okay from Eloise, Jimmy hurried out the door and hustled down two flights of stairs to the ground floor. When he popped out the building's front door, he saw the happy faces of David, his parents, and his two younger sisters, all patiently waiting for him.

"Hi, Jimmy, good to see you again," David's father, James Whitefeather, said, shaking his hand.

"Oh, hi, Mr. Whitefeather," Jimmy said, looking up at the tall stately man with shoulder-length, raven-black hair and a kind face. "—and hi, Mrs. Whitefeather."

"Glad you could come, Jimmy." David's mother said, with a warm smile.

"Me too, I'm very hungry." He made her a happy face.

Both of David's parents were full-blooded Hapua Indians, which meant, of course, he and his sisters were also full-blooded Hapuas. David had lived on the Hapua Indian Reservation in the Southwest till shortly before his sixth birthday, at which time his parents moved to Alexandria. His

75

father, a medical doctor, had run a medical clinic on the Hapua reservation where David was born. He took his family to Alexandria after accepting a job at the Headquarters of the Bureau of Indian Affairs in Washington, D.C. David's mother, who worked as a nurse at the reservation clinic, had taken a part-time job at a clinic in Alexandria. His grandfather, the Hapuas' shaman, still lived on the reservation. Each year, David spent one month with him during his summer vacation, learning about shamanic healing, and honing his ability to mentally communicate with beings and spirits in other dimensions. His grandfather, a serene man, taught him the Hapua way of life embraced love and peace, and fostered harmony with the planet and its environment.

Jimmy and David got to know each other in first grade of elementary school about six years ago and became friends almost immediately. Giving David a bear hug, Jimmy said, "Hey, thanks for the invite, I'm really starving."

"So am I," David said, grinning mightily, happy his friend decided to come along. The same age as Jimmy, he already stood six feet tall, with the same color shoulder-length hair as his dad. Proud of his Indian heritage, he sported a small braid on his left side, in which he had fastened a rare all-black eagle feather given him by his grandfather.

"Come on, I'll race you there," Jimmy yelled as he took off running towards Bennant's.

Jimmy could run, but when it came to sprinting, he was no match for the taller boy, who easily caught up with him. His friend purposely slowed down to stay even; but when they got to within half a block or so of Bennant's, he kicked in the afterburner and got there several seconds before

Jimmy. Winded and laughing, they put an arm around each other and sat down on the curb to wait for the others.

While they waited, Jimmy said to David, "Uncle John wants to take you and me skiing for the day next weekend. I sure hope you can make it."

"But I don't know how to ski," his friend said. "And where would we go?"

"We're going to the slopes in western Virginia, and I don't know how to ski either. But not to worry; Uncle John said, knowing the two of us, he could teach us in no time."

"Sounds like a great adventure. I'd love to go, but I need to ask my parents first."

The dozen freshly baked doughnuts David's mother purchased at Bennant's disappeared in no time—with Jimmy and David each making short thrift of three of them.

"And how are you doing in school these days?" David's father inquired of Jimmy, watching the two boys savor their hot chocolate at one of the tables in front of the bakery's counter. "Still keeping up the grades?"

"School is great, and I'm doing really well," Jimmy responded. "But I like the weekends much better, especially when we get to come to Bennant's."

"Oh, yeah, what we get at Bennant's beats anything we get in the school cafeteria," David added, laughing.

"That's putting it mildly," Jimmy said. He normally brought a nutritious lunch prepared by his grandmother to school, because he found school food lacking both in variety and taste. The exception came on Fridays, when lunch in the school cafeteria included "pizza extravaganza"—a lunch featuring several varieties of pizza that had, by Jimmy's standards, "great taste."

David's father and mother were aware Jimmy excelled in all of his classes. Because of this, they considered him a

77

good role model for their son and encouraged David's friendship with him. They knew Jimmy had made the honor role at school for the past five years and expected him to do so again this year. It also sat well with them that Jimmy participated in several of his school's extracurricular activities; he played violin in the strings ensemble and saxophone in the band, and attended the school's after-hours Spanish language program.

Having to adjust to an environment radically different from the Indian reservation, David had struggled in his new school for the first two years; but then he improved his grades each year as he tried to keep up with Jimmy. Last year, to his parents' pleasant surprise, David had also made the honor role; and, because Jimmy played in the band, David had decided to join, too, and took up playing the drums.

"And how are your grandma and uncle doing?" David's father asked.

He asked about them not to make polite conversation, but because he truly cared about both people. He liked and respected Jimmy's grandmother immensely for the way she raised her grandson, and he appreciated John for the effort he put forth in trying to be a good father-figure in Jimmy's life.

"They're doing great," Jimmy said. "Grandma made a new quilt for Uncle John's birthday tomorrow, and you'll see him at the game this afternoon."

He was referring to the indoor soccer match David and he planned to compete in later that day. With John's encouragement, Jimmy had decided to get into various sports, and David had eagerly joined him in a number of them. On Saturdays, the two of them played together on a youth team in the county soccer league. Because of his size, David played goal-keeper; and Jimmy, because of his nifty foot work, passing skills, and good understanding of the game, played center mid-field. In the winter time, they played indoors; and in the fall and springtime, outdoors. Both Uncle John and David's father always came to as many games as possible to show their support, and having them at the game meant the world to the boys.

"I'm so glad he's coming," David's father said. "We love watching the two of you play."

Since they talked about Jimmy's uncle, David made use of the opportunity to tell his father about John's offer to take both of them skiing. "Whaddaya say, Dad?" he said, looking at his father, hoping for a favorable response. "It is next weekend, and we have no plans."

His father shot a glance at his mother, who overheard what her son had said and nodded her head in approval. She generally supported him taking on new challenges, or learning new skills such as skiing, as long as it did not interfere with his schoolwork. She felt that way about the once-a-week tae kwon do karate classes David and Jimmy attended in the nearby county recreation center. They had participated in these classes for the past five years and managed to earn several advanced karate belts. She had supported their participation, because it not only presented them with a continuous challenge to reach higher skill levels in the sport, but it also nurtured skills needed to effectively deal with the adversities and stumbling blocks of daily life.

"Sounds like a good time, Son," his father said of the proposed ski trip. "And we can use all of next week to get you outfitted."

"*Yes!*" David exclaimed. "You're the best." He then said to Jimmy, "Please tell your uncle, it's a go for next weekend."

"Okay, he'll be glad to hear that," Jimmy said happily.

79

When Uncle John came to Jimmy's soccer game that afternoon, he and David's father cheered on the two boys in a match their team won handily. Then, they accompanied them to the usual after-game pizza-and-root beer get-together with the rest of the team at Fabulous Phil's Pizza Parlor.

"Have you decided on the ski resort to take 'em to next week?" David's father asked John, as they watched the boys finish the last two slices of their deep-dish pepperoni pizza.

"I think we'll go to Green Mountain," John replied, "if they have enough snow there."

"I've heard about that resort; and if I remember correctly, it's only a couple of hours west of here."

"Yes, that's right."

"Is that why you want to go there…Uncle John?" Jimmy asked, swallowing his last bite of pizza.

"Well, besides being close by, the resort also has several excellent beginner slopes, great for teaching the basics," John responded. "It has quite a few chair lifts too, which keeps the waiting time to a minimum. And it further appeals to me, because it's a *truly-green* resort. "

He explained Green Mountain not only had beautiful evergreens and green shrubbery all over it, but windmills as well. "When we get there," he told the boys, "you'll see high up on the mountain over a dozen windmills quietly generating green electricity for the ski lifts and the resort's other equipment and facilities."

"I'm glad to hear that," David's father said. "I strongly supported making electricity from renewable resources on our Indian reservation in Arizona."

"And so does Grandpa," David added. "He always complains that burning coal to generate electricity pollutes the air on our reservation and dumps acid rain in our streams and waters. He also hates strip mining coal; he says it will destroy our lands and hurt our planet."

"Your grandfather has it right, Son," David's father said, looking proudly at him. "Destroying the land and polluting the air is bad for our people and our planet. The wind, given to us by our Creator, makes pollution-free electricity; and harvesting the wind does not destroy our lands."

"You speak with words of wisdom we can all appreciate," John said. "Someday soon, I would love to hear more about how you use renewable energy on your reservation; but for now, unless the boys want some more pizza, what do you think about heading home, James?"

"Yes, I think this is a good time," David's father said, getting up. "They've had a long day and they look full—right boys?"

"Yep, I'm completely full," David said.

"And so am I," Jimmy joined in. "Filled to the brim."

"Okay, then," John said, also getting out of his chair, "let's hit the road. And by the way, James, why don't you come along on our trip, too?"

"Wish I could," James said, appreciating the offer. "But next week will be a busy one for me—maybe next time?"

When the two boys walked out of Fabulous Phil's a short while later, feeling good about their win, David told Jimmy, "I can't wait to learn how to ski and see that mountain with all the windmills on it."

"Me, too," Jimmy said, hugging his friend goodbye. "I hope next week will go by really fast."

During the whole week, Jimmy constantly wished for time to hurry by and endlessly counted the days and hours until his first-ever ski trip. But Father Time took his time, and it seemed to take forever for Saturday morning to roll around. When it finally did, he got up at the crack of dawn; and before too long, he stood all bundled up in his new scarf, ski pants, and ski jacket on the balcony of his condominium, looking for his uncle, who planned to pick him up at eight o'clock in the morning. Because he was staring down the street intensely, he never even noticed the black van with the darkened windows parked again across the street from his condominium.

Seeing John's sports utility vehicle coming down the road, Jimmy shouted to Eloise, "Grams, he's here," and hurried back inside to grab his ski cap and gloves.

After gratefully accepting the munchies and juice drinks his grandmother had readied for the two-hour drive to the ski resort, he kissed her on the cheek and went down on his knees to hug Sparkles. "Good girl," he whispered, while the dog jumped all over him.

"I think you look really terrific," Eloise said affectionately, when he stood back up.

"Well, thanks, Grams," Jimmy said, pleased to be wearing his new colorful ski outfit.

"And I know you will have lots of fun out there on the slopes with John and David."

"Yes, I think so, too."

"But, please, be careful; I've heard about people getting hurt by reckless skiers."

"Of course, Grandma, I'll promise."

Jimmy gave Eloise a big hug before getting out the door. Once outside, he spotted his uncle's SUV parked a little ways down the street and quickly ran up to it.

John noticed the black van the minute he parked his car; and as soon as he saw it, he got an eerie feeling its occupants were up to no good. He contemplated getting out of his SUV and walking over to the van to confront them about lying in wait again in front of Jimmy's condominium. But when he saw him sprinting in his direction, he decided to stay in his car.

John bent over and opened the passenger-side front door to let Jimmy in.

"Howdy, partner," he greeted his young cousin, who quickly climbed into the seat next to him. "Ready for some *skiing*?"

"*Of course,* I am!"

"Then, let's *blast outa here!*"

"Yeah, man—*let's get outa here!*" Jimmy said, playing along. "Can I drive?"

"Perhaps another day," John replied. "But if you want, you can be the designated backseat driver; and when you get *really* good at it, I'll give you some real driving lessons."

"Oh, shucks, you're not much *fun*," Jimmy lamented, jokingly.

"But—enough fun to go skiing with, right?"

"Yeah, I guess so."

"Well, in that case, let's get out of here!"

John started up his car and waved to Eloise, who along with Sparkles stood on the balcony. She waved back and said a quick prayer for their safe return. As they pulled out, Jimmy turned in his seat and also gave a wave to his grandmother, who by now strained mightily to keep a hold of Sparkles' collar. With both front paws on the railing, the dog looked like she wanted to jump off the balcony and follow Jimmy down the road; but Eloise was not about to let that happen and grabbed her collar even tighter.

When John drove his SUV to the high-rise where David lived, he watched the black van in his rear view mirror as it pulled out of its parking spot and started trailing them down the road. It stopped on the side of the road after they entered the driveway to David's condominium. Along with his dad, he had patiently waited for them in the ground-floor lobby of his building; but the moment he saw John's SUV, he rushed outside, obviously excited about the upcoming trip. His father followed right behind him, carrying David's AWOL bag containing his ski jacket and other warm outdoor attire, and the huge bag of cookies and pastries his mom had also prepared for the trip.

"Let's give 'em a hand with his stuff," John suggested, opening the automatic rear door of his SUV before getting out.

Having also stepped out, Jimmy hugged his friend and helped his dad put the big AWOL bag in the back of the car.

"Thank you, Jimmy," James said. "You look like you're ready for the slopes."

"Yep, I've been ready all week."

Turning to John and shaking his hand, Mr. Whitefeather confided, "David looked forward to this trip all week, too. I can't tell you how much his mother and I appreciate you taking him along."

"We're glad he could come," John said. "Too bad you can't come, also."

They all waved goodbye to Mr. Whitefeather after John put the SUV in gear and slowly pulled out of the driveway. It didn't take long before they reached the main highway outside of town, leading to the Green Mountain resort. Shortly thereafter, John spotted the black van again, following them at what the two occupants considered a safe distance; they mistakenly thought they had not been noticed.

The two hour ride to the resort was scenic. The two boys, riding in the back, had panoramic views of the snow-covered hills, interlaced with gently sloping fields, also blanketed in white. While every now and then flurries of snow engulfed their car, the main roads, snowplowed and salted earlier in the day, remained clear.

Before too long, David, who had never ridden in John's SUV before, noticed the car's engine only made a soft humming noise.

"This car sounds a lot like the cart my dad lets me drive when we play golf," he said, wondering why it rode so quietly.

"Yes, it does sound like a golf cart," John said.

"How come?" David asked.

Before John could answer, Jimmy replied, "Because it also has an electric motor."

"Does it run on a battery like a golf cart?" David also asked.

"No, it doesn't," Jimmy told him. "It runs on a fuel cell."

Jimmy had asked John the same questions when he first rode in his SUV several years ago and, by now, knew all about fuel cells. Not wanting to let on he had no idea what a fuel cell entailed, David just nodded his head. Suspecting this, John came to his rescue.

"As you probably know," he told him, "a fuel cell acts just like a giant battery. The main difference between the two is that a fuel cell uses hydrogen to produce the electricity which runs the electric motor in my car. And, because it has a fuel cell, my car only exhausts small drops of water from the tailpipe—instead of the dirty exhausts produced by the gasoline engines of some other SUVs."

Wanting to contribute to the conversation, David said, "I remember our science teacher, Mr. Bartles, telling us in class how dirty exhausts pollute the air everyone breathes and damage the environment."

"That's right," John agreed.

"And he also said," David added, "polluted air gives kids asthma, especially those living in the big cities."

"Right again," John said.

"When I buy my own car, I'll definitely get one with a fuel cell in it," David proclaimed.

"Me, too," Jimmy agreed, "but I want to have an SUV with a fuel cell in it." He liked riding in his uncle's car because it not only had lots of room and comfort, but also allowed him to sit up high, making it much easier to see the area around him.

"Good for you guys," John said. "And the sooner you save your money, the faster you can get one."

Both boys nodded their heads and visualized driving their own fuel cell cars.

During the remainder of the two hour trip, Jimmy and David mostly chatted about downhill racing, snowboarding, and various other ways of speeding down the mountain. They also feasted on the pastries and other goodies Eloise and David's mother had packed for them. In the meantime, John took in the beautiful scenery and enjoyed the quiet ride of his car, complemented by the tranquility of the countryside. He continued to keep an eye on the black van in his rear view mirror as it trailed them all the way to the ski resort's parking lot. After he parked his SUV, he saw the van enter the lot and come to a halt on the far side from where he had parked. And it just sat there while he and the two boys headed for the lodge to pick up their ski equipment.

They spent quite a bit of time in the rental office of the ski lodge because John wanted to ensure their equipment fit them properly.

"Make sure your boots feel comfortable," he advised. "Unhappy feet make for very unhappy skiers."

Once fitted with the right size boots, the boys had little trouble locking the buckles and tightening the power straps; but getting used to walking in the tight-fitting contraptions, latched way up above their ankles, was another story. John had to laugh at the awkward expressions on their faces as they took their first steps.

"Do we have to wear *these monstrosities* all day?" Jimmy asked, laughingly, taking elephant steps in front of the rental desk. "This is hard work."

"Actually, this is the easy part," John said. "Moving about with your skis on is going to be a bigger challenge— until you get the hang of it, that is."

Outfitted with the proper equipment, they lumbered from the equipment room to the large veranda outside the lodge, each carrying a helmet and their own set of skis and poles. There, they briefly sat down on one of wooden benches to look at the brochures they had gotten from the rental office, showing the location of the various ski trails. The veranda afforded a breathtaking view of the snowy mountain and the resort at its base. It also gave a clear view of the dozens of windmills standing majestically on top of the mountain about two hundred feet apart, with their huge blades catching the wind and turning slowly.

"Wow," Jimmy let out, marveling at the sight of dozens of skiers zigzagging down the mountain on the long meandering trails.

Having acquainted themselves with the layout of the resort, they stepped down from the veranda directly onto the snow-covered staging area. There, skiers readied themselves to glide down a short trail to the chair lifts, which would take them up the mountain to the jump-off points for the various ski trails. It was also the place where all the trails came together to a joint finish, and where the expert snowboarders, having traversed back and forth across the slopes without any ski poles, executed hockey stops at the end of their runs.

As he watched their amazing balancing acts on a single board, Jimmy nudged David with his elbow. "Look at those guys," he said excitedly. "That's going to be us in no time."

"Yes, you're right; we'll soon be skiing just like 'em," David said, feeling similarly exhilarated.

Looking at John, Jimmy asked, "Can you teach us that?" He pointed to a ski-boarder who came to a perfect hockey stop only a few yards away from them, sending a stream of snow spraying upward in their direction from the edge of her board.

"Sure, later," John responded, "but, first, we shall go to the bunny hill."

"The bunny hill—we have to go to the bunny hill?" Jimmy moaned. "Uncle John, we're not little kids anymore."

"Don't worry," John explained, "It's not just for little kids. All skiers start with a basic lesson on the bunny hill— over there." He pointed to a small elevation off to the side of the beginners' trail. "You start your practice sessions over there and get used to being on your skis."

Tracking up to the bunny hill, they carried their poles in one hand and steadied their skis on one of their shoulders with the other. On the weekend, with the slopes crowded, accidents happen more frequently; and so, even though both boys griped about it, John had insisted that, while on the slopes, they wear their helmets at all times. Having reached

88

the bunny hill, he showed them how to snap on their skis, and started their first lesson.

"You first need to know your basic stance," John explained. They quickly understood—legs slightly parted, knees bent, and hands centered over the skis. "Next you must learn how to snowplow down the hill." With the tips of his skis close together and ends wide apart, John demonstrated how to slowly slide straight down the hill—just like a snowplow. He also showed them how to change direction by putting their weight over one ski, and go the opposite direction by shifting their weight to the other. "To come to a full stop," he told them, "you must position yourself perpendicular to the hill and, then, center your weight over both skis."

As good athletes do, the two boys easily followed his lead, and the class proceeded smoothly as they snowplowed down the bunny hill. Then, things deteriorated. When John showed them how to take a sideways fall with their skis on without getting hurt, Jimmy pounded him with a snowball just before he got back on his feet. Laughing heartily, he retaliated; and in no time, a full-fledged snowball fight had erupted, with all three of them flinging dozens of snowy projectiles at each other.

Having declared a truce, John started another lessons and showed them how to sidestep up the hill. Things deteriorated again when, trying to follow his lead, the boys tripped over each other's skis and ended up sliding down the bunny hill on their backsides—skis sticking up in the air. This time, John initiated the battle by hurling two well-placed snowballs at the tangled-up boys. Jimmy and David quickly responded and war had started. When things had settled back down again, both boys quickly mastered their sidestepping technique; and after taking a little breather, the three of them walked up the beginners' slope for their next lesson.

After they reached the top of the slope, Jimmy said to his uncle, "Thanks for your help, Uncle John. I think we can ski down this trail by ourselves."

David nodded his head in agreement.

John had his doubts but appreciated their confidence; and when they started to snowplow down the hill, he remained at the top. He tried not to laugh when a short while later they both wiped out and splashed head-over-heels into a snow drift at the edge of the trail—arms, legs and skis flying everywhere. He hurried down to make sure they hadn't hurt themselves and was glad to see the smiles on their faces. Thanks to the safety features on their equipment, their skis immediately detached from their boots as they went tumbling down the hill. With only their pride slightly injured by the fall, they both started to laugh and made snow angels in the foot-deep snow.

"Yes, I can tell you're ready." John said, bursting out laughing—causing them to laugh even harder.

A little while later, having brushed off the snow, Jimmy and David got back on their feet and quickly snapped their skis back on. Then, they happily continued plowing down the hill again, wiping out a few more times before reaching the end of the trail.

After a rather shaky start, they both learned to keep their balance and, to John's pleasant surprise, completed several runs down the beginners' slope without crashing into the powdery white stuff again. It also didn't take very long before they managed to safely ski down the intermediate slope, with John trailing slightly behind them, feeling like a proud parent. Since they both appeared ready and able to ski by themselves, he decided to take a break and give them some time on their own.

"I'm going to the lodge to warm up a little," he told the boys, as they stood in line for another ride on the chairlift to the top of the intermediate slope. "So, please, be careful."

"Don't worry, Uncle John," Jimmy said, elated David and he would soon zoom down the trail by themselves—just like two experienced skiers. "We'll be fine."

As they went up the mountain on the chairlift, they both waved at him a few times. Watching them disappear from view, John felt pleased. The two boys thoroughly enjoyed themselves; and Jimmy had not once mentioned anything during the trip about his strange dreams.

Having detached his skis and standing them upright in one of the racks along the edge of the staging area, John walked over to the veranda and headed for the lodge's cozy restaurant. Accessible from an outside entrance on the veranda, it allowed a good view of all the trails, the staging area, and the chairlifts. He intended to keep an eye on the boys from one of the restaurant's several bay windows.

Once inside, John walked up to the raging fire burning in the open fireplace in the center of the restaurant for a quick warm-up. Turning his back towards the fire, he looked the place over and couldn't help but immediately notice the two men in cowboy outfits standing right in front of the large center bay window. Except for the huge silver belt buckles, their attire was all black: black dress jeans, black western shirts, black corduroy sports coats, black Stetsons, black cowboy boots, and black sunglasses. One of the men, a short, chubby, bald person, with broad shoulders and hardly any neck, constantly fidgeted with his Stetson, lifting it up to run his thick fingers across his bald head to wipe away the sweat.

91

John thought, judging by his built, he might have been a wrestler in his younger days. The other man, tall, skinny, and sinister-looking, with long dark hair protruding from underneath his Stetson, constantly stared out the window. Because of their outfits, they couldn't help but stand out in a crowd of skiers—all wearing brightly-colored skiwear.

Not too long after he first noticed the two urban cowboys, John moved away from the fireplace and sat down at a table near one of the other large bay windows.

"Can I help you, sir?" a young waitress asked.

John quickly looked through the food menu and responded, "Yes, please, I would like a hot chocolate and a couple of your warm oatmeal cookies."

When she returned with his order, the waitress said, "Can you believe those two strange guys over there?" She rolled her eyes in the direction of the two cowboys. "They've just stood there in front of that window for almost an hour, staring at someone out there, without ever ordering anything."

"Yeah, they didn't come here to ski—that's for sure," John said, before he thanked her for his hot chocolate and cookies.

Having observed the two men for a while, he all of sudden realized the person they were constantly watching through the bay window was Jimmy. Using binoculars, and paying no attention to the stares of the people around him, the tall, skinny man—apparently in charge—kept track of him every time he rode the chairlift up, and again as he skied down the mountain. He seemed to pay attention to every move Jimmy made on the ski slope, pointing out his exact location to his colleague, who for no apparent reason, all of sudden, started to nervously pace back and forth in front of the table in back of them. As the chubby man's restless pacing ramped up, he lost his Stetson when he tripped over one of the chairs and fell over backwards, knocking down the table and several other chairs. This drew even more attention from the restaurant's patrons, but both men seemed oblivious to the wondering stares they drew.

"Is there anything I can get you, gentlemen?" the young waitress asked, after she helped right up the knocked-over table and chairs and handed the chubby man his hat. He scared her when, without saying anything, he chirped like a bird and rubbed one of his hands several times over his bald head and across his portly face. The waitress quickly ran off, praying he would not come after her when she heard another chirp. The tall man, seemingly unaware of what was happening around him, continued to watch Jimmy closely— not knowing John was now watching both of them closely too.

It didn't take too long for him to figure out these two men occupied the black van that had followed his SUV to the resort. While keeping an eye on them, he took out his cell phone and dialed the number of the Piedmont International Academy. When the school's operator took his call, he asked to speak to the director again and was quickly connected.

"At least two operatives followed us all the way from Alexandria, and they have kept Jimmy in their sights with binoculars ever since we arrived here," John told her, having explained he and the boys came to Green Mountain on a ski trip.

"VARS?" she wanted to know.

"Judging by their looks, most likely humans in their employ. They keep track of every move he makes. After the boys finish skiing, I wanted to take them to the park just down the road to look at the deer; but now I'm a little concerned about it."

"I'm glad you called. Don't worry about stopping by the park. I'll send help—enough help to overpower them if things get out of hand. They should arrive within the hour. Also, for your information, we've checked into how the VARS could have found out about Jimmy; we suspect treason within our own ranks. I will tell you more about it when we confirm our suspicions. We also contacted our friends in Egypt regarding any sightings of the Peacemaker or rumors of its presence in that part of the world; they're still looking into it."

"Please, let me know when you hear back from them."

"Of course, I will do so. Did you drive your SUV?"

"Yes, I did. And thank you for your assistance."

"You're welcome. Watch your back, and call me if you have any problems."

"Okay."

When she hung up the phone, John took a deep breath. He was shocked by her revelation. He didn't want to believe corrupt Atlanteans might have aided the enemy. He realized this possibility would change the way in which he fulfilled his mission to keep Jimmy safe and prepare him for his leadership role. The VARS might be tipped off about the safeguards he put in place to keep them away from him, and they would do their best to circumvent them. And any concern about whom to trust, even the slightest one, would make it more difficult to pick the right individuals to help train him safely. Even though John trusted the Piedmont director beyond a shadow of a doubt, he wondered if there could be an enemy collaborator among the help she promised to send his way.

Chapter 8: In the Park

Still thinking about his conversation with the director, John walked out of the restaurant and positioned himself at the edge of the veranda, so he could spot the boys as they completed their runs down the mountain. It didn't take long before he saw the two of them coming down the intermediate trail, and he started waving his arms to catch their attention. When he did, they both headed in his direction.

As he approached his uncle, Jimmy said enthusiastically, "Hey, Uncle John, why don't you put your skis back on and race us down the hill one time?"

"Yes, and let's all go down the advanced slope this time," David suggested, ignoring his body's signals telling him to slow down.

Having skied for over two hours, both boys felt tired and needed a break. Even though they would never admit it, snowplowing down the slopes had taken a toll on their legs; and their feet had numbed from continued restriction in their tight ski boots. But their eyes still shone bright with excitement; and if it were up to them, they would gladly make a few more runs down the mountain.

Not wanting them to overdo it during their first ski-outing, John said, "No thanks, guys; but why don't we get the two of you something to eat?"

Being both hungry and thirsty, they agreed—though reluctantly. A short while later, after they devoured their hamburgers and French fries in the lodge's restaurant while being watched by the two cowboys from across the room, John had a suggestion. He told them if they returned their equipment now and got on the road with plenty of daylight left, they could drive home a slightly different way and briefly drop by a nearby state park to look at the deer.

"In the winter," he said, "they congregate on the side of the park's main road in the hope of getting some handouts from the park's visitors."

"Aren't they afraid of people?" Jimmy asked.

"Normally, yes," John replied, "but not in the winter time."

He explained during the winter months the deer cannot find in the park the food they depend on for much of the year, such as acorns and beechnuts. And because park visitors feel sorry for them and give them people-food to eat, the deer won't dart off at the sight of humans as they would normally do.

"Maybe we can give them some of our munchies?" Jimmy wondered out loud, knowing the three of them could never eat all the cookies and other snacks they had in the back of the car.

"That's probably not a good idea," John said. "Feeding the deer makes them dependent on people for their food and keeps them from searching for the few remaining natural food sources available in the winter time—like the buds and twigs of small plants."

He told them park rangers posted signs discouraging visitors from feeding the deer, because they can actually get most of their daily energy requirements for making it safely through the winter from their own fatty tissues accumulated during the summer and fall months—provided they eat their natural foods in sufficient quantities.

"Well, even if we can't feed the deer," Jimmy remarked, "I'd still love to see 'em."

"Me, too," David said. "And I should also tell you when we lived on the reservation, my grandfather also told us not to feed the deer for the same reasons."

"That's it, then," John said. "To the park we go."

He did not tell them about the real reason he wanted to get back on the road with plenty of daylight left: the presence of the two cowboys.

The Piedmont International Academy, a secondary co-educational boarding school for students—seventh grade and up—had opened its doors a little over fifteen years ago in a location about an hour's drive from the Green Mountain resort. John expected the "help" the director had referred to, said to arrive within about an hour, to come from the school. When he and the two boys walked from the ski lodge to their SUV about an hour and a half after he talked with the director, John noticed the two cowboys scurrying to their van—still parked in the same spot at the far end of the parking lot. He'd gotten a call on his cell phone from Piedmont saying the "help" had arrived. As they drove out of the ski resort's parking lot, John noticed the black van started to depart too. He also saw a white van leaving from the opposite end of the parking lot. When they got to the main road, it positioned itself directly behind them, in front of the black van; John correctly assumed this white van contained the "help" from Piedmont.

It took about twenty minutes to drive to the state park where hundreds of white-tailed deer roamed around in the fields adjacent to the main road and further down in the wooded areas. When John stopped his SUV on the shoulder of the road to allow Jimmy and David to get a closer look at the deer, the white van stopped about twenty car lengths

97

behind them; and the black van, in turn, stopped at a similar distance behind the white van.

"Wow, look at all those beautiful deer!" Jimmy let out, "They're all over the place." He loved being around animals and marveled at the opportunity to see the deer up close.

It was then he heard the soft little voice for the first time.

"Go visit the deer," it whispered softly in his ear, "the ones in the field staring at you. Go see them."

Looking out of the rear-passenger window, Jimmy saw a dozen deer grazing in a nearby field off the side of the car. All of a sudden, they raised their heads in unison and stared at the SUV, as if it startled them. With a very surprised look on his face, Jimmy shot a glance at David and then at John to see if they might have also heard the little voice. Neither one of them gave an indication of having heard anything unusual; both had focused their attention on a large group of deer mulling about in the fields further down the road. The little voice had sounded feminine and trustworthy, and reminded him of his mother's voice. As he contemplated what the little voice just said, he heard it again.

"Go now," it said tenderly.

Feeling awkward about a little voice whispering in his ear, telling him to go look at the deer in the field, Jimmy hesitated to follow its advice. Then, one of the deer that had stared in his direction started to walk towards the car. When she got to within thirty feet of it, she looked straight at Jimmy and then turned around and headed back towards the other deer in the nearby field. Jimmy, suddenly, realized she looked just like the doe he had flown on in his dream about the Great Pyramid.

"Yes, that's her, the one in your dream," the little voice said. "Now, please, go over there."

This time, Jimmy didn't hesitate. He got out of the SUV and calmly walked towards the small group of deer staring intently at him.

"Hey, where're you going?" John asked, surprised Jimmy had not requested his permission to get out of the car. He lowered his car window and shouted, "Please, don't go too far."

Jimmy stopped and turned round. "Okay, I'll stay close," he yelled back.

"I think you better stay put," John cautioned David, knowing he just itched to also jump out of the car and follow his friend into the nearby field. John had seen the black van stop a ways back of them and thought it better for the boys to watch the deer from the car, rather than venture amongst them.

When Jimmy continued walking slowly towards the deer, John and David were surprised to see the animals starting to move towards him, even though he did not have any food or treats in his hands to give them. Some of them came so close Jimmy reached out and softly stroked their foreheads. John became concerned when, all of a sudden, many of the other deer tracked over from nearby fields and also started to crowd around him. One of the deer gently nudged the others out of her way to get closer to him; and when she got to within a few feet, Jimmy noticed her. There was no doubt in his mind—this was the doe from his dream. After nudging her way next to him, she raised her head and blinked one of her big brown eyes, as if to wink at him.

"There you are," Jimmy said warmly, reaching out and hugging her gently with both arms around her neck. "I'm so glad to see you."

When she let him touch her, he realized his dream had a real purpose and meant to convey something important to him. Then he heard the little voice again.

"Please get back into the car," it said softly.

Having just met the doe of his dream, Jimmy wasn't quite ready to go back.

"I can't leave her now, I just found her," he said almost pleadingly, looking around carefully to see where the voice came from—but detecting only lots of deer around him.

"Better get back," the little voice urged. "Your uncle will worry about you."

Okay, I'll tell him about my doe and then come back here again, Jimmy thought.

With a happy smile on his face, he turned around, intending to walk back to the SUV; but he could only take a few steps, because the herd of deer surrounding him effectively kept him from moving any further.

"I can't move, Uncle John," he shouted in the direction of the car, thinking, *Now what do I do?*

Even though all of this occurred rather unexpectedly, Jimmy at no time felt any of the animals threatened his safety. Then, a series of startling events unfolded that took him way out of his comfort zone. All of a sudden, after swerving onto the main road and racing around the white van, the black van drove directly into the field where Jimmy stood. The deer at the edge of the road scampered out of the way; luckily none of them got hurt as the van headed straight for the boy. When it got to within fifty feet of him, the chubby cowboy jumped out and, huffing and puffing, began wading fiercely through the dense herd surrounding Jimmy—with the obvious intent of grabbing and dragging him into the black van.

As soon as the cowboy got out of his van, two other things happened almost simultaneously. Out of the corner of one eye, Jimmy saw three men jump out of the white van and immediately race towards him. Out of the corner of his other eye, he saw John jump out of his SUV and also rush towards him.

"Jimmy, come back *now*!" John shouted, waving his arms wildly and motioning him to come back to the car.

"Ok, I'm coming, I'm coming," Jimmy yelled back. He could see the cowboy and the three other men jostle with the deer, trying to get closer to him. Not knowing who these men were and what they wanted, but sensing something was not quite right, Jimmy did what his instinct told him: he dropped to his knees and out of sight.

Seeing Jimmy disappear in the middle of the herd of deer, and watching the chubby cowboy and the men from the white van push and shove their way towards the spot where his friend ducked down, was too much for David to take sitting down. Wanting to come to Jimmy's rescue, he decided to disregard John's warning to stay in the car and quickly got out. Once outside, he could see the deer scampering around, trying to get away from the four men. He knew he had to do something to stop the men before they got to Jimmy and could think of only one thing to do—something he had learned from his shaman grandfather during the many days he spent with him on the reservation.

When Jimmy dropped out of sight, John contemplated how to best navigate his way through the throng of deer so he could get to the boy before the cowboy did. Not knowing what Jimmy tried to do, he decided to start tackling the deer too and head for the spot where he disappeared. He cast a quick glance back over his shoulder to make sure David had stayed put. A puzzled look spread over his face when he noticed the boy had ignored his caution and stood next to his SUV with his eyes closed. Perplexed, John turned around completely to get a better look at David. Facing in his direction, he stood straight-up with his arms outstretched over his head, his thumbs intertwined, and his other fingers spread wide apart. The way in which he held his hands depicted a bird in flight. Keeping his eyes closed, he slightly tilted his head forward as if praying and, then, slowly lowered his arms in front of him while continuing to use his hands to portray a bird in flight.

Deciding not to interrupt David's concentration, John turned back around, intending to muscle a path to the center of the herd. Just then, another puzzled look appeared on his face when he noticed the deer no longer scampered away from the other four men but had started to surround them—restricting their movements. And to his biggest surprise, instead of also surrounding him and constraining his movement, the deer in front of him backed off to let him pass through.

In the meantime, finding himself surrounded by the deer and not sure where Jimmy was, the chubby cowboy stopped shoving the deer. Frustrated by what happened, he chirped like a bird, took off his Stetson, and rubbed his hands over his bald head and down across his face—just like he did earlier in the ski lodge. Having decided Jimmy most likely headed towards John's car, he leaned his bald head forward and, like a wild bull, charged at the deer huddled together between him and the SUV. His frantic, out of control charge caused him to trip over his own feet and crash to the ground. Startled, he pulled himself up, wiped the mud and grass from his face, and pressed his Stetson back on his round head. To his astonishment, he noticed the deer had gathered even closer together and tightly surrounded him—actually preventing him from moving at all. Even his loud shouts and wild shoves did not deter them from blocking his path to the boy.

After he hit bottom, Jimmy started to crawl furiously on his hands and knees through the grass towards John's SUV while repeating, "I'm coming! I'm coming!" The grass was wet and the ground underneath it muddy, but Jimmy didn't care; he just wanted to get safely back into the car. In his hurry, he didn't notice the deer started to move away from him, giving him more leeway to maneuver in his scamper back to the SUV. It startled him when, all of a sudden, he crawled in between two human legs and got grabbed by the back of his belt and hoisted upward. He closed his eyes and held his breath, expecting the worst. Then he heard John say, "Quickly, get back into the car."

Jimmy had never felt so glad to hear his uncle's voice as at that very moment, and to his great relief it was John, not one of the other men, hoisting him off the ground. After he took Jimmy by the hand and quickly guided him to his SUV, John noticed David had abandoned his stance and sat in the rear of the car with the back door wide open. Motioning his friend to get into the back seat, he shouted, "Jimmy, come in here!"

"Hey, David, you are so not going to believe what happened back there," Jimmy said, piling in, breathing heavily from his fast track to the car.

"You can tell me later," David said, pulling the SUV's rear door closed.

Anxious to get everyone in the car as soon as possible, he then reached over and from the inside opened the SUV's front door to let John in. After he slid into the driver's seat,

John closed his door, turned on the engine, told the boys to buckle up, and silently sped off.

Realizing the animals made it very difficult for them to get close to Jimmy, the three men from Piedmont had stopped jostling with the deer and positioned themselves directly between the chubby man and the black van. If he had been able to grab Jimmy and tried to force him into his van, they would have interfered and kept him from doing so. When John took off in his SUV, it didn't take very long for the three men to get back into their white van and tell their driver to follow him down the road. As they drove off, they could see the chubby cowboy still struggling to get away from the deer, so he could get back into the black van and join his frustrated compatriot—who by now appeared to be very, very angry, and growled, "We'll get you the next time…Jimmy Starlight."

"*What* in the world was that all about?" Jimmy said, after they had left the park and drove on the main road heading back towards Alexandria. He felt still a little bewildered by everything that had happened earlier.

"Yes, *who* were those guys?" David asked.

"The four men in the white van were my colleagues from work," John replied, "but I do not know who the chubby guy in that cowboy outfit was."

"Do you have any idea why he acted so crazy?" Jimmy wanted know.

"Not exactly," John said. "I spotted the black van following us when we drove to the resort. And just in case the people in it were up to no good, I called my colleagues to come and help me keep an eye on things; I'm glad I did."

104

Not wanting to worry Jimmy too much or cause him to have nightmares about the episode, John did not tell them they spied on him with their binoculars at the ski resort.

"So you don't know why those scary guys followed us?" Jimmy said, with a shiver.

"Not really," John replied. "But when I find out, you'll be the first to know."

"I'm not sure I really want to know," Jimmy worried out loud.

"By the way, what motivated you to jump out of the car like that?" John asked, still wondering why Jimmy had suddenly gotten out of the car without warning to mingle with the deer.

"I'm sorry, I don't really know," Jimmy responded, not wanting to tell him about the little voice. "But guess what—I saw the deer from my dream."

"You saw what?" David wanted to know.

"I saw the deer from my dream." Wanting to make sure his uncle believed him, he reiterated, "Honestly, Uncle John, I really saw her."

"I believe you," John said. "But the next time, please, ask me first before you go charging off like that."

"Yes, I promise," Jimmy said quietly.

"So, what deer was that anyway?" David asked.

Jimmy told him about the strange dreams he had, and what John had said about the anti-gravity technologies and the large crystal.

Having briefly thought about what Jimmy just told him, David said, "My grandfather once told me that strange dreams often bring us important messages from the spirit world. I'm sure, someday soon, you'll figure out why you had 'em."

"Your grandfather is a wise man," John said.

105

"Yes, he *is* a wise man," David said, feeling proud of his granddad.

"And thank you for what you did back there," John told him. "Whatever it was, it worked. Your grandfather must have taught you that too."

"Taught him what? What did he do?" Jimmy asked.

"Why don't you tell him," John suggested to David.

Feeling a little awkward talking about himself, David hesitated.

"Go ahead, tell him what you did," John encouraged him.

"Yeah, please, tell me," Jimmy pleaded.

Giving in, David finally said, "I got out of the car and made our tribal signs—asking the spirits of my people to tell the deer to protect you."

"You asked your spirits to talk to the deer so they would protect me?"

"Yes, I did."

"Where did you learn how to do that?"

"My grandfather taught me."

"Did it work?"

"It sure did," John said.

"Wow, thanks for your help," Jimmy said to David. "Someday, you'll have to show me how to do that."

"Okay, someday I will," David promised.

On the rest of the way home, both boys fell silent and remained in thought. Noticing a troubled expression on Jimmy's face, John told him not to worry about what happened in the park.

"I'll find out who those men are and why they followed us," he assured him. "In the meantime, my

106

colleagues and I will keep a close eye on you and not let them get anywhere near you again."

"Thank you, Uncle John," Jimmy said. "This makes me feel a whole lot better."

While John didn't know who the two men were, he felt sure they acted on behalf of the VARS. And he was also pretty sure they tried to nab Jimmy because the VARS knew and worried about the Atlantean Prophecy. As before, he didn't think it advisable to let Jimmy in on all of this without properly preparing him to deal with it. Later that evening, having dropped David and Jimmy off at their respective residences, he noticed the white van parked not too far from Jimmy's house and called Piedmont.

When the director got on the phone, she said, "I heard about your troubles in the park and the deer protecting Jimmy. What happened there could mean the Prophecy has started to unfold—what do you think?"

"Yes, I agree," John said, "and I should probably tell you something else."

He explained to her that, while in the park, Jimmy actually saw the doe he flew on in his dreams.

"I'm not surprised," the director said. "This also seems to point to the Prophecy coming about."

"That's right," John said. "And, by the way, did you hear back from our people in Egypt?"

"Yes, I did," she said. "They've had no reported sightings of the Peacemaker, and they've not heard any rumors about its whereabouts either, except for what they considered the useless ramblings of a crazy old man. He claims that, when he fell seriously ill as a child, they used a large crystal—the size of a soccer ball—to save his life."

"Do they believe him?"

"No, they don't; they actually consider him raving mad. And according to the people in the village where he lives, not too far from Giza, he can't remember what he said or did from one minute to the next. They wonder how he can remember anything about an illness he endured many years ago."

"Well, as far as I know, just because someone's short term memory has stopped functioning doesn't necessarily mean he can't recall things that happened many years ago."

"Yes, you're right, of course."

"And did you say he lived near Giza?"

"Yes."

"That's where the Great Pyramid stands. In Jimmy's dream, it looked like they built the Pyramid with the help of a large crystal."

"I remembered you telling me that. So, I asked our people to give this old man the 'once over' one more time and probe a little deeper into his background."

"I think that was a very good idea."

Knowing the VARS had tried to nab Jimmy, and would undoubtedly conspire to do so again, had made the director very edgy about his safety. "Now that they know who Jimmy is and where he lives," she said, "they'll continue to come for him. I hope to bring him to Piedmont as soon as possible, so we can safely train him and get him ready to help us decimate the whole bunch of them."

"So, do I," John said, "but if it's alright with you, I would like to wait until the end of the school year before we bring him in. It would disrupt his life quite a bit if we pulled him out of school right now. And with the help of our people, I can watch over him closely and keep him safe."

"If you can do that, it's okay with me," the director said. "It will give us more time to root out the conspirators here at Piedmont, and deal with other traitors in our midst, too. In the meantime, I will assign additional 'help' for you—in addition to what we sent today."

"I appreciate that very much," John said. "And, please, keep me abreast of how you plan to deal with these turncoats."

"Yes, I'll do that," the director promised before she ended the call.

After John got home, he replayed in his mind the events of the day and contemplated what the director had said about rooting out conspirators at Piedmont and dealing with other traitors in their midst. To him, her words seem to imply there might be several Atlanteans, both here on Earth and on Atlantis, collaborating with the VARS.

If that's the case, he thought, *and officials on Atlantis are also involved in this conspiracy, it will complicate my job enormously; and I'll have to watch out for my own safety, too.*

One afternoon, several weeks after his ski trip, Jimmy looked at himself approvingly as he stood in front of the mirror in his bedroom and finished tying his little red silk bowtie. The tie, and his white shirt, black pants, and black shoes were required attire for his performance in the annual Spring Concert of his school's strings program. It was scheduled to start at six-thirty that evening in the cafeteria of Belleview Elementary School. He really looked forward to playing in the concert because his violin teacher, Mr. Becksbury, had asked him to play a violin solo towards the end of the program. After practicing his solo at school for over a month, Jimmy was eager for Eloise and John to hear him play it. He also looked forward to attending an additional event after the concert: the official kickoff of the school's solar energy project, organized by the PTA. Since his uncle served as the PTA president, the principal of Belleview had asked John to make a brief presentation about the project and the benefits of using renewable energy. He had also asked that John make himself available afterwards to answer any questions about the project.

Even though the two urban cowboys had stayed out of sight since the scary episode in the park, and Jimmy constantly tried to put it behind him, he couldn't help feeling unsettled whenever his eye caught something that reminded him of them—like a person wearing a black cowboy hat, a black van driving by, or one parked in the lot of the shopping center a few blocks from his condo. He had loving memories of the deer surrounding him and coming to his rescue. But his recollection of the chubby man aggressively pushing his way through the herd of animals, in what he understood to be a brazen attempt to haul him into the man's car, made him feel so uncomfortable it raised goose bumps all over. He had no idea what the man wanted from him; but no matter what, he had no doubt this person was up to no good. One time, having relived this scary episode, Jimmy couldn't calm down until he remembered John's promise that he would always look after him and never allow the two cowboys to get near him again. And he firmly believed his uncle always kept his promise.

Knowing John's colleagues also watched over him helped ease his mind too. He could tell they kept an eye on things because he often noticed the white van parked down the street from his condo and correctly assumed they were there to keep him safe. But he never noticed two other white vans parked around the block from his street; and he didn't know John's friends from work followed him whenever he left his condo—no matter where he went. Nor did he realize that the young couple who recently moved into the condo below him also worked for John. As Jimmy would soon find out, however, the two cowboys were more determined than ever to get their hands on him. And unless he followed John's instructions closely, it was going to be very difficult to prevent this from happening.

After he finished dressing, Jimmy went looking for his grandmother, hoping for something to eat; she always prepared a meal before his concerts. This time, knowing that during the after-concert party the kids would be treated to a potluck dinner, Eloise had only made a snack for him. Since all parents and guests were bringing a favorite dish or some finger food for the potluck, she had Jimmy's favorite dish ready to take along.

Finding Eloise in the kitchen, he asked, "Whaddya have for me, Grams?"

111

"One of your favorites—a peanut butter and jelly sandwich," she replied. "But only a half, because I don't want to fill you up before the party. Also, here's another one of your favorites to bring to the potluck dinner—pasta primavera."

"Thanks, Grandma, that's perfect!" Jimmy said, giving her a big hug. "And guess what?"

"What?"

"That means later today I get to do my two favorite things: play my violin and eat the best pasta *in the world.*"

"I can't wait to hear you play," Eloise said, "especially your solo segment."

"And *I* can't wait to play it for you."

Jimmy loved playing his violin, not only because he loved the elegant sound of the instrument, but also because it brought back fond memories of his mother. In his room, several framed pictures of her holding or playing her violin hung on the wall and sat on his night stand. He knew his love of music came from her. Prior to his birth, she had played the violin professionally. Eloise often recalled her days as a well-respected violinist with the National Symphony Orchestra. On several occasions, she had been a featured soloist at the Kennedy Center in Washington, D.C.

After Jimmy was born, she had left the NSO to devote herself fulltime to raising her only child. He still remembered how she would play lullabies on her violin for him at bedtime. When she finished playing, she would always whisper, "Remember, my child, playing music keeps you happy, and happiness keeps you healthy." He always heard her.

"I always loved listening to your mother's solos," Eloise couldn't help but reminisce.

"I know," Jimmy said softly, noticing a tear in her eyes. "She and Dad will be listening this evening from above."

"Yes, they will," Eloise said.

"Do you remember how happy I was when you gave me a violin for my birthday?" Jimmy asked her, wanting to cheer his grandmother up by reminding her of a happy occasion.

"Yes, I do," she said, wiping away her tear. "When I bought it, I wasn't even sure you would ever want to play your violin."

"But after you gave it to me, I knew I would always want to play it."

When he started second grade, Jimmy joined his elementary school's strings program. He took up the violin and showed the talent and passion to master some of the more difficult musical scores and progressions. He quickly became one of the favorite pupils of Mr. Becksbury, who taught all the school's strings classes. After three years of playing the violin, Jimmy was accepted into the county's Youth Symphony Orchestra, due in no small part to a glowing recommendation from his violin teacher. At age ten, he was the orchestra's youngest violinist. Playing in the YSO twice a week, while continuing to participate in his elementary school's strings program, allowed him to advance his skills well beyond what either of the two programs by themselves would have enabled him to do. The strong bond he developed with Mr. Becksbury influenced his decision to continue to participate in his school's program. The music teacher considered Jimmy his protégé and continued to go out of his way to help him develop his playing technique with the kind of artistry that makes young violin players get noticed by professional orchestras. Two years after joining the youth orchestra, Jimmy realized one of his aspirations and became its lead violinist.

"I'm going to call David to make sure he still plans to come," Jimmy told Eloise after he finished eating his PB&J.

David could always be counted on to come and hear his friend play. "I'll stop by your place so we can walk over together," he told Jimmy when they talked on the phone.

"Great," Jimmy said, "Uncle John and Grandma are coming, too."

Shortly after John arrived, the four of them walked over to the school cafeteria, about a five minute stroll from Jimmy and Eloise's condominium.

"I hope you're ready to *rock 'n roll* this evening?" John told him jokingly, as they crossed over the small foot bridge spanning the large drainage ditch running alongside the school's playground.

"Yeah, that's for sure," Jimmy said, playing along. "But Mr. Becksbury won't be, he has a different agenda."

"I guess we should invite him to visit our basement someday and show him our stuff," John said, laughing heartily.

Considering his quiet demeanor, one would never guess John loved rock and roll. He and Jimmy frequently jammed together in the basement of his townhouse where he had hooked up his electric guitar to a professional sound system, including a state of the art amplifier and wireless microphone system. An accomplished guitarist, John enjoyed playing country rock, especially when Jimmy accompanied him by playing country fiddle on his violin. Whenever he could, David would join them and bring his drums; and Eloise would play the adoring audience, cheering them on.

As a trio, they sounded good enough to have sparked talk of someday recording a CD together.

"Mr. Becksbury would never come to our basement," Jimmy said, chuckling.

"And if he did, he'd probably have a heart attack hearing us play," David added, jokingly.

Jimmy had it right—Mr. Becksbury would never accept an invitation to come and listen to country rock played anywhere. He enjoyed only classical music and always made it perfectly clear that, as far as he was concerned, only classical music was real music—not rock, rap, country, or any other dissonance, as he called non-classical forms of music.

They joked and laughed all the way to their destination. Having crossed the footbridge, they walked past the playground and entered Belleview Elementary School through its rear entrance. Once inside, they passed through the front end of a long hallway and stepped into the large cafeteria where the concert was being set up. There, John took Jimmy aside and cautioned him to be careful and not go off on his own, and to stay in the vicinity of the adults he knew, at all times.

As Jimmy walked to his seat in the front section of the cafeteria where four rows of fold-up chairs had been set up for the concert's twenty string-players, a black sedan pulled into the parking lot in front of Belleview Elementary. The car's driver, a tall man wearing dark sunglasses and a blue sports jacket with a long-sleeve white shirt underneath, parked in a spot close to the lot's street entrance. Before getting out, he opened the small storage bin between the two front seats and took out a rolled-up, four foot piece of heavy-duty metal picture wire, which he stuffed in the inside pocket

115

of his jacket. He then exited the vehicle and slowly walked over to the school's main front entrance. Having removed his dark sunglasses, he calmly entered the building and smiled at the security guard standing just inside the entrance.

"Are you here for the concert, sir?" the guard asked him politely.

"Yes, I am," the man said with a deep growly voice.

"Do you know where to go?"

"Yes, I do."

Seeing a nicely dressed man who knew his way, the guard bade him, "Have a pleasant evening," and let him pass by. After walking through the large hallway, the man entered the cafeteria where he sat down in a chair at the end of the last row of the three-hundred audience seats neatly arranged for the concert in the center of the cafeteria. While waiting for the music to start, he repeatedly fingered the roll of picture wire in his pocket. And every time he touched it, he looked at Jimmy with an evil grin on his face, thinking, *All I need, Jimmy Starlight, is a few seconds with you by myself, and my job will be accomplished.*

Mr. Becksbury became an instructor at Belleview Elementary when Jimmy first enrolled there six years ago. He was well-suited for teaching young children, with an easy-going personality and soft-spoken mannerism. The following year, he detected Jimmy's sincere interest in learning to play the violin and appreciated his eagerness to excel in doing so; he soon considered him his star pupil. Because this would be Jimmy's last concert under his tutelage, Mr. Becksbury wanted to feature his star pupil in a short violin solo he had composed specifically for the occasion.

"Good evening, ladies and gentlemen," he said elatedly to the audience of almost three-hundred people. "Welcome to the last concert of this school year—our Spring Strings Concert."

Speaking into a small condenser microphone secured on a stand in front of him, he told them the hour long event, which also included performances by the school's chorus, would adhere to the nicely printed Program handed out earlier, listing a mix of popular strings and choral compositions.

"As you can see in our Program," he said, "our concert includes a brief solo performance of one of my short compositions by our talented young violinist, Mr. Jimmy Starlight."

He mentioned that, as usual, after the concert, a potluck dinner would be served in the rear of the cafeteria.

"And after that," he informed them, "we'll all go to our school's computer lab across the hall from here to help Principal Dorsey and Mr. John Parker, our PTA president, kick-off our school's solar energy project."

The concert started well, with the properly attired string virtuosos—including violin, viola, cello and bass players—and all chorus members giving it their very best. The parents and guests of the performers responded enthusiastically to each number; and Mr. Becksbury, also in formal attire and tirelessly waving his little director's baton, was ecstatic. Jimmy's violin solo—his first—played at the end of the concert, got the loudest applause. Performing with a creativity and technique beyond his years, Jimmy kept the audience totally spellbound for ten minutes. It brought tears to Eloise's eyes, because he reminded her so much of his mother, who had similarly captivated her audiences with her violin solos. David's finger-whistling and several "Bravos,"

"Yeahs," and "Atta Boys," accompanied the loud applause, and Mr. Becksbury—now even more ecstatic—felt extremely proud of his young protégé.

After the concert, school staff served the potluck dinner, including deserts and refreshments, as proud parents and guests mingled with the musicians and singers, still glowing from their successful performances. Most of them, including John, Jimmy and David, took their food and drinks outside to the picnic tables surrounding the playground in back of the school, so the students had an opportunity to get some fresh air and unwind after hunkering down in place during the hour-long concert. The three of them took a seat at an empty table at the edge of the playground around the corner from the school's rear exit, where the youngest kids had a great time climbing up and down the various play stations while loudly squealing their delight to the rest of the world.

"May I join you?" Mr. Becksbury asked, as he walked by their table shortly after they sat down.

"Please, do," John answered. "We would be honored to have the maestro sit with us—right, boys?"

"Yes, for sure," Jimmy hastened to say, happy Mr. Becksbury chose to sit with them.

"Jimmy, that was quite a performance you gave," Mr. Becksbury said with a serious face, sitting down on the table bench. "I'm very proud of you."

"Thank you," Jimmy said shyly. "I love playing your music."

"And you played it beautifully," John added. "And the others played beautifully too. *And you*, Mr. Becksbury, did a *great* job teaching all these young musicians how to put on a *great* concert. I can't tell you how grateful I am for all the help you have given Jimmy these past five years."

"Well, it certainly was my pleasure to have him as my student," Mr. Becksbury said appreciatively. Looking at Jimmy, he went on, "If you choose music as your career, you'll have a very bright future, indeed."

Jimmy glowed.

Wanting some peace and quiet and hoping to talk with some of the other grandmothers attending the concert, Eloise decided to eat her potluck dinner in the school's cafeteria where only a few tables were occupied—including one where the tall stranger who came in the black sedan sat. This quickly changed as darkness fell and all the picnickers relocated indoors to continue the celebration a little longer. After they came back inside the school, Jimmy and David mingled with some of the other students while John sat down at a small table not too far from where Eloise sat. She had just finished her plate and was chatting happily with three other elderly ladies, who had asked her to join them at their table. Except for her family, nothing made Eloise happier than socializing with people her own age, and John could see she was thoroughly enjoying herself. Realizing the VARS might have conceivably entered the school under the guise of being parents or guests of one of the students, he kept a close eye on Jimmy at all times. At one point, when he looked over at the table near the cafeteria entrance where the two boys had seated themselves with some of their classmates, he noticed David getting up and rather frantically searching through his pockets. The boy then pulled his chair back and looked underneath their table.

"I can't find it," David said to Jimmy, with desperation in his voice, reaching for his back pocket.

"Can't find what?" Jimmy asked, wondering about the painful expression on his friend's face.

119

"My billfold, it must have dropped from my pocket somewhere, and I don't see it under our table."

"Uh, don't worry, we'll look for it."

"Okay, let's do that now."

Both boys got up and retraced their steps from the moment they came back into the cafeteria, along the way asking their classmates and others if they had seen David's wallet. When they walked out of the cafeteria into the hallway leading to the school's rear entrance, John shot up out of his chair and hastened after them. When he walked out of the cafeteria, the driver of the black sedan also got up from his chair and followed him into the hallway.

"We shouldn't go outside, it's almost dark," Jimmy told David, who intended to open the rear-exit double door leading to the playground and look for his wallet in the area around the picnic table where they had eaten their potluck dinner.

"But we have to go outside and look for my billfold," David said worriedly. "It has all my valuable stuff in it."

He wasn't referring to the twenty or so dollars he had in his wallet, but to the Hapua peace shield and other tribal protection amulets he kept there. He, and all other members of his Hapua tribe, considered these to be priceless talismans for guiding them into the New Epoch—the era after the destruction of the current ineffectual world order, as predicted by Hapua elders. David treasured these charms more than any of his other worldly possessions.

"Before we do that, let's ask my uncle or Mr. Becksbury to go with us," Jimmy suggested, minding John's caution not to go off on his own.

Just as he said that, John came hurrying into the hallway and walked over to the two boys, standing by the rear exit. Jimmy wanted to tell him about David's inopportune loss, but his school's principal preempted him.

"Hi, John," Mr. Dorsey said, approaching him from behind. "Ready for your presentation?"

"Oh, hello, Ted," John said, turning around and shaking the principal's outstretched hand. "Yes, I'm ready whenever you are."

"Hi, Jimmy; hi, David," Mr. Dorsey said, noticing the two boys who stood rather restlessly next to John. "Are you alright?"

"Oh, hi, Mr. Dorsey," Jimmy said. "I'm just fine."

"Hi, Mr. Dorsey," David also said. He wanted to say something about his lost wallet, but before he had a chance to say anything, the principal spoke up again.

"I hope you enjoyed the concert and Jimmy's performance as much as I did," he said to John.

Having overheard what he said, Jimmy glowed again.

"I sure did," John said, looking proudly at Jimmy. "I loved the whole program, and I thought Jimmy played beautifully."

Jimmy glowed once more.

"You're quite right," the principal said. "We're very proud of all of our musicians, and our singers too."

He and John had known each other for many years, ever since Jimmy started school at Belleview; and they had struck up a solid friendship. Putting his hand on John's shoulder, he guided him across the hallway to the computer lab. John turned around and motioned Jimmy and David to follow them. As he did so, he caught sight of the black sedan's driver just hanging around in the hallway. John had never seen him before; but since several other individuals, with whom he was also not familiar, lingered about in the hallway, he didn't think anything of the tall stranger.

121

"Why don't you get your presentation up and running," the principal suggested to John as they walked into the computer lab. "I'll go to the cafeteria and let the students and their parents know we're ready to start the remainder of this evening's program, and that you can't wait to tell them about our solar energy project."

"You're absolutely right," John said, "I'm sitting on pins and needles to do just that." Then, on a more serious note, "It should only take me a few minutes to get my PowerPoint ready."

After the principal left, Jimmy asked his uncle what he meant by "getting his PowerPoint ready."

"I was talking about the solar energy presentation I prepared a few days ago on my laptop computer," John replied. "It's a PowerPoint slide show illustrating how the school's solar energy system works. Earlier this afternoon, I hooked my laptop up to the equipment here in the lab; and when we're ready, I can present my slide show to the audience."

As he talked with the boys, John noticed the tall stranger entering the room and intensely scrutinizing some of the computers and other equipment in the lab. It seemed to John that, for whatever reason, he was trying hard to give the impression he was only interested in looking at the computer hardware, and the man purposely avoided making eye contact with him—and John wondered why.

"So, did you create this solar energy project yourself?" David asked.

"No, I didn't," John responded. "A renewable energy company designed it and then put it together, and they plan to donate all the equipment to the school."

"That's mighty nice of 'em. Why are they doing that?"

"Because I asked 'em to. It just so happens, the company's owner is a good friend of mine."

"So, why did you ask 'em to build it?"

"Because I want kids like the two of you to know how solar energy works, and that it can supply the world with plenty of much needed clean energy."

"Well, it sure pays to have good friends," Jimmy said. "Does he also work with you—like the ones who helped us in the park?"

"Yes, he does," John replied. "I've worked with him for quite a long time."

He walked over to the small stand in the front of the room on which he had deposited his laptop and hit a few keys, powering it up, and launching his presentation.

"You're the first ones to see this," he told the boys standing next to him, as he brought up several windows simultaneously on his laptop screen.

"Great, what are these?" Jimmy asked, looking at the equipment and numbers appearing on the screen.

John explained the windows displayed the major components of the school's solar energy system and its energy outputs.

"The first few slides," he said, "show how the solar energy panels installed on the school's roof generate electricity from sunlight—without polluting the air, of course—and how this solar electricity runs the school's computers and all the other equipment in the lab. Some of the other slides in my presentation talk about the monitoring device also installed on the roof; it measures the amount of sunlight shining on the panels throughout the day, and it shows you that the more sunlight the panels receive, the more electricity they produce."

Having tapped two laptop keys simultaneously, the windows all popped up on a large LED screen attached to the wall on the side of the room. Clicking a few more keys, he then displayed each of the windows individually on the LED in larger font. "The big screen over there will allow everyone in the room to get a good view of my presentation," he said, pointing to the LED.

While discussing his slide show with Jimmy and David, John occasionally cast an eye in the direction of the tall stranger, who continued to avoid making eye contact with him, and appeared to focus his attention solely on the big screen. John couldn't help but notice the man had no family members or students near him, and this made him wonder why he was there. John decided to track the man's movements more closely, especially if he got anywhere near Jimmy.

After he walked back into the cafeteria, the principal picked up the microphone and invited everyone to join him across the hall in the school's computer lab to watch John's presentation. It didn't take long for the lab to fill with parents and students eager to hear what he had to say. After Mr. Dorsey introduced him, John walked over to the small stand containing his laptop and, making eye contact with the two boys, signaled them to sit near him. He then took his audience through the slide show displayed on the large screen, telling them about the workings of solar technologies and all the ins and outs of the school's solar energy project— all the while keeping track of the tall stranger out of the corner of his eye. The man stood motionless in the back of the room, with his angry stare focused on Jimmy, who, along with David, had taken a seat behind one of the computer stations in back of his uncle.

John wrapped his presentation up by explaining that during the day the solar panels could actually generate more electricity than needed by the lab, and that any excess would keep the huge battery pack in the school's basement fully charged.

"These batteries," he said, "will supply the electricity for the lab when the solar panels aren't generating electricity, either because it's nighttime or the sun's rays are being blocked by a heavy cloud cover."

As much as David liked learning about solar energy, he was glad John finished his presentation and hoped he could soon go outside and look for his wallet. To his disappointment, after he finished his presentation, John asked the audience if they had any questions, and more than a dozen hands went up. While he was answering their questions, John didn't see or hear David get up, take Jimmy by the hand, and quietly lead him out of the lab to the school's rear exit. There, David briefly paused to cast a glance in the direction of Eloise, who was still sitting in the same seat, to see if she could see him. She couldn't, so he carefully pushed open one of the double doors and stepped outside.

"I need to find my billfold before it's too late and someone takes it," he whispered to Jimmy. "You don't need to come, but I have to go look for it."

When David closed the door and headed towards the picnic table where they had earlier eaten their potluck dinner, Jimmy couldn't stay inside and let his friend go off in the dark by himself. After he opened the door, ready to go outside, Jimmy heard the little voice again—the same voice that had gently urged him to get out of the car when they were in the State park a few weeks earlier.

125

"Don't go outside; it is dark and your uncle said not to go off on your own," the voice whispered.

Jimmy hesitated, but as he watched David disappear from view in the dark, he decided to ignore the little voice's advice and ran after his friend, not heeding his uncle's caution. "David, wait," he yelled, "I'm coming to help you look for it."

David stopped and turned around. "I knew you'd come," he said, as a breathless Jimmy caught up with him right in front of their picnic table.

As soon as the two boys walked out of the lab, the tall stranger started to edge his way from the back of the room towards the door in front. He moved slowly but deliberately as he passed through the jam-packed room, with John tracking his every move. At one point, the man looked at John to see if he was watching him, and for the first time their eyes met. John's steely gaze told him he was a man to be reckoned with, and to get to Jimmy he would have to go through his uncle first. John continued to watch the stranger squeeze through the crowd until he exited the room. After the man passed from his view, John got the surprise of his life when he turned around and saw two empty chairs where Jimmy and David had been sitting. After frantically scanning the lab and not seeing them anywhere, he abruptly stopped answering the last question posed by one of the students.

"Please excuse me for having to briefly attend to a personal matter," John told the audience, realizing he needed to locate his nephew fast to keep him out of danger. He caught the principal completely off guard by what he said next. "I'll return shortly to continue with our project's kickoff, but in the meantime, Mr. Dorsey will answer any other questions you may have."

Before the stunned principal could say anything, John walked away from the podium and went out the door.

Moments earlier, the tall stranger hurried down the hallway, not seeing the boys anywhere. Thinking they may have gone outside, he ran to the rear exit doors and looked out. With no indication of them being out there, and noticing the outside area was only sparsely lit by the small outdoor light over the rear entrance and an even smaller one on the light post in the playground, the man assumed Jimmy and David went somewhere else. After walking into the cafeteria, and casting a quick glance around, he realized they weren't there. He turned and walked across the hall to the small stairway leading down to the school's gym. Just as the man reached the stairway entrance, John came out of the lab, and they locked eyes briefly before the stranger darted down the stairs.

John quickly followed him down, ready to confront the man about his reason for being at the school. When he entered the gym, the stranger was nowhere to be seen. Wondering where he disappeared to, John looked around for an answer and quickly found it—three doors along the far wall. Having walked across the gym, he read the nameplates on each of the doors. The doors on the left and right provided access to the boys' and girls' locker rooms and the one in the center to the equipment storage area. He realized, in order to flush the man out, he would have to enter the rooms one by one and risk being jumped by the stranger from his hiding place. Not hearing voices or other sounds, John thought it unlikely the boys had gone into any of the rooms; but on the outside chance they were in there hiding somewhere, he was willing to take that risk and conduct the search.

After carefully opening the door to the boys' locker room, John ran his eyes across the tiled space and, not seeing anyone, stepped inside and cautiously checked each of the locker room stalls. Having found no signs of the man and the two boys, he calmly retraced his steps and headed for the girls' locker room. There he conducted a similar search, yielding the same result. He knew the man had to be holed up in the third room.

On a second plate on the storage room door John read the words "Off-Limits to Students," which reinforced his initial doubt the boys had walked into the gym; he nevertheless continued his search. The door squeaked ominously as he slowly pushed it open, revealing a large storage area equal in size to the locker rooms. As before, he let his eyes wander across the room before entering it. Two large metal cabinets behind which the man could easily hide caught his attention immediately. One stood up sideways against the front wall about five feet to his right and the other sat in the center of the room. He also noticed the large metal racks covering the back wall, one of which held what looked like cleaning supplies. John surmised these might well contain materials that could be used to blind him. To his immediate left, also up against the front wall, he saw three large wire bins: one filled with an assortment of basket- and soccer balls; another with a variety of field hockey and lacrosse sticks; and a third with what looked like a hodgepodge of lost-and-found items, including old tennis shoes and other used sportswear. A little further to his left, up against the side wall, he could see several stacks of exercise mats sitting in between other gymnastic equipment.

"I know you're hiding in here, so you might as well come out, right now," John shouted forcefully from where he stood, hoping the stranger would show himself. Since the man did not respond, he added loudly, "You'll eventually have to come out." Getting no response a second time, he knew he would have to flush him out. He also knew, to keep Jimmy safe, he would have to face the man sooner or later— so he carefully entered the room.

John didn't see nor hear the old tennis shoe flying over his head. The stranger lobbed it across the room from behind the cabinet next to him as soon as John walked in. But he did hear the sound of it hitting the left wall. He instantly turned his head in the direction of the sound, and therefore was taken by surprise when the man jumped suddenly from behind the cabinet on his right, forcefully swinging a hockey stick at his head. It hit him in the neck at the base of his skull and sent him stumbling forward, smashing into the metal cabinet in the middle of the room with enough force to tip it over. With stars swirling through his throbbing head, he tried to stay on his feet but lost his balance and ended up tripping over the cabinet and crashing onto the concrete floor. As John struggled to get back up, the man walked over and whacked him across the head once more, sending him face down to the floor again. He then took the roll of picture wire from his pocket and, after unraveling it, stretched the steel cable between both hands, intending to use it as a garrote to strangle John.

With an evil grin on his face, the would-be assassin got down on one knee, ready to perform his grisly deed. Expecting no interference with his horrid work, he was caught by surprise when John, using his forearms, suddenly elevated his upper body and twisted it around. Before the assassin had a chance to loop the wire around his neck, John thrust the heel of his upright left palm in the man's direction while intensely focusing his thoughts on delivering him a mental blow to his chest.

If Jimmy had witnessed what happened next, he would not have believed his eyes. As if struck by a bolt of lightning,

129

the man was suddenly lifted two feet off the ground and went flying backwards until he crashed into the middle stack of exercise mats piled up high along the left wall. He hit the stack with such force it knocked the wind out of him and scattered the mats all over the floor. Collapsing against the wall, the man lay gasping for air. Fortunately for him, he was in excellent physical shape and after a few minutes caught his breath and stumbled back to his feet. Shortly thereafter, still groggy from the earlier hockey-stick shellacking, John started to pick himself up and sat up straight on the floor. The assassin looked at him in total bewilderment, wondering what awesome power John possessed that knocked him clear across the room without having been physically touched. When he noticed John slowly turning to face him, the man regained his composure, picked up his cable wire, and quickly bolted out the door.

Seeing him flee the scene, John staggered to his feet and hobbled across the storage room, preparing to send another mental blow the assassin's way. But by the time he stepped into the gym, he only caught a glimpse of the man scrambling up the stairs.

"Hey, you—stop," John yelled as he pursued him.

When he reached the hallway, he caught another glimpse of the man hurrying around the corner at its other end, heading towards the school's front exit. Having shaken off most of the ill effects of the blows to his head, John continued his pursuit and started to run down the hallway. By the time he turned the hallway corner, he ground his teeth as he caught a final glimpse of the man dashing out of the school.

The guard at the school's front entrance was one of John's colleagues from work. It was his job to keep an eye on the people coming into the school and alert John if any suspicious characters appeared. Feeling pretty much his old self again, John yelled at him, "Grab that man!" The guard was surprised by John's urgent request and for a few seconds just looked at him. But then, seeing John come barreling towards him, he turned and rushed outside to see where the tall man went. It didn't take the assassin long to make it to his car. By the time the guard came out the front door, he had crossed the school's parking lot and jumped in the black sedan. When John made his way outside shortly thereafter, he had started it up and, peeling rubber, blew out of the lot, making his getaway.

"Who was that?" the guard asked as they walked back into the school. "Why did you want me to grab him?"

"VARS," John said. "He was after Jimmy."

"I'm sorry I couldn't keep him from getting away. When he first came in, he knew where to go; I assumed he had been here before and had a legitimate reason for coming."

"Yes, he seemed to know his way around here alright. Anyway, thanks for keeping an eye on the front door for me."

"You're welcome," the guard said. "Hmm, look at this. I saw him drop it as he went out the front door."

He showed John a four-foot piece of heavy-duty picture wire. They exchanged knowing looks.

"I need to find Jimmy," John said, starting to walk back up the hallway to look for the boy.

"Let's look around quickly and hurry back to the computer lab," Jimmy said to David while he searched the ground around the picnic table for his friend's billfold. He did not say anything about the warning the little voice gave him before he stepped outside. "We can probably get back

131

there before Uncle John finishes answering all of their questions, so he won't even know we left."

"Good idea," David said, walking around the table, scouring the ground for his stuff.

"Boy, we sure could use some more light out here," Jimmy said, straining his eyes as he continued to search the area barely illuminated by the faint light coming from the playground.

Not having any success, they both dropped to their hands and knees and inched their way around the space underneath the table—to no avail. Before long, they stood back up empty-handed and turned ghostly white when they noticed the two urban cowboys, black Stetsons and all, standing across the table from them, blocking their way back to the school. Ready to fulfill the mission they failed to complete during their previous encounter in the park, the two men came at them menacingly—each from a different side of the large nine-foot picnic table. They were after Jimmy but also intended to grab David to keep him from alerting anyone else. The tall man slowly circled around the table towards Jimmy with great deliberation, like a sleek jungle cat moving in on its prey. The chubby one, however, still embarrassed from having been waylaid by a bunch of deer in the park, was much less deliberate. Anxious to get his hands on the boys, he suddenly charged blindly around the table, chirping loudly. In his haste, he didn't notice the sharp corner edge of the bench attached to the table in front of him. When his knee hit the edge, he fell, wincing in pain, allowing both boys to jump up and over the table and make a beeline for the school entrance around the corner.

When they reached the double doors—out of breath and shaking all over—and yanked both handles, they didn't budge. Because of school safety measures, after dark the doors only opened from the inside. Jimmy and David froze. Realizing the boys had nowhere to go, the two cowboys slowly advanced towards them. They wanted to make sure they got their prize this time and covered any angle that might allow for an escape route. With his eyes closed, Jimmy leaned back against the door, thinking they were done for; David, however, was not willing to give up so easily. He assumed his karate stance, ready to defend both himself and his friend. Even though he was almost six feet tall, he would have been no match for the chubby man. Though still in pain, the cowboy started to chirp once again, intending to forge ahead and finish the job.

Once in a while, miracles do happen. All of sudden, the door Jimmy leaned up against was pushed open from the inside, shoving him forward in the direction of the two cowboys. But, as soon as the door opened far enough to let him inside, David grabbed Jimmy by the arm and pulled his friend with him as he quickly re-entered the school.

The minute they got inside, Mr. Becksbury said, with a stern voice, "For heaven's sake, what are the two of you still doing outside—by yourselves, no less—when you should be inside listening to Mr. Parker's presentation?" When he saw the two cowboys, he shuddered and closed the door with a look of disgust on his face. Nodding at David, he said to Jimmy, "You both need to get back to your family."

The two boys couldn't thank him enough, and Jimmy gave him a big hug. The whole frightening incident had taken less than ten minutes. As they scurried back into the school cafeteria, Mr. Becksbury was all smiles again and started talking to some of the parents and guests who had decided to forego John's talk. And Jimmy and David, knowing they had dodged a bullet after going outside by themselves, quietly sat down at Eloise's table.

"What's up with you two?" she wanted to know, noticing their awkward silence.

"I lost my billfold outside somewhere," David said, feeling terrible about the loss.

"Oh, I'm sorry to hear that," Eloise said. "You can look for it when John finishes his presentation; and if you can't find it tonight, we can look again tomorrow."

Neither Jimmy nor David mentioned anything to her about their encounter with the two cowboys. Both men were still standing on the school's playground, just staring at the closed door through which their quarry had disappeared. They didn't notice the four men and three women—all colleagues of John—standing almost invisibly among the trees at the edge of the playground, with their night-vision equipment on and flex weapons ready to fire. Each of these weapons, attached to a strap around the waist, resembled a small belt buckle with a tiny camera lens attached to it. They were mind-controlled and could shoot hot or cold lasers at any object if mentally directed to do so. When a flex weapon's engagement button was switched on, its computerized control system could read the user's mind and instantly follow a mental directive to unleash a laser at the desired target. John's colleagues would have overpowered the urban cowboys if the men had gotten their hands on Jimmy. They wouldn't have seriously hurt them, but they would have stunned the cowboys with enough force to incapacitate them for an extended period of time.

After Jimmy and David's safe re-entry, John's colleagues stayed put for a while before quietly retreating across the little foot bridge. As they left, the two cowboys continued to stare annoyingly at the closed school door. In his frustration, the tall man, even more furious than the last time they tried to snatch Jimmy, jabbed the chubby man with

134

the palm of his hand on his forehead, letting him know he was to blame for it all. He then growled, "We're still going to get you, Jimmy Starlight...it's just a matter of time."

When John walked back into the cafeteria, he quickly spotted Jimmy and David sitting at Eloise's table.

"Where did you guys go?" he asked, sitting down next to them.

"David lost his billfold outside somewhere," Eloise told him.

"Sorry to hear that," John said to David. "We can look for it before we walk home."

"Uhh…that may not be a good idea," Jimmy said, feeling apprehensive about running into the two cowboys again.

"Why do you say that?" John asked, wondering why Jimmy would hesitate to look for his friend's personal belongings.

"Uhh…because it's probably too dark to see anything," Jimmy replied, not yet ready to tell him about their unfortunate encounter.

"Oh, no need to worry about that, my dear," Eloise said, reaching in her large handbag and pulling out a small flashlight. "I brought four of these for our walk back home."

"Fantastic, we'll look for David's billfold when we leave," John said, getting up. "But now, I must go back to the computer lab to see how Mr. Dorsey is doing. The two of you should stay put right here with Eloise until I get back."

John entered the lab just in time to hear Mr. Dorsey say to the audience, "Well, if there are no more questions, we can get our solar energy project officially up and running— just as soon as our PTA president returns." Seeing John walk towards him, the relieved principal raved, "And *here* he comes now, ready to kick it off."

When John moved next to him in front of the small podium, Mr. Dorsey took him briefly aside and whispered in his ear, "Everything alright?"

"Yes," John also whispered. "Sorry to have left you stranded like that. I'll explain later."

"Don't worry. I answered most of their questions, thanks to the earlier briefing you gave me on the project."

"Great, I knew you could handle it."

Stepping back in front of the podium, the principal said in a loud voice to John, so the audience could clearly hear him, "Well, Mr. Parker, I understand, to get this project officially started, our school has to agree to fulfill certain requirements—is that right?"

"That's right, Mr. Dorsey," John said, also in a loud voice. "If Belleview agrees to keep all the students up-to-date on the project's status, maintain all the equipment in working order, and integrate the project into the school's science curriculum, the company that built the system will donate all solar equipment to the school."

"That's fantastic," the principal proclaimed. "I'm happy to promise all of those things."

"Then, on behalf of the company, I'm happy to donate it all to Belleview Elementary," John said.

The audience applauded as John and the principal shook hands, and Mr. Dorsey announced the demonstration project was now officially underway.

"Well, folks, this concludes tonight's program," he told them. "A great big thanks to Mr. Parker for arranging this, and thank you all for coming."

Because John was not in a position to discuss Jimmy's problems involving the VARS with anyone but his closest associates at his work, he decided not to tell Mr. Dorsey about the assassin and what had transpired in the gym. Instead, he attributed interrupting his presentation and leaving the principal by himself in the computer lab to having to deal with an urgent personal issue.

"Unfortunately, it required my immediate attention," he told Mr. Dorsey, as they walked back towards the cafeteria, without explaining what the fuss was all about. "Sometimes duty calls when you're out having fun."

"No problem, I know what you mean," the principal said. "That happens to me all the time."

Spotting grandma and the two boys in the cafeteria, they walked over to their table.

"How are you, Eloise?" Mr. Dorsey asked. "Did you enjoy the evening?"

"I sure did," she replied, "and I especially enjoyed the music."

To forestall having to give any further explanations regarding his sudden departure from the lab, John decided to call it an evening. "David lost his billfold and may have dropped it outside," he said to the principal. "So the boys and I are going to take a quick look around the playground before we head for home."

"Sorry to hear that," Mr. Dorsey said to David. "If you dropped it around here and don't find it tonight, there is a good chance it will be at our Lost and Found tomorrow. Our kids are usually pretty good at bringing in any lost items they find."

"Thanks," David said to the principal. "If we can't find it, I'll be sure to check with 'em in the morning."

"Would you like to bring your flashlights and help us look?" John asked Eloise.

"Sure, I love to," she replied, grabbing her bag and taking out the flashlights.

Shortly thereafter, having said goodbye to Mr. Dorsey, the four of them searched for David's wallet in the same area where the two boys had looked earlier. Actually, John and Eloise did most of the searching, because the two boys spent most of their time nervously shining their flashlight on the trees and bushes surrounding the playground, praying they wouldn't get any more unwanted visits from the two cowboys.

Ten minutes later, after another unsuccessful search, Jimmy and David trailed closely behind John and Eloise when they walked across the little foot bridge. John knew that somewhere in the surrounding darkness his colleagues kept track of them while they made their way home. He didn't know they also kept an eye on the two cowboys, also standing in the dark at the edge of the large drainage ditch. The two men quietly watched Jimmy cross the foot bridge, knowing there would be other opportunities to accomplish their mission.

After John said goodnight to Jimmy and Eloise in front of their condominium unit, he walked David home. On his way back to his townhouse, he touched base by cell phone with the leader of his colleagues.

"Any surprises?" John asked.

"Just those two cowboys," she responded.

She described what transpired on the playground when Jimmy and David were there by themselves.

"I'm glad Mr. Becksbury came to their recue, and you did not have to intervene." John thanked her and the rest of her colleagues for their vigilance and then called Piedmont to bring the director up-to-speed on the evening's incidents.

"Are you sure he was after Jimmy?" she asked, when John told her about the assassin.

"Without a doubt," he replied. "Fortunately, I fended him off with a mental strike after he jumped me from behind."

"Are you alright?" she wanted to know.

"I'm fine, but the guy got the shock of his life when I sent him flying across the room. Too bad he got away; he will most certainly inform the VARS about our martial-arts techniques."

"Don't worry, they would have found out about them sooner or later anyway. The important thing is that you and Jimmy are safe. And the VARS may not believe the man anyway when he tells them you smacked him with an invisible punch."

"Yes, you're probably right," John said, snickering a little.

"I'll ask our sources to check out those two cowboys; we should keep a close eye on them."

"That's a good idea."

"And now that we know they're also well-informed about the activities at Jimmy's school, we must be even more vigilant to keep him safe."

"I couldn't agree more. Do you want me to bring the boy in now?"

"No, not yet; we're still working on identifying the traitors in our midst. We now suspect the collaboration with the enemy goes all the way to the highest levels of our own leadership. Until we pinpoint this connection, it won't be much safer for him here at Piedmont than where he is right now. I'll let you know when to bring him in. Hopefully, it will not take too long."

139

"Okay, I'll wait to hear from you," John said, before hanging up.

The morning after Jimmy's violin concert, he and David agreed to search the playground for David's billfold one more time before class started. As they walked to school, he still felt immensely grateful to David for having the presence of mind to drag him safely back into the school when the two cowboys tried to pounce on him the evening before. *He kept them from getting their hands on me,* Jimmy thought, *just like he did in the park when he kept the chubby guy from nabbing me.* Reliving these events, Jimmy started to feel rather uneasy about walking to the playground by themselves. He would have felt better had he noticed the young couple who lived in the condominium below him were trailing them at a safe distance. It was far enough for them not to get noticed, yet close enough to quickly come to Jimmy's assistance if needed. He would have felt even better had he known about the two white vans. One was parked in the parking lot next to his school and the other a block away. And the vans' occupants constantly communicated with the young couple by means of two-way portable communication devices.

"Thank you for saving me from those goons last night," Jimmy said, smiling wearily. He was worried but tried not to show it.

"Oh, it was nothing," David said gently, noticing concern on Jimmy's face. Then he added a little more forcefully, "Don't you worry, you're my best friend, and I will *never* let them get you."

"Gee, thanks for letting me know that," Jimmy said, "You're making me feel better already!"

Jimmy was not surprised by his friend's protective attitude. David acted the same way at school. Soon after they first met and quickly hit it off, David had taken it upon himself to look after Jimmy; and he let it be known to all the students at their elementary school he considered him "family." What this meant was "*if you mess with Jimmy, you're also messing with me.*" And since David was a foot taller and twenty pounds heavier than most students his own age, this was not something to be taken lightly by any kid wanting to pick on Jimmy for whatever reason. However, in keeping with his karate training, fighting was never his first option for solving a disagreement or dispute; Jimmy felt the same way. While appreciative of David's protective attitude, when it came to his own wellbeing in school, Jimmy always felt more than capable of standing on his own two feet.

In view of the events of the previous evening, he realized he had to pay very close attention to his uncle's advice on how to best avoid those two dangerous cowboys. It was also clear to Jimmy, these individuals were not interested in John and David, just him; and not knowing why made him feel very uncomfortable every time he thought about it. Furthermore, he didn't know what to think of the little voice he first heard in the park and again the evening before when it urged him not to step outside the school. It had given him sound advice both times, but the very fact he twice heard a voice made him wonder about his state of mind; and he didn't think it wise to let anyone know about it—not even David.

"Last night, I talked with my grandfather by phone and told him about your dreams," David said as they crossed over the little bridge onto the playground.

"Did he think they were stupid dreams?" Jimmy asked.

"No, he didn't. He thought they were very special; the kind that are trying to tell you something."

"Did he tell you what they meant?"

"No, but he did say you'll eventually find out yourself why you had them. He also told me about Hapua legends that talk about flying machines with no engines."

"What legends?"

"Ancient legends—like the one about two Hapua children, lost and left behind after a flood destroyed their village. When they couldn't find their parents, they made camp for the evening out in the wilderness. They heard a noise in the air and saw a sky-god land in front of them on his paatuwvota."

"Pa-what?"

"Paatuwvota—something like a huge flying shield."

"Why did he fly on a shield?"

"We don't know. We do know he gave them food and the next morning took them high into the air on his paatuwvota to look for their parents. And when they saw 'em, he took the children back down and reunited 'em with their parents."

"Then, what did he do?"

"He said goodbye and flew back up into the clouds, and the children were forever grateful to him."

"That's a great story, or legend, or whatever! Do they know where this sky-god came from?"

"Sort of; my grandfather said there are many other old Hapua legends about men on flying shields, and many tribal elders believe they all came from Atlantis."

"Are you talking about the city that sank to the bottom of the ocean?" Jimmy asked. He had read in the library about the legendary City of Atlantis and that some people believe it sank underneath the Atlantic Ocean thousands of years ago.

143

"Yeah, that's the one," David responded. "He also said some elders believe the Hapuas received assistance from the Atlanteans in traveling to the Americas, and others think the Hapuas actually came from Atlantis in air ships after the Great Flood."

"Please, tell your grandfather 'thanks' for letting me know about these paatuwvotas and all. And what did you tell him about those two goons?"

"I haven't told him anything about 'em. To be honest, I don't have the faintest clue why these guys want to bother us, but I have a feeling they're not so much interested in me as they are in you. And I don't want my family to have to worry about those crazies; and I'm certainly not going to worry too much about 'em myself."

Jimmy felt the same way as David about not wanting to worry his family, and he also decided not to let his worries about the two cowboys overwhelm his own life; so he put them out of his mind—for the time being, anyway.

Their search of the playground was again unsuccessful. But later that day, they checked with the Lost and Found office after school let out and got good news: one of the students had just turned in a billfold he found the evening before in the school cafeteria. Since it had David's ID card in it and contained all of his important stuff, the boys soon cheerfully made their way home, starting their weekend off in a very pleasant manner.

Jimmy always looked forward to the weekend because on most Saturdays John would take him to Woodlawn Farm to ride his horse, Spirit. Woodlawn Farm—or just Woodlawn, as the locals called it—was a horse farm with a riding stable where Spirit was boarded, and where Jimmy often took horseback-riding and show-jumping classes. It

144

was located in the western Virginia countryside, about an hour from Jimmy's house. On this particular Saturday, since a nearby town was hosting a weekend art festival, Woodlawn had no scheduled riding or jumping classes; and he and John went there primarily to see his horse and let Jimmy practice his jumping skills. Spirit, a beautiful Thoroughbred Jimmy started riding when he turned six, had belonged to his father, who had a passion for horseback riding and trained her for Olympic competition. He won a silver medal riding her in the Olympic Show-Jumping event. Jimmy kept his father's riding helmet on a shelf in his bedroom bookcase and the medal hung from his bedpost. He looked at them almost every night before going to bed, hoping some day he would also ride in the Olympics.

At the age of seven, Jimmy started taking horse-jumping lessons at Woodlawn, wanting to become a champion show-jumper just like his father. By the time he turned nine, he started competing with Spirit in junior show-jumping events and did rather well, judging by the trophies displayed on his bedroom dresser.

As they drove to Woodlawn in John's SUV, Jimmy told him what David's grandfather had to say about flying paatuwvotas and other Hapua legends involving Atlanteans.

"What do you think about those paatuwvotas, Uncle John?" he asked.

"They sound fascinating."

"So, do you think it might be true that Atlanteans helped those children and other Hapua people as well?"

"Could well be," John said. "I've heard many stories about Atlanteans helping people all over the world. It has been said they helped ancient civilizations build their large monuments—like the Mayans, and the people on Easter Island, and the ones who built Stonehenge. And some people claim—they also helped the Egyptians build the large Pyramid at Giza."

"Wow!" Jimmy exclaimed. "Maybe that's what they were doing in my dream. Those might have been Atlanteans flying those little airplanes and helping people build that Pyramid."

"Could well be," John repeated.

"But why would I dream about Atlanteans?" Jimmy wondered out loud, just as they drove onto the grassy field serving as Woodlawn's parking lot.

That's a very good question, John thought, wondering himself how to best respond if Jimmy actually asked him that question directly.

But Jimmy didn't ask and quickly jumped out of John's SUV as soon as he parked it. He already had his riding helmet and boots on, and he couldn't wait to get back in the saddle.

"I'll meet you at the corral!" Jimmy shouted excitedly, heading for the barn where Spirit and all the other horses at Woodlawn were stabled.

"Okay, okay," John said, waving him on. "I'll see you there."

Spirit noticed Jimmy the minute he opened her stall door; with her ears pricked up, she nickered to let him know how happy she was to see him.

"Hi, Spirit," he said tenderly, hugging her and gently stroking her forehead. "I missed you and brought your favorites—some carrots and apples."

Spirit gulped them down in no time and showed her appreciation by nudging him slightly with her nose, as if to say, "thank you."

She was the kind of horse anyone would love to own, and Jimmy was extremely proud of her. Spirit looked beautiful and majestic with her shiny chestnut-colored coat, dark eyes, long neck, long legs, thick flowing mane, and long wavy tail. John had measured her at seventeen hands—horse talk for over five and a half feet tall. Since she was not only tall but also had very strong legs, jumping came naturally to her. On numerous occasions, Jimmy had cleared four-foot high obstacles while jumping her in competition.

Spirit was also a very gentle horse. When Jimmy was only three years old, his father, with his mother's reluctant approval, put him on top of Spirit in a western saddle and secured the reins in his tiny hands. They both watched—she with bated breath—as Spirit walked all by herself slowly and carefully around Woodlawn's large indoor riding ring, fully aware of her precious cargo. And when Jimmy was a year older, she frequently showed her gentle side by standing perfectly still after he gingerly walked up to her and gave her a big hug by wrapping both arms tightly around one of her legs. Nowadays, she would also stand totally still while he carefully lifted up her legs, one at a time, to check her horseshoes for signs of looseness and her hoofs for needed trimming or cleaning. Their closeness could be seen, too, on days she'd been let out to pasture. At the first sound of his telltale whistle, letting her know he had come for her, she would quickly trot up to him and follow him to the stable, so he could take her for a ride.

After combing Spirit's mane and tail, Jimmy went to the tack room, where Woodlawn garnered all riding equipment and accessories. There, besides various other pieces of horse tack, he retrieved the old English saddle, bitless bridle, and leather reins once belonging to his father, who had boarded Spirit at Woodlawn a decade before he was born. Understandably, these three pieces of tack were some of Jimmy's most prized possessions; and even though each piece had yielded over twenty years of use, all three were still in good enough shape to safely equip Spirit. After tacking her up, he quickly jumped in the saddle and made a beeline for the old corral behind the farm's stables, where a group of well-behaved kids were taking turns jumping various obstacles.

As soon as Jimmy went looking for Spirit, John got on his cellphone and made three quick calls to three of his colleagues. When they answered, he asked each of them the same question, "Are you in place?" Each time he got the same answer, "Yes, we are." Then, he got out of his SUV and walked over to Woodlawn's administrative office to see Edward, the farm's manager. Woodlawn Farm had been recently purchased by the Piedmont International Academy. Edward managed the day-to-day activities of the farm for the Academy's director, who had final say on all of Woodlawn's operations. If Jimmy had overheard his uncle's conversation, it would most certainly have caught him by surprise.

"Hi, Ed," John said, "How's everything?"

"Great," the manager responded, "We have some of the kids from Piedmont here for the first time. They're just out there riding by themselves; as you know, no classes today. I have two of our hands, Marion and Terry, keeping an eye on them. How are things with you and Jimmy?"

"We're both fine. Right now Jimmy is getting Spirit ready to do some jumping in the corral."

"Wonderful. We just finished laying out a new practice course in the corral for our young show jumpers."

"That's great. I'm sure Jimmy will love it. You should know our guys are watching the farm's access roads until he finishes riding. I just talked to 'em by phone, and they're in place at your three entrance ways."

John explained he had requested his colleagues from Piedmont to keep an eye out for a black van with two cowboys in it, and let him know immediately if they spotted such a vehicle, or any other suspicious-looking automobiles, entering the property. He had asked them to drive to Woodlawn in three of Piedmont's all-terrain SUVs, instead of their minivans. These SUVs, similar to the one he drove, would allow them to speed cross-country to anywhere on the farm in case he and Jimmy needed assistance. As a further precaution, he had emailed each of them a map of Woodlawn he had drawn up, so they would be familiar with the layout of the farm's riding facilities and trails.

"That was a good idea," Edward said. "I was at Piedmont yesterday for a meeting with the director, and she told me about those cowboys stalking Jimmy the other day. She also asked me to keep an eye out for any strangers whenever the kids from Piedmont are here; that's why I have Marion and Terry out there."

"I'm glad they're out there, we can never be too careful," John said, before he excused himself and walked over to the corral to look for Jimmy.

A little while later, leaning on the corral's plank fence, watching Jimmy and a dozen other students from the Piedmont International Academy practice their jumps, John couldn't help but notice how relaxed he was as he effortlessly guided Spirit over the cross rails and other obstacles making up the new practice course. He also noticed, while the course presented a real challenge to the junior jumpers, many parts of it would undoubtedly require advanced riders to put forth their very best efforts too.

149

Besides the four-foot high straight-ahead obstacles, the course had tight turns; and some of the double- and triple-combination jumps required riders to change direction between jumps. Several obstacles had shortened distances between them, making the correct timing for starting the jumps all the more challenging.

Applying what he learned in his riding classes, Jimmy constantly talked to Spirit and calmly encouraged her to approach the various jumps head-on. Then, using a gentle nudge with the heels of his boots, he made her forcefully launch herself across the obstacles. As his instructor had encouraged him to do, he always thanked Spirit for her efforts by stroking her neck and affectionately whispering sweet nothings in her ear.

Since the students from Piedmont used the same practice course as he did, Jimmy frequently had to wait his turn to jump. He didn't mind waiting, because he thoroughly enjoyed just being around Spirit. He loved sitting high up in the saddle and feeling her strength beneath him; and in between jumps, he appreciated how quickly she responded to his small and gentle directional cues and stop-and-go signals. While watching the other kids, he noticed all of them wore colorful sweatshirts with a big emblem on the front. It depicted a majestic blue spruce standing in a green field with silvery mountains in the background and a blue planet hanging far off in the sky; all of this was encircled in large black letters by the name "Piedmont International Academy." Jimmy thought he wouldn't mind owning one of those shirts himself. He not only liked the emblem, but the blue spruce reminded him of the Christmas tree John had dragged into their condominium at the start of the last holiday season. He had helped his grandma decorate it and been proud of the glittery end result of their efforts. Because the tree made their condo look so festive, he had asked Eloise if they could keep it up for another week or so past the holidays; she had happily obliged him. To his delight, they didn't actually take it down until well into February.

Jimmy couldn't help but particularly notice one of the students from Piedmont—a flamboyant young girl about his age, wearing a bright-red sweatshirt, with long dark hair flowing from underneath her riding helmet. She exhibited real jumping talent, much more so than the others. She would often shout directions at them about which obstacles to jump and whose turn it was to do so. Every now and then, she would give Jimmy a fleeting glance as she blew by him on her tall black stallion and successfully completed various combination jumps. She noticed he was an accomplished rider too, and really enjoyed himself moving around the practice course from one series of obstacles to the next.

After practicing for almost an hour, Jimmy needed a break; and he considered bringing Spirit alongside John, who was sitting on the corral's fence, talking with some of the kids from Piedmont.

"Hi, I saw you jump," the flamboyant girl said to Jimmy out of the blue, pulling her stallion next to him and giving him a nice smile. "You're pretty good, and I like your horse."

"Thanks, you're not too bad yourself," Jimmy responded, noticing her pretty dark eyes. "And I like your horse, too. He looks pretty spirited and seems to enjoy jumping."

"Yes, he does, but I'm still getting used to him. My brother just sent him to me from Egypt—for my birthday."

Surprised by what she said, Jimmy only managed to repeat some of her words. "From Egypt?...For your birthday?…From your brother?…Wow! Oh, yes, happy birthday, of course!"

"Thank you," she said, with a twinkle in her eyes. "My birthday was last week."

"He sent you the horse all the way from Egypt?"

"Yes, my brother, who is the kindest soul in this world, wanted me to have a real big surprise for my birthday."

"Can't get any bigger than a horse," Jimmy said, laughing. "So, what's your brother doing in Egypt?"

"He runs a business there, in Alexandria. I'm going to boarding school here—close by—at Piedmont. I used to ride a lot back home in Egypt, in the same place where my brother lives—but I just started riding here recently."

"Wow," Jimmy said, "you're from Alexandria…in Egypt? That's funny. I'm from Alexandria, too—Alexandria, Virginia, that is."

"Small world," she said, with an even bigger smile. "Oh…my name is Mirah."

"Nice to meet you, Mirah; I'm Jimmy—Jimmy Starlight."

As soon as he mentioned his name, her smile faded away, and a startled look came over her face.

"You're Jimmy Sta…!" she said, flustered for some reason, not able to fully pronounce his last name. When she finally composed herself, she said almost nonchalantly, "So, you're Jimmy Starlight?"

"Yes," Jimmy said, "that's my name. You sound surprised. Have you heard it before?"

"Uh…no," she said, "…I've never heard it before…but I like it. It's such a different name—Starlight, light from the stars. Yes, I really like your name."

"Thank you, I like it too," Jimmy said a little awkwardly, wondering why his name seemed to startle her.

Mirah thought for a minute and, then, with a smile back on her face, she said, "I have a stopwatch in my saddle bag. Would you like to time some combinations with me?"

"Oh…sure," Jimmy said, wondering what she had in mind.

"Let's jump those three over there, and time each other's jumps…and see who does it the fastest," Mirah said, pointing to three combination jumps at the end of the practice course—the last one of which required a big change in direction between jumps.

"Sounds good," Jimmy said, knowing this was the most difficult part of the course, but feeling up to the challenge.

"Here, I'll start, and you time me," Mirah said, handing Jimmy her stopwatch. "You can tell me when to begin; and when you do, press this button here at the top— just once. And when I complete the last jump, press the button again, and tell me what my time is."

"Okay," Jimmy said, already looking forward to his turn. "Are you ready?"

After she said, "*Yes*," he shouted, "*Go*," pressed the button, and watched her take off.

When she completed her round, he showed her the elapsed time on the stopwatch and took his turn. When he finished, rather than showing him his time on the watch, she clicked it twice, erasing his time, and just told him what it was—a few seconds more than her time. "I win," Mirah said, smiling jubilantly. "Let's do it again."

The result of the second round of jumps was the same. "I win again," she announced triumphantly, telling him his time was again a few seconds longer than hers—without showing him the elapsed time on the watch. "Let's do it one last time to see if you can do any better."

"Ok," Jimmy said, "but would you mind, this time, showing me my *actual* time on the watch?"

"Sure," Mirah said as she bolted off.

Jimmy quickly pressed the button. But he had a sneaky suspicion that the watch didn't matter; she would find a way to win.

"You lose again," she told him wryly, even after her horse had initially refused to jump over the last obstacle because her timing was off, and she had to move back and start the jump again.

"But you didn't show me my time like you said you would!" Jimmy protested.

"Oh, don't worry, little man," she said laughingly, "I wouldn't lie to you."

Jimmy was about to say something, but thought better of it. *She surely must be putting me on*, he thought.

"And by the way," Mirah then said, "right after we have our snacks, most of us are going for a ride in the pasture and, after that, probably for a gallop along the trails. Want to come along?"

"Oh...yeah, that sounds...like fun," Jimmy said hesitantly, "but let me ask my uncle, first."

When Jimmy asked him for permission to go trail riding with the kids from Piedmont, John started to say "no," preferring to have his young cousin within eyesight at all times. But he reconsidered his decision when he realized, if he said "no," he would have to come up with some explanation for saying so; and this would be difficult without first telling him about the VARS and the Atlantean Prophecy—a discussion he was still not ready to have. Knowing his colleagues from Piedmont were keeping a close eye on the access roads to the farm and could render assistance on short notice made John lean towards letting him go. And when he also realized Marion and Terry would be riding along to keep an eye on all the kids, he decided to allow it.

"Okay, go ahead," he ended up saying, "but let's, first, get you something to eat."

"How about a sandwich from one of the vending machines here in the snack room," Jimmy suggested.

"Good idea," John said.

Not long thereafter, Jimmy galloped Spirit around in the pasture next to the corral, and he had a great deal of fun playing "horse tag" and various other games on horseback with the students from Piedmont. Marion and Terry kept an eye on the kids and were a big hit when they organized a few competitive events.

Jimmy particularly enjoyed the barrel races, wherein each rider had to complete, in the fastest time possible, different patterns around three large plastic barrels. Having demonstrated how to best maneuver one's horse around and in between the barrels, the two farmhands gave the students plenty of opportunity to practice their skills before they took turns timing the races. In one of the races, the students had to complete a double figure-eight pattern in between and around the three barrels, lined up in a row, with a few horse-lengths in between them. In another one, they had to execute a cloverleaf as they circled around the barrels, this time arranged in a triangle.

When it was his turn, Jimmy completed his patterns without necessarily trying to post the fastest times. Never having ridden Spirit in a barrel race before, he focused his efforts on maneuvering her evenly around the barrels and controlling her speed in the turns so as to not get her feet tangled up and risk possible injury. Mirah, however, was determined to post the best time in both events; and she did so by speeding aggressively through her patterns and making her turns so tight, she frequently scraped her legs against the barrels.

When all the kids had taken their turn, in what was overall a very cordial and fun event, she approached Jimmy and tauntingly said, "Sorry, you lost again, Starlight; better luck next time."

What's with this girl? Jimmy thought, thinking it better not to respond to her taunting. But this time he knew for sure she was not just putting him on; something made her very antagonistic towards him. "Maybe it's my bad breath," he jokingly told himself.

The kids thoroughly enjoyed playing games in the pasture for over an hour; then, Mirah suggested they take a trail ride. With all in favor, she led her horse to the three-mile-long trail that started at the corral and wound through mostly open terrain to the other end of the two-thousand acre farm. Despite some initial misgiving, Jimmy decided to follow her when she sped off. In no time, he, the other kids, and the two ranch hands also raced their horses down the trail, trying to catch up with Mirah, who constantly fired up her stallion to stay ahead of the rest of the pack.

Mirah's horse was young and fast, but Jimmy knew once Spirit got in a steady beat, his long-legged friend could outrun her stallion. Galloping along, he stood up in his stirrups, slightly raising himself above the saddle and sinking his weight into the balls of his feet. Before too long, he outdistanced the other kids and caught up with Mirah. Not wanting to upset the girl by passing her by and make her even more antagonistic towards him, he slowed and stayed slightly behind her. A little while later, the two of them reached a small narrow bridge located on the side of the trail, spanning a spring-fed stream that crisscrossed the length of the farm. They dismounted and waited for the others to catch up.

Not too long after they arrived and had the opportunity to give their horses a brief rest, Mirah walked her stallion, without warning, across the bridge to a larger trail on the other side of the creek. There, she quickly mounted up again and took off while Jimmy and the others scampered to get across the narrow bridge. The trail sloped up and across a rather steep hill and then passed by several large fenced-in fields before eventually looping back to the old corral. Having crossed the bridge, Jimmy noticed Spirit was still a little winded, so he waved the other riders by, dismounted, and walked her up the hill, intending to let her steady her breathing for a few more minutes. When he got close to the top of the hill and contemplated mounting Spirit, he heard the little voice for a third time. It spoke a bit louder and sounded more urgent than before.

"Let the girl go for now," it said, "and rest your horse a while longer in the shade up ahead."

A bit flabbergasted, Jimmy said, "Let the girl go…rest my horse…in the shade…why?"

"It's better not to follow her. A little ways further down the path, there is a field on the left side, with some shade trees in it—go there, please."

Jimmy looked around, trying to locate the source of the unsolicited advice. "Where are you? …And *who* are you?"

"Never mind where I am—you can't see me anyway. I am Tooku, your Celestial Guardian."

Jimmy couldn't believe what he heard—a Celestial Guardian named Tooku? He looked around again, not noticing anyone or anything near him. He also didn't see any places close by where a person, or whatever it was, could hide. Not knowing why the voice spoke to him again made him feel rather uneasy.

"So, you're my Celestial Guardian," Jimmy said slowly, "...now why in the world do I need a Celestial Guardian?"

"I'm supposed to give you advice and keep you out of trouble," the voice replied.

"I didn't know I could be in trouble," Jimmy said. "And who *are* you to give me advice, anyway?"

"You are not in trouble yet, but you will be if you don't do as I say," the voice said calmly. "As I already told you, I'm your Celestial Guardian, and we're supposed to give people advice. Now, please, go to the field; we don't have much time."

"Not much time for what?" Jimmy asked. "And I didn't ask for a Celestial Guardian, so why do I need your advice?"

"As your Guardian, I will advise you how to best reach your destiny. Like your forefathers, you are destined to become a great leader of your people—sometime soon. And, as I tell all future leaders, great leaders need advice on how to become great and, then, even more advice on how to stay that way."

"Me...a great leader...soon—*no way*," Jimmy said, feeling amused.

"You will be."

"And how do you know that?"

"The Prophecy."

"What Prophecy?"

158

"The one that says you will become a great leader of your people and someday lead them deep into the universe."

"Come on, stop kidding me. I'm not going to be leading anyone, anywhere. And I'm certainly not traveling deep into any universe."

"Yes, you are—I would never kid you about that."

"So, where can I find this Prophecy?"

"In the Book of History."

"Book of History? And where can I find this Book?"

"On Planet Atlantis."

"Planet Atlantis? Where is that?"

"You'll find out someday soon."

"Why can't you just tell me where to find it?"

"I'm not allowed to. You'll have to find it yourself."

"This all sounds very farfetched and very confusing. So how do I know you're really my Celestial Guardian, and not just some crazy spirit who's trying to fool me?"

"You'll find out soon. Now, please, go!"

"Wait...first answer this. If you're supposed to be my Guardian, wouldn't it be better if I could see you?"

"No, you won't be able to see me."

"Why not?"

"Because I'm from another dimension, and you cannot see it. You can hear me, but you can't see me—yet. Some day you will!"

While he conversed with the voice, Jimmy continued walking Spirit up the hill. When he reached the top, he noticed a little ways further down, on the left side of the path, a huge wooden barn filled with hay, sitting at the edge of a large grass field. Tall trees shaded the area in front of the barn, and a wide-open gate provided access to the field, which had a six-foot wooden perimeter fence surrounding it. In its center stood a quarter-mile lap track, further fenced off by a low railing fence. Like the perimeter fence, it was well-maintained and nicely painted in white.

"Tooku, I can see the field," Jimmy said, feeling a bit more at ease now that he saw the field and the shade trees the little voice had mentioned. "Now, why do you want me to go there?"

"Just go, you'll see," the voice replied.

Jimmy was about to pass through the wooden field gate when he heard another voice.

"Hey—Starlight, what happened to you?" Mirah shouted, riding back down the trail.

"Oh…nothing," Jimmy replied loudly. "I'm just going to give Spirit a little more rest…under those shade trees over there."

"Why…? Cause you couldn't keep up with me?"

"Not really," Jimmy said, "Spirit is still hot from running so fast, and she needs some time in the shade to cool down."

He wasn't about to tell her a little voice had advised him to go to the field.

"Shame on you, Jimmy Starlight," she said, again taunting him. "You couldn't keep up with me, and now you're trying to blame it on your horse."

"Give me a break!" Jimmy let out.

He wanted to ask her why she was so nasty to him, but she had already turned her stallion around and started to gallop down the trail again. Wondering what Mirah's problem was, he led Spirit to the shaded area under the trees and sat down on the ground next to her.

"Hey, Tooku, since you're supposed to be my advisor, please tell me why this girl has such a bad attitude and dislikes me so much," Jimmy said, looking around, hoping the little voice could hear him.

160

"She's mad at you," it said.

"Why?" Jimmy asked.

"You'll find out some day. It actually has nothing to do with you, per se."

"What's that supposed to mean?"

"You'll find out."

"You're not much help you know. I'm just going to have to stay away from that girl."

"No, that's not a good idea. You'll soon visit a place called Piedmont where she and the other kids go to school. And when you do, you'll have to become friends with her."

"Why should I do that? She doesn't even like me."

"Because she will help you find the underground passageway."

"Find an underground passageway? Why do I need to find that?"

"It will take you to Planet Atlantis."

"Why can't you just tell me where the passageway is?"

"As I told you earlier, I'm not allowed to do your work for you. You must find it yourself."

"You're still no help."

"Just go to Piedmont and look for it."

"Go to Piedmont and look for it? I've got better things to do than look for an underground passageway at some school called Piedmont."

"No, you don't."

"Yes, I do. For your information, I have a big problem to take care of before I start looking for anything. I need to know why two very scary guys want to kidnap me. And I also have to figure out why I had two very strange dreams."

"I know all that."

161

"If you know all that, and you're supposed to be my Celestial Guardian, then tell me what to do about these things."

"Find the underground passageway, and you'll find the reason behind their attempts to get you," the little voice said calmly. "Then you must go right away to Planet Atlantis and look for the Prophecy; and when you find it, you'll discover what your dreams are all about."

While Jimmy was talking to the little voice, John stood next to the corral, staring at the spot on the trail where the group of kids had rounded the bend and disappeared from sight. As he stood there, an eerie feeling crept up his spine; it felt like he was being cautioned not to underestimate the VARS' determination and ingenuity to achieve one of their main objectives—grab Jimmy. He wished Jimmy would come back from his trail ride, and he wondered if he should have taken additional measures to ensure his safety. Short of having followed him around on horseback or in his SUV—which without a doubt would have made Jimmy very uncomfortable, and to which he would have vehemently objected—he could not think of anything else he could have done. Then, he heard the sound of a helicopter passing high overhead, and he immediately realized what he'd overlooked—VARS coming through the air.

Not wasting any time, John ran to his SUV, jumped in, and sped down the trail the kids had used. When he saw the narrow bridge Jimmy had crossed earlier, he noticed all the horse-tracks leading directly to it. Because the bridge was too narrow for his car to pass over, he got out and ran across to determine if the tracks on the other side followed the trail up the hill or veered off into the rough. Since all riders appeared to have stayed on the trail, he had a decision to make. He could either run to the top of the hill to see if he could spot them nearby or quickly drive back to the corral and come up the trail from the opposite direction, in hope of catching them as they looped around and headed back to the stables. In the middle of making this decision, he heard the loud "whup, whup, whup" sound of a helicopter coming in for a landing; he instantly knew the VARS had spotted Jimmy.

When he heard the helicopter, John correctly assumed the pilot intended to land at the lap track; and he immediately got on his cell phone to notify his colleagues about this unpleasant development. He had indicated the location of the track on the map of Woodlawn he had drawn up for them. And because they had such a map, he was able to precisely direct his colleagues to the track—all the while running up the hill as fast as he could.

Perplexed by Tooku's urging to look for an underground passageway to another planet, Jimmy thought, *Why should I listen to him? He talks in riddles, and all of this sounds really farfetched.* He was about to tell him so when he heard the "whup, whup, whup" sound of a helicopter's rotor blades and the piercing noise of its engine coming towards him. Shortly thereafter, he saw it land on the trail, just in front of the wooden gate. Even before the helicopter's cockpit door swung open, he knew who his visitors were.

The first person to exit the chopper was the tall sinister-looking cowboy, wearing his black Stetson and dark sunglasses. He smiled when he caught sight of Jimmy, thinking, *This time I will get this little lamb for sure.* After he cautiously stepped down and surveyed the situation around him, he heard a big yell as his partner in crime tumbled out of the helicopter. While getting out, the short, chubby

163

cowboy got one of his feet tangled up in the restraining gear of the rear passenger seat; and with a big thud, he fell right on top of the tall man—knocking him flat on his face. The takedown sent the man's Stetson and sunglasses spiraling into the dirt three or four feet in front of him. After knocking his partner to the ground, the chubby cowboy ended up sitting on the tall man's back, with both of his big feet planted on the rear of his head.

"Oops…sorry…boss," he stammered, dazed by the jolt he had taken to the back of the head in his dive from the helicopter.

"Get off me—you fool," the tall man said harshly.

Totally frustrated, he rolled over and forcefully shoved the chubby man aside. He quickly got up and dusted off his sports jacket and jeans. After walking over to where his hat and sunglasses were laying in the dirt, he picked them up and blew the dust off the lenses, while slapping his hat forcefully against his hip to rid it of the dust too. With a look of disgust, he slid his sunglasses back on and carefully repositioned the Stetson on his head.

Turning around, he looked at the chubby man still sitting on the ground and calmly said, "Let's go, Happy."

"Ok, Sam," the chubby man said, stumbling to his feet. As soon as he got up, he looked around for his own Stetson, dislodged during his painful tumble. Spotting his hat underneath the helicopter, he got down on his hands and knees and crawled between the landing skids. Having retrieved it, he put the now crumpled Stetson on his shiny head, crept from underneath the helicopter, and stood back up. He chirped, proud he had managed to keep his sunglasses on during the entire episode. He, then, falteringly trailed the tall man in the direction of Jimmy, oblivious to the fact he looked like a destitute person, with his clothes and hat totally wrinkled and covered with dirt.

As soon as he saw the helicopter land, Jimmy quickly got on his feet and grabbed Spirit's reins. He put his foot in the stirrup and, taking hold of the pommel, pulled himself up and into the saddle.

"Now look what you've done…you Celestial Guardian, you," he said, irritated about the turn of events. "I don't really think it was a very good idea to come here…To be honest, it was a real bad idea…And I wouldn't call this keeping me out of trouble…would you?"

"Everything happens for a reason—you'll see," the voice countered. "It's better to deal with them here than out there on the trail with all the other kids around. Since there are no trees on the trail, they could have come in low and easily knocked you off your horse with the helicopter's skids."

When the two cowboys started to walk towards him, Jimmy quickly cantered Spirit around the lap track to the far side of the field, away from the two men. There, he took stock of the situation—judging it as "pretty bad."

"Things are not looking overly good—my dear Tooku," Jimmy said, worrying. "You got me into this mess; now what are you going to do to get me out of it?"

"*You* will get yourself out of it," the voice said firmly.

"That's easier said than done," Jimmy protested, not liking his chances of keeping himself out of the grip of the two cowboys, this time.

As he saw it, judging by Spirit's stance, he was surrounded by a fence at least six feet high—too high for him to jump over. And two "very-unfriendlies" were now approaching him from different sides of the lap track, while the helicopter, standing just outside the field in front of the wooden gate, blocked the only exit. To his astonishment, that gate was now being closed by a third man, the copter's pilot.

Even though there was enough space between the boards of the perimeter fence for him to climb through and make a run for it, Jimmy would never leave Spirit behind. He also realized, if he did make a run for it, the tall man would, most likely, outrun him and quickly track him down.

"So, how do I get myself out of this mess?" he asked the voice.

"Jump," Tooku responded, "with your horse *over* the fence."

"No way," Jimmy said. "It's over six feet high. I've never jumped that high, never higher than four feet."

"You can do it."

"No, I can't."

"Yes, you can! You have *no choice*!"

Those words got Jimmy's attention, and he realized Tooku was right—he had no choice. He had to jump the six-foot fence. There would be no room for mistakes, and he didn't have much time to decide how he was going to do it.

As he pondered how best to make the jump, he remembered the advice of his riding coach at Woodlawn— about getting mentally prepared to make a challenging jump. *Think about going forward and, actually, visualize making the jump,* she had said, *and do not visualize your horse refusing to jump, or she will do so.* To this she had added, *and be confident, because your horse can't be confident if you aren't.*

Jimmy took her recommendations to heart and, with his eyes closed, visualized himself making the six-foot jump with room to spare. He felt confident Spirit could jump that high because John had told him, when his father rode Spirit

166

competitively, she had made jumps over seven feet high on several occasions. Based on what he had seen as a spectator at various competitions, Jimmy also knew he wouldn't need more speed to make a successful six-foot jump than a four-foot jump; but he would need to time his launch with precision and attain a much steeper launch-angle than he had ever attempted before.

After an exhausting sprint, John reached the top of the hill while Jimmy contemplated how best to make his jump. Out of breath, John waved his arms, trying to get his cousin's attention, but Jimmy didn't notice him. He sat motionless in the saddle with his eyes closed, visualizing a perfect jump. When he realized Jimmy planned to jump the fence, John stopped his arm-waving so he wouldn't break Jimmy's concentration. He took a few deep breaths and started to sprint again towards the field where Jimmy was now prepared to make his escape—about a hundred yards further down the trail from him.

Having picked a part of the fence where a head-on jump would land him on soft grass on the other side, Jimmy patted Spirit's neck and nudged her gently with the heels of his boots to make her trot. After he nudged her again, she started to canter. In preparation for the jump, he slightly raised himself in his stirrups, convinced, if he timed his jump correctly, Spirit would deliver the needed launch-angle and fly them over the fence.

Just as the two cowboys rounded the lap track, Jimmy sped by them; all they could do was give him a look of frustration as he aimed straight for the perimeter fence. John stopped running when he got to within thirty yards of the field and saw Jimmy tap Spirit with both knees, signaling her to start her jump and launch herself into the air. He took another deep breath and held it while he watched the boy and Spirit fly over the fence and land safely on the soft grass in front of him—almost running him over in the process.

Jimmy was ecstatic about his successful jump, and really, really glad to see his uncle just when he needed him desperately. He leaned over in the saddle, hugging and patting his horse, and repeating several times, "Good girl, Spirit, you're the best horse in the whole world." Then, he jumped off, ran up to his uncle, and gave him a big hug, too. "Thank you for coming," he told him. "Am I ever glad to see *you*!"

Putting his arms around the boy, still marveling at what he had just witnessed—Jimmy jumping a six-foot perimeter fence—John hugged him back. "That was some jump you made."

Jimmy started to explain how the two cowboys had arrived by helicopter and began chasing him. John interrupted. "Yes, I saw the helicopter, and I can see them standing right over there," he said, nodding towards the lap track. "We need to get out of here, right now." Grabbing the horse's reins, he said with a serious voice, "We must ride Spirit quickly back across the bridge, tie her behind the car, and then hurry back to the stables."

Jimmy didn't appreciate the idea of tying Spirit to the SUV, even though he knew his uncle would drive carefully, so as not to hurt her. He was about to voice his reservations when John jumped in the saddle and extended his arm towards him; he grabbed it with both hands. After pulling him up, John set Jimmy right behind him on Spirit's bare back. Being a strong Thoroughbred, she could easily handle the double load; and when John nudged her, Spirit trotted towards the bridge. At the same time, the first of the three

SUVs with John's colleagues at the wheel came into view, racing towards them on the same trail he ran down earlier. Seconds later, coming from opposite directions, the other two SUVs could be seen speeding through the rough terrain, also heading towards them.

Having taken to the air before John and Jimmy reached the bridge, the helicopter screamed by right above their heads just as they passed over it. The chopper came so close it looked like the pilot had considered knocking the two of them and Spirit off the bridge with his skid but decided against it when he noticed the three SUVs coming to the rescue. When the helicopter banked away, the two cowboys sat quietly, looking down at them from their passenger seats, realizing they were in serious trouble for failing for a third time to bring Jimmy in. They knew their masters despised failure at any time, never mind three times in a row; and their punishment would be swift. They also knew the VARS would send others to get rid of Jimmy—and the next time, they would send a horde.

Chapter 11: Atlanteans on Planet Earth.

Having crossed the narrow bridge, Jimmy and John dismounted Spirit. Shortly thereafter, the three SUVs driven by his colleagues roared onto the scene and skidded to a stop. John explained to Jimmy he had asked his men to come to the rescue when he heard the sounds of a helicopter getting ready to land near the lap track, and he immediately suspected the two cowboys planned to pay him another unwelcome visit. Listening to his uncle, Jimmy recalled the pledge he made, after their run-in with the cowboys in the park, not to let them get anywhere near him again. Even though John had a tough time delivering on his promise, and Jimmy had to jump himself to safety when he was trapped inside the fenced-in field, he was very grateful for his uncle's efforts to keep him safe. He was especially appreciative John showed up right after his jump and kept the bad guys from making a further nuisance of themselves.

Deep in thought, Jimmy rode Spirit back to her stable as the sound of the helicopter carrying the two cowboys faded away. John drove behind him. Jimmy thought about the turmoil these men had brought into his young life, and right then, he wanted to know, more than anything else, why they were so desperately trying to abduct him. Because of the latest episode with the two cowboys, he had a feeling his uncle had not been as forthcoming with him as he could have been. He had no doubt, however, John always had his welfare at heart, and when the time was right, he would voluntarily disclose everything he knew about these two extremely annoying characters. But he felt really uneasy about not fully understanding the events unfolding around him, and he wished his uncle would confide in him sooner rather than later.

As all these thoughts swirled through his head, he also thought about the words of the invisible Celestial Guardian, and he decided not to mention to John what the little voice had said to him. *He will find it hard to believe,* he thought, *a little voice told me to search for an underground passageway, and go to another planet to look for a prophecy about me becoming a leader of my people—even David will have a giggle about all this leader stuff.*

Jimmy didn't know John had already decided to tell him everything he knew about the two cowboys and their masters, the VARS. He was ready to tell it all, except for the facts pertaining to the Atlantean Prophecy.

When he got back to the stable, Jimmy put first things first; and before asking John for answers to the questions occupying his mind, he gave Spirit a thorough grooming. The work had a calming effect on him, and he was happy to be doing something to reward Spirit for her magnificent jump.

In the meantime, while Jimmy undertook his labor of love, John got on the phone with Piedmont's director to brief her on their latest go-around with the VARS.

"It was a close call this time," John told her, having explained how Jimmy was nearly trapped by the two cowboys at the lap track.

"The VARS are getting bolder, and more aggressive," the director said. "How could they have known where he was?"

"I don't really know. They may have someone on the inside at the Farm, who let them know we came here."

"I'm hoping we can bring Jimmy in pretty soon," the director said, sounding very concerned. "Have you talked with him about this yet?"

"No, not yet," John replied, "but I plan to talk with him about it later today. His school will be finished in a couple of weeks, and I intend to bring him to Piedmont shortly thereafter—assuming, of course, you have been able to remove the traitors in our midst."

"Good. We'll all breathe easier when he arrives safely on *our* grounds, out of the reach of the VARS. After all, once we have taken care of the turncoats, there is no better place to look after his welfare than here."

"True. Just so you know, when I talk to Jimmy about coming to Piedmont, I also plan to tell him about all of us, and, of course, the VARS, and those who work for them."

"That's a very good idea. What about the Prophecy?"

"I don't think it's the right time yet to let him know about that. I'm concerned about how he might react to hearing about it if we don't properly prepare him for the awesome responsibility it puts on his young shoulders. I think it would be best, for a while at least, if I prepare him for it without letting him know I'm doing so. What do you think?"

"Yes, perhaps it's better to wait. But I should tell you, we may not have as much time to get him ready as we originally thought. We recently picked up some chatter among the VARS indicating they're planning to bring their new spaceship *Eliminator* here from New Varsius."

"That sounds pretty ominous. Do we know why?"

"No, we're not entirely sure. But whatever the reason, if they bring this highly advanced spaceship to Earth, there will be lots of uninvited mayhem for all of us—especially since it's able to cloak itself."

"We better get ready for that then. And before I forget, I should mention that when Jimmy comes to Piedmont, he'll probably want to bring his grandma and his dog, too."

"Wonderful, that won't be a problem. They can use the cottage where you and his father used to stay."

"Great, she'll like that. There is one other thing I wanted to ask you. When I tell him his father used our portal, he'll probably want to use it himself as soon as possible, too. What do you think?"

"Better wait till we solve our problem with our own Leadership on Atlantis."

"That makes sense. I'll tell him we can't use it for a while, but I'll give him a reason other than us having a Leadership problem right now."

"Okay, you can let me know later what you said to him."

After John got off the phone with Piedmont, he headed for the snack room, wanting something to drink and some time to formulate his thoughts about how best to bring Jimmy up to speed on all the happenings impinging on his young life.

Having finished grooming Spirit, Jimmy gave her some oats from his grain bin, hugged her "goodbye," and went looking for his uncle. When he located him in the snack room, savoring a fruit punch, he wasted no time unloading the things he needed to get off his chest.

Jimmy took a deep breath and, without an exchange of greetings, said, "Uncle John, I'm *really worried* about those two guys in the helicopter, and I *really want to know* who they are, where they are from, and why they're trying to kidnap me? Why me, Uncle John, *why me?*"

With his major worries out in the open, Jimmy took another deep breath and, looking pleadingly at his uncle, said, "Uncle John, I would appreciate some straight answers, 'cause I really need to know why these guys keep coming after me!"

John could hear the frustration in Jimmy's voice; and he intended to not only respond to his questions, but to also clarify for him all the confounding cards he had been dealt as a result of events that took place many, many years ago.

"I'm going to give you some straight answers," John said, "but I'll have to warn you—what I'm going to say to you will sound like something straight out of the movies." He laughed. "And if anyone else hears this, they *will* think I need to be committed somewhere. So it's probably best for us to talk about this in the car, and if need be, continue our chat at home."

"Okay, I can't wait," Jimmy said. "This *should* be good."

John called his backup team at their lookout positions to let them know he and Jimmy were leaving. He was looking forward to ending the charade regarding "my colleagues from work," and relieved to be able to tell Jimmy the truth—that they were Atlanteans. He knew Jimmy would be astonished to learn there were lots of them running around on Earth, ready to welcome him into their midst.

As soon as they got in the car, Jimmy decided, before anything else, to tell John about the encounter with the two cowboys after the Spring Concert at his school.

"They also showed up the other night...those two cowboys...outside my school...after the concert," Jimmy said. "I'm sorry it took me so long to tell you."

To his surprise, John said, "Don't worry, Mr. Becksbury already told me about it."

174

"Mr. Becksbury…he told you?" Jimmy said, with a puzzled look on his face.

"Yes, he did," John said. "For your information, Mr. Becksbury is also one of us. He became a music teacher at your school at my request, so he could watch over you at Belleview."

Jimmy's eyes grew large at that surprise announcement, and they would grow even larger when he heard the rest of what John had to say.

As they drove out of Woodlawn's parking lot, John told him, "Like I said before, what you're about to hear will sound so unbelievable, you may think I'm putting you on. But as unbelievable as it may sound, you'll soon experience some pretty amazing things, which will help convince you I'm telling the truth."

All Jimmy could say was, "Great," thinking, *After having had two cowboys chase me in a helicopter, a deer wink at me, and an invisible Celestial Guardian talk to me, nothing can really surprise me.*

"Do you remember a long time ago, while we were in the library, I gave you an article to read about Atlantis?" John asked.

"Yep," Jimmy responded.

"And do you also remember reading in that article that ever since Atlantis sank beneath the ocean so long ago, people have searched for it seemingly forever—for its underwater ruins, that is?"

"Yep."

"And because they've not been able to find these ruins anywhere, most people believe Atlantis never existed?"

"Yep, I remember reading that."

"Well—it did exist and descendants of its people are still alive and well, and living on our planet—also called

Atlantis—out there, far away in the solar system." John pointed to the sky as he said that.

An alert Jimmy questioned him. "You said *our* planet...whose planet are you talking about?"

"My own planet, and...actually...it was your dad's planet, too. We were both born there and came to Earth some twenty-five years ago."

"My dad's planet!" Jimmy exclaimed, shaking his head and squinting his eyes at John in total disbelief. "My dad was...an Atlantean?"

"Yes, he was. A full-blooded one."

This revelation shook Jimmy to the core, not only because it was totally unexpected and so unbelievable, but also because of what Tooku had told him earlier—that he needed to go to Planet Atlantis to look for a prophecy. *If Dad was an Atlantean,* he thought, *could this mean this prophecy is about me becoming a leader of these Atlanteans?* Having entertained this notion, he launched another stream of questions at his uncle.

"Are you putting me on?" he asked, still reeling from John's surprise announcement, "Did Dad really come from another planet?"

"Yes, he did," John said. "And no, I'm not putting you on."

"And, what about my mother. Was she also...Atlantean?"

"No, she was born on Earth—as were you and your grandmother."

"Wow, so I'm part Atlantean...because of Dad," Jimmy said, now grinning from ear to ear.

"Right you are."

"So, where's this Planet Atlantis, anyway?"

"It circles the Sun in the same orbit as Earth," John explained. "And it's always located in this orbit at a distance from Earth that is slightly larger than the distance from Earth to the Sun."

"If Atlantis orbits our Sun…how come I've never heard of it before?" Jimmy asked, sounding skeptical.

"Because it's located in another dimension and is not visible from Earth," John responded. "Nor is it visible, for that matter, from any of the other planets in our solar system."

Hearing that blew Jimmy's mind again.

"You and Dad came from an invisible planet in another dimension?"

"Yes, we did."

"So, why did you two decide to come here?"

"To help save Planet Earth and protect it from the VARS."

"The VARS, who are they…and why does Earth need to be protected from them?"

"The VARS are archenemies of Atlantis, and those two cowboys we saw earlier are humans working for them."

Jimmy listened quietly as John told him all about the lost City of Atlantis—when and where it existed, what its civilization was like, and how the VARS destroyed it many years ago. He explained where these aliens came from, and that they came to Earth after destroying most of their own planet. He also told him about Atlantis' crystals, its energy shield, and its ancient bases on the Moon and Mars; and how the Atlanteans on the Moon migrated to Planet Atlantis after the City of Atlantis on Earth was destroyed.

John was right—Jimmy could hardly believe what he heard.

"And how did Dad and you get here?" Jimmy asked.

"Portal," John said, "Space portal."

"Space portal…what's that?"

"It's an entranceway through Space, which allows you to enter into another dimension and instantaneously travel from one planet in the universe to another."

John explained that by using their crystals, the Atlanteans—not too long after they traveled to Planet Atlantis from the Moon—built a space portal connecting their planet with Earth. He also told him about Planet Atlantis' first Leader, Antonius Starlight.

"His name was Starlight, just like mine?" Jimmy asked, pleasantly surprised.

"Yes, that's right. He was a very distant forefather of yours, and he served as Leader of Atlantis for a very long time. After his death, one of his sons became Atlantis' Leader; and ever since that time, quite a few of Antonius' descendants have also served as Leaders; including your grandfather, Marcus Starlight, who passed away three years ago."

"So, how come you know so much about Atlantis and the Atlanteans' migration to their New Planet, thousands of years ago?"

"Because the Atlantean struggle against the VARS and the demise of their City, and their subsequent travel to Planet Atlantis, have all been documented in the Atlantean Book of History."

John told him this Sacred Book contained all the Ancient History of Atlantis, and that it was stored as a hologram in a large display case in the main library of Poseidon, the capital city of Planet Atlantis. When John mentioned the Book of History, Jimmy recalled Tooku had also talked about it.

"Wow, I can't wait to find out more about this Book and go to Atlantis to read it, and learn everything there is to know about the place," Jimmy said, as John parked his SUV in front of Jimmy's condominium building. "But for now, please, tell me more about Dad growing up on Atlantis—and about the rest of your family."

"I'll tell you when we get inside," John promised, after he got out of the car and waited for Jimmy to grab his riding helmet from the back seat.

"Are you sure you're not making all this up?" Jimmy joked as they strolled up the concrete path leading to his building.

"No, but even if I wanted to, I couldn't make up a fantastic story like this; and just wait 'til you hear the rest of what I have to tell you," John said.

He took a key out of his pocket and opened the building's front door. Having stepped inside, they walked up a flight of stairs to the second level, where John used another key to open the door to Jimmy's condominium unit.

"Grandma, guess what—I'm Atlantean," Jimmy said excitedly, when he walked through the door and noticed Eloise sitting in her favorite chair in the living room, reading the local gazette.

Sparkles, sitting on the carpet next to her, jumped up as soon as she heard the key turn the lock, and rushed to greet Jimmy as he walked in.

"Hi, Sparkles," Jimmy said lovingly, embracing her after she got up on her hind legs and playfully put her front paws on his chest.

"And what makes you think you're Atlantean?" Eloise said.

"Uncle John just told me. He said Dad was an Atlantean, just like him; and Mom was an earthling, just like you—which makes me half-Atlantean."

"Well, that's some awfully big news," his grandmother proclaimed, getting up and walking to the kitchen. There, she started to heat up some water for the tea she planned to make for John and herself, and fetched a glass to pour her grandson some cold lemonade.

Dying to hear more about his father's life on another planet in another dimension, Jimmy beseeched his uncle, "Please, Uncle John, tell me about Dad and you growing up on Atlantis." Hoping for a quick response, he eased Sparkles slowly back down to the floor and plopped himself on the thick rug next to John, who had seated himself in a comfortable chair in the living room.

Knowing how his little cousin felt, John quickly came through for him.

"Well, we grew up in Poseidon," he told him. "During the school year, we studied in the morning and played sports in the afternoon."

"What sports did you play?" Jimmy asked.

"When we were your age, we played mostly a game similar to soccer."

"You played soccer?"

"Yes, we did. Atlanteans have been kicking a ball around for at least five thousand years. They played soccer in the City of Atlantis when it existed on Earth, but their rules were slightly different from those of the game that you play."

"I can't wait to see Atlanteans play soccer. What else did you and Dad do?"

"During our summer breaks, we frequently went on camping trips together to make videos in some of the most scenic and remote areas of our planet."

"Did you sleep in a tent and roast marshmallows over a campfire, just like you and I do?" Jimmy asked.

"Yes, we brought our own tent and made campfires, but we had no marshmallows. We often swam in crystal clear lakes, though, and lived mostly off the land by catching fish and searching for wild berries and mushrooms, and digging for edible plant roots."

"That must have been fun, but what would you do if you couldn't catch any fish or find any other food?"

"We seldom had such a problem, because the lakes were teeming with fish, and once we figured out where to look and dig for plant food, we had little difficulty putting a meal together. But nevertheless, we always brought a back-up supply of food and water with us."

Jimmy thought for a second and then said pensively, "It must have been hard for the two of you to carry all of your stuff on your backs all the way into those remote areas."

"Not really," John said, "we carried hardly anything on our backs, just our video cameras."

"But what about your food and water supply, and your tent, your fishing gear, your clothing, and whatever else you brought with you, like batteries, and towels for when you went swimming?"

"We kept all of those in our cargo carrier."

"Your cargo carrier? How could you bring that with you on camping trips in remote areas?"

"It floats in the air."

"A floating cargo carrier, you must be joking?"

"No, I'm not. It's a remotely controlled anti-gravity baggage and equipment carrier, powered by a small Atlantean crystal."

"And you can put all of your stuff in it?"

"That's right. It's about double the size of a car's rooftop carrier, and streamlined just like it. Using a remote control, we can make it hover in the air or send it in any direction we want to, or lower it to the ground, so we can unload its cargo. On Atlantis, we use these enclosed carriers when we're hiking or trekking and don't want to carry our luggage on our backs."

"Wow, I can have a lot of fun with one of those cargo carriers here on Earth. Not only can David and I go on long camping trips with it, like you and Dad did, but we can ride on it, just a few feet off the ground, and not have to walk too much."

"Yes, there are all kinds of neat things you can do with it. Your dad and I had two harnesses made that we attached underneath our carrier so it could take us high up in the air. That allowed us to take videos in places we couldn't have filmed otherwise."

"It sure sounds like the two of you had a lot of fun on these camping trips."

"Yes, we did. The only thing we had to worry about was staying out of the way of the dinosaurs and flesh-eating hoppers."

Jimmy held his breath and gave his uncle a rather bewildered look. *"What...you have dinosaurs and flesh-eating hoppers on Atlantis?"*

"Yes, we do," John said, amused by Jimmy's reaction. "But not to worry, our dinosaurs are only slightly larger than an iguana and eat only plants and berries; and the flesh-eating hoppers are about the size of a squirrel and eat only rodents and dead animals. Actually, both are deadly afraid of humans, and the reason you want to stay away from them is that they smell really bad."

"Thank goodness they aren't dangerous," Jimmy said. "For a few seconds, I was really worried for you and Dad, out there in the wilderness all by yourselves."

John made him laugh with funny camping stories about them being chased by huge mountain goats and giant wild turkeys. Then, he told him about their days at the Technical Institute of Poseidon.

"We studied physical sciences there," he said, "and after two years received our science degrees. Eventually, your dad became an architect, and I became an engineer. In those days, your grandfather was the Leader of the Supreme Council of Atlantis, and your grandmother was the head librarian in the same place where the Book of History is kept."

"Is she still alive?" Jimmy wanted to know, recalling John had told him earlier his grandfather had passed away.

"Yes, she is, and she's dying to meet you—and so are your dad's sister, Maryka, and her three young children, Irene, Dax and Patricia."

"Cool—I have cousins," Jimmy said jubilantly.

Except for his grandmother, he had no living relatives on his mother's side that he knew of. And, as far back as he could remember, he'd always wanted to have more family than just his granny and his uncle. It wasn't that he was unhappy with either one of them; he loved both of them dearly. It was just that, since he had no brothers or sisters, he'd always hoped someday an unknown relative would show up—someone his own age, with whom he could share secrets and confide in, just like he would do with a brother or sister. Having just heard his aunt and her young children were living on Atlantis made that wish unexpectedly come true. Jimmy couldn't wait to meet them, even though he might have to travel to another planet to do so.

While he was fascinated by what John had to say about his dad's younger days, Jimmy was also very curious about why his father had decided to leave Atlantis—why he had left what appeared to be a safe place to come to Earth and confront the dangerous VARS.

"So, how come you and Dad were so interested in saving our planet?" he asked, "and how were you planning to protect it from the VARS?"

"Well...before I answer those questions," John replied, "Let me tell you a bit more about the centuries-long struggle between us, Atlanteans, and our enemies, the VARS; so that my answers will make more sense to you."

"That would be great," Jimmy said. "Please, tell me more."

John told him, after arriving on the New Planet, the Atlanteans were obsessed for a long time with plotting revenge for the Varsian annihilation of their City on Earth.

"They would have liked nothing better," he said, "than to engage the VARS in a major inter-galactic battle and, in retaliation for having lost everything they held dear, totally annihilate both them and their planet."

"So, I take it they probably didn't do that," Jimmy said, paying close attention to what his uncle was saying.

"You're right. They knew the VARS were a very powerful opponent who maintained heavily armed spaceships, while the Atlanteans only possessed unarmed space shuttles. So they decided instead to use guerrilla tactics to make it very unattractive for the VARS to continue living on Earth, and thwart any intention of further Varsian colonization of the planet. And having built their space portal, they sent small teams of highly-trained commandos to

Earth to constantly harass the VARS with daring and exceedingly annoying guerrilla raids."

"Were you and Dad guerrilla fighters?" Jimmy asked excitedly.

"No, we weren't," John quickly replied, "Actually, we were far from that."

Without elaborating on what he meant by that, he continued telling Jimmy about the Atlanteans' guerrilla raids.

"Our forefathers," John said, "knew the VARS were most vulnerable, not at their major Earth Bases, protected by their lethal spaceships, but at their smaller forward bases and rural outposts in newly occupied areas."

He explained, after blending in with the native, rural populations, the Atlanteans continuously mounted small operations against these bases and outposts, and avoided direct confrontations with reinforcements brought in by the VARS to counter these quick strikes.

"It turned out," John said, "by launching this full-scale guerrilla war, the Atlanteans were able to inflict many casualties among the VARS, while minimizing the number among their own."

"Did they actually kill many of them?" Jimmy wanted to know.

"Yes, many VARS were slain," John replied.

"Did that scare 'em away from Earth?"

"Not really. What the Atlanteans didn't count on was that, instead of being bothered by the many confrontations, the VARS loved the skirmishes and kept bringing more of their compatriots to Earth to make up for the casualties they incurred in the fighting. It was like pouring gasoline on the fire; every time we inflicted casualties on them, they brought in twice as many people to replace the ones they'd lost."

John mentioned this went on for years, until the Atlanteans finally became convinced the continued fighting—producing suffering on both sides—was no longer in their best interest. And they also realized, the continued fighting had changed them from a peace-loving people into a war-making society.

"Just like their enemies, right?" Jimmy noted. "They were becoming just like the VARS."

"That's right," John said. "Eventually, the Atlanteans stopped their guerrilla warfare and, not too long thereafter, their intense hatred of the VARS diminished, and their will to fight started to decrease. And when that happened, they became a peace-loving people again."

John also explained that the fighting between the VARS and Atlantis decreased unexpectedly when, as a result of their continued exploration of the galaxy, the VARS discovered several other Earth-like planets where they could fight with the native populations. The fighting further waned when, because of the continued presence of Atlanteans on Earth, the VARS no longer considered this planet their best option for a new home. When their old planet, Varsius, became unlivable, they migrated instead to one of their newly discovered planets, which they named New Varsius.

"Did many of the VARS living on Earth at that time also travel to that other planet?" Jimmy asked.

"Yes, many did," John responded, "but the majority stayed here."

"Why was that?"

"Two reasons: First of all, they really enjoyed making all sorts of bad things happen around here—the more havoc they created on Earth, the better they liked it; and second, after having lived on our planet for so long, many of them considered Earth their home and married earthlings."

"So, since the VARS started all of this havoc many, many years ago, how come it still goes on today?" Jimmy asked. "I think they would have gotten tired of it by now—considering their intermarriages and all."

"Yes, one would think so," John replied, "but that has not happened. It's in their nature to sow discord and hatred wherever they are, and this has not changed over the years. Sadly, it doesn't take much for earthlings to turn against their fellow human beings. When the VARS encourage it, or create an opportunity for it, human beings will, at the drop of a hat, murder, plunder, and destroy without remorse—this has gone on for ages."

After John had given Jimmy this rather somber account of the struggle between Atlanteans and the VARS, Jimmy came up with an obvious question. "So what have the Atlanteans been doing on Earth to help us humans, after they stopped actively fighting the VARS?"

"Well, we have always kept very close tabs on what goes on all over the globe," John said. 'We know most, if not all, of the really bad things happening on Earth—such as war, atrocities, terrorism, and violent crime—come about, in large measure, because humans listen to the ill advice given them by the VARS. And we also know the Varsian leadership on New Varsius controls much of what goes on with their fellow countrymen living here on Earth. They constantly send their representatives to Earth to check up on things and make sure their compatriots here continue to tow the party line—which is to make as much trouble as they possibly can. They understand, as we do, if earthlings ever decide to put their differences aside, it wouldn't be long before they boot all the VARS off this planet."

"So, if that's the case, how can we keep the VARS from spreading so much discord all around the world?" Jimmy asked sincerely.

"We can't prevent them from constantly trying to lead humanity down the wrong path, but we can make it more difficult for them to be successful at it."

"And how do we do that?"

"By continuing to do what we Atlanteans have been doing for centuries—actively encouraging the human race to live in peace and harmony; and promoting love, consideration, and generosity among all the people, regardless of their cultural and ethnic differences."

Jimmy fell quiet for a moment as he thought about the implications of what John had just told him. He then surprised his uncle by what he said next.

"So, the struggle on Earth between the Atlanteans and the VARS became and continues to be a struggle for the minds and hearts of the people—right?"

"Exactly," John said.

"And the reason you and Dad came to Earth was to help win over all those minds and hearts, so the VARS can't have them."

John smiled and admired Jimmy for this insight.

"Yes—*you are absolutely right!*" he said.

"So how, exactly, did the two of you plan to do that?" Jimmy asked.

John looked at him for a few seconds, thinking about how to best answer him. "Our plan was to win over the minds and hearts of as many kids as possible."

"And how did you plan to do that?"

"By building international schools where kids from all over the world can come and learn to live together in harmony."

"And then what?"

The answer to this question brought out the passion John had for his work here on Earth.

"Our schools are meant to be places where we teach boys and girls from many different countries—with different racial, ethnic, religious and social backgrounds—how to get along and respect and appreciate each other's differences. They're also intended to be places where we teach them to take care of each other and their planet; and instill in them the seeds of kindness, generosity, and responsibility."

John told him their schools are also meant to foster an environment in which students learn to clearly distinguish between right and wrong, and are given the opportunity to envision a much better world where everyone is taken care of, and to become part of an Atlantean-supported movement actively working to make this happen.

"So, why do you want to teach these things to kids, rather than adults?"

John found it hard to believe he was actually conversing, in a rather sophisticated manner, with a twelve year old kid.

"Kids' minds are open and, in most instances, have not yet been exposed to- or manipulated by- destructive forces like the VARS. If we are successful in teaching them the right values, they can pass these on to their parents and other adults in their lives; and they will grow up and become responsible leaders in their communities. And just so you know, Atlanteans are also involved in many efforts to convince adults to change their destructive ways."

"So, did you and Dad build these international schools?"

"We built the first one in Middleburg—Middleburg, Virginia—about an hour's drive from here."

"Do the kids know this school was built by two Atlanteans?"

"No, they don't—and they also don't know all the school's teachers and administrators are Atlanteans, too.

"So, what is it called?"

"Piedmont International Academy. This is the model for the others we planned to build all over the world."

"Piedmont…did you say Piedmont?"

"Yes, why?"

"That's the school…eh…the little voice told me to visit."

"A little voice told you to go to Piedmont?"

"Yes."

"What little voice? You hear voices?"

"Just one, my Celestial Guardian."

"Your Celestial Guardian? Well, I wish I had one of those."

Thinking his uncle did not take his comments about the little voice seriously, Jimmy regretted telling him about it and decided to steer the conversation in another direction. John had actually taken him very seriously and believed him; and he had also decided not to bring the Celestial Guardian up in the conversation, because he wanted to avoid having to answer any potential questions about the Prophecy.

"Well, since you and Dad built Piedmont, I think that's where I want to go to school," Jimmy said.

"Great."

"So, when can we go there to look at it?"

"Soon."

"How soon?"

"Perhaps after school is out. If you like, you can sign up for one or two of the great camps held there during summer break."

"Gee, thanks, Uncle John. I would love to do that. Can David come too?"

"I'll talk to his dad."

"And while I'm at Piedmont, can we use the portal to go to Atlantis?"

"We may have to wait for a while before we can do that," John said, mindful of what the director had told him earlier that day about having to solve a problem concerning the Atlantean leadership.

"Why is that?"

"I've been instructed not to use it for a while. But as soon as I find out that we can use it again, I will let you know."

"That will be great."

Feeling understandably upbeat after learning genuine information about his dad's life and his praiseworthy intentions in coming to Earth, Jimmy wanted to ask John many more questions about Piedmont and Planet Atlantis. But there was a real concern he still needed his uncle to address—the two cowboys.

"Uncle John, you haven't told me yet why those two shady characters are trying to grab me," Jimmy said.

Again, John gave his young cousin a sincere response without getting into what he knew all along was the main reason why the VARS wanted to kidnap him—they had learned about the Prophecy.

"Those two cowboys work for the VARS and get paid to carry out their dirty little tricks, designed to create problems on Earth," John told him. "And because they have somehow found out you are the son of an Atlantean, the VARS see you as trouble in the making, and they instructed the cowboys to abduct you, so they can make sure you will not interfere in their earthly affairs."

"If they do catch me, what will they do with me?" Jimmy asked, with a shudder.

"Most likely, they will try to get you to join them."

"And if I won't?"

"They'll probably force you to work in one of their factories producing the arms and ammunition they secretly sell to third-world countries and terrorists organizations."

"Will I be safe from the VARS if I go to Piedmont?" he asked.

"That would be the safest place in the world for you."

"Then, I should go there for sure."

"That would be great," John said, noticing the eager look on Jimmy's face.

Even though Jimmy wondered why the VARS were so concerned about a twelve year old kid, he decided, for the time being, to let it go and not asked any more questions. A couple of days later, Jimmy confided in David during recess at school what his uncle had told him about his father and the fighting between the Atlanteans and the VARS.

At first, his best friend just looked at him rather skeptically, wondering if Jimmy was putting him on. "You're kidding me, right?"

"I swear I'm telling the truth," Jimmy said, looking as serious as possible. "I've told you exactly what Uncle John told me—you must believe me!"

"Okay, I believe you. After all, I saw those two goons myself."

"Wanna come with me to summer camp at Piedmont, then?"

"Of course, someone needs to look after you."

"Terrific," Jimmy said. "But I don't think I'll need much looking after, because once we're there, we'll be safe and sound."

"I certainly hope so," David said.

Chapter 12: The Smithsonian

At Jimmy's elementary school, the sixth graders were traditionally treated to a fun school trip during the last week of classes. During his last week, they were going to Washington, D.C., to visit the National Air and Space Museum of the Smithsonian Institution. Air and Space is a bustling place; it has the distinction of being the most visited museum in the world since it opened in 1976. It is also a huge place, stretching out over three whole blocks between Independence Avenue and the National Mall, less than a quarter mile from the Smithsonian's administrative building.

School officials had arranged for the students to spend part of their day on a guided tour of several of the museum's exhibitions dealing with the History of Flight, including the ones on How Things Fly, Space Science, and Astronaut Travel to the Moon. The students had to bring their own sandwiches and other snacks for their lunch in the museum's food court after completion of their guided tour.

"I asked Grandma to pack me my favorite lunch," Jimmy said to David as they rode the school bus to the Air and Space Museum. "I have two peanut butter and jelly sandwiches, two oatmeal cookies, and an orange drink—what do you have?"

"I'm not as lucky as you," David said. "My mom insisted on packing me a healthy lunch today." He opened his brown bag and checked its content. "It's mostly rabbit food," he said, with a little let-down in his voice. "I can see some carrots, a couple of celery sticks, a few radishes, some kale chips, a bag of nuts…and what looks like some goat cheese wrapped in lettuce leaves, and a bottle of water. If my grandpa were here, he would have included my favorites:

buffalo jerky and dried venison strips—*much* better tasting than this other stuff."

"Your mother loves you—that's why she feeds you healthy stuff," Jimmy said. "But don't worry, I like veggie sticks and chips; and I'll gladly trade you a peanut butter and jelly sandwich and an oatmeal cookie for some of those."

"I can't thank you enough," David said, accepting the sandwich and cookie his friend handed him, and putting them in his lunch bag.

Jimmy really looked forward to visiting the Air and Space Museum because of what John had told him about his dad and Planet Atlantis. He hoped to become much more knowledgeable about the planets in the solar system.

"Yesterday, I got on the Internet on my I-phone to see if I could find any useful information on planets in other dimensions," he told David. "But as I expected, I didn't find anything. Then, I went to the Smithsonian website to see what the Air and Space Museum has to offer us."

"So, what did you find out?" David asked.

"I learned it has an exhibition on planetary exploration in our solar system and another one on exploring the universe."

"Great, let's visit those. And let's also go to the IMAX Theater. Dad told me we can watch 3D movies there about deep space and distant galaxies."

"Okay, that sounds like a good plan."

John intended to keep a very close eye on Jimmy throughout the whole school trip. He and several of his colleagues had followed the school bus in two vans since it left the school parking lot at nine thirty in the morning. They stayed close to the bus as it traveled along Mount Vernon Parkway, passed through Old Town Alexandria, and continued on past National Airport to the Fourteen Street Bridge. Having crossed the Bridge into Washington, D.C., the bus made a right turn and proceeded slowly up Independence Avenue. To get to the Air and Space Museum, it had to pass by several other Smithsonian buildings, including the administrative building, nicknamed the Castle, the Arts and Industries building next to it, and a building about three hundred yards further down the road, known around Washington as the Bunker, which houses the Hirshhorn Museum.

John, who drove the first van, all of a sudden, heard several police sirens wail as he was about to pass by the Castle. Seconds later, two burly, motorized District of Columbia cops maneuvered their motorcycles rather bluntly in front of his van and signaled him to stop. Having come to a complete halt, he ground his teeth as he watched the bus continue down the road past the Arts and Industries building.

John quickly lowered his window and said loudly to the policeman nearest him, "Officer, why are you stopping us? We need to follow that bus. Please, let us proceed!"

"Don't move!" the officer hollered at him.

Seconds later, two Secret Service SUVs, their sirens blasting away and red lights flashing, also pulled up in front of him and started to block traffic on both sides of Independence Avenue.

John jumped out of his van and approached the officer.

"Sir, please, let us go. We really need to follow that bus!"

He pointed at the bus as it passed by the Bunker and made a left turn so the passengers could exit the vehicle at the Mall-side entrance of the Museum.

"Sorry, no can do," the officer said harshly.

"But sir, my little cousin is on that bus, and we can't leave him by himself."

"He is not by himself if he's on the bus."

"But he may be in danger if we're not there to look after him."

"In danger of what?"

"Some really bad people!"

"Aren't we all? As I told you before, you need to stay put!"

John relented and got back in his van.

L'Enfant Plaza, which intersects Independence just across the street from the Castle, is home to several large government buildings, including the sprawling complex taken up by the U.S. Department of Energy. From where he sat, John could see the reason why all traffic on Independence Avenue had come to a halt. Half a dozen Secret Service SUVs and limos lined the front of the Energy Department along L'Enfant. Judging by the flurry of activity around them, he concluded they were about to transport a group of high-level bureaucrats from their meeting at the Department to their next destination—quite possibly the White House. In front of the line of SUVs and limos, a dozen or so motorized D.C. policemen had started their motorcycles, ready to perform their escort duties. The size of the escort and the number of Secret Service agents standing around the limos, carefully scouring their surroundings, told John this group of bureaucrats included very high-ranking government officials, perhaps the Vice-President, or even the President himself.

Worried about Jimmy, and not knowing exactly how long it would take for the traffic to start moving again, John gave his colleagues an order.

"I want everyone except the drivers to exit and proceed on foot to the museum. Please, get there as fast as you can and look for Jimmy. When you find him, stay close and let the rest of us know. *Now, please, go!*"

John instructed the man sitting next to him in the passenger seat to take the wheel, and he got out of his van. He wasn't prepared for what happened next.

Noticing five men jump out of John's van and, then, five more out of the second van, the Secret Service agents in the two SUVs blocking traffic on Independence Avenue also jumped out of their vehicles. They suspected foul play aimed at the group of high-ranking officials who coincidentally exited the Department of Energy at the very same time John and his men jumped out of their vehicles. The agents, their weapons drawn, screamed at the Atlanteans to sit down on the ground with their hands behind their heads. Seconds later, three other SUVs loaded with more agents pulled up, and the drivers of the Atlantean vans were instructed to get out of their cars and sit down on the ground, too, hands behind their heads. John and his colleagues obeyed their commands and, without complaints, allowed them to conduct body searches. When the searches turned up laser-based stun guns, the twelve Atlanteans were quickly arrested and soon found themselves in a paddy wagon, heading for a D.C. jail.

In the meantime, Jimmy and David had entered the Air and Space Museum. Even though it was a weekday morning and schools across the country had not yet let out for summer recess, hundreds of tourists had streamed in before them. The chaperones from Jimmy's school told the students they had one hour to look around by themselves before the guided tour would start in the central gallery of the museum. In awe of the building's enormous glass walls and ceilings, and the dozens of aviation and space displays around them, including airplanes and spacecraft hanging from the roof trusses above the entrance, the two boys just looked around for a while, wondering what direction to go in. Having spotted the Welcome Center, they strolled over, all the while looking up admiringly at the striking shape of the X-15 hanging above.

"Could you, please, tell us where we can find the gallery on planetary exploration," Jimmy said to the elderly gentleman behind the counter.

The man pulled out the museum's floor plan and showed them where it was located on the second floor. He then nodded to his right and said, "And over there is the escalator; it will lead you to it."

After they thanked him and started to walk in the direction of the escalator, Jimmy, all of sudden, froze in his tracks.

"David...look there," he said, with a shudder, pointing in the direction of the museum entrance they had passed through less than fifteen minutes earlier.

At first, David wasn't quite sure what Jimmy was pointing at. Then, he saw what caused his friend to tremble. Two familiar-looking characters had entered the museum and, taking in their surroundings, stood next to each other in the central gallery, directly underneath the "Spirit of St. Louis." They were, unmistakably, the two cowboys the boys had encountered before, except this time they weren't wearing their Stetsons and other western attire. Like many of the younger tourists, they wore tennis shoes, tee shirts and baseball caps.

"Oh, my goodness...where in the world did they come from?" David wondered, as he pulled Jimmy with him and quickly hid behind the exhibit of John Glenn's Mercury capsule, Friendship 7.

"I don't know," Jimmy said, "but how could they have known we were going to be here? And where is Uncle John when we need him?"

For a short while longer, the two cowboys just stood around, apparently conversing about how to best achieve the objective they came for—to catch Jimmy.

"They're not moving," David said, taking a peek at them from behind the capsule.

"Before they start looking around, let's quickly hide upstairs in one of the movie theaters until Uncle John gets here," Jimmy suggested.

"Good idea," David said, tiptoeing to the nearby escalator—with Jimmy on his heels.

Both boys ran up the escalator, looking back several times over their shoulders to see if the two cowboys had noticed their getaway. Near the top, Jimmy took one last glance behind him, hoping they had made it to the second floor unnoticed—only to see the tall man looking directly at him from below.

"They've seen us!" he shouted, jumping off the escalator.

"You're kidding, right?" David uttered.

"No, the tall one saw us."

"Then, let's get in there! Quickly."

David pointed to the IMAX Theater located on their right in the middle of the hallway. It had a big sign in front, announcing a free showing of the "Stars Tonight." Judging by the number of people filing in, they could tell the show was about to start. After they entered the theater, the boys looked around and noticed the only empty seats were all the way down in front. They let out a sigh of relief when they sank into two seats at the far end of the first row; shortly thereafter, the lights dimmed.

The movie, which portrayed a journey to the stars and constellations lit up in the night sky, would normally have gotten their complete attention. This time, however, they frequently took turns looking over the backs of their seats, praying the two cowboys would not show up suddenly and begin a row by row check of the theater; unfortunately, that was about to happen.

"They're here," David whispered.

When Jimmy peered over the back of his seat, he saw the tall man slowly walk down the side aisle, checking each row meticulously for any signs of the two boys.

"Let's go," he said softly, sinking to his knees and starting to crawl alongside the stage beneath the theater's screen. David quickly followed.

In less than ten seconds, Jimmy came to the door with the "Emergency Exit Only" sign lit up above it. Still on his knees, he reached up for the door's metal opening bar. Considering their situation a real "Emergency," he carefully pushed the bar back and opened the spring-loaded door just far enough for him and David to crawl into the small corridor behind it. After he let it close silently behind them, they both ran to the end of the corridor. There, they quickly walked down a concrete stairway, which took them to a large, empty backroom illuminated by florescent lights. They could see what looked like a door to a vault on one side of the room and a large double door at the end.

Jimmy walked over to the double door and looked through one of the small glass windows at the top of its panels.

"Whaddya see?" David asked.

"It's the ground floor," Jimmy said, gazing at the open space in front of the museum's first floor galleries. "I can see the old man we asked for direction."

Not sure if the coast was clear, he slowly pushed one of the door's panels forward. When it opened far enough for him to get a side view, he gasped and froze for a second time in less than fifteen minutes. The chubby cowboy was standing about ten feet from the double door, with his back angled towards him, keeping an eye on the two lower wings of the museum from behind a giant V-2 rocket. Pulling himself together, Jimmy gently let the panel, which was also spring-loaded, come back to a close; then, he slowly exhaled.

"Now whaddaya doing?" David whispered.

"They've split up," Jimmy said softly. "The fat guy is lurking out there, right next to the door."

They heard the emergency door in the theater above slam to a close, letting them know the tall man would be coming down.

"We're trapped!" Jimmy said. "Whaddawe do now?"

They both looked around, desperate for an escape route.

"Let's go over there," David said, pointing to the vault door on the side of the room. "Whaddaya think that's for?"

He rushed over and grabbed the door's five-pronged spindle, expecting to open the door by turning it; but it didn't budge. Noticing what looked like a scanner, with the image of a hand on it, attached to the wall next to the door, he put his right hand, which matched the image, against the scanner. He hoped this might unlock the door's safety mechanism; but when he tried to turn the spindle once more, it still didn't budge.

"It won't open for me," David said. "Perhaps you can try it."

Knowing they were running out of options to get away from the two cowboys, Jimmy quickly walked over and put his hand on the scanner. He had never experienced anything more unexpectedly when the green light lit up on the scanner and a loud click signaled the safety mechanism had turned itself off.

"Look, I did it," he said proudly, after he turned the spindle and pulled the door open.

"Wow, I can't believe you got us in," David said, shaking his head. "How is this possible?"

"Dunno," Jimmy said, "I can't believe it either."

"So, what's inside?"

"I can't exactly tell," Jimmy replied, "it's dark in there."

Seeing a light switch on the wall next to the scanner, David flipped it on, lighting up what turned out to be a humungous vault. The boys hurried in and Jimmy quickly closed the door. They had walked into a tightly sealed space, loaded with artifacts. These items were part of the Air and Space collection that, due to space limitations, could not be displayed in the museum's galleries. They both shivered, because the fully air-conditioned, humidity-controlled storage area was kept very cool to ensure the artifacts remained well-preserved.

After Jimmy had pulled the door shut, neither one of them had noticed the safety lock button on the wall next to it. They couldn't have known one push on this button would have locked the vault door again and kept any undesirables out. A second push would have unlocked it, allowing them to exit safely.

As they walked towards the back of the vault, they saw row after row of large storage racks, crammed full of metal containers. Each had a label on it, identifying in large print the collection inside. There were moon rocks, meteors, astronaut gear, aerial cameras, pilot uniforms from both

World Wars, and many other artifacts—too many for them to venture a guess as to the exact number.

"Do you know how they collect all of this stuff?" Jimmy asked.

"No, I don't," David said. "But, I do know we need to find a good hiding place in here quickly. Maybe we should climb inside one of these boxes?"

"Maybe we don't have to," Jimmy said. "I can see another door over there, right behind the last storage rack."

They soon found out this door was exactly like the one through which they entered, and this time they did detect the safety lock button on the wall next to it. When they pulled the vault door open, they noticed a large platform right in front of them, and two side-by-side tunnel entrances about a hundred feet away. The tunnels appeared to be dimly lit and had small railroad tracks running down their centers. On one of the tracks sat an open railcar with two sets of back-to-back benches in it. The railcar reminded Jimmy of the times he had ridden Capitol Hill's famous trolleys through the underground tunnels connecting the Congressional office buildings and the Capitol building. He had enjoyed those rides because of the well-known politicians he met onboard the railcars. Looking at the two tunnels in front of him, he wondered who had built them and what their purpose was, and how many people even knew they existed. He would soon find out and, at the same time, learn why the hand scanner on the other vault door had recognized his palm's heat signature and allowed them in.

Just as they stepped outside onto the platform, Jimmy and David heard loud voices inside the vault.

"I told you they must have come in here," they heard one voice say.

"Yeah, no other place for them to go to. I stood there the whole time."

"They must still be in here. Let's see if we can find 'em."

That conversation painted frantic expressions on the boys' faces.

"Hurry, let's hide in the railcar over there," Jimmy urged, pulling the door closed, and running to his hiding place.

Once inside, he quickly crouched down in front of the closest bench, right behind the car's four-foot-high back retaining panel. David was going to suggest hiding further down in one of the tunnels, but then thought better of it. He followed Jimmy into the car and crouched down beside him.

Tucked face-down in the railcar, they could hear the vault door open and the two men talk as they walked onto the platform.

"They must be out here somewhere."

"Yeah, let's take a look around."

The tall man, with a devilish look on his face, motioned the chubby one to look in the railcar, saying deceivingly, "I think they got away—must have gone into one of the tunnels—might as well get out of here."

When Jimmy heard those words, a feeling of relief came over him, and he briefly closed his eyes, thinking, *Thank you, Lord, they'll be on their way shortly.*

His relief was short-lived, because a second later, he felt a hand grabbing his shirt collar in the back. After the chubby man reached over the railcar's back retainer and got a hold of Jimmy, he also grabbed David by the collar with his other hand. The man was strong—strong enough to lift both boys by their shirt collars simultaneously out of the railcar.

While continuing to hold on to their collars, he set both of them down on the platform in front of the tall man.

Jimmy and David were baffled by what just happened, but neither of them stayed that way for long. Knowing his freedom was at stake, Jimmy grabbed a hold of the chubby man's leg and bit it. In pain and cursing him, the man let go of both boys and grabbed his leg with both hands. In a second, David was on his feet and delivered a karate round-house kick to the chubby man's groin; the cowboy cursed him as he tumbled forward holding his privates. Encouraged by what David did, Jimmy quickly jumped up and also assumed his karate stance, ready to give both cowboys as dogged a fight as he possibly could. Fortunately, further action was not warranted; the tall man completely surprised them by what he had to say.

"Hey, you two, stop hurting my friend here," he said. "We mean you no harm."

Not believing what he said, the two boys just looked at him—then, at each other—and, then, again at him.

"Yeah, stop biting and kicking me," the chubby man said.

He chirped as he got up off the ground and started rubbing his hands over his bald head and across his face again.

The two boys didn't know what to think.

"If you don't mean us any harm, then what do you want from us?" Jimmy asked, distrusting them.

"And why are the two of you following us all over the place?" David added.

"Just now, we came to warn you and help you get away safely from here," the tall man replied in a pleasant tone of voice.

"We don't need you for that," Jimmy said, with a look of disgust on his face. "My uncle will get here any minute and keep us safe from *you*!"

"Your uncle won't be coming," the tall man said. "They will have arrested him by now."

"You're lying!" Jimmy said, frowning.

"No, we're not," the chubby man chimed in.

Then, he started to chirp again.

"Stop that chirping and rubbing your head all the time," an annoyed David told him. "You make me nervous when you do that."

"Sorry, but I can't help it," the chubby man said emotionally. "I have to do that when I get excited."

"We're not lying," the tall man said. "They've arranged to stop your uncle's van and arrest him and the other Atlanteans before they can get to the museum."

Jimmy was surprised the man knew his uncle was Atlantean.

"So, who's *they?*" he asked.

"The ones we came to warn you about—the VARS, of course," the tall man replied.

"You came to warn us about the VARS! That's *not* very likely!" David blurted out. "*You work for them*!"

"Not anymore," the chubby one said, trying not to chirp again.

"We made a mistake by going to work for them," the tall man explained. "They lied to us about *you* and the Atlanteans."

When he said that, he looked straight at Jimmy.

"They lied about me?" Jimmy asked. "What did they say about me?"

"They said you are big trouble," the chubby one chimed in again, this time trying consciously not to rub his head.

"What kind of trouble?"

"They said there is a prophecy, about you causing destruction on Earth, and they want to keep you from doing that."

"Me…causing destruction? How in the world would I do that?"

"We're not sure," the tall man said, "but that's what they told us. And they showed us film of Atlanteans bringing airplanes to Earth to make war—film that had your uncle in it."

"Airplanes? Where?"

"At the Atlanteans' military base."

"And where's that?" David asked.

"We don't know. We recently learned, however, they brought those planes to Earth to defend it, not to cause its destruction."

Jimmy didn't know what to make of all this; his head started to spin.

"How do we know you're telling us the truth?" he asked.

"You just have to trust us," the tall man said.

"And why should we do that?" David asked. "You've been constantly harassing us."

"We're sorry for that." Motioning to the railcar, he said, "We arranged for this, and we need to use it right now."

"You've got to be kidding," Jimmy said. "We're not getting in there with you."

"You have no choice, my friend, and we don't have much time to get you out of here."

"You're not my friend, and I'm not going anywhere 'til my uncle gets here."

"We told you before, he's not coming," the chubby one said.

Just then, they heard footsteps and voices in the vault.

"They're here," the tall man said. "We've got to go."

"Who's here?" David wanted to know.

"The VARS," the chubby one replied. "We saw them enter the museum shortly after we did."

"And they'll be here in no time," the tall man said, sounding urgently. "You must trust us and come now!"

The two men rushed to the railcar and jumped in, seating themselves on the front bench. Jimmy and David looked at each other and, hearing the clatter of many feet running down the vault, followed them and also jumped onboard. Even before they sat down on the rear bench, the tall man had pushed the starter button on the railcar's automated control system, engaging its electric motor. As they pulled away from danger and moved further into the tunnel, Jimmy saw a dozen or so men with sunglasses charging out of the vault. They could only watch him, David, and the two cowboys accelerate out of view. He noticed all of them were dressed nicely, like office workers, wearing long-sleeved white shirts and colorful ties. What he didn't see was that, moments later, they started to run after them on the narrow walkway alongside the tracks, at a speed as fast as that of the railcar itself.

Because the tunnel was part of the Smithsonian's air conditioned space, the air smelled fresh and felt cool as the railcar quietly made its way down the tracks. Besides the whooshing of the air rushing past their ears, the two boys heard only the humming of its electric motor. For a while, the two boys sat quietly, hoping they had made the right decision getting in the railcar with the two cowboys, not knowing if Jimmy's uncle and his colleagues would show up.

"Where're we going?" Jimmy asked, wondering what the men had planned for them.

"This tunnel takes us to the National Gallery of Art," the tall men replied.

"Why are we going there?" David asked. "That place is full of paintings and other artsy stuff."

He had learned about the Gallery's masterpieces in his art class in school, where they had shown a video describing the works of Rembrandt, da Vinci, and several other great masters on display there.

"Because just down the road from there, we've parked a car we intend to use to take both of you to the Piedmont International Academy in Middleburg."

"You want to take us to Piedmont!" Jimmy exclaimed. "Why in the world would you want to do that?"

"We figured it's the safest place for you, and maybe for us too," the chubby man chuckled.

The tall man elaborated. "We hope, by bringing you safely to Piedmont, the Atlanteans will be grateful enough to give us asylum there, so we can escape retribution from the VARS for not bringing you in."

"So, that's why you're doing all this, asylum?" David grumbled.

"Well, yes—we're no dummies," the tall man fumed. "You need us, and we need you."

We don't need, or want, them, Jimmy thought. He had another question. "How did you know we intended to go to the museum?"

"They've got a canary at your school," the chubby man chuckled.

"The VARS have an informant at your school and knew about your school trip," the tall man added. "You're lucky we heard about their plan to grab you here."

"An informant at our school…who is it?" Jimmy wanted to know.

"We don't know. But we do know it's the same person who told them about the concert at your school."

"And how did you know where I was when you helicoptered in at Woodlawn?"

"Another canary," the chubby man chuckled again.

All this talk about canaries worried Jimmy, and he wished his uncle would show up soon and sort this mess out. But he realized, if the two men were telling the truth, and the VARS had waylaid John on his way to the Air and Space Museum, his uncle might not be showing up anytime soon. In that case, he and David would have to depend on these men for their safety—not something he looked forward to. A few moments later, their destination came into view.

The National Gallery of Art, located directly across the Mall from Air and Space, consists of two large structures— the East and West Buildings, connected by an underground concourse. The railcar's automated control system quietly applied the brakes and brought the vehicle to a halt in the basement of the Gallery's West Building. In front of them, Jimmy noticed a vault door similar to the ones they saw earlier.

After getting out of the railcar, the tall man said, "Please, Mr. Starlight, do us a favor and open this door."

Without saying anything, Jimmy walked up and put his hand on the scanner. When the green light came on, and the safety mechanism turned itself off, the chubby man turned the spindle and opened the door, revealing another huge storage space—this one filled with eight-foot-high racks, loaded with crated-up paintings, drawings, sculptures, tapestries and other works of art. Many of these would be exhibited in the National Gallery at a later date; others were awaiting restoration or shipment to exhibitions in other locations.

Having entered the vault, they suddenly heard sounds echoing in the tunnel behind them—unmistakable sounds of quite a few runners barreling down the tunnel's walkway.

"The VARS, they followed us," the tall man yelled, pulling the door shut and pushing the button that locked it again. "Come with me."

Even though he felt confident the VARS would not be able to enter the area, he led the others quickly towards the other end of the vault. The racks had been arranged in two columns of fifty rows, with space to walk through in between the columns and along the walls of the vault. They had progressed along the center pathway past all the rows but two, when the vault door behind them swung open with a loud bang. Shocked, they all turned around as the VARS burst in.

"Run for your lives," the tall man shouted, racing to the door on the other end of the vault. He touched the safety lock button that instantly unlocked it. Without looking back, he shoved the door open, rushed to the freight elevator across from it, and pushed the up-button—luckily it opened right away.

When he saw the VARS pile in, the chubby man froze, finding it difficult to move his legs. "Hey…wait for me," he begged. He spoke so softly none of the others heard him. Trying to follow them, he tripped over his own two feet; and struggling to keep himself from falling, he grabbed a hold of a large rack in the first row. Unfortunately, he couldn't keep his balance and went crashing to the floor, pulling the rack with him. Crates went flying as it heaved over and tumbled against the rack behind it. This started a domino effect, as one rack after another tumbled over against the one behind it—until all the racks on one side of the room lay on the floor with their crates strewn all over the vault, including the center walkway. Because the crates were made of very sturdy materials, held together by nuts and bolts, and lined with thick foam and other cushions, all of them survived smashing onto the concrete floor—as did the masterpieces within them.

When Jimmy heard all the commotion, he stopped and turned around. Seeing the chubby man try to disentangle himself from the rack that pinned him down, he hurried back to help him. Following his friend's lead, David also rushed to lend a helping hand, and together they were able to pull him from underneath it. They both grabbed the chubby man by the arm, and after getting him back on his feet, swiftly led him to the elevator where the tall man was waiting. Hearing all the commotion, and seeing his colleague in trouble, he wanted desperately to come to his aid. But that meant he would have to let go of the elevator door he kept open and risk losing their only means of escape. He was about to charge out of the elevator to help his friend, when he saw Jimmy and David coming to man's rescue. He could see the VARS rapidly gaining on the three of them, but there was nothing he could do except push the up-button inside the elevator and wait for them to get safely inside.

Jumping left and right over the crates and racks scattered around, the VARS were desperately trying to reach the elevator before the doors closed. They got there a second too late and, with great consternation, saw their catch wave them goodbye as the elevator doors sealed shut right before their eyes.

Jimmy and the others rode the elevator two floors up and got out right in front of the Gallery's exit to the Mall.

"Hurry," the tall man urged, taking the chubby man by the arm and leading him to the exit. "Our car is parked outside—just one block away."

Concerned about his uncle, Jimmy hesitated at first, then rushed to the exit, with David on his heels. They hurried past the guard in charge of checking the bags of visitors entering the Gallery, and almost bumped into the tall man who had suddenly come to a complete stop just before exiting the building.

"Look, over there—more VARS," he said worriedly, pointing to the five men with long-sleeved white shirts and sunglasses who were standing outside on the sidewalk.

"What's with those guys and their long-sleeved shirts and dark sunglasses, anyway?" Jimmy asked.

Having regained his composure, the chubby man said, "They don't want you to see the scaly skin on their arms and the big pupils of their eyes."

"Scaly skin and big pupils," David said, "how'd they get those?"

"Evolution on Varsius."

"And that's how you can always tell them apart from humans," the tall man said. "I could tell you a lot more about them; but right now, we have to hurry to the other exit on the floor below."

"Wait," Jimmy said. "Please, tell me, first, how those VARS could enter the vault down below after you locked the door?"

The tall man looked at him pensively.

"They had an Atlantean traitor with them."

"Atlantean traitor? What do Atlanteans have to do with this?"

"They are the only ones who can open the vault doors to the tunnels underneath the Mall."

"Why are they the only ones?"

"Because they built the tunnels."

"But I can open those doors."

"Yes, 'cause you're Atlantean. Now, please follow me."

The tall man led them down a marble staircase next to the elevator. It took them to the ground floor, to the exit onto Constitution Avenue. There, the situation was the same. They noticed five more VARS, standing on the sidewalk, closely scrutinizing people coming out of the Gallery.

"Now what," Jimmy said, restlessly.

Because he had mentally scripted the various escape routes from the Gallery, the tall man had another solution, precisely for this situation.

"It looks like they've covered all the exits from this building," he said calmly. "We'll have to go through the underground concourse to the East Building and leave from there."

He led the two boys and his partner to the ground floor escalator, taking them to the concourse. When they walked by its self-service restaurant, the Cascade Café, Jimmy realized, due to their hasty retreat, they had left their lunch bags in the IMAX Theater.

"Let's stop by that café and quickly pick up a sandwich," he suggested.

"Better not," the tall man said, not wanting to take any chances on his ticket to asylum falling into Varsian hands. "We must get out of here."

He proceeded to lead them towards the museum's glassed-in waterfall in the center of the concourse. From there, he planned to go through the underground walkway to

215

the stairwell and go up to the East Building's ground level. From there, they could leave through the 4th Street exit and run around the corner to the car.

Even though he had prepared a number of contingency plans for getting Jimmy out of the building, the tall man was not prepared for the large number of foot soldiers the VARS had committed to bringing Jimmy in this time. As he and the others reached the waterfall, the hair on his neck started to rise when he saw five VARS coming straight towards them from the East Building, through the underground walkway. His first instinct was to turn and run. But before he could take a single step, he saw five more VARS coming down the escalator from the West Building.

"Follow us," he yelled, grabbing the fat man by the hand, pulling him into the Cascade Café.

He intended to make their getaway through the emergency exit in its open kitchen. Seeing the clearly marked exit, Jimmy and David sprinted by them, and set off the door's alarm when they burst through it into an open brick pit with a brick stairway, leading up to the street above. Their jaws dropped when they noticed five other VARS standing along the railing at the top of the stairway, looking at them menacingly.

We're done for, the tall man thought, resigning himself to captivity when he looked through the emergency exit and saw the VARS.

As usual, Jimmy and David were not about to give up. Not wanting to confront the VARS in a cramped stairwell, Jimmy pulled the emergency door closed, shutting off its alarm, and they hustled back to the open space in the concourse in front of the restaurant. Reluctantly, the other two joined them. With five VARS coming at them from one side, and five more from the other, and nowhere else to go, the two boys assumed their back-to-back karate stance, ready to defend themselves and make the VARS pay a price for grabbing them.

Just when he started to wonder what it would be like to work in one of the VARS' arms factories, Jimmy heard a commotion in the underground walkway. Looking over at the source of the noise, he saw people getting out of the way of a group of men running in his direction. Having just passed through the walkway, the five VARS coming from the East Building turned around to see what the fuss was all about and noticed twelve men running straight at them. Moving closer together, the VARS braced themselves for a head on collisions with the group—especially with the one leading them. He ran several paces in front of the group, coming at them with fire in his eyes. Jimmy's face lit up when he recognized the man.

"Uncle John," he yelled as he ran right by the VARS into the open arms of his uncle.

With their flex weapons strapped on, the Atlanteans came to a stop right in front of the VARS. Realizing their catch might get away, the VARS started to reach for their laser weapons, concealed in their ankle holsters.

Having steered Jimmy to the back of the group, John warned them, "Drawing your weapons is not a good idea and will only get you seriously hurt."

After he said that, John focused his thoughts on destroying one of the chairs around a group of empty tables in the restaurant and touched his flex weapon's engagement button. Reading John's mind, the weapon's control system instantaneously identified the chair as his designated target and fired a hot particle beam that blasted it to pieces.

217

Temporarily outnumbered and having witnessed the destructive power of the Atlanteans' flex weapons, the five VARS decided not to engage them—at least not until their five compatriots coming from the West Building could join them. An alert David and the other two men made use of VARS' temporary unfavorable position to also run quickly past them to the rear of the group of Atlanteans.

"Who are these men, Jimmy?" John asked, without taking his eyes off the VARS, referring to the tall man and his chubby companion.

"They've helped us, Uncle John…they helped us escape from the VARS," Jimmy responded. "They used to work for them, but now they hope to get asylum at Piedmont in return for giving us a hand."

Before long, standing side by side, the Atlanteans faced ten VARS, also abreast, in a standoff in the concourse. Knowing their opponents had awesome fire power, none of the VARS had the heart to be the first one to reach for his weapon. Bemused, the tourists walking by didn't know what to think. Noticing all the VARS had long-sleeved white shirts and dark sunglasses on, some of the onlookers had the impression this was a staged performance by the Smithsonian. Others thought it was some kind of spiritual exercise put on by some New-Age group. When John gave the order to leave, the Atlanteans moved backwards in unison till they were almost halfway down the walkway. Then, they surrounded Jimmy as they hurried to the escalator and rode it up to the East Building's ground floor. There, they exited to the Mall and continued on to the two vans parked a few blocks away. After a quick headcount, all of them, including the boys and the cowboys, piled into the vans and, before too long, they were on their way out of the nation's Capital.

Back home in Alexandria, after dropping David off at his condominium, John told Jimmy about his run-in with the Secret Service and his subsequent arrest by the D.C. police.

"You were set up by the VARS, Uncle John," Jimmy said. "They told us there's an informant at our school."

"Who told you that?"

"The two guys you met earlier, who helped us get away from the VARS at the Air and Space Museum and the National Gallery."

"They were right. Someone most certainly set us up."

"And you should also know, they told us the VARS had an informant at Woodlawn."

"Thanks, I actually suspected that."

"So, where did you take 'em...those two guys?"

"My men took them to a secure place where we can question them."

"You're not gonna hurt them, are you?"

"Of course not. We just listen to what they have to say about their involvement with the VARS, and to whatever else they're willing to tell us about the VARS' secret operations here on Earth."

"Are you going to give 'em asylum at Piedmont?"

"I'll have to talk to the Academy's director about that. We'll have to make sure they aren't part of a Varsian plot to get two of their people inside our school."

"That's exactly what I'm worried about, Uncle John; and because they've caused me so much grief, I could never ever trust them."

"Yeah, I know what you mean."

"How did you get out of jail, anyway?"

"Some of my people work for the D.C. Court system, and they quickly arranged for bail."

"And how did you find me at the National Gallery?"

"Tracer—there's a tracer on your belt. I put it there, so I always know where to find you."

Jimmy took off his belt and carefully studied it, trying to locate the tracer; he could not find it.

"Where is it?"

John showed him a tiny micro dot, pasted to the inside of his belt—practically invisible.

"Wow, I'm glad you knew where to find me."

"So am I."

Later that evening, John called Piedmont to inform the director what had transpired at the Smithsonian that day.

"I plan to bring Jimmy in at the end of this week," he told her.

"That's great. We'll make everything ready for him."

"And those two cowboys I just told you about, they would like asylum at Piedmont."

"We will need to check them out thoroughly before we promise them anything, but I guess we owe them for taking care of Jimmy."

"Yes; and hopefully, they will tell us what the VARS are up to, and who the traitors in our midst are."

"Why don't you bring 'em over tomorrow, so we can talk to 'em."

"Okay, I'll do that. I mentioned what happened in D.C. to David's father. He would like to bring his son down this weekend, too."

"Wonderful. They will be happy here, together."

"By the way, neither one of the two boys knows David's father is working for us."

"Good, we'll keep it that way."

"Before I forget it, I should also tell you Jimmy confided in me a few days ago that a little voice told him to go to Piedmont."

"A little voice told him to go to Piedmont? What little voice?"

"He claims it was his Celestial Guardian."

"His Celestial Guardian told him to come here; *my goodness—that is great news!*"

"That's what I thought when he told me. I remembered Jimmy's dad telling me his father had a Celestial Guardian, who advised him on being the Leader of our people."

"He was right, only Atlantean Leaders have Celestial Guardians. What this means is that Jimmy will be our Leader someday soon—and the Prophecy is coming true."

After she finished talking with John, the director was overcome with emotion. *Finally, all the work we have done is starting to pay off,* she thought. *Now that the Prophecy is being fulfilled, we have to get ready for an all-out offensive against the enemy—I have to get Jimmy ready for war.*

Chapter 13: Piedmont International Academy

On the Saturday morning after his Smithsonian adventure, Jimmy Starlight felt great as he and his uncle drove west on Route 50 to the rustic little town of Middleburg, Virginia. He looked forward to participating in the two-month long horseback-riding camp at their destination, the Piedmont International Academy, located just outside of town on 2000 acres of scenic land. He had brought his violin and three suitcases: a large one, stuffed full with his clothes, shoes, socks, and the like; and two smaller ones for his riding boots, books, video games, and musical scores. After finishing the camp, he planned to stay at Piedmont to start high school.

"Your dad really loved western Virginia," John told him, "because of its natural beauty and quaint little towns."

"Then, I will love it too," Jimmy said. "Hopefully, David and I can visit some of these towns while we're at Piedmont."

David's parents had also enrolled their son in the horseback-riding camp; they intended to drive him down later on in the afternoon. The two boys hoped to play polo during the camp and compete in polo matches with teams from neighboring clubs. They also planned to refine their jumping skills and compete in local jumping competitions. Excited about going to camp, Jimmy had all but forgotten dashing wildly through the Air and Space Museum and the National Gallery of Art while barely slipping away from the VARS.

As they approached the town's outskirts, Jimmy asked his uncle, "Why did you and Dad decide to build your school in Middleburg, anyway?"

"Horses and history," John responded. "Your dad loved anything having to do with horses, and I love history and historical places."

He explained that Middleburg was one of the nation's foremost places for horse racing and thoroughbred breeding, and his dad had been involved with both.

"If that's what he did, then I want to do it too," Jimmy said.

Then, John had a question for him.

"Can you guess where Middleburg got its name from?"

When Jimmy pleaded ignorance on the matter, John told him that in 1787, at the time of its establishment, the town was named after its location—on the old Ashby Gap Turnpike, midway between the Port City of Alexandria, where Jimmy lived, and the City of Winchester, Virginia.

"In those days," he said, "The Ashby Gap Turnpike was the major stagecoach thoroughfare between the western areas of the country and its eastern seaports; it is now part of Route 50, the highway we're driving on."

"You sure know your history, Uncle John," Jimmy said, grateful for having learned a few historical tidbits about the place his dad loved.

As they drove along Washington Street, the main thoroughfare running through the center of Middleburg, John pointed out several buildings dating back to the late 1700s and early 1800s, including the oldest original inn in America—the Red Fox Inn.

"That's where your dad and I stayed when we first came to this planet," John said.

"Great, I'll plan to stay there one day."

A few minutes later, John made a sharp right turn on a narrow winding road; shortly thereafter, they arrived at the only entrance to the Piedmont International Academy.

Tall oak trees flanked the open entrance, and two elegantly curved six-foot high brick walls funneled the paved road through it. A brick guardhouse sat a few feet off the entranceway on the driver's side of incoming traffic. One person stood guard while another attended to the computer terminal in the guardhouse. The school's computer system contained all information on individuals cleared to enter the campus, and it was standard operating procedure for the guard to run a check on his computer terminal before letting anyone unfamiliar to him onto the school grounds.

When, recognizing John, the guard motioned them through, Jimmy was in for a real surprise. Standing next to the guard house, waving at them with both hands, trying desperately to get their attention, was…?

"Mirah…! What do you suppose she wants from us?" Jimmy exclaimed, gawking at her with misgivings on his mind.

With a nice smile on her face, in contrast to the rather snide looks she had given him the last time he saw her at Woodlawn Farm, she shouted, "Hey, Jimmy—Jimmy Starlight—wait."

After John pulled over to the side of the entranceway and lowered his window, she ran up to the car.

"Hi, it's me…Mirah," she said, noticing the surprised looks on their faces. "I'm Jimmy's 'Welcome to Camp' CIT. I'm supposed to let him know where to go for registration and show him around campus."

"Oh, that's really nice," John said. "So, what do we do now?"

"If it's okay with you, I'll just jump in the back of the car and show you where to go."

"Great, hop in."

John knew the school grounds and buildings' locations inside out, but he decided to let Mirah guide them onto the campus. After Jimmy's father died, he was reassigned from his job as co-director of Piedmont by the High Command of the Atlantean Civil Service Corps, shortly before the current director was appointed to her position. The High Command, which oversees all earthly matters involving Atlanteans, informed him they needed him to fill an important intelligence position in Washington, D.C. There was another reason for his reassignment, but it was not conveyed to him; they understood he needed time away from the school to heal the mental wounds he incurred when a boating accident robbed him of his best friend and longtime partner, who shared his vision of transforming Planet Earth—Jimmy's father.

Seeing Mirah again, Jimmy didn't know what to think. He learned later, CIT stood for "counselor in training." It referred to students who were being trained to become paid summer-camp counselors the next year. As part of their training, they were assigned various camp chores, such as welcoming new campers.

"I'm so glad you could come to Piedmont," she said pleasantly, handing him a little booklet. "As your CIT, I'm supposed to give you this brochure. It has a map of our campus in it and tells you a little about our school and the area in which we're located. Later today, I'll give you a tour of the place."

"That sounds…interesting," Jimmy said.

Wondering how he could have been so unfortunate as to have Mirah as his personal greeter, he felt, at first, terrible

225

about the prospect of having to spend time with her touring the campus. But then, recalling what Tooku had said a few weeks ago at Woodlawn—about making friends with her, and letting her help him find an underground passageway to take him to Atlantis—he started to feel better about it.

"Actually, it would be useful for me to know more about this school," he said, trying to sound upbeat. "A tour would come in handy."

"Great," she said. "Let me tell you a few things about our school."

She told him the school was named after the area in which it was located—Piedmont.

"The Piedmont region, which includes the Virginia Piedmont in the western part of the state, stretches all the way from New Jersey to central Alabama," she said, giving him a scholarly look. "It sits in-between the Atlantic Coastal Plain and the Appalachian Mountains. You should also know, even though this name translates from French as *foothill*, it was, according to historians, actually named after the Italian region of Piemonte."

"You don't say," Jimmy said. "I'm so glad you told me that."

"Furthermore, it's called an *International* Academy because we enroll students from all over the world."

"From all over the world, that's amazing."

Glad she had Jimmy's attention, she said, "The next thing I'm going to do is register you at the summer-camp office and find out what dormitory room you've been assigned. The office is just down the road in the admin building, next to the big parking lot we're going to."

Fox Chase Lane is a narrow, uphill, mile-long curvy road leading north from the Academy's entrance, through some heavily wooded acreage of pine trees, to the area where

226

the majority of the school's buildings are located. As they drove up the road, Mirah continued her CIT briefing.

"When we get to the top of the hill, you'll see our campus and the Blue Ridge Mountains behind it. Unfortunately for you, but fortunately for the students of Piedmont, most of the campus is off-limits to automobile traffic."

She told them they would have to park their SUV in the large visitor parking lot at the end of Fox Chase Lane and then proceed by foot to the admin building.

"After you have registered, we'll take our regular means of transportation to your dorm."

"What regular means are you talking about?" Jimmy wanted to know.

"You'll see when we get there," she replied, with mystery eyes and voice.

As they cleared the heavily wooded area and reached the top of the hill, Jimmy got his first glimpse of the Piedmont campus. What he saw took his breath away. John stopped the car on the side of the road, and all three got out so Jimmy could get a better view of what lay below. Stretched out in front of them, in a valley with grass-covered rolling foothills, sat a sprawling campus, containing the most unbelievable assortment of futuristic buildings he had ever seen. Interspersed between the buildings, he saw dozens of ponds, fed by a slow-flowing creek that crisscrossed through the whole campus. Several small elegantly covered wooden footbridges curved over the creek in the grassy fields, and stone arched bridges allowed the narrow brick campus roads to cross over it.

"Wow," was all Jimmy could say, as his eyes moved from one intricately designed building to the next. Feeling elated and struck by the beauty of it all, he turned to John and said, "So, you and Dad built all this?"

"Yes, we did. Your dad designed and I constructed it."

"*That's so cool*," Jimmy said, turning back around, so he could take in the whole panoramic view once again.

"I'm glad you like it." John said.

Feeling so proud of the place his family built, Jimmy couldn't help posing Mirah one question after another.

"What's that?" he asked, pointing to the campus' tallest structure, sitting off to his right.

The building had three circular bottom floors layered at its base, and a tall helical-shaped glass tower resting on top of it. The opaque glass tower spiraled three hundred meters upward, tapering to a large pointed cone.

"That's our admin building," Mirah replied. "That's where we're going to register you."

"And what about those big buildings over there?" he asked, nodding towards four large shiny multi-story buildings, further down to his left.

These elegant, elongated structures had long concave roofs, and large floor-to-ceiling glass windows on both sides. They struck Jimmy as having the shape of his grandmother's bread canister with its long slightly oval top.

"Those are the boys' and girls' dorms."

"Is that where I'll be staying?"

"That's right. Your dorm is the one closest to us."

"And what's that over there," Jimmy asked, pointing to a ultramodern building sitting down below in front of them, surrounded by several small ponds. From where he was standing, the building looked like a tall plant stem, with a dozen or so beautifully shaped multi-colored lily pads sprouting out of it in several directions.

"That's our art center," Mirah said. "It's hard to tell from here, but inside those lily pads you'll find our art classrooms and studios. And the tall tower to the right of it is our science building."

That building really had his attention. It had the shape of a long, thin hourglass, with a large disk on top, and another one, slightly smaller, surrounding its thin waist about halfway up. Like the admin building's tower, it was made out of opaque material; but in addition, it had colored lights continuously streaking through its outer shell, in different symmetrical patterns and shapes.

"Wow, look at all those beautiful colors!" Jimmy marveled. "What's inside those saucers at the top and in the middle?"

"Those saucers are our science library, classrooms, and laboratories," Mirah replied.

"And what about those guys over there on the right?" he asked, continuing his barrage of questions.

The "guys" he asked her about were four eye-catching spring-green structures. All of them had a slim central tower, to which—at five different levels—four covered platforms were attached, in a four-leaf-clover design, by four curved walkways.

"Those are our liberal-arts classrooms," Mirah responded, patiently. "The platform furthest to your right houses our regular library."

Jimmy saw several more dazzling structures he really wanted to ask her about, especially the deep-blue one with a large silver dome at its top. But before he had a chance to do so, Mirah suggested he keep any other questions for the tour and they proceed to the summer-camp office to register him. She took Jimmy by the hand and led him back to the car.

When they reached the visitors' parking lot a little while later, Jimmy was in for another surprise. The lot was more than halfway filled with colorful golf carts—most of them connected with plug-in electrical cords to outlets mounted on dozens of lamp posts, scattered throughout the lot. He saw quite a few kids driving the carts to and from the parking lot, and using them to zip around on the roads surrounding it. He also noticed dozens of bicycle racks, lining the curbs around the lot. They were filled with all-terrain bicycles, and many kids were biking and walking on the bike paths that ran along both sides of the campus' roads.

"Look at all those carts," Jimmy chuckled. "So, where's the golf course?"

Happy that Jimmy showed a sense of humor, Mirah said, "They're not for playing golf, silly—they're the regular means of transportation I told you about, for students and teachers to get around campus."

"Am I allowed to drive 'em?"

"Yes, of course. Anyone can use the carts anytime they want to, and the bicycles too. But after you use 'em, the bikes have to be placed in the bike racks, and the carts must be plugged into the electrical outlets to make sure their batteries remain sufficiently charged for their next use."

"You should also know," John said, "that besides shading their occupants, the carts' small vinyl canopies serve another important function. Because they have a layer of thin-film solar cells glued on top, the canopies generate electricity during the day, and serve as an alternative power source for charging the carts' batteries."

After John parked the car, they walked over to the school's admin building. It towered over the rest of the campus; Jimmy almost got a crick in his neck when he looked up at the top of the building. While they climbed the granite steps to the building's ground floor, Jimmy wondered what purpose the three hundred-meter-high glass tower might serve. Its translucent glass allowed light to stream in but kept anyone from noticing what went on indoors. When he queried Mirah about it, she said the tower served as office space for Piedmont faculty; but she had actually never visited any of the offices, since the tower was off-limits to all students. It seemed to Jimmy, the large tower had probably enough office space not only for all of Piedmont's teachers, but for all of its students as well. He was right—and one day he would discover what other purpose the huge tower served.

Because it was the weekend, most of the admin offices were closed. After they walked through the main entrance, Jimmy suddenly got a sensation resembling a burst of energy streaking through his body. It gave him the same feeling of elation as when he first laid eyes on the Piedmont campus. Wondering what had instigated this most pleasant experience, he stopped and scrutinized his surroundings. Unable to determine its cause, he then hurried after Mirah as she escorted them past the office of the Piedmont Director to the winding marble staircase that took them up to the second floor. There, she led them to the end of the hallway, and into the summer camp office.

"This is Jimmy Starlight," Mirah informed the secretary at the front desk in a pleasant manner, taking Jimmy by the arm and gently nudging him closer to where the nicely dressed woman was sitting. "He's here for the horseback-riding camp." Motioning John to also step forward, she said politely, "And this is his uncle—Uncle John."

"So very nice to meet you, Jimmy," the secretary said, looking at him with admiration in her eyes. "We've been expecting you." Then, turning to John, she said, warmly, "And, so nice to see you again, director."

"It's certainly nice to see you again, too, Evelyn," John said.

They had known each other for many years—ever since he hired her as a summer intern when he and Jimmy's dad were co-directors of the school.

"I will let the camp director know you are here," Evelyn said. "In the meantime, please make yourselves comfortable over there." She pointed to two couches in the guest area in the back of the office.

As Jimmy looked around, he saw many pictures on the walls of kids enjoying their summer camps, including pictures of previous horseback-riding camps. He knew that this year, besides the one he was going to attend, the school offered a number of other camps, covering a variety of interests; such as drama, jewelry, photography, music, sports, and science camps. *Enough choices,* he thought, *to keep myself busy during future summer months.*

"How are ye, John?" a boisterous voice reverberated through the room, as the camp director walked out of his private office and gave John a great big bear hug.

He was a huge man, over six and a half feet tall, with long, curly, gray hair and hands that, to Jimmy, seemed the size of grizzly-bear paws.

"Great. And how are you, professor?" John replied, happy to see his old friend again, with whom he had spent many a day discussing ways to save the world's beleaguered dolphins.

"Well, who do we have here?" the director asked jokingly, looking at Jimmy, pretending not to know who the child standing in front of him was—even though Jimmy coming to Piedmont had been the most discussed topic among the Academy's faculty for the past year.

"This is my young cousin, Jimmy Starlight," John said. "He's here for the riding camp."

"Of course—*I knew that*," the director said, with the biggest smile Jimmy had ever seen. "Hi, Jimmy—they call me Professor Brassner—B. Brassner—but you can just call me *professor*."

"Nice to meet you, *professor*," Jimmy said, gingerly shaking his huge outstretched hand.

He couldn't help but like the man right from the start. The professor had a handsome caring face that seemed to say, "*I'm glad you're here—welcome to my world.*" He wondered what his initial "B" stood for, but was not about to ask him about it so early on in their acquaintanceship. He would learn later nobody at Piedmont, including John, knew what it stood for. And Professor Brassner had never given even the slightest of hints to anyone about its meaning—not even to those who offered him riches if he were to divulge his secret. A few months down the road, on the day Jimmy fought his first battle against the VARS, he would find out what the "B" stood for.

"And how has young Mirah been treating you, gentlemen?" the director asked, looking proudly at the girl. "Well, I hope?"

"She's been wonderful," John replied. "We're very grateful for her help."

Mirah beamed.

I wonder how long she'll keep this up, Jimmy thought, suspecting Mirah would revert to her old ways as soon as John and the professor were out of sight.

"I'm going to ask Evelyn if she can take your picture now and make you a camp ID," the professor said, turning to

233

his secretary. She nodded her head affirmatively, letting him know she heard him. "She will let you know what dormitory room we have assigned to you, and Mirah will show you where it is."

While Jimmy had his picture taken and Evelyn made his ID card, John and Professor Brassner, sitting on one of the couches in the back of the office, had a quiet conversation, the topic of which Jimmy could not discern. When he approached them, wanting to show John his new ID, they stopped talking and stood up.

"You and I will see a lot of each other while you're here at Piedmont," the professor told Jimmy. "I'm sure you're going to love our camp. I can tell you that, besides polo and show jumping, we will have a cross-country treasure hunt—on horseback, no less—which should be loads of fun."

Jimmy just knew that was going to be the case. Before they left the office, the professor told John the school's director also wanted to see them after Jimmy had registered, so she could welcome him to Piedmont.

"You seem to know the professor rather well," Jimmy mentioned to John as the three of them walked down the staircase to the school director's office.

"Yes, I have known him for a long time—ever since I met him over ten years ago at a conference on dolphins."

John told Jimmy both his father and he had had deep concerns about the slaughter of dolphins all over the world and the distinct possibility that many of the thirty-six species of dolphins could soon become extinct due to ocean pollution and harmful fishing practices. Wanting to learn more about protecting the only known wild animals to come to the rescue of human beings, he had attended a conference where the professor made a presentation on how to stop the slaughter of these marine mammals and alleviate many of the practices fostering their extinction. Impressed by what the professor had to say, John invited him to come to Middleburg and make a similar presentation to the students at Piedmont.

"Did he accept your invitation?" Jimmy asked.

"Yes, he did," John replied. "And our kids liked him so much, they asked him to help them start up a Save-the-Dolphins Club, right here on our campus."

"And did he do that?"

"Yes—and much more. He not only started up our Club, which helps educate people all over the world about the need to protect the dolphins, but he also organized our marine-science program, which educates our students about the need to protect our oceans and all of its creatures, including the dolphins."

"That was awful nice of the professor. Then what happened?"

"We hired him to teach our marine-science classes and oversee our summer-camp program."

"I belong to the Save-the-Dolphins Club," Mirah let it be known.

"Can I join, too?" Jimmy asked.

"Of course," John said, "as soon as the new school year starts."

"So, you will be coming to school here in the fall?" Mirah inquired.

"Yes, I will," Jimmy responded proudly.

Just as they were about to enter the office of the director, she walked out to run a small errand down the hall. To Jimmy, she looked every bit a private-school headmistress—stern-looking, neatly-dressed, very little make-up, with her long hair folded in a halo, kept in place by a hairnet. Her long-sleeve black dress, with lace around the collar and padded shoulders, almost touched her ankles, barely showing her black, shiny, low-heeled shoes.

Seeing John, she started to give him a big hug, but then thought better of it in front of her students.

"Good to see you again, John," she said in a proper tone, holding out her hand for him to shake.

"Good to see you too, director," John said, gently shaking her hand.

"Hello, Jimmy," she said, also shaking his hand and looking at him in the same caring way the professor had looked at him. "I'm so happy to meet you and glad you're here!"

"I'm also glad to be here," he responded.

"And how are you, my dear?" she said, turning to Mirah.

"I'm fine, ma'am," Mirah said timidly.

"Why don't you take them inside and ask my assistant to seat you in my private office while I run my errand," she suggested, and quickly hurried off.

After the young assistant had seated them comfortably in the director's large office—stylishly decorated with a thick carpet, an antique mahogany desk, leather sofa and chairs—Jimmy glanced at the framed pictures hanging on the walls. He saw several pictures of steeplechase races and show-jumping competitions in the Middleburg area, and famous personalities, like the Kennedys, riding their horses in local horse shows and parades.

"Hey, Uncle John, *look at those!*" Jimmy let out, all of a sudden.

He got out of his chair to look more closely at a group of black and white pictures hanging next to a large oil painting portraying the serene countryside around Piedmont.

236

"Those are pictures of Dad, and he's riding Spirit."

Just as he said that, the director walked in.

Having overheard his remark, she told him, "Yes, that's your father competing in the Olympics and riding in the Upperville Horse Show and Tournament, just a few miles down the road from here—he was such a great champion."

Now, Jimmy beamed.

The director didn't take much of their time. From her previous conversations with John, she already knew much about Jimmy's interests, and his likes and dislikes. So, she just made some small talk, wanting to make him feel at home at Piedmont. She knew, while the Prophecy played itself out, the days ahead would be challenging for him, and she wanted him to feel comfortable enough to come to her for advice, if he needed it.

"Make sure you let me know if there is anything I can do for you," she whispered to him, as they were leaving.

"Let's put your luggage in the golf carts," Mirah suggested when they got back to the parking lot.

Five minutes later, they were on their way to Jimmy's dormitory. Mirah led the way, driving a cart with Jimmy's big bag loaded in the luggage bin in back of the cart, and one of his two smaller bags sitting on the seat next to her. A highly excited Jimmy, his face glowing, drove the second cart, with John sitting next to him and his other small bag stowed in the bin behind them. As Jimmy saw earlier, when he looked down on the school from the top of Fox Chase Lane, most of Piedmont's buildings, including the four boys' and girls' dormitories, were clustered inside the brick mini ring road circling the center area of the campus. From the parking lot, they made a left turn and headed west on the ring road. A short while later, Jimmy noticed hundreds of large

237

wind turbines sitting on top of a long mountain ridge, far out in the distance straight ahead of them, their blades turning at full speed.

"What are those for?" he asked John, pointing at the turbines.

"Those windmills belong to the school's wind farm," John replied.

"The school has its own wind farm? Why?"

"Because it uses a lot of electricity for lighting, cooking, air conditioning, and many other things, such as charging the batteries on the cart we're driving."

"So, why does it produce its own electricity? Isn't it cheaper to just buy it from the electric company, like we do back home?"

"Not really; making electricity using wind power costs about the same as buying it from the electric company. And as you already know, wind power does not pollute the environment. Your dad and I wanted to show the world that schools like ours can produce their own electricity cheaply, and we also wanted our school to be a showcase of what we can do to make life on Planet Earth as environment-friendly as possible."

"That's also why you drive a fuel cell car, right?"

"That's right; my car doesn't pollute the environment either. And, if you look to the right of those windmills, you can see the solar power tower that is part of our solar farm. It also produces electricity for our school without polluting the environment."

When Jimmy looked to where John pointed, he could see a large tower sticking up in the air like a tall pillar. John explained that, from their viewing position, it was not possible to see the five hundred sun-tracking mirrors— arranged on the ground in concentric circles around the fifty meter high tower—that focused sunlight on a receiver at the tower's top.

"The heat from the sunlight in the receiver is used to make steam," John said, "and the steam is used to make electricity."

After he thought for a while, Jimmy said, "I'm glad you and Dad built the wind and solar farms, because it's important to protect the environment we live in—and protecting the oceans and the dolphins is very important, too."

Now it was John's turn to beam, elated over his smart, young cousin, who already understood the importance of protecting Earth's environment at his very young age.

Before long, Mirah made a sharp right turn into the parking lot of Jimmy's dormitory building. As he made his turn into the lot, Jimmy did a double take when he recognized the two men dressed in overalls, tending to the dormitory's garden patches—the two cowboys.

"Look there, Uncle John," he said, pointing at the men and stepping on the brakes.

He got out and walked towards the men, wondering what they were doing close to the place where he would be staying. The chubby one, glad to see Jimmy, started to run towards him; but in his haste, he tripped over the rake he was using to spread some dirt around. He ended up diving headfirst into a pile of manure, dumped at the end of the parking lot. When he got back on his feet with the tall man's help, he started to chirp again; and with a sheepish grin, he pulled the manure from around his ears and wiped it from his face and the top of his head.

"What are you guys doing here?" Jimmy said, laughing at the antics of the chubby man. "You smell terrible," he told him.

"We got asylum," the tall man said solemnly.

"How did you manage that?"

"We told 'em everything," the chubby one said jubilantly. *"Everything we knew."*

"We told the director and your uncle everything we know about what the VARS are doing, where they are doing it, and when they are going to do it," the tall man explained.

"Then they gave us asylum, and we had to promise we would never work for any bad guys again," the chubby one added.

"That's great," Jimmy said. "So, why are you working in this yard?"

"We're under the cover," the chubby one whispered, secretively.

"He means we're working *undercover*," the tall man corrected him. "It looks like we're doing yard work, but in reality we're keeping an eye on your dormitory—so you'll be safe when you're in there."

"That's good…to know," Jimmy said, starting to feel rather uncomfortable about their undercover business around his dormitory. "Seeing you're looking after me, I probably should know your names…don't you think?"

"He's Sam and I'm Happy," the chubby one said, shyly.

"I'm happy, too," Jimmy said. "So, what's your name?"

"My name is *Happy*."

"Ohhh…that's nice. Happy to meet you Happy…and Sam," Jimmy said, grinning with difficulty, as he shook their hands.

"Hey, Jimmy, Mirah is waiting for you," John shouted from the cart.

Jimmy saw Mirah had unloaded his bags in front of the dormitory entrance and was patiently waiting for him and John to come and carry them in.

"I've got to go now," he told the men, "but I'll see you again. Bye."

Jimmy ran back to the cart, and he drove John and himself to where Mirah was standing.

When he got there and grabbed his bag from the back of his cart, Mirah said curiously, "You seem to know our gardeners." Then, laughingly, "And what did you say to make one of them jump into that pile of manure?"

"I told him there was treasure in it," Jimmy said, jokingly. Not wanting to take the time to explain to her how and where he met Sam and Happy, he added, "And some day, I will tell you all about 'em."

"I can't wait for you to do that," Mirah said, also jokingly. Sensing his reluctance to come clean with her about the two men, she changed the topic. "I'm sorry I can't help you take your bags to your room; girls are not allowed in the boys' dorms."

"No need to worry," John said. "You have done enough to help us."

"I'll come back in an hour and meet you right here," she told Jimmy as she got into her cart. "Then, I will show you the rest of the campus, okay?"

"Okay," Jimmy said.

She gave them a short wave and drove off.

As soon as he walked into his dormitory carrying his two small bags, Jimmy felt the same sensation flash through his body as when he first entered the school's admin building. He stopped to look at his uncle to see if John had experienced anything similar. As John passed him by, toting his big bag, Jimmy gave him the once-over, but John gave no indication of being infused with an analogous burst of energy. Jimmy quickly walked after him.

Because the room Evelyn assigned him was on the first floor, close to the dorm entrance, they didn't have to carry Jimmy's bags very far. After they dropped anchor in the room, John helped him unpack his bags. Like all the others in the dorm, his room contained turnkey furniture for two people: two bunk beds with night stands, two dressers, two small desks with drawers and chairs, a sofa, and a wall mirror. It also had a private bath and a small kitchen with a compact refrigerator, electric stove, and microwave in it. The large floor to ceiling windows had translucent glass that afforded privacy during the day, while letting the sunlight pass through. At night, long curtains could be pulled shut, isolating the room from outside view.

At John's request, Evelyn had assigned Jimmy and David the same room. Upon hearing this, the boys had agreed to give the room their own personal touches. To make the dorm room feel a little like home, Jimmy had brought his family pictures and his violin; he wondered what David would bring to—as his friend called it—jazz up his side of the room.

While Jimmy neatly arranged the framed pictures of his parents, family, and Sparkles on his night stand, and stored his books in the desk drawers, John hung some of Jimmy's clothes in the walk-in closet, and put others, nicely folded, in his dresser. When they finished putting Jimmy's belongings away, John looked around for something else he could do for him, but there was nothing else to be had. He really wanted to spend more time with him, seeing this was the first time Jimmy would be away from home for an extended period of time. He had intended to give him a tour of the campus; but that was not an option anymore, since Mirah planned to do that in about half an hour. John was about to say goodbye and let Jimmy know he would drop by the school occasionally to make sure he was doing alright, when Jimmy caught him by surprise with a question that had been on his mind since he talked with Sam and Happy.

"Why are Sam and Happy working around my dormitory?"

After he thought for a moment, John said, "We told 'em they could do yard work for us. I'm not sure who asked 'em to work around your dorm. Why do you ask?"

"They said they're keeping an eye on my dorm to keep me safe, but I don't really trust them."

"I know what you mean. For you information, they've been very forthcoming with us and given us a lot of valuable information."

"But it gives me the creeps to think they'll be watching me all the time, especially at night. Are you sure I'm going to be safe here with those two around?"

"Don't worry. Piedmont is the safest place in the world for you. We're keeping them under constant surveillance."

"Do you think the VARS might try to come here and grab me?"

"They may try, but with the number of people we have looking after you, and the shield activated twenty-four hours a day, they will not be able to get anywhere near you."

"What shield?"

"The energy shield."

John explained that, instead of building a large fence around the school to protect it from unwanted intruders, the Atlanteans surrounded the campus with an energy shield.

"The shield," he said, "keeps people not only from wandering onto the school's grounds, but also protects it from ground assaults and aerial attacks by planes, missiles, or spaceships."

"Can people see the shield?" Jimmy asked.

"No, they cannot."

"So, if they can't see it, how do they know it's there?"

John told him the Atlanteans had posted many signs in the areas bordering the shield, letting people know they were trespassing on private property and should not proceed any further.

"If they ignore the signs," he said, "anyone getting anywhere close to the shield will instantly experience dizziness and disorientation. This is normally enough of an incentive to turn back and leave the premises."

John also explained that, for those still not willing to withdraw and refrain from entering school grounds, the shield will dispense remotely a series of electric shocks—similar to the small jolts delivered by an electric fence—causing further discomfort. For any remaining diehards who continued to approach the shield, dead-set on entering school grounds in spite of these deterrents, the shield will induce total immobility before they made contact with it. They are then subject to arrest by the school's security force, and arraignment by local authorities.

"Rest assured, nobody can get in, unless they are let in by the guards through the same entrance you came through," John said. "And they won't let anybody in, unless we tell them to."

"That's good to know," Jimmy said, feeling relieved by what John had to say about the energy shield, but still worried to have Sam and Happy prowling around in his neighborhood.

Hoping Jimmy's concern about his safety at the school was alleviated, John suggested it was time for him to hit the

244

road and pay a brief visit to Eloise, prior to going home. As John walked over to give Jimmy a goodbye hug, he decided to ask his uncle one last question.

"Did you feel different when we first walked into my dorm?" he asked, with an inquisitive look on his face. "And also, right after we first entered the admin building?"

John looked at him thoughtfully. "You mean like feeling more energized and invigorated?"

"Yes, like that," Jimmy said, expecting to get some confirmation of his experience.

"And feeling really good about the place you just walked into?"

"Yes, yes—that exactly how I felt," Jimmy said excitedly.

"No, I didn't feel anything like that at all," John said, trying not to laugh.

When he saw Jimmy's face registering some disappointment, John quickly said, "Just kidding." Then, he added, "To be honest with you, I always feel really good as soon as I walk into any one of our campus' buildings."

Hearing those words, Jimmy's face perked up a little.

"Are you sure? You're not kidding me again, are you?" he asked, skeptic about his uncle's sincerity.

"That's the honest to goodness truth," John responded. "These buildings will give anyone a lift in spirits."

"How come?" Jimmy asked.

"Because—" John paused. "I want you to promise me, you will not tell anyone what I'm about to tell you."

"Not even David?"

"That's right, not even David."

Since he had never kept a secret from David before, Jimmy had to stop and think about this. He quickly realized, however, if his uncle asked him to keep a secret, he would have a very good reason for doing so.

"Yes, I promise not to tell," Jimmy said.

"These buildings increase your energy levels because—they're alive and full of oxygen."

"What! The campus' buildings are alive?"

"Yes, almost all of them."

"Not nice to kid me again, Uncle John."

"I'm not."

"You're not?"

"That's right. They're alive."

"Come on, Uncle John. Tell me the truth."

"I am telling you the truth!"

When Jimmy realized his uncle was serious, he didn't know what to think.

"They're alive? But how can that be?"

"Your dad designed 'em that way. And when we built 'em, we followed his designs."

Jimmy was dumbfounded. "That's so hard to believe," he said.

"Push against the wall, then," John suggested.

When Jimmy carefully put his whole hand against the wall, it felt soft; and when he pushed against it, the wall felt strong and seemed to be pushing back.

"How did you and Dad know how to build this?" he asked, quickly pulling his hand back.

"We Atlanteans have known how to do this for centuries."

John told him the Atlanteans had the technology to make plants grow quickly into any desired shape and height by manipulating their DNA and changing their genetic blueprints. He explained that plants receive genetic instructions from their seeds on how to grow, for example,

246

corn stalks, tree trunks, and leaves; but they can also be given genetic instructions on how to grow a building's foundation, and make the construction materials needed to build the rest of the building.

"Genetically-engineered foundations and materials," John said, "grow quickly and are a thousand times stronger and more flexible than traditional foundations and building materials. Like other living things, buildings that are alive are full of energy and, because they are large plants, they can also produce lots of oxygen—in much larger quantities than smaller plants."

"So, you are telling me," Jimmy said, "that when you walk into a living building full of positive energy and oxygen, it will increase your own energy level and make you feel really good."

"That's right," John said. "And I should also tell you that some people are much more sensitive than others when it comes to feeling and absorbing the positive energy in our buildings. I think you are one of those very sensitive people."

Jimmy took a deep breath and briefly reflected on the sequence of events catching him by surprise that day: Mirah showing up out of nowhere; getting a breathtaking view of the Piedmont campus; his father's pictures hanging on the wall in the director's office; driving a golf cart; Sam and Happy making an unexpected appearance; and now, hearing about living buildings. He felt a little dizzy and wondered what else might be in store for him at Piedmont.

"Why can't we let the rest of the world know about these buildings?" Jimmy wanted to know.

"We will, in due time," John replied. "But for now, the people on Earth are not yet ready to hear about living buildings, and if they did, they might not believe us and try to shut the school down."

"Are there going to be any other big surprises for me here?" Jimmy asked, feeling overwhelmed by it all.

"Yes, there will be a few more zingers coming down the pike," John said, with a wink. "But don't worry. I know you and David are going to have a great time this summer."

When Jimmy followed John out of the dormitory, Mirah was already waiting outside in her electric cart to take him on his tour of the campus. Having said goodbye to his uncle and promised to make timely phone calls to his grandma, Jimmy popped into the passenger side. Mirah told him to hold on tight as she sped out of the dorm's parking lot.

The first place Mirah drove by was her dormitory, located across the parking lot from his own. After she pointed to the two windows of her room on the second floor, she drove out of the lot and turned right onto the ring road. She followed it around the bend, affording him another clear view of the Blue Ridge Mountains and the Piedmont wind farm, and continued east on the ring road to the area in the center of the campus. There, she parked the cart so Jimmy could get a firsthand look at some of Piedmont's unique buildings.

Several of the buildings were located along the edge of the ring road itself; others were situated along the smaller brick roads curving through the center area. Most of them were surrounded by tall pine trees and mulched garden patches full of flowering plants and small evergreens. All buildings had small ponds close by and plenty of parking for the campus' two main modes of transportation—electric carts and bicycles.

The first building they visited was the art center. As he saw it up close, Jimmy couldn't imagine having ever seen such stunning architecture and was immensely proud of his dad for having designed it. What earlier in the day had looked like a tall plant stem, when he had first seen it from the vantage point of Fox Chase Lane, turned out to be a long, greenish center tower, with the shape of a lighthouse. Its elevators and stairs provided access to ten large, multicolored, enclosed platforms, attached along its sides at different heights. The platforms, shaped like lily pads, made up the building's ten floors. Three of them housed the school's two theatres and large auditorium; the others contained the art department's classrooms and studios.

"Let's ride up in the elevator to the first floor," Mirah suggested, "and I'll show you some of the classrooms."

"Yes, let's do that," Jimmy said.

As soon as they walked into an empty classroom, he could feel the positive energy in the building permeating his body, adding to the mind-set of bliss he derived from seeing his father's legacy. He pushed on the wall and quickly withdrew his hand when it pushed back. *Plants*, he thought, trying to act casually.

"What's the matter?" Mirah queried. "Why are you pushing on the wall?"

"Nothing," Jimmy responded. "I just wanted to see if the walls here were as soft as those in the dorm."

"Yes, most of the walls of the buildings on campus are soft," Mirah said. "I'm not sure why."

"I don't know either," Jimmy said, still not fully convinced he was actually standing inside another living building.

After they looked into a few of the other classrooms, all of them empty, they decided to mosey up to the second floor.

"Art camps," Mirah said as they stepped out of the elevator. "All of these studios have artisan activity going on inside."

"Can we look?" Jimmy asked.

"Sure, but we have to be very quiet." She opened the door of the studio nearest to the elevator far enough for Jimmy to see inside. "This is a jewelry camp," she whispered, pointing to a dozen or so students sitting in front of laptop computers, looking at holograms of jewelry, rotating in the air in front of them.

"What are they doing?" Jimmy asked, also whispering.

"They're using computer-assisted design programs to build different styles of jewelry and displaying them as holograms to see what they have created. After completing the designs, they will use 3D printers to make the jewelry, including its precious stones."

"Wow, David is so not going to believe me when I tell him about all of this."

"Who is David?"

"He's my best friend. He's coming here this afternoon."

"Oh, that David." Mirah seemed to know about him coming to Piedmont.

Without further comment, she continued the tour. After she slowly opened the next studio's door, she motioned for Jimmy to peek inside. "This is pottery camp," she whispered.

In the back of the studio, Jimmy noticed several kids focusing their attention on what was being molded from a lump of clay on the instructor's pottery wheel. Overhead, a variety of pottery designs, for use later during the class, also floated around as holograms.

"Will they use the same 3D printers to make their pottery?" Jimmy whispered.

"No, but many of the other art camps use them."

After they went up a few floors, Mirah showed him one of the theaters hosting drama camps. Then, they stopped by the large auditorium on the art center's top floor, before riding the elevator back down and walking around the block to the school's science building.

With colored lights streaking through the opaque plant material that made up its outer walls, the science building reminded Jimmy of a kaleidoscope version of the Seattle

251

Space Needle. He had seen it in the movies, and on TV. Like the Space Needle, the science building's top disk was shaped like a flying saucer and contained an observation deck, but not at its top level. It was not only one of Piedmont's most colorful buildings but, at one hundred fifty meters high, also its second tallest building—only the admin building reached higher in the sky.

"Why all the colored lights?" he asked as they rode the elevator up to the building's first level, in the middle disk, to look at the school's science library.

"I'm not really sure," she replied, "but when I come here, seeing all those beautiful colors continuously fading into one another really makes me feel like wanting to study science. And all the different symmetrical patterns and shapes changing constantly into other intricate patterns and shapes make me want to learn more about what allows all of this to happen."

"Yeah, I know what you mean," Jimmy said. "I feel the same way right now."

After briefly visiting the library, they took the elevator to the top disk's lower level, which made up the building's second floor and contained the schools science laboratories.

"We have two science camps here this summer," Mirah said when they exited the elevator. "Over there is Quantum Camp." She nodded to a lab where several kids huddled around a giant microscope. Every now and then, they gazed upwards at a hologram showing a projection of the very tiny objects magnified by the large scope. "I attended this camp last summer. We looked at nanoparticles, using an electron microscope."

"I have *never* seen such a big microscope as that one in my whole life," Jimmy let out. "Is that also an electron microscope?"

"Yes, it is," Mirah said. "It magnifies twenty million times, and you can watch little particles move around, one atom at a time."

"Wow, I wish David could see this."

"Don't worry. He'll get the same tour as you, from his CIT. But this is nothing compared to the next camp."

She led him to another lab, filled to the brim with campers, all sitting cross-legged on the ground around a circular platform, above which a hologram containing a projection of a bearded Swami-like wise man floated. He was dressed in a flowing, white robe, sandals, and a turban; and he communicated with the campers in broken English.

"What sort of a camp is this?" Jimmy whispered.

"This one studies the science and spirituality behind the power of the mind, psychic abilities, and distance healing and viewing," Mirah replied, in a soft voice. "During one part of the camp, by means of satellite communication and hologram projections, mystics and shamans from all over the world demonstrate for the students the ability to make the mind control matter; they do all this from their own sacred grounds and temples in their own countries."

As she said that, the man in the hologram took off his sandals. After briefly meditating, he lifted up his robe above his knees and stepped barefooted, without hesitation, into a bed of burning coal. The whole room fell totally quiet, everyone holding their breath. The mystic remained stationary for a while, with his eyes closed, before stepping out of the bed and showing everyone the bottoms of his feet; they had no burns or any other marks on them. The room exploded with applause, and loud expressions of wonder and disbelief filled the air. They could hardly believe their very own eyes.

"Wow, did you see that?" Jimmy uttered out loud. "How did he do that?"

"Mind control," Mirah whispered. "He showed them the mind is able to control what we feel or don't feel, and how we physically experience things. Other mystics and shamans will show them later how the mind can be used to cure sick people from a distance, and how it can also be used to see things mentally as they happen many miles away, all without the use of electronic or other equipment."

Having overheard part their verbal exchange, an older gentleman, sitting on the ground in back of the kids close to the doorway, got up and slowly walked over to them. He had long hair and a beard and looked like a mystic himself. Seeing Jimmy, he apparently recognized him from somewhere and, with a kind expression on his face, whispered, "Please, come and sit down, Mr. Starlight. We've been waiting for you to come to Piedmont. And you, too, Mirah, please, come in."

"This is Professor Martindale," Mirah whispered in Jimmy's ear. "He's one of our science teachers, and in charge of this camp."

"Please, sit down behind the other kids, and let's hear what else our guest from India has to say," the professor said.

Really surprised the professor knew his name, Jimmy wanted to ask him about it. He thought better of it when he heard the mystic say, again in broken English, with a slight British accent, "We will now see if any of you have psychic abilities. I want each of you to close your eyes, and not say or do anything except focus your thoughts on me, and send me a mental message introducing yourself by name, and letting me know how old you are and what you look like. In turn, I will focus on receiving your messages and let you know what I have learned. So, please, start now."

With that, the whole room got totally quiet again. While everyone focused intensely on sending him their messages, the mystic, with his eyes also closed and sitting cross-legged on the floor, applied his telepathic power remotely to the group of kids trying to connect mentally with him. He soon started to utter some words.

"Nothing…nothing…nothing…yes, here it comes. One of you is called Mirah…a girl…thirteen years old and wearing jeans and little earrings."

As soon as he said that, Mirah waved her hands in the air, saying. "That's me—that's me." Elbowing Jimmy in his side, she said elatedly, "Can you believe it, I'm psychic!"

When they heard what she said, the kids in the room let out a collective, "Ooooh."

It soon got really quiet again, when the mystic continued his uttering, with his eyes still closed, "Yes, here comes another one—a very powerful one—and very clear—Jimmy Starlight, twelve years old, with khaki shorts on."

Then, Jimmy was hit by a real zinger when the man said falteringly, "And there is more…. But wait, this did not come from him….Actually, I'm not sure where it came from….It just appeared in my mind." He raised his hands above his head, and looking straight up said, "The boy will bring peace and love all over the world and travel far into the universe." After he said those words, he lowered his hands and sat very still for a while, with his eyes closed again. Then, he said, very quietly, "There are no more messages. Thank you, goodbye until next time."

As the hologram of the mystic faded away, Jimmy didn't know what to think about his message and sat pensively, not saying anything.

"Well, folks, that's it for today," Professor Martindale announced. "We'll see you all tomorrow, at the same time."

Everyone got up slowly, conversing with one another about the astonishing events that unfolded in the camp and speculating who Jimmy Starlight was. For all of them, learning his identity would have to wait until a later day.

When Jimmy stood up, the professor came up to him and gave him a pat on the back. He then told him, "You're welcome to drop by my camp anytime."

"Thank you very much, sir," Jimmy said, "I would love to do that."

After they had left the laboratory, he said to Mirah, "Thanks for bringing me here. I really hope I can participate in these science camps again someday."

"You will," she said, motioning him to follow her to the elevator.

"Where are we going next?"

"To the observation deck. You'll love the view from there."

While they rode the elevator up, Jimmy realized she had not expressed any curiosity about the mystic's prediction that he would bring peace and love to Earth and travel far into the universe. He was curious why she had had no reaction whatsoever about it. *If I were in her shoes*, he thought, *I would have most certainly said something by now—she must have had a good reason for not having done so. Could it be she has heard it before?* He wondered from whom.

The enclosed deck was two floors up, just above the floor containing the science class rooms. Its glass windows allowed a 360 degree view of the entire campus. The view exhilarated Jimmy yet again. From where he stood he could look down upon the four identically-shaped liberal-arts buildings, located down the road from the science building.

256

"Look at those beautiful clovers," Jimmy said, admiring the buildings whose spring-green color reinforced the artistic quality of their four-leaf-clover design. "And over there, look at *that* beautiful blue building!"

The building he referred to sat outside the ring road, due north of the science building. He had noticed it earlier in the day when he first saw the campus. It was shaped like a huge tripod, with three thick legs supporting the building's three painter-pallet platforms. Above the top platform, at the building's apex, sat a large silver dome.

"That's our observatory," Mirah explained. "That's where our astronomy camp is held. Inside that dome sits a very powerful telescope. We'll drive by it later on, so you can get a closer look at it. But first, let's get something to snack on at our coffee shop; and then, on our way to the observatory, we can stop by our gym, which is my favorite place on campus."

Pointing to a large complex in back of the liberal arts buildings, she said, "That's our Student Activities Center; the coffee shop is in the bookstore right next to it." Then, she nodded to the large brick building sitting outside the ring road at the eastern edge of the school grounds. "That building with the huge glass atrium in front is our gym." The final building she brought to his attention was the huge dome-like structure far out at the campus' north end. "You are going to spend a lot of your time over the next three months in that building over there; that's our equestrian center, where your horseback riding camp will start in a couple of days."

"I can't wait to see it," Jimmy said. "Let's get going!"

Having decided to forego a visit to the liberal arts buildings, Mirah took Jimmy to the elevator, intending to ride back down to the ground floor and go straight to the

Activities Center. As they entered the elevator, Jimmy noticed an up-button.

"What's above this observation deck?" he asked.

"I don't know. That's another area where students are not allowed to go."

"If we push this up button will the elevator take us there?"

"No, that won't work. If you press it, which I've done before, the elevator won't go anywhere."

To demonstrate the validity of what she told him, Mirah pushed the button; nothing happened, the elevator didn't move.

"The next time I see him, I'll ask Uncle John about it," Jimmy said, playfully touching the same button.

The elevator responded immediately and started moving...upward!

This time, Mirah was caught by surprise. "What did you do to make it go up?"

"Nothing, I touched that button by accident." Jimmy stared at his hands— what had happened in the Air and Space Museum, when he unlocked the vault door, flashed before his eyes. *The elevator moved because I'm Atlantean.* He was sure of it.

When the door opened, Mirah hesitated to exit because it was pitch-black on the floor. "Let's go back down," she said, reaching for the elevator's ground-level button. "We shouldn't be here."

"Wait," Jimmy said. "There has to be something secretive here, otherwise they wouldn't have restricted it. Let's look."

Before she could say anything else, he stepped onto the floor, intending to look for a light switch—that's when another zinger came down the pike.

They both gasped when, all of a sudden, the lights came on: red ones, green ones, purple ones, yellow ones, and white lights—all flashing throughout the place. Sunlight penetrated through the small circular skylights in the ceiling and the porthole-shaped windows along the wall. Previously, something had prevented it from streaming in; what that was, was not immediately clear to either one of them. It was clear, however, this was not your average high-school science laboratory or classroom.

"My goodness…what kind of a place is this?" was all Jimmy could say.

"I told you—we should not have come here," Mirah said sternly.

The circular floor was filled with dozens of computer consoles, display screens, and other freestanding super computers. Except for the small windows, every inch along the walls was taken up by pieces of equipment, which were loaded with monitors, gauges, digital displays, indicator lights, switches, and various controls. Shortly after the lights came on, a soft humming sound enveloped the area as all of the computers and other equipment powered on. Monitors lit up and displayed their startup screens, while indicator lights blinked and came to rest in a variety of colors. All the gauges and digital displays responded to the signals of the equipment's self-tests to show their status. A few feet from the wall, directly across from the elevator door, a giant freestanding screen came to life, presenting live views, in four quadrants, of the outside areas around the science tower, including the skies above it and the area directly below the top disk.

Jimmy walked across the floor to take a closer look at the high-back swivel chair, secured on a podium about twenty feet in front of the giant screen, and another high-back chair, surrounded partially by a huge console, sitting to the side of the podium. He closely examined the console's monitor, depicting the same views as the giant screen, and the array of gauges, digital displays, knobs, and dials on the instrument panel built into the console—it struck him as some sort of electronic navigation system.

"Mirah, this could be the bridge of a spaceship," he said. "It kind of looks like the ones I have seen in my videos about space travel."

"We must go," she said, not having ventured far onto the floor. "I have been told this area is off limits to all students, and I don't want us to get into trouble; it could cost me my job."

Too absorbed by what he saw, Jimmy didn't hear her and continued looking around the place. "This here could be the commander's seat," he said, standing next to the high-back swivel chair in front of the giant screen. He touched the chair next to it. "And this could be the pilot's seat; it has a flight screen and a navigational console in front of it."

"Console or no console, we have to leave." Mirah walked over, grabbed Jimmy by the hand, and led him to the elevator.

"But Mirah, we need to check this out," he protested. "This could be a flying saucer." She ignored him.

As they rode the elevator back down, all Jimmy could think about was what he had seen on the top floor. *I will have to ask Uncle John about this, for sure,* he thought. *If it is a real flying saucer, why would the Atlanteans hide it in a school?*

After they got into their electric cart, they drove further east along the ring road until they arrived at the busy parking lot of the Student Activities Center. They were fortunate enough to secure a parking spot quickly. The single-level Activities Center had a large concrete square directly in front of it. Like all other buildings on the Piedmont campus, it had a beautiful design, with bright colors popping up everywhere, and ponds with small fountains in the middle, bubbling soothing and enhancing sounds into its environs.

"This is where the kids at Piedmont spent most of their free time," Mirah said, nodding towards the large, colorful building before them that had two smaller pinkish circular structures sitting alongside of it. "What do you think?"

"I think it's beautiful, like all the other buildings here," Jimmy replied as he got out of the cart. "And will you look at that roof. I've never seen one quite like it."

He referred to the huge deep-purple catenary-shaped suspension roof. It ascended fifty feet at the front, dipped lower in the middle, and rose upward again in the back, but not as high. A row of ten outward-sloping columns, set about thirty feet apart, supported it in the front; a similar support structure, not visible from where Jimmy stood, held up the rear. As soon as they started to walk across the square in front of the Center, Jimmy noticed that, besides making up its front wall, the fifty-foot panels in between the front columns also served as large outdoors LED screens.

"Look, they're showing movies over there," he said, pointing at the screens.

"Actually, the three screens in the middle are showing nature videos," she said. "The others display still images of scenic areas across the country."

When they came closer to the building, Jimmy saw, on the middle screen, dolphins and other sea creatures swimming in the ocean. On the screen to the right of it, wildlife foraged around in what looked like virgin rainforest;

and on the third center screen, caribous trekked across the arctic tundra. All the way on the left, a still image of the Everglades spanned across three screens, and a picture of the Alaskan wilderness covered the three screens on the far right. Underneath both pictures, it said in large script: *These unspoiled vistas may not be around for your children to enjoy if the degradation of our environment continues at its present pace.*

"These pictures are so peaceful," Jimmy said solemnly, "and so are the videos."

"If you like *these* videos," Mirah said, "just wait till this evening; you'll see the weekend's summer concert on all nine screens together."

"A summer concert? We can go to a concert this evening?"

"Yes, if you like. During the summer, they show concerts every Friday evening, after dinner is served in the school cafeteria. The cafeteria is located in that pink round building, over there on the right."

"Dinner and concerts…do we have to pay for 'em?"

"No, everything is *on the house.*"

"Wow, free dinners and concerts—wait 'til David…"

Before Jimmy could complete his sentence, Mirah interrupted. *"Yeah, yeah, I know,"* she said abruptly, "w*ait—until—David—hears—about—this.*"

"Sorry," Jimmy said, grimacing slightly. "He's a really good friend, and sometimes I can't wait to tell him about exciting things."

"Yeah, I understand," she said, her voice gloomy. "Sometimes, I wish I had a friend like that."

"I'm sure you will someday; and if you like, I'll be your friend, too."

"We'll see," Mirah said, still sounding down. "In the meantime, let's go to the coffee shop and get some of their free pastry and cookies to cheer me up. It's in the bookstore in the other pink building, over there on the left."

"Great, I could use a little something right now," Jimmy said. Not seeing an outside entrance to the bookstore, he asked, "So, how do we get there?"

"Through here," Mirah replied, as she opened one of the double doors to the Activities Center and entered the building. "The entrances to both the bookstore and our cafeteria are inside."

"Wow, this place is huge," Jimmy said, having followed her in, trying to sound upbeat. "What all do we have here?"

"Lots of different things," Mirah responded, sounding rather terse. "Enough to keep even someone of your standing occupied most of the time."

"And why is that?" Jimmy asked, thinking, *The real Mirah is finally coming out.*

"Because there are quite a few places in here that I'm sure you'll like," she responded.

"Please, tell me about 'em."

"Well, over there in the middle is our international food court, with a dozen or so healthy eating places. And to the right of it is our convenience store. Over on the left, there are some small clothing stores, and even a little sports store with tennis stuff and running shoes." Pointing to the far end of the Center, she said, "And way down there is our *free* movie theater, and next to it is our *free* bowling alley."

"My goodness, you're not kidding! Who wouldn't like this place? There are so many free things to do here." He tried to sound even more upbeat. "And everyone in here seems to be having a terrific time," he said, watching the

263

other students laughing and kidding around while they went about their business—mostly eating or just strolling around.

"Yes, there's enough here to keep all of us entertained," Mirah said. "Come with me."

She took Jimmy by the hand again and led him to the coffee shop. Having spotted an empty table, she asked him to sit there and wait for her while she got something for them to snack on. Before long, Mirah returned with a small plate of free pastries and cookies, and two juice drinks purchased with her own money, and sat down next to him.

"How long have you been at Piedmont?" Jimmy asked as he enjoyed his free treats.

"This is my second year," Mirah replied.

"Do you like it?"

"Yes, I love it here."

"I remember you told me you came here all the way from Egypt. Don't you miss your parents and your family, and Egypt, too?"

"Yes, I miss my country. But both of my parents are dead, and I have no family except for my brother; and he is too busy with his work to worry much about me."

Jimmy couldn't help but notice the bitter tone in her voice when she said that.

"Oh, sorry to hear about your parents; I lost mine too."

"I know," Mirah said coldly, with her face showing anger. "They were killed for no reason, just like mine."

Startled by this comment, Jimmy was about to ask her what she meant by that, when without notice, she stood up and headed for the bookstore's exit. Caught off guard by her sudden departure, he stuffed the remainder of his pastry in his mouth and quickly followed her out of the store. Without slowing down, she made her way unceremoniously through the Activity Center's main hallway and, with Jimmy trailing a ways behind her, walked out of the building.

As he stepped hurriedly outside onto the brick square in front of the Center, still wondering what she meant by her comment about their parents, he bumped into a person about to enter the building. He started to apologize to the man for doing so when, to his great surprise, he recognized his face.

"Mr. Becksbury…what are *you* doing here?" Jimmy blurted out.

"Oh, hi, Jimmy," Mr. Becksbury said, equally surprised.

Jimmy wrapped his arms around him and said, "I can't believe you're here; how nice of you to stop by."

"Well, uhh…I'm not just stopping by. I will be working here."

"You're going to be working here? Wow, that's terrific. Will you be teaching music?"

"Yes. I hope in this upcoming school year you'll be one of my students again."

"You bet I'm going to be. You can't believe how happy I am to see you."

"I'm very happy to see you, too."

"My uncle told me you're one of us Atlanteans. Is that true?"

"Yes, yes," Mr. Becksbury whispered, "but don't let anyone else know, okay?"

"Okay," Jimmy also whispered.

"That's good. So, now, be on your way and keep our little secret a secret."

"Okay," Jimmy said. He hurried off to catch up with Mirah, who had already gotten into their electric cart.

"I see you have acquaintances all over this place," she said, with a gloomy expression on her face, as he sat down next to her.

"That's Mr. Becksbury, my violin teacher at Belle View Elementary School."

"So, what's he doing here?"

"He's going to teach music. Isn't that great?"

She didn't reply and instead started up the cart and zoomed off. Jimmy considered asking her to clarify her earlier comment but, not wanting to upset her again, decided to leave it until later. He also decided not to let her sometimes moody behavior interfere with the nice time he was actually having at the school his father built. *Later today, after the tour,* he thought, *David and I can head to the concert on our own, and I will not have to worry about her moods anymore.*

A little ways down the road, she broke her silence. "That's one of my favorite buildings on campus." She pointed down the road to the building Jimmy recognized as the gym. "It's sunny and has an indoor pool and fitness center inside, and basketball courts, too."

"You like to play basketball?"

"No, but I love to watch our school's basketball team play. I also love using the pool and the fitness center. And I really like the building itself—just wait until you see it on the inside."

Judging by the large number of carts parked in the adjacent parking lot and the many bicycles sitting in the bike racks on the sidewalk, other Piedmont students also really liked their gym. Having parked their cart in the lot, Mirah and Jimmy walked into the gym's large atrium where several students stood in line in front of the information booth, looking for a schedule of the gym's summer fitness programs or other informational materials. Other students lounged in the Atrium's comfortable chairs, enjoying the beauty of the massive glass structure and its many large tropical plants, potted in huge decorative containers. Mirah told him to grab a chair while she joined the line to obtain a general information brochure about the gym.

"You should keep this," she said, handing him the brochure she just picked up from the booth. "It has lots of good stuff in it about this building."

Glancing through it, he noticed that, besides information on operating hours and rules for the facility's use, it also had a small section explaining some of the characteristics of the building itself.

"It says here the gym is a zero-energy building, one that uses no electricity from outside sources," Jimmy said, with an inquisitive look on his face.

"Yes, amazing, isn't it? The solar panels on the roof and in the racks on the land in back of the gym generate all the electricity the building uses. It also tells you in the brochure, the gym itself, unlike the other buildings on campus, is made out of earth bricks."

"What in the world are earth bricks?"

Mirah showed him the page in the brochure where it explained earth bricks are made from compressed soil, and the soil used to make the gym's bricks came from the hole dug to pour its foundation.

"If you look over here," she said, showing him another page, "it explains a large geothermal heat-pump system heats and cools the gym, and is three times more efficient than regular heating and cooling systems."

Jimmy thought about what she just told him. "That must save this building a lot of electricity."

"Yes, it does, and there is more." Pointing to the top of the atrium, she said, "In the summer time, the type of glass the atrium is made out of blocks the sun's ultra-violet rays, keeping the building cooler; and during the winter months, it lets those rays come in to help heat it."

"That's so fascinating," Jimmy said. "I can see why you like this building so much. How do you know so much about it, anyway?"

"CIT training," Mirah said, with a wink. "I have more to show you, so come with me, please."

Grabbing Jimmy by the hand for a third time that day, she led him through the atrium to a long hallway where large glass panels afforded a full view of the indoor pool. He didn't know what to think about her on-again pleasant demeanor, but wasn't about to say or do anything that might cause it to change.

"That pool is awesome," he said, looking at the Olympic-size pool, which had a full-length pyramid-shaped skylight overhead, flooding it with natural daylight. Several students were swimming laps or just sitting in the hot tub adjacent to it; others had passed through the pool's sliding glass doors and were sunning themselves on the outside veranda in comfortable chaise lounges.

"Yes, you're right," she said. "And what makes it even more awesome is that the pool's and hot tub's water is heated by all those solar hot-water panels sitting over there next to the veranda."

Jimmy began to understand what made this a zero-energy building, and that the school was, in fact, a zero-energy school. He hoped that one day, like his dad, he could design buildings like this and others on the Piedmont campus.

After a brief look at the fitness center, they returned to the cart and continued their tour. The road to the observatory led them past two smaller brick buildings, sitting alongside each other in back of the gym.

"That's where we play indoor soccer and tennis," she told him, pointing at the two buildings. "Besides horseback riding, those are my favorite sports. And in case you're wondering, these buildings are also made of earth bricks."

"Thanks for letting me know," Jimmy said. "I'm glad you like to play both sports, 'cause I like 'em, too. Perhaps we can play tennis some day?"

"Yes, that would be fun," Mirah said. "Or on a nice day, we could just kick the soccer ball around."

"Yeah, I would like that, too," Jimmy said, glad they had something in common besides liking to ride horses.

A little further down the road, she pointed out the school's outdoor soccer fields and tennis courts; and before long, they chatted about their favorite professional soccer and tennis players, as they continued on their way. By the time they pulled into the parking lot of the observatory, Jimmy started to think that, in spite of her mood swings and sometimes cranky behavior, she was not so bad after all.

The observatory, located on the same road as the school's equestrian center, reminded Jimmy a little of the Eifel Tower. He had seen pictures of it in his geography class. Even though the observatory was blue and shorter, had three legs, and contained a telescope on top, it looked every bit as stately as the Parisian tower. Just after they had parked their cart, another one entered the lot and came straight towards them.

"Look, that's Professor Brassner," Jimmy said. "What's he doing here?"

"I don't know," Mirah said nervously, wondering if her director was checking up on her.

"Professor, what brings you here?" she asked him, as he pulled up next to them.

"I'm having a brief get together with Dr. Jason," the professor responded. "Please, don't pay any attention to me and continue with your tour. I'm sure you're doing a great job." Turning to Jimmy, he asked, "How is everything with you? Enjoying your tour?"

"Oh, yes, professor, I'm having a great time," Jimmy replied.

"Wonderful, I know you're in good hands. Just keep on exploring."

With that, he turned and quickly walked over to the outside stairway leading to the observatory's first floor, and headed up. After passing through the glass double door at the top of the stairway, he took an elevator up to Dr. Jason's office on the second level.

"Who is Dr. Jason?" Jimmy asked, as he and Mirah walked across the parking lot to the same stairway the professor used.

"He's the director of the observatory," she responded.

"Does he teach the astronomy camp?"

"No, his staff does."

"So, where is it—this camp?"

"In the Discovery Room; we can go there and see if the camp has started yet."

While they walked up the short stairway, she told him the Discovery Room took up most of the space on the observatory's first floor. When not in use for camps or other astronomy programs, students could come there at any time during the day and watch videos of the Moon, the Sun, and the planets. They could look at images of other star systems in the Milky Way Galaxy and other faraway places—images beamed down by the giant telescope on the third floor. She also mentioned the observatory's laboratory and staff offices occupied the second floor; and on the third floor, they could visit a small viewing room from where they could take in the inner workings of the telescope.

"Here it is," Mirah said, after they entered the first floor and stood in front of the entrance to the Discovery Room. "Let's go inside."

"Oops, it's closed," Jimmy said when he tried to open the Discovery Room's door for her. "Now, what do we do?"

"They keep the door closed because the hallway lights interfere with stargazing, but we can peek inside through the wall slits."

Mirah showed him the narrow horizontal glass viewing-slits in the wall next to the door. Even though the room was darkened, when they looked through the slits, they could make out a dozen or so campers standing next to each other, gazing at a huge screen against the far wall of the Discovery Room. Hundreds of different-size light particles, several linked together in simple patterns by thin light streams, dotted the screen. Every now and then, all the dots disappeared, and a new set of dots, linked in different patterns, popped up on the screen.

"They're looking at past depictions of the night sky captured by the telescope," Mirah explained. "Those light dots are stars and the lines connecting them show the locations of various constellations in the night skies over our northern and southern hemispheres at different times of the year. Many of those you can locate yourself at night. When I participated in this camp last year, they told us that, on a clear night, away from light pollution, you can see over four thousand stars at any one time."

"I don't think I have ever seen *that* many stars," Jimmy said. All of sudden, several colorful images floated across the room over the heads of the campers. "Wow, what are those?" he asked.

"Those are holograms of nebulae and quasars, and other objects from deep space," Mirah told him. "Our telescope also developed those."

"These camps are so cool," Jimmy exclaimed. "Why does Piedmont have so many of 'em, anyway?"

"In our regular classes, our school provides us with a basic education, so we can be successful in finding good jobs," Mirah said. "But our camps and other extra-curricular activities teach us how to be successful in other aspects of life, like getting along with one another and taking care of those less fortunate than us. They're also meant to help us understand that the power of your mind is unlimited, which is true for all people on our planet; that the beauty of art transcends all cultures and brings us peace of mind; and that sportsmanship defines your character and teaches you how to face adversity. In addition, they teach us respect for our environment, and that the universe is self-correcting."

"That sounds a lot like what my uncle told me, except for the part about the universe being self-correcting," Jimmy said. "What does that mean?"

"It means the universe is alive and will remove anything that threatens the wellbeing of any of its parts," Mirah said. "If we destroy our planet, the universe will eventually destroy us."

"That sounds pretty scary," Jimmy said. "How do you know all these things?" He quickly answered his own question, "Oh, yes, I forgot—CIT training, right?"

Mirah gave him a high-five as she took him by the hand again and led him to the elevator. "Let's go and look at the lab," she said, "that's where you'll find all of the observatory's computers, databanks, spectrometers, and calibration equipment."

"Okay, that should be interesting," he said, glad she seemed to be in a good mood.

Having ridden the elevator up to the second floor, they exited directly across from the lab's entrance and noticed its door was also closed. Through the door's glass panels, Jimmy could see Professor Brassner and another person, with a white lab jacket on, engaged in a lively conversation, amidst tons of electronic equipment, stacked high all around the lab.

"I'm sure the professor and Dr. Jason probably don't want us interrupting them right now," Mirah said. "Let's go up to the viewing room on the next floor, so you can see what our telescope looks like on the inside."

"Good idea," Jimmy said. "I have never seen one of those before."

As Jimmy followed Mirah back to the elevator, the two men in the lab continued their conversation.

"So, you're telling me those two cowboys gave us very useful information," Professor Brassner said.

"Yes, they did. Based on what they told us, we were able to track one of the Varsian spacecraft as soon as it entered our solar system. Through the use of our satellite-surveillance systems, we followed it all the way to the VARS' new underground base in the Pacific, which was exactly where they said it was located."

"And are these the pictures of their underground base with its camouflaged dome?" the professor asked, looking at several colored frames Dr. Jason had arranged in time-sequence on one of the tables.

"Yes, our satellites and anti-gravity drones took all of these. We didn't really know what they were doing until we saw these pictures of the dome opening up to let one of their spacecraft land inside their base. As you can see, it's huge and big enough to accommodate hundreds of their spaceships."

"And based on what those two had to say, you believe the VARS are planning an attack on our Earth Base?"

"Yes, I do."

"If they attack, our energy shield will protect us."

"Yes, our shield should keep us safe. But, nevertheless, our people must be ready to defend us just in case they're able to circumvent it—don't forget about the traitors in our midst."

"And do you think, if they attack us, this could be the beginning of the fulfillment of the Prophecy?"

"Yes, I think so. We have to get Jimmy Starlight ready to fulfill his mission."

"And you also believe what those cowboys told us about the VARS planning to invade Earth?"

"Yes. Why else would they build such an enormous underground facility and bring new spaceships to Earth. I'm sure they're up to something big. And if they do invade, the only thing that can stop 'em is the Peacemaker—Jimmy must find it."

"I will talk with John about getting him ready and let our High Command know about what you just showed me. Thank you for your vigilance. And by the way, Jimmy is visiting your facility as we speak. One of my CITs is giving him a tour of our campus. I think they may be on their way upstairs to look at the telescope, because I saw them glance at us a minute ago through the glass in the door. They must have decided not to interrupt us."

"Great, I will go and say hello to him."

The two men shook hands, and they both headed for the elevators.

Seeing the inner workings of the observatory's telescope from the viewing room fascinated Jimmy. He had no idea it took so many different pieces of equipment and gadgets of all sizes to make it work.

"What exactly are all those mirrors for?" he asked Mirah, looking at the base of the telescope.

"I'm not sure," she replied, "but I know the telescope can't operate without 'em."

"I can tell you what they're for," a voice interjected.

Turning around, they saw the observatory's director standing behind them.

"Hi, I'm Dr. Jason," he said to Jimmy, with a stern expression on his face.

He held out his hand, which Jimmy shook.

"Oh, hi, I'm Jimmy Starlight; nice to meet you."

Turning to the girl, the director said, "And how are you, Mirah?"

"Just fine, doctor."

"Good." Turning back to Jimmy, he said, "You wanted to know about those mirrors?"

"Yes. I didn't know telescopes needed all of those. I thought they just needed lenses—telescopic lenses."

"Large telescopes actually need them both," the director explained. "They need the mirrors to receive the light signal or image from space, and they need a lens to magnify the signal so we can see the image."

He further explained that, in general, the larger the mirrors, the more light the telescope collects and the brighter the final image will be; and that the telescope's magnification—its ability to enlarge an image—depends on the type and strength of the lenses used.

"We are very fortunate to have an observatory that can not only give us very clear images of objects in deep space, but also allows us to determine the wavelength of the light emitted by these objects. This tells us what an object is made of. And our telescope also lets us receive radio waves and other communication signals, like video broadcasts."

Since Mirah was in their presence, the director, in spite of being very proud of his observatory, didn't reveal all of its uses and capabilities. He didn't tell them, for example, that it was part of the Atlantean intelligence-gathering system and that Atlantean crystals powered it. He also didn't divulge it could closely track any object moving through the solar system, and instantaneously detect and analyze any form of communication beamed across Earth's airspace or traveling through landlines.

"If you would like to learn more about our observatory and objects in outer space, please come see me any time," he told Jimmy. He said goodbye and quickly returned to his laboratory to keep an eye out for other Varsian spaceships sent to destroy his home away from home.

Since I'm Atlantean, Jimmy thought, *I need to know a lot more about our solar system and the rest of our galaxy.* He intended to come back soon.

"We have one more stop on our tour—our equestrian center," Mirah told Jimmy as they walked back to their cart. "It's just down the road. But if you're tired of all this, we can go there tomorrow if you like—your choice."

Captivated by the tour, Jimmy considered it one of the highlights of his young life. "No, let's go there now," he said eagerly. "I'd love to see more."

They were soon on their way again, but this time, Mirah had not gotten behind the wheel. She had asked him if he would like to drive, and he had jumped at the chance. Letting out a yell, he pushed down on the accelerator as hard as he possibly could. They screeched out of the parking lot and in no time buzzed along at the cart's top speed; five minutes later, they reached the equestrian center. It had been designed and built as a state of the art riding facility, with a large indoor riding ring, two outside rings, a one hundred-stall stable, an outdoor jumping course, and a professional polo field.

As they drove by the first of the two outside rings, they heard the loud neighing sound of a horse vociferously complaining about something it did not want to do. Looking over to where the complaints came from, they could see a young horse being ridden around the ring by a determined female trainer. She had attached two extra lead ropes to the horse's rein rings; and two handlers, walking alongside the horse, assisted in keeping the animal under control, with tight grips on the ropes. Judging by his loud complaints, wild bucking, and frequent rearing on his hind legs, the horse really objected to having to carry a load on his back. Several kids, some dressed in formal riding attire, sat on the top railing of the ring, intensely watching the trainer as she tried to calm the horse down.

"That's Ms. Mayberry," Mirah said, nodding her head in the direction of the trainer. "She's the head counselor of your camp. Let's find out what she's doing."

Before Jimmy could say anything, Mirah jumped out of the cart and ran to the ring where she also climbed onto the railing.

"Hi, Ms. Mayberry," Mirah shouted to the trainer, who, in spite of the horse's frequent rearing, stuck to the saddle like glue. "Is there anything I can do to help?"

"Oh, hi, Mirah," she shouted back. "It's probably best not to come into the ring because this little horsie is not cooperating very well."

Having parked the cart in the equestrian center's parking lot, Jimmy followed Mirah to the ring, wondering why the trainer insisted on making the young horse do something he clearly did not want to do. Then, Jimmy heard the little voice once again.

"Tell her you would like to ride him," the voice urged.

"Is that you, Tooku?" Jimmy whispered, hoping Mirah and the other kids could not hear him talking to the invisible spirit. "I wondered when you would show up again."

"Yes, it's me. Ask the woman in the ring if you can ride the horse."

"That's a very wild horse...I don't think I want to ride it."

"Take my word, you'll like riding him."

"Maybe...but *he* won't like it."

"Yes, he will."

"And how do you know that?"

"Because."

"Because what?"

"Because I know he'll enjoy being ridden by you."

"And how do you know that...now?"

"As I told you before, I live in a dimension where the present, future and past are all the same—so I know now, what that horse will enjoy later on."

"I wish I lived in the same dimension as you do. Then I wouldn't have to worry about the future either."

"Not possible."

278

"Why is that?"

"Never mind, just tell her you would like to ride the horse. He will save your life one day."

"Well, if you put it that way, I'll go and ride that horse!" Jimmy said a little louder.

"What did you say?" Mirah asked, as she turned towards Jimmy, having overheard his last comment.

"Uhh...I said I like that horse."

"How can you? You don't even know Prince."

"Prince who?"

"The horse—his name is Prince."

"He looks like a very nice horse."

"Believe me, he really is *not* a very nice horse."

"But I would like to ride him anyway," Jimmy said as he climbed on the railing next to her. He intended to follow Tooku's advice.

"That's suicide!"

"Why?"

Mirah explained that Prince was a very temperamental three year old Arabian stallion. A local riding club had donated him to the school because none of the club's members could ride Prince without having others help rein him in. Many of their riders had tried to break him, but no one had been able to—most of them ended up on their behinds in the ring dust.

"So, if you want to kill yourself, go ride that horse."

Then, something happened that surprised everyone. When Ms. Mayberry rode past Jimmy, with the two handlers hanging on to the extra set of leads, Prince looked at him and, instantly, stopped his antics. The horse pulled the handlers with him as he moved to within a hair's length of Jimmy and put his nose on the boy's chest—all the while resisting Ms. Mayberry's attempts to make him back away.

279

"Oh, I'm so sorry," she said to Jimmy, as she tried to rein Prince in, wanting to turn the animal's head away from the boy and lead him back to the center of the ring.

Pulling with all their might on the lead ropes, the two handlers also tried to get Prince to back up, but the horse refused to budge from his stance. Eventually though, with three people pulling on him, Prince could no longer keep his head from being turned aside and started to neigh loudly again, registering his protest.

"Please, don't hurt him," Jimmy begged of Ms. Mayberry.

Caught off guard by the suggestion she was hurting the horse, Ms. Mayberry immediately loosened her grip on the reins and motioned the two handlers to do the same, allowing Prince to put his nose back against Jimmy's chest. Glad the horse had stopped complaining, Jimmy started to gently rub Prince's forehead.

"I'm not trying to hurt him, young fellow," Ms. Mayberry said. "I'm only trying to ride him safely. I hoped to use him as a polo pony for our students some day; but that's probably out of the question, because it seems Prince definitely does not like anyone riding him."

"Yes, he does! Can I ride him, please?"

Mirah could not believe her ears when he said that.

"Jimmy, what are you thinking?" she blurted out. "Do you really want to get hurt?"

"He will not hurt me," Jimmy assured her. "He will never do that."

"Who is this confident young man?" Ms. Mayberry asked Mirah, actually amazed at having witnessed Prince's change in demeanor when Jimmy came on the scene. Before her eyes, the horse had, all of a sudden, changed from an animal wild with fury, wanting to buck off any and all riders

280

daring to mount him, to a docile little munchkin, wanting to show affection to a young boy by rubbing his nose against him.

"Oh, this is Jimmy Starlight," Mirah replied. "He's going to be in your camp this summer."

Ms. Mayberry instantly recognized the name.

"Hi, Jimmy, nice to meet you. I'm Helen Mayberry."

"Nice to meet you too, Ms. Mayberry. Can I ride your horse?"

"Jimmy, no…not now," Mirah pleaded.

Even though she heard Mirah's plea, Ms. Mayberry did not hesitate to grant him his request. "Sure, why don't you give him a try," she said kindly. "He seems to like you."

"But Ms. Mayberry—" was all a worried Mirah could utter, wanting to keep Jimmy from getting hurt.

"Don't worry, Mirah," Ms. Mayberry said. "Prince will not hurt him."

How can you be so sure? Mirah thought.

Having dismounted, Ms. Mayberry asked her handlers to remove the extra set of lead ropes; and after Jimmy lowered himself into the ring, she handed him the reins. She then quickly climbed onto the railing and sat herself next to Mirah. It got totally quiet at ringside when Jimmy slowly raised himself into Prince's saddle. Holding the reins in one hand, he stroked the horse's neck with his other and then lightly tapped him with the heels of his tennis shoes. Prince immediately responded by going into a slow trot around the ring as Mirah and the other students sitting on the railing collectively held their breaths. When, having circled the ring once, Jimmy brought Prince to a canter, they let out a collective, "Ohhh!" Then, after he led the horse to a full gallop, they, at first, nervously watched him dash along the far end of the ring; but as he passed by in front of them, they

281

broke out in a loud ovation. Everyone was astonished at how Prince had instantly obeyed even the slightest of Jimmy's commands. He didn't seem to be the same horse who earlier had tried to buck Ms. Mayberry out of the saddle.

"Thank you, Prince," Jimmy whispered in the horse's ear, as he brought him to a halt in front of Ms. Mayberry.

Mirah jumped off the railing and patted Prince on the side of his neck. Shortly thereafter, Jimmy and the horse were surrounded by a flock of students, all trying to pat Prince.

"Nice going, Jimmy," Ms. Mayberry told him. She did not begrudge him for accomplishing instantly what she had tried to do for days: ride Prince peacefully around the ring. "I can see our horsie might become a polo pony after all. And I know just the person who can help me train him."

"I'd really like that," Jimmy said, feeling extremely happy.

"Before camp starts, you and I will have to figure out what we need to do to make him the best polo pony in the bunch," she told him, with a wink. "And if he's a fast learner, as I suspect he will be, he can be your polo pony during camp. But for now, why don't you and Mirah walk him to the stable where she can show you what stall to put him in."

"Great—and thank you for letting me ride him," Jimmy said, not believing his good fortune at having Prince as his own polo pony.

After Jimmy dismounted, Mirah gave him a big hug. "How did you do that?" she asked, looking at him with a glint of admiration in her eyes.

"Do what?"

"You know, get Prince to let you ride him, without any bucking or rearing."

"I don't know. I think he just likes me."

"Why would he like you when he doesn't even really know you?"

"I don't know why. I just know he does."

"And why did you want to ride him anyway?"

"I just thought it was a good idea," Jimmy said, not wanting to tell her about his conversation with Tooku.

Having said goodbye to Ms. Mayberry and taken Prince to his stall, Mirah and Jimmy walked over to the indoor riding ring, the last area she wanted to show him. It was larger than each of the two outdoor rings and completely lit up by the two-dozen oval skylights in its vaulted ceiling. Along the side sat a row of bleachers, from where spectators could watch the horse jumping and showing events; and inside the ring, several jumping fences had been erected on its custom made rubber-and-dirt footing.

"This is where Ms. Mayberry will teach you and the other campers how to become champion jumpers," Mirah told him, as she walked to the center of the ring and playfully spun herself around a couple of times, with her arms outstretched.

"I can't wait to get started," Jimmy said, following her into the ring and looking appreciatively at the jumping fences. "I want to become an Olympic champion someday, just like my dad." With a smile, he added, "And I hope Ms. Mayberry's jumping horses are all as well-behaved as Prince is."

"You mean the way he behaves when *you* are riding him—not when *she* is in the saddle," Mirah said, breaking out laughing.

As they walked back to their cart, Jimmy thought about all the people he had met at Piedmont and how nice all of them had been; including Mirah, at various times. A short while later, they were zooming along in their cart, with Mirah back behind the wheel. Jimmy noticed the happy expression on her face, much in contrast to the gloomy look she had shown earlier when they left the bookstore. He again pondered her startling comment at the time, about both his and her parents having been killed for no reason; and he contemplated asking her what she had meant by that. However, this would have to wait once more till another time.

He was ready to ask her about it, when she said, "I'll drop you off back at your dorm, so we can both get refreshed and take a breather. The main cafeteria will start serving our dinner in about an hour, and if you like, we can eat there together."

"Great, I'm starting to get a little hungry."

"And if you feel up to it, after we eat, we can catch this weekend's summer rock concert on the screens outside the Student Activities Center."

"Me, feel up to it; of course I do! I wouldn't miss this for anything in the world!"

"Yeah, I know what you mean. I feel the same way about our concerts."

A little ways further down the road, they passed by what looked like a medieval tower, with small merlons and crenels at the top, and arrow slits in its walls. It stood across the road from Mirah's dormitory at the edge of a level grass field, a hundred acres in size. At the end of the small parking area next to this square structure, stood a tall water storage globe, with the name "Piedmont International Academy" prominently displayed on it.

"What's that over there?" Jimmy asked, pointing to the tower.

"That's our water tower," Mirah replied. "It has big pumps inside, which provide our school with its own well-water."

"Can we look inside?"

"No, for some reason, we're not supposed to go in there. There's probably not much to see on the inside, anyway."

As soon as she said that, Jimmy immediately thought of the other area where students were not allowed to go—the top floor of the science building.

I'll definitely have to check this tower out real soon, Jimmy thought. *Who knows what secrets the Atlanteans could be hiding in there?*

Chapter 15: The Passageway

When she dropped him off at his dorm, Mirah told Jimmy she would be back in one hour to take him to dinner. A short while later, as he opened the door to his room, he got a little jolt from seeing the unexpected setup in front of him. In the middle of the room sat a teepee, reaching all the way to the ceiling, taking up almost half of the dorm space. Lying on his back on the floor right next to it, with a pillow under his head, a familiar figure gave him a little wave with one hand, while holding the small book he was reading in the other.

"*David, you made it,*" Jimmy said loudly, delighted to see his friend.

"Hey, Jimmy, this room is perfect—big enough for our teepee," David said, as he stood up and gave Jimmy a big hug.

"*Our* teepee?" Jimmy let out, not knowing what to think of it. "It's so huge…but it looks nice, and it will come in handy for…something."

David's parents left him in the room about an hour before Jimmy showed up, shortly after they finished helping him put away his belongings and set up his teepee. When she kissed him tearfully goodbye, his mother had surprised him with the book he was reading—about the history of Middleburg.

Jimmy recognized the teepee as the one David kept in his room at home. He used it to store his valuables: his tribal protection amulets, his dream catchers, a feathered Hapua headdress, an antique tomahawk, a Swiss army knife, and all his books on Hapua history. Jimmy noticed David had hung one of his dream catchers on the wall above his bed. Wondering what other prized possessions David might have brought with him, Jimmy opened up the flap of the teepee and looked inside. It was empty, except for a Hapua headdress carefully laid out on a small colorful blanket.

"Remember you said we should make it so we feel at home here. Well, I wanted to bring my drum set, but Dad said that was probably not a good idea."

"He's a very smart man," Jimmy said.

"If you don't like having the teepee in here, I can take it down."

"No, it's okay. Come to think of it, having a teepee in our room will… uh… give us some privacy when we need it. Good idea of yours…bringing it."

"Great, so I can leave it up?"

"Of course, we'll leave it up."

Jimmy told him about his campus tour with Mirah and seeing the two cowboys outside his dorm.

"I can't believe you saw Sam and Happy, and Mr. Becksbury, too," David said. "And Prince sounds like a great horse…and the girl sounds nice, too. I'm looking forward to meeting all of 'em."

"You'll meet Mirah in about an hour when she takes us to dinner, and we can visit Prince tomorrow morning."

"I'm supposed to go on a campus tour with my welcome-CIT tomorrow morning. Maybe we could visit Prince in the afternoon?"

"Don't worry. I'll take you on the campus tour myself. You won't believe all the things they have here. You can call your CIT in the morning and tell him he's not needed. He'll probably thank you for that."

"Sounds like a good plan to me," David said.

"And I should also tell you, they're showing a concert on the big screens outside the Student Activities Center this evening. We can go see it after we eat. You're so not going to believe the size of these screens."

"Cool, I can't wait. By the way, there is something about this room that really gives me lots of positive vibes, just like I get on the Hapua reservation. Did you notice anything?"

"Yes, I can feel it, too," Jimmy said, without elaborating on it.

When Mirah called from her cell phone to let Jimmy know she had arrived, the two boys had already showered, changed clothes, combed their hair, and brushed their teeth. They hustled out of their room, down the hallway, and out of the building. After introducing David, Jimmy motioned him to sit next to Mirah on the front seat and climbed in the luggage bin. Without engaging in conversation with David, she drove straight to the cafeteria, where they had a tasty evening meal, including dessert, provided at no charge to all students and summer-camp participants. During dinner, Jimmy took it upon himself to tell her a few things about David's background. Appearing to be quite taken with his Hapua ancestry and him having lived on an Indian reservation, she started to ask him many questions about his tribe's customs and history, and his family, especially his grandfather. Flattered by her attention, David meticulously responded to all of her queries and gave her a vivid account of the days he spent on tribal grounds in New Mexico. Happy they seemed to hit it off so well, Jimmy just listened.

After dinner, they headed for the area in front of the Student Activities Center to watch the concert. When they got to the Center's brick square, Mirah asked them to stay put briefly, while she ran a little errand. Waiting for the concert to start, hundreds of students had already congregated on the square or seated themselves on blankets spread out on the grass field just beyond it. To Jimmy and David's pleasant surprise, when Mirah returned, she pulled a blanket, big enough for the three of them to sit on, out of the large shopping bag she retrieved from their cart.

"Now, let's get comfortable over there," she said, pointing to a grassy area near one of the ponds with a small fountain in its center.

"What's on the program tonight?" David asked Mirah, after they spread out on the blanket. "And when do you think it will start?"

"It's a rock concert, with some big-name oldies on stage," she replied, "and it should start in about fifteen minutes or so."

"We love to play country rock," Jimmy said, excited by the prospect of seeing the concert.

"No kidding, who's we?" Mirah asked.

"David, my uncle, and I," Jimmy said. "David plays the drums, my uncle the guitar, and I the violin."

"That's great. I love country rock myself. I learned to play the keyboard at Piedmont."

"Well, you'll have to join our band, then."

"Yeah, that's a great idea," David seconded. "Then we can play right here on campus—whaddya say, Mirah?"

"Okay…," she said slowly, not sure what she might be getting herself into. "That sounds like fun."

All three of them thoroughly enjoyed the concert and afterwards stopped by the international food court for a late-night snack. When she took the two of them back to their dorm, both Jimmy and David agreed their stay at Piedmont could not have started off in a better way. And when they told her so, and Jimmy in particular thanked her for the wonderful tour, she blushed slightly and gave them an appreciative look.

Back in the dorm, still highly excited about being together at camp, neither one of the two boys felt ready for bed, even though it had been a long day for both of them. Jimmy sat down at his desk and started to pen some musical scores for the violin, and David grabbed his pillow and lay down next to his teepee to continue reading his book about Middleburg. Before long, however, their eyelids grew heavy, and they had a tough time staying awake. After a valiant struggle, they both conceded defeat and crawled in between the sheets. In no time, they fell asleep—not knowing their adventure of a lifetime was about to begin.

The serenity of the boys' room came to an abrupt end when Jimmy's cell phone jingled in the middle of the night. Half asleep, he answered it and heard Mirah's voice on the other end; she sounded very excited.

"Jimmy, I'm at your front door. Please, come outside. I need to show both of you something."

"Outside, you want us to come outside?" he asked, with a drowsy voice, slightly annoyed at having been awakened from a deep sleep. "But Mirah, we're in bed."

"Yes, never mind that. Hurry, I need to show you something."

"Okay, we'll get dressed. Give us a few minutes."

Awakened by the jingle, David tried to return to dreamland; then Jimmy gently shook his shoulder.

"Hey, David, wake up. We need to get dressed. Mirah wants us to meet her outside."

As soon as Jimmy mentioned her name, David sat up, still groggy, trying to decide what to do.

"She wants what?"

"She wants us to come outside."

"Why?"

"I don't know. She wants to show us something."

"Okay, then. Let's go."

David jumped out of bed, and they both dressed quickly. When they appeared outside, a few minutes later, Mirah was waiting for them in her cart.

"Please, get in," she said, with a secretive look on her face. "Once we get going, I'll explain everything."

"But Mirah, it's the middle of the night," Jimmy said, not wanting to get into any trouble driving around at bedtime. "Should we be doing this?"

"Don't worry, we won't go very far. *You are so not going to believe what I have to tell you.* Please, get in quickly."

After David took the initiative and climbed into the luggage bin, Jimmy slid in next to Mirah. With a determined look on her face, she drove out of the parking lot onto the ring road, which was well-lit at night by fluorescent street lights, like all other roads and parking lots on campus.

"So, where are we going?" Jimmy asked.

"There," she said, pointing to the water tower.

"The water tower…why?"

"Because that's where your two friends went."

"Which two friends?"

"The two gardeners."

"You mean Sam and Happy?"

"Yes—whatever their names are. And two others went inside too!"

Mirah explained that after she had come back to her room that evening and happened to look out of her window, she saw Sam and Happy standing right underneath Jimmy and David's dorm window.

"What were they doing there?" David asked.

"Nothing, they just stood there—for almost two hours."

"Then, what?"

"They walked across the road to the water tower."

"What for?"

"I don't know. They've been in there for over an hour."

"That's weird," Jimmy said. "I knew those two were up to something, just like I knew there was something going on in that tower."

"Yes, and it gets even weirder," Mirah said, mysteriously. "After they disappeared into the tower, your teacher…Mr. Becksbury…came out of nowhere, crossed the road in front of your dorm, and also walked to the tower. And he, too, went inside."

"Mr. Becksbury? No way—why in the world would he be going there? Are you sure it was him?"

"Absolutely—it was him." Mira took a deep breath. "And you are also not going to believe who else came from behind your building a little while later and, just like the others, walked over to the tower."

"*Who?*" both boys asked simultaneously.

Mirah waited a few seconds before answering—to increase the suspense.

"Professor Brassner."

"*No!*" the two boys exclaimed, also simultaneously.

"Yes—it was Professor Brassner," Mirah said, as she stopped the cart next to tower under one of its outside lights. "*And they all went in there!*" She pointed to the tower door.

Both boys looked a little skeptical, not knowing what to think of all this mysterious night action.

292

"Well—don't just sit there," Mirah said, getting out of the cart, walking over to the tower door. "Let's take a look inside."

"Wait…what if they're still in there," Jimmy said.

"They're probably in there somewhere, since I didn't see them come out," Mirah said, carefully turning the handle on the thick tower door. "But I really want to know what they're up to, don't you?"

She didn't get an answer. When she opened the door partially and peeked inside, they could hear the humming of a water pump.

"What do you see?" David whispered.

"Nothing, just a dimly-lit room and some pumping stuff, and another door," she whispered back.

Mirah then opened the tower door a little further, so the two boys could also look inside.

In the back of the room, they could see what looked like two huge pumps and large water pipes running from each of them into a well hole in between the two pumps. Other large pipes ran from each of the pumps into the back wall (and from there, presumably, to the water storage globe outside). Judging by the sound, only one pump appeared to be operating. To their right, they saw the door Mirah mentioned.

"They must have gone in *there*," Jimmy whispered, nodding towards the door.

"Yeah, let's take a look," Mirah said softly, stepping inside, determined to get to the bottom of why the four men snuck into the tower in the dark of night.

All three held their breath as she slowly opened this door. Behind it, the only thing they could see was a small lit-up hallway, with two more doors. Mirah walked over and tried unsuccessfully to open one of them. Then, she tried to open the other—again, no success.

They must have gone through one of them, Jimmy thought. *Perhaps they had a key.*

He noticed, however, there were no cylinders to hold a lock on the two doors and no key slots in the door handles. He walked over and tried to open up one of the doors himself—and, lo and behold, when he turned the handle, the door gave way.

"How did you do that?" Mirah asked, puzzled—like she had been when he made the elevator go up to the top floor of the science building.

"I don't know. I just turned the handle."

After Jimmy opened the door completely, they could see a brick stairway, leading down to a well-lit underground passageway about ten feet wide and eight feet high. Feeling slightly irritated because she could not open the door herself, Mirah quickly tiptoed down the brick steps.

"Come on," she called out to the two boys, as she reached the bottom step and noticed their hesitation in following her down. "Let's get going."

When they saw her continue down the passageway without looking back, Jimmy and David hurried down the steps to catch up with her.

"Mirah, please, wait," David said, in a low, but urgent, voice. "It may be dangerous down here."

Not wanting to let anyone dissuade her from probing the men's secretive behavior, Mirah ignored David's caution and kept going, until she came to a side tunnel, displaying a sign on its wall reading "Equestrian Center." The sign had an arrow at the bottom, pointing in the Center's direction. She waited until the two boys caught up with her.

"Now what?" she said quietly.

"Let's keep going straight," Jimmy suggested. "There's no reason for the four of them to go horseback riding in the middle of the night."

A little while later, they came across another side tunnel, with a similar sign, saying "Gymnasium."

"I don't think they're going swimming tonight, either," Mirah said as she kept walking down the passageway. She did the same thing when they passed by a third side tunnel, leading to the Student Activities Center. She couldn't resist saying, "I don't think they planned to go to the movies and bowl a few frames afterwards, do you?"

A little ways further down, they came to the end of the passageway, where they saw a door with a sign reading "Training Center." Mirah tried to open the door but could not. Then, David tried, but it didn't budge either.

"You try it," she said to Jimmy. When he did, it opened without a hitch. "Boy—you've got the touch," Mirah said, moving in front of him and slowly pushing the door all the way open.

The lights in the space in front of them were turned off, and they strained their eyes to see what was inside. Not enough passageway light leaked through the doorway for them to make anything out, so Jimmy ventured into the room and felt for the light switch on the wall next to the doorpost. After locating it, he turned on the lights.

"Wow—it looks like a computer-gaming center in here," Jimmy uttered, looking at the two dozen or so back-to-back cubicles sitting in the room. Separated by three-feet-high, orange dividers, the cubicles were aligned in a row along both sides of the room, about ten feet from the wall. Inside every one of them stood a white, oval pedestal desk, with a high-back arm chair in front of it, and a thin-screen monitor on top. Next to each of the monitors lay what looked like an oversized pair of sunglasses, with very thick temples.

"If this is a Training Center, like it says on the sign, what do you think these sunglasses are for?" Mirah asked the boys.

"Perhaps they're visors for virtual-reality games," David replied, not knowing they were indeed virtual-reality visors, but not for the kind of games he had in mind.

Also wondering what the glasses were all about, Jimmy decided to take a closer look at one of them. He sat down in a cubicle and picked up a pair, looking for markings that might indicate their use As soon as he seated himself, the monitor in front of him lit up with a greeting, *Welcome to Wander World.*

Jimmy didn't know what to think of this, but it got his complete attention. It also got David's attention; he sat down in the cubicle next to him and looked at his own thin-screen—nothing happened.

"How did you power yours up?" he asked Jimmy.

"I'm not sure. When I sat down, the words just popped up." *Must be an Atlantean thing*, he thought.

Just when Jimmy had that notion, the greeting disappeared, and his monitor displayed a directive:
Employ visor
Understanding it was prompting him to use the glasses, Jimmy put them on and settled back in his chair. For a few seconds, he sat in darkness. But then, the visor's built-in miniature 3-D screens lit up in front of his eyes with another directive, and a choice-menu appeared below it:
Focus your thoughts on one task below

Times Past
Pilot Training
296

For no particular reason, Jimmy focused his thoughts on the first task, *Times Past*. He was completely unprepared for what happened next.

Suddenly, his surroundings lit up, sunshine warmed his face, and fresh air entered his nostrils. He stood behind the wheel in the cockpit of a large sailboat, wearing a bright orange lifejacket.

"You're doing great, Son," his father said. He had seated himself on the cockpit bench upwind from him, keeping an eye on the watercraft crowding the waters around them.

Jimmy looked at his father affectionately. His mind wandered back to the times when, as a little boy, he played with him on the beach in Florida and walked hand-in-hand with him at Woodlawn Farm in Virginia, looking at horses.

"Don't forget—red, right, return," his father reminded him.

"Yes, Dad, I won't forget."

His father had taught him many years ago that when returning to port, you had to keep the red channel-markers to your right and the black ones to your left to avoid running aground. And when leaving port, you had to do the opposite and always keep the red markers to your left and the black ones to your right. These red and black buoys, with red and white lights on top, marked the channel running from open waters to the harbor entrance and guided sailboats, day and night, safely to and from their destinations.

In five hours, they had sailed their thirty-six foot Endeavour sailboat across the Chesapeake Bay, from their home on the South River to the town of St. Michaels on

Maryland's Eastern Shore. Having reached the entry channel to the town's harbor, they got ready to drop their sails and motor to the local marina, with the hope of finding a slip large enough to safely dock their boat.

"I can't wait to visit this beautiful little town again," his mother said, comfortably stretched out on the bench opposite his father. "It's been almost three years since we last visited here."

Jimmy also looked at her affectionately, remembering her cheering him on when he played soccer in the Little Kickers League, and tucking him in at bedtime, after placing his soccer ball next to his pillow

"Go ahead and point her into the wind, Son," his father instructed him. "Let's reel in the jib and lower the mainsail."

"Okay then, ready to come about," Jimmy cautioned, as he changed the Endeavour's course so her bow faced against the direction of the wind.

"Good job, Jimmy," his mother commended him, when the boat slowed to a near standstill. "I'll take care of the jib, if you and Dad handle the main."

"Cool, Mom," he said, "I'll let it down and Dad can tie it up."

After his mother reeled in the jib, he climbed out of the cockpit onto the deck and, holding on to the mast, loosened the mainsail's up-haul from its cleat.

"Ready, Dad?" he asked, holding the line as tight as he could, feeling rather proud for knowing what to do in situations like this.

"Yep, ready Son," his father replied, "Let her rip."

As Jimmy fed the line upwards so the mainsail could slide down the mast, his father grabbed the sail and, after rolling it up, tied it to the boom with several small nylon sail ties. Having tied the last one, he reached down in back of the steering wheel and started the Endeavour's diesel engine.

"You can take her in now," his father advised him, as he sat back down on his bench.

"Thanks, Dad," Jimmy said happily, scooting back behind the wheel. He pushed the gearshift on the side of the steering column into the forward position, which started the propeller turning and powered the Endeavour down the entry channel toward St. Michaels. Having entered the town's small port, it didn't take them long to locate a proper size slip and safely moor the boat inside of it.

"Are you guys up for a stroll?" his mother asked, when they finished securing the docking lines. "I would love to go ashore and look at some of the shops and visit a few of the museums and galleries—what do say?"

"Great idea," his father said. "After Jimmy closes the hatches and I grab my billfold, we'll be ready to go."

Having briefly visited the Chesapeake Bay Maritime Museum, they thoroughly enjoyed exploring the galleries, boutiques, and pottery stores along the many picturesque streets around the harbor of St. Michaels. After eating dinner in one of the town's many seafood restaurants, they returned to the ship at nightfall, tired and sleepy, and all but collapsed on the cockpit's benches.

Even though he felt dead tired, Jimmy was not ready to call it a day. "Let's play cards," he said, not wanting to let go of the enjoyable time he was having, with both parents giving him their fullest attention.

His mother was about to suggest saving the card game for the next evening, when the noise of two motorboats simultaneously entering the harbor got their attention. The huge boats, all black in color, looked like two Offshore Grand Prix Racers and made just as much noise. After motoring up and down the marina, apparently searching for safe spots to tie up to, but not finding any, the ships' helmsmen maneuvered their vessels next to each other in the middle of the harbor and dropped anchor not too far from the Endeavour. When Jimmy stood up to take a better look at the two noise makers, he saw only a single person in each of their cockpits. The two men left their engines idling loudly while they tied their vessels together. As he watched them go below deck after finally shutting their engines down, he suddenly had a foreboding feeling of evil lurking inside the two boats.

Not wanting to disrupt an otherwise perfect evening, he said nothing about his misgiving to his parents and shut it out of his mind. Having given Jimmy his wish, they happily huddled in the cockpit and played cards until late into the night. When they finally decided to hunker down, the relaxing sound of waves lapping against the boat's hull lulled all three of them to sleep in no time.

"Rise and shine," Jimmy heard a voice say, as he lay curled up in his sleeping bag on the cushions of the starboard bench in the cockpit of the Endeavour. Having pushed back the sliding hatch-cover, his father had climbed the small steps of the boat's cabin and stuck his head in the cockpit. "It's time, Son," he said, "time to head back across the Bay."

Jimmy remembered their plan called for sailing back during the day across the Chesapeake to scenic Annapolis—capital city of Maryland—and spending the night in the inner-harbor aboard ship. They intended to return home the following day.

"Dad, please, another half hour," he pleaded sleepily, wanting a little more sack time in his warm, comfortable sleeping bag.

"You can have five more minutes," his father said, looking at him fondly.

"How about twenty?"

"Alright, I'll give you another ten."

"How about fifteen? Pleaaase."

"Okay, fifteen minutes, then."

"Thanks, Dad," Jimmy said, pulling his sleeping bag's hood all the way over his head and closing his eyes again.

"Your fifteen minutes are up, sweetheart," his mother announced a little while later, as she climbed into cockpit from the cabin where she and his father had slept in the forward berth. "Let's go and take our showers at the harbor-house."

"That's a great idea if you're able to get him out of his bag," his father said, joining her in the cockpit. He grinned when he noticed the only response she got was a growl from somewhere deep inside the sleeping bag. It was not until she sat down on the opposite bench and tickled him with her toes that a head with a sleepy face popped up out of the bag.

"Okay, okay, Mom; please stop," Jimmy grunted. "I'm coming, I'm coming."

As the father started to loosen the Endeavour's port-side life line to allow the three of them to step unhindered from the boat onto the dock, Jimmy was happy to see the black boats had left port. He'd heard their engines crank up real early in the morning but had been too sleepy to sit up and watch them leave. Soon after the life line had been lowered, they went to the harbor-house at the town's dock where boaters who had paid their overnight docking fees to the harbor master could avail themselves and their families of private shower stalls. Having showered and picked up some sandwiches, juice boxes, and an assortment of cut veggies from the harbor food pavilion, they returned to the boat. There, they leisurely consumed half of their purchases for brunch, keeping the other half for their four hour journey across the Chesapeake. After filling his stomach, Jimmy helped his mother stow away all loose items aboard ship. With the prevailing winds blowing gently in a westerly direction, his father took time out to rig up a large spinnaker before they got underway. With this large balloon sail fully extended in front of the boat, they could maximize the aerodynamic push on their sails and make best use of the modest winds.

"Can I take the wheel again and bring her out?" Jimmy asked, after his father started up the ship's engine.

"Sure," his father said, "I'll loosen the dock lines and then you back her out."

"Great," Jimmy said excitedly, slipping behind the wheel again.

"Before we head out, we should take on some diesel," his father recommended, pointing at the refueling station further down the dock.

"Okay, Dad, can do."

Jimmy had no problems backing the boat out of the slip and motoring over to where a line of other boats awaited their turn at the pump. It took until early afternoon for them to top off the Endeavour's fuel tank and motor over to the shipping channel leading out of St. Michaels' harbor. As they continued motoring down the channel towards the open waters where they intended to raise the sails, Jimmy kept close track of the dozens of little day-sailers in their vicinity. These little boats had the right-of-way over the motoring sailboat because they were under sail. The Endeavour had to slow down or change course several times to avoid interfering with their tacks—bringing the boy appreciative looks and gestures from the young kids skippering them.

Jimmy did a double take when he detected, several boats back, two familiar-looking black speedboats, chugging along noisily in the same direction and at the same speed as their sailboat.

"Look over there, we saw them come in last night," he said to his parents, pointing to the two vessels.

He remembered the premonition he had the evening before and wondered why the two ominous-looking ships came out of nowhere and followed them to open waters.

"You're right, that's them," the father said. "I heard 'em leave early this morning and have no idea where they just came from."

"I think they're awful-looking boats," the mother added, with a shiver, as she made an ugly face. "And they sound even worse than they look."

"You can say that again," the father said. "They bothered my ears both coming and going, and I wonder why they're back."

Both Jimmy and his mother noticed he looked pensively for a while at the two speedboats, which slowed down and fell back several boat lengths.

"Honey, I'm going below for a few minutes," he said to his wife, with a worried look on his face. After she nodded her head, understanding his intent, he told his son, "In the meantime, please, put a lifejacket on."

"Okay, Dad," Jimmy said agreeably. Watching his father move down the cabin entryway and disappear below deck, he asked his mother, "Mom, can you take care of the wheel for a minute, please?"

"Of course," she responded, as she got up from her bench and grabbed ahold of the wheel, surveying the waters around her.

Letting go of the helm, Jimmy turned around, lifted up the cover of the aft storage bin right behind him, and grabbed one of the lifejackets stashed inside. Quickly slipping it on, he secured the snaps and took the wheel back from his mother. Standing alertly at the helm again, he could hear his father below talking to someone in a rather urgent tone on his cell phone. Not able to make out what or with whom he was communicating, he wondered why his father decided to go below to make the call; he assumed it had something to do with the two black boats.

Before the boy had a chance to give it any further thought, his father climbed back into the cockpit and announced, "It's time to man the sails, let's raise 'em up."

It didn't escape Jimmy that his father seated himself across from his mom and gave her a little reassuring nod, as if to say, "All is well." She then flashed him a "thank you" smile back.

"Now that we've reached open waters," his father said to him, "let's head our boat into the wind and slow the engine down, so we can raise the main."

"Good idea, Dad," Jimmy said, ready to follow orders.

"If you don't mind letting Mom have the wheel again, you can come on deck and help me put the sail up. I can feed it to you after I untie it from the boom."

Jimmy did as his father requested and crawled on deck next to the mast where his dad handed him the winch handle he would need to crank up the mainsail. He had sailed with his parents for most of his life and had no problems getting the sail in place. Before long, they headed downwind, and his father hoisted the red-white-and-blue spinnaker that quickly rounded in front of the boat. With Jimmy back at the helm, both parents settled in for what they hoped would be a peaceful crossing to Annapolis.

Over the next hour, their spinnaker stayed full intermittently; every now and then when the wind died, it would collapse and fold back on itself. Jimmy wasn't exactly pleased with the slow progress they made due to the off and on winds, which also brought almost no relief from the rising humidity. While he was savoring a nice cold juice drink, all of a sudden the wind really picked up, and the Endeavour surged forward—its brightly colored spinnaker leading the way. Shortly thereafter, he noticed dozens of birds crowding each other as they swooped up and down over the surface waters further downwind from them.

"Look over there, Mom and Dad," he said, pointing to a spot less than a quarter mile away. "There are those gulls again, fighting over bait fish." He had seen these frenzies on previous trips, but not as frantic as this one.

"That must be a really big school of little fish swimming near the surface to attract so many birds over there," his father said. "I'll bet ye the big sea basses are herding 'em up."

"If that's where the big fish are, that's where those fishermen should be going," his mother reasoned, as she watched a motorboat with two men inside trawl for fish off the Endeavour's starboard side. "Be careful, Son, 'cause we're on a collision course with that boat."

"Of course, Mom, I'll watch it," Jimmy said. "And don't worry; we have the right-of-way because we're under sail."

"Well, please, be careful anyway," she said. "Always remember what happened to the guy who insisted to the very end he had the right-of-way over the truck that ran over him."

"Okay, Mom, I'll be careful."

Jimmy kept a close eye on the motorboat until it slowed down and gave way. As the Endeavour passed in front of it, he waved at the two young fishermen, who returned his greeting.

"I think those boys just saw the feeding frenzy over there," his mother said, shortly after they passed by the motorboat. "One of them is standing up in the boat and seems to be looking through his binoculars at where the fish are."

"You're right, Mom," Jimmy said, "and he just gave 'em to the other guy to look too."

Because the Endeavour had picked up speed and moved a good distance downwind, the flock of birds now took care of their business only a few hundred feet off the portside of the ship. After the two fishermen cranked up their boat's engine and headed there, Jimmy noticed his father focusing his attention not on the fishermen, but on another motorboat speeding in their direction from the Eastern Shore.

"What ye looking at, Dad?" he asked, watching him stare across the stern of their boat.

"I'm watching that black boat over there coming towards us," he replied, trying not to look too concerned in front of his son. Scanning the eastern horizon, he added, "I wonder if there is another one somewhere nearby."

Having overheard what the father said, the mother stood up and looked at the boat he'd been watching. Because it looked like one of the black racers they had seen at St. Michaels, she asked, "Do you think this could be one of those boats we saw last night?"

"It looks like one of 'em, but I'm not sure," he replied. "It's by itself and running quietly, and it has a fishermen's sunscreen overhead, which the other two didn't have."

"It's probably just another fishing boat then," she said. "It seems to be heading more in the direction of those birds than towards us."

"Could be," his father said. "It does look like it's heading for the fishing spot."

Jimmy and his parents watched with some apprehension as the black boat approached the area where the other two fishermen were ready to cast their fishing lures. All three of them expected the boat to slow down and shut off its engine, so it wouldn't chase the big fish away. But it soon became apparent the black boat was not out to catch fish.

Jimmy couldn't believe his eyes when he observed what happened next. Instead of slowing down, the black boat accelerated, racing right by the two stunned fishermen, heading straight for the Endeavour. As soon as his father noticed the boat speeding up, he pulled out his cell phone and, after hastily pushing a few buttons, shouted into the device, "Mayday, Mayday, we need help." Also sensing danger behind him, he turned around and discovered a second black boat speeding towards them from the opposite direction.

"I should have known they disconnected their mufflers last night before they came into the harbor," he said apologetically to his wife and son. "That's why those boats were so loud. They reinstalled 'em after we saw them today, so they could run much quieter. Those crooks tricked us and fooled me completely. Sorry, I didn't figure it out earlier."

"Don't worry, honey," the mother beseeched her husband. "Help is on the way."

Less than twenty seconds after his father's emergency call, the first black boat raced to within thirty feet of the Endeavour and showed no signs of slowing down. The father grabbed Jimmy's hand and pulled him from behind the wheel. He kissed him on the forehead and, after taking hold of him with both hands, lifted him over his head and tossed him overboard across the stern.

Jimmy floated in the water, watching his father embrace his mother, shielding her with his body just before the black boat crashed into the Endeavour amidships. A second later, he saw the huge explosion that blew both boats to pieces—then, everything around him went totally dark.

Surrounded by darkness, Jimmy reached for his visor. After he ripped it off, the first thing he saw was the white pedestal desk in front of him with the thin-screen sitting on top; it read, *You have left Wander World. Thank you for visiting.* Breathing heavily, totally stunned by what he had experienced, he tossed the visor on the desk, leaned back in his arm chair, and buried his face in his hands. With his eyes closed, he reflected on what had been the most horrific experience he had ever gone through—seeing his parents engulfed by a huge explosion that, in his mind, most certainly blew them to bits.

This must have been a virtual-reality video, he thought, *but not like any I've ever seen before. How is it possible I saw myself about to be knocked unconscious and my parents being killed right before my very eyes?*

Jimmy had seen virtual-reality videos before. In his science class in school, students had taken turns strapping on a head-mounted display—or as his teacher called it, an HMD. It allowed them to see virtual-reality videos containing computer-generated images of people living and playing in many different cultures. But this virtual-reality occurrence had been different; he had been part of it himself and experienced every sensory perception in it as if it was really occurring all around him. His virtual-reality parents had looked just like his real parents who died in a boating incident seven years ago when he was only five years old. He couldn't understand how they had ended up together in the virtual-reality episode he just witnessed, and how this episode just happened to be one of the selections in the choice-menu that popped up after he sat down in one of the cubicles and put the visor on.

When he lowered his hands and opened his eyes, he saw David's concerned face.

"Hey, buddy, are you alright?" his friend wanted to know.

"Not really," Jimmy answered, looking pale. "I just witnessed my parents being assassinated."

"What?"

"Yes, I saw a black boat crash into ours on purpose and kill them."

"You saw that? How?"

"I saw it in Wander World."

"What's Wander World?" Mirah wanted to know, also looking concerned. "And what exactly happened to your parents?"

Jimmy gave them a rather extensive account of what happened to him after he put the visor on and was transported to a virtual-reality world.

"You were on that boat for two days?" David asked.

"Yes, I was onboard that ship when we motored into St. Michaels and stayed there till I was tossed overboard by my father the next day."

"That's strange," David said. "You had your visor on for only two or three minutes. I just happened to look at my watch when you put it on, and that was, at most, five minutes ago."

"He's right," Mirah said. "When I saw him look at his watch, I looked at mine, too."

"I swear I'm telling the truth about what I saw and when I saw it," Jimmy said defensively, concerned his friends might think he was making the whole thing up.

"Don't worry, I believe you, no matter what," David reassured him. "But what's really strange is how you could have become a part of that Wander World virtual-reality video—if that's really what it is."

"Yes, why do you think that video is on a computer here in this room?" Mirah asked. "And why is it about you?"

"I wish I knew that," Jimmy said. "All I know is, I don't ever want to go through an experience like that again."

"I know how you feel," she said quietly. "I felt the same way when my parents were killed."

"I'm sorry to hear that," Jimmy said, sensing the pain in her voice. "What happened?"

"I'd rather not talk about it," Mirah replied.

"Sure, I understand," Jimmy said, wondering if that lay behind her strange behavior from time to time.

Wanting to get their minds off their unpleasant experiences, David walked to the entrance at the opposite side of the room and suggested, "Let's check out what's behind this door." Turning to Jimmy, he then said, "Perhaps, you can open it?"

After Jimmy opened the door, they walked into a hallway looking very familiar to all of them.

"This is the main floor in the admin building," Mirah said, recognizing the entranceway at the end of the hallway and the stairway going up to the Summer Camp office on the second floor. Just when she said that, they heard footsteps coming down the stairway; all three retreated quickly back into the room.

Listening through the crack of the door for an indication of where the footsteps were going, they quickly realized the person making them was coming straight towards the room they were in—they urgently needed a place to hide. Having quietly closed the door, Jimmy looked around the room and decided the best place to hide was for each of them to crawl underneath a pedestal desk in one of the cubicles facing the side walls of the room.

"Let's duck down there," he said, pointing to the row of cubicles facing the wall farthest away from the hallway door.

Tucked face-down underneath their pedestal desks— each in their own cubicle—they stopped their breathing when the door opened.

"I could have sworn I turned off the lights in here," a deep voice grumbled. Jimmy recognized it as belonging to Professor Brassner. He seemed to hesitate at first, but then quickly walked across the room and opened the other door. Before exiting, he briefly paused again. He turned off the lights, closed the door behind him, and hurried to his destination. The sounds of his footsteps echoed in the tunnel. They all took a deep breath.

Shortly after the door closed, Jimmy crawled carefully from under his pedestal desk and felt his way over to the door leading to the passageway. He opened it slowly and peeked out; not seeing any signs of the professor, he turned on the lights.

"He's gone, you can come out now," he told the others.

Mirah crept out of her cubicle and straightened out her hair. With a determined voice, she said, "I really want to know what he's up to—and where he's going. Let's follow him *right* now."

Seeing signs of hesitation on the faces of both boys, she added, with a hint of desperation, "Look, guys, he went to his office in the middle of the night and didn't use the front entrance to the admin building. Instead, he used a secret passageway, and now he went back the way he came. There's something fishy going on here. *Let's find out where else he might be going!*"

Wanting to give her some support, David said, "Yes, there's obviously something going on here they don't want anyone to know about."

"But what if he sees us?" Jimmy asked.

"Don't worry, he won't," Mirah replied. "Just open the door, before he gets too far."

After Jimmy did so, she rushed by him into the passageway. Knowing she had made up her mind to chase after the professor, Jimmy and David followed her out of the room. Before he closed the door behind him, Jimmy took one last look at the cubicle in which he had experienced the unfortunate accident on the Chesapeake Bay. As he did so, he had a feeling he may have actually experienced it in reality not too long ago. He tried to suppress it, telling himself it was impossible for this to have actually occurred, because his uncle had told him his parents died seven years ago in a boating accident—when he was five years old. However, for whatever reason, he couldn't get rid of it.

"We need to hurry," Mirah said, when he caught up with her. "I think I may know where he's going."

"And where might that be?" Jimmy asked.

"The same place where the other three went."

"You mean Mr. Becksbury—and Sam and Happy?"

"Yes, those three."

"And where do you think they went?"

"Just follow me, and you'll see."

Motioning them to step lightly, Mirah started to speed-walk down the passageway.

Every great civilization has great men serving it, but there are always a few rotten apples that use their positions to serve themselves. One of those rotten apples on Planet Atlantis was Traitus Deliritus, the Regent of the Planet. He was not at all happy with the way things had been going recently. Even though the Planet's last leader, Marcus Starlight—Traitus' deceased uncle—had passed away three years ago, the approval of the Regent's appointment to become the next Leader of Atlantis' Supreme Council, the most powerful job on the Planet, was still stalled in the Council's legislative process. And, it would most likely not get acted upon any time soon.

Like a trapped mouse in a cage, the tall, skinny Regent—with a long, pointed face, slicked down, black hair, and angry eyes—paced back and forth on the thick carpets covering the floor of his ornate office in the Starlight Mansion. This huge mansion, located in the center of Poseidon, had served for hundreds of years as both the Executive Building and private quarters for Atlantis' Leaders.

"I can't believe the Council has not acted on my appointment because of some prophecy," he squealed to his aide—a bald, muscular man, built like an avid weightlifter. "How do you think the numbers stand right now?"

"As of right now, over ninety-five percent of the Council still wants to wait and see if the little guy, Jimmy Starlight, will step up to the plate and show signs of being capable to become our next Leader," his aide responded, with a deep, growling voice and a look of disgust on his face.

His answer sent Traitus into a tirade.

"Him, our next Leader. *Over my dead body!* He will never, ever be our Leader—not if I can help it! *And I'm tired of just being this child's regent!*"

"Don't worry, he has never even lived on Atlantis; so how can he become anything here at all?" the aide sneered.

"You tell that to all of those fools delaying my appointment and see if that makes any difference to them— *probably not.* The only way they will change their votes and make me their new Leader is if the boy does not live up to their expectations." *Or is not around to do so,* he thought, with an evil grin on his face.

"Well, I'll talk to them again and rattle their cages to see if I can change any minds."

"You do that, and also check with our man at the Civil Service Headquarters to see what their latest plans are for the boy."

"Yes, sir; I will see to it," the aide said, as he bowed slightly and quickly left through the office's main entrance— glad to get out of there.

A little while later, there was a tiny knock on one of the side doors of the Regent's office. Traitus walked over and opened it to let the person in.

"I came as soon as possible when I learned you wanted to see me."

"Yes, I want to know why it's taking so long for them to grab the boy."

"The people in their employ tried several times but were not able to do so."

"If they don't grab him soon, I want *you* to get rid of him."

"That may be difficult."

"I'm sure you can do it; just like you got rid of the other three."

"I'll give it my best shot."

"That's not good enough. Either *he* or *you* will not be around."

"Understood, my Leader; and by the way, today I learned that two men, who used to work for our collaborators, came to the home of one of your relatives. I thought you might want to know."

"Unbelievable," the Regent said, after he was given the name of this relative. "Besides the boy, we may have to get rid of a few other pests."

As the assassin left quietly through the same door he came in, a conversation took place between two men and Traitus' relative.

"Thank you for bringing me up to speed on our little one," she said. "You gentlemen did a great job, and I will be eternally grateful to you. Please, go back there and keep a close eye on the boy for me."

"Of course, my Lady, we'll watch him closely and keep you informed," the taller of the two men said, respectfully.

"Yes, don't you worry, we'll protect him," the second man said, fidgeting with his fingers.

Not wasting any time, Mirah hustled back down the passageway, with the two boys trying hard to keep up. Hearing the faint sounds of Professor Brassner's footsteps in the distance, straight ahead of her, she again motioned to the boys to step lightly. Then, she continued her brisk pace and passed by each of the three side-tunnels without slowing down. Having reached the brick stairway leading back up to the small hallway in the water tower, she paused to take a breath and allow Jimmy and David to catch up with her. By then, the sounds of the professor's footsteps had faded away.

"He went up there," she whispered as she started to slowly climb back up the stairs. "There's nowhere else for him to go."

The two boys quickly followed. At the top of the stairs, she motioned for Jimmy to open the door. He slowly turned the handle before cautiously pulling it open and letting Mirah pass by. When she stepped into the small hallway, she immediately went to the door Jimmy had not opened before.

"This is where they all went," Mirah said, looking at Jimmy, and nodding towards the door. "And I just know you can open this one for us, too."

When Jimmy started to open the door, the three of them didn't know what to expect, except that they would find, most likely, something totally unexpected behind it— just like when they discovered the underground passageway.

If Mirah is right, Jimmy thought, *and all four men went looking in the middle of the night for whatever is behind this door, then it has to be something truly out of the ordinary.*

What they found was not only something out of the ordinary, but something out of this world. When Jimmy pushed the door open, they saw…another passageway—very narrow and only about twenty feet long. That was, of course, not something out of this world, but what they saw at the end of it was—an entryway of glitter, with columns of white light streaming up and down, and up and down, inside of it. This resemblance of an entrance into heaven radiated a bright glow into the passageway, seemingly inviting them to come forward and step inside.

317

"What in the world is that?" Jimmy said, staring at the curtain of streaming lights.

"Entrance point," David said. "This looks like an entrance point into another dimension."

"What...? Into where...?"

"It's an entry from our world into another one."

"You can tell that just by looking at it?" Mirah asked.

"My grandfather told me about entrance points—they talk about 'em in our Hapua legends. And they all have streaming lights inside of them."

"Are they dangerous?" Jimmy wanted to know.

"That depends."

"On what?"

"On the kind of world they take you to. If they take you to an underworld—that would not be good." Turning to Mirah, he asked, "So, what do you want to do now?"

"Uhh...I'm not sure," she said, having lost some of her drive to discover where the four men had gone. "You said this could take us to an underworld?"

"We should go through it, of course," Jimmy said, recalling what Tooku had said about a passageway leading him to Atlantis, a Planet in another dimension. "The others must have gone through it already, including the professor." He passed by his friend and walked confidently towards the lights.

"Jimmy—be careful," David said, hesitating briefly; then, following him down the narrow passageway.

"Hey, wait for me," Mirah said, quickly pursuing them, having regained some of her confidence from Jimmy's determination to pass through the lights.

When he reached the entryway, Jimmy stopped and looked over his shoulder to see where David and Mirah were. Seeing them closely behind him, he grabbed their hands, took a deep breath, and, without saying anything, led them through the curtain of lights. While they passed through it, the lights streamed so brightly they had to close their eyes. A few seconds later, the intensity of the lights diminished as they stepped out of the entryway; and when they opened their eyes, they found themselves in another dimension.

The first thing Jimmy saw when he opened his eyes was the gazebo-like, glass structure they were standing in. He could tell it was glass because the second and third things he saw were the brightly lit concourse in front of the gazebo and the stars in the night sky above it. The square concourse was full of parked aircraft with the same shape as the ones he had seen in his dream about the Pyramid. Some of them were about the same size as the ones in his dream, but others were two, or three, or even ten times larger. The fourth and fifth things he saw were the relieved faces of David and Mirah, who were very glad to have made it safely past the bright lights.

"We made it through," Jimmy said, letting go of their hands. "But the question is, *through to what?*"

"Thank goodness, we did," Mirah said. "Where do you think we are?"

"I'm not sure," David replied, "but we are most certainly in another dimension somewhere."

"Could be," Mirah said, "but I can see the tower we were in…right over…there…" As she spoke, her last words almost got stuck in her throat. She pointed to the water tower, which sat, all lit-up, quite a ways to the right of the gazebo's exit. "My gosh…how did it get way over there?"

"That's not all," David said. "I can see our dorm and some of the other campus buildings behind it, but the large grass field that was next to it is gone."

"Yes, the area with the planes in front of us is where the grass used to be," Jimmy said. Noticing three huge buildings, with wide hangar doors at the front, sitting along the edges of the concourse, he suggested, "Let's go outside and take a peek inside those hangars."

When they stepped outside, they discovered the concourse was made out of a soft rubberized material, and all the planes were neatly parked in rows along its perimeter. Next to the first hangar they came to, stood an obelisk with a large pyramid-shaped glass apex that glowed. The four-sided pillar looked like a smaller version of the Washington Monument. As they would learn later, the glass apex was actually a large crystal that provided the electric-power needed to operate Piedmont's energy shield, and all the power for the immediate area surrounding the concourse, including the curtain of lights.

"These thingies parked here don't look like planes," Mirah said. "They don't seem to have any engines, and they don't have wings. I really wonder if they can fly."

"I think they can," Jimmy said. "I saw 'em fly in my dream."

"What dream was that?"

"He had a dream not so long ago about those planes being used to help build the Great Pyramid," David said.

"*What!*" Mirah exclaimed. "There were no planes when the Great Pyramid was built. What kind of a silly dream was that?"

"Yeah, you're right; it was just a silly dream," Jimmy said, not wanting to get into a debate with Mirah about his dream.

"Planes or no planes," David said, "this place is unreal. We appear to be on the same campus with the same buildings and streets, but now there are planes—or whatever they are—and hangars sitting where the empty grass field used to be."

Just as he said that, a small door inside the large hangar door on the building in front of them opened up and out stepped…?

"*Sam and Happy…what in the world are you guys doing here?*" Jimmy said loudly, totally astonished to see them.

He frowned at the two men, who were just as surprised to see him and his two friends—and seemed temporarily dumbfounded.

"Uhhhh…we might ask you the same question," Happy said.

"Come on, tell us. Where did you guys go?"

There was a brief awkward silence.

"Well…we went home," Sam replied, finally, with a serious voice.

"Yeah, we went home," Happy reiterated, "to see the family."

"Home…? Home where…? To see what family…?" Jimmy asked, skeptically.

"Your family," Happy replied.

"My family…? Where…?"

"Your—family—on Atlantis," Sam said, slowly.

"Wait a minute." Jimmy sounded puzzled. "*You went to Atlantis to see my family?*"

"Yep, we sure did," Happy said, with a serious look on his face.

"You're kidding me right?" Jimmy said, looking at them disbelievingly.

"Jimmy, I don't think they're kidding," David said. "I think this *may* have something to do with this other-dimension thing."

"Nah—they're just kidding," Jimmy said.

"We're not," Sam said, "we're *not* kidding."

"Yes, you are—you must be—how could you have gone to Atlantis…?

"Through the space portal," Happy piped in.

Knowing his father had come to Earth from Atlantis through a space portal, Jimmy's heart started to beat faster.

"Is that the one my dad used to come here?"

"Yes, it is," Sam said.

"That's the one," Happy restated.

"Wow, I can't wait to see it," Jimmy said.

"Will one of you, please, explain what you're talking about?" Mirah interrupted. She felt very confused about all the talk about portals and Atlantis, and Jimmy's family living there.

"Oh, sure, Mirah," David said. "They're talking about another planet—Planet Atlantis." Looking up, he continued, "It's way out there, in Space. And Jimmy's father came to Earth from Atlantis through a portal—an entranceway through Space from another dimension."

"Now, *you* are kidding, right?" Mirah said.

"No, he's not," Jimmy said. "That's where my dad came from. And there are many Atlanteans walking around right here on Earth."

"And we're two of 'em," Happy said.

"You're Atlanteans?" Jimmy sounded really amazed.

"Yes, we are," Sam replied.

"But you worked for the VARS."

"We worked undercover," Happy said. "The VARS thought we were earthlings, and they asked us to work for them and kidnap you."

"So, if you worked undercover, why did you try nabbing me in the park, and at my school, and also at Woodlawn?"

"We didn't try to nab you at all," Sam said. "We were watching over you. We tried to warn you about them, and about the assassin they sent to your school, but we could never get close enough to you."

"And the VARS thought you were helping them?" Jimmy asked.

"That's right," Happy said. "Those dummies got madder and madder at us for not bringing you in—not knowing we would never do that."

"So, why do you guys want to help me?"

"Because your dad's sister asked us to keep an eye on you," Sam said.

"My aunt, Maryka? Why would she ask you to do that?"

"Because we work for her," Happy said.

"What do you mean, you work for her?"

"He's her chauffeur and I'm her butler," Sam said.

"Do you know my Uncle John came from Atlantis?"

"Yes, we do."

"Did you meet him there, at Aunt Maryka's house?"

"No, we never met him on Atlantis. The first time we saw him was when we had parked our van in front of your house."

"Why didn't you talk to him then and tell him who you were?"

"Your aunt did not want us to disclose to anyone she sent us here to keep an eye on you."

"Why was that?"

"She never told us why, but we think it was to protect her own family."

"Well, it's sure nice to have you look after me," Jimmy said. "But why does my aunt want you to do that?"

"She told us it has to do with the Prophecy," Happy said.

"Prophecy, a prophecy about what?" Jimmy asked. Because he did not want to tell anyone he had heard about the Prophecy from a little voice, he acted like he had not heard about it before.

Instead of answering Jimmy's question, Happy queried him. "You mean you don't know about the Prophecy?"

Before Jimmy could say anything, Sam said, "Of course, he doesn't; he's never been to Atlantis."

"So, tell us about this Prophecy," Mirah interjected, wanting to join the conversation. "Where can we find it? What does it say?"

Sam felt hesitant to talk about it, but Happy had no reservations doing so.

"It's in the Book," Happy said.

"What book?" Mirah asked.

"The Book of Prophecies, of course."

"And where is this book?"

"In our main library—in Poseidon."

"And where is this Poseidon?"

"On Atlantis—it's our capital city."

Mirah was determined to get to the bottom of this Prophecy business. "And what *exactly* does this Prophecy say?"

Having thought briefly about how to answer her question, Happy started to say something, but Sam cut him off. "Maybe it's better if his aunt explains this directly to Jimmy."

Now Mirah started to get a little frustrated.

"Why can't you tell us now?" she asked.

"Because the Prophecy will affect the lives of many people in many different ways, and his aunt can explain all of this much better than we can."

"So, what does all of this have to do with Jimmy?"

"It has a lot to do with him," Sam said softly, without further elaborating.

"*With me!* Why me? I don't even live on Atlantis," Jimmy complained.

"I know. That's why it's better for your aunt to explain this to you."

"Then, let's go and see her, right now," David said.

"But it's the middle of the night," Mirah interjected.

"Not at his aunt's house," Happy said. "We just came from there and it's daylight."

"That settles it then," Jimmy said. "We're going to Atlantis."

"Okay, where is this portal?" Mirah asked.

"It must be in there," David said, pointing at the small hangar door through which Sam and Happy had appeared on the scene. "Let's take a look."

Without waiting for a response from anyone, David walked over to the door and tried pushing the door handle down to open it. The handle stayed put, no matter how hard he tried.

"I'm so sorry," Happy said, with a sad face. "Only Atlanteans can open it."

"That's why we brought Jimmy," Mirah said, jokingly, finally understanding why only he could open the doors in the passageway.

"Before we go anywhere else," Jimmy said, "please, explain to us what this place here is all about?"

"This is our Earth Base," Sam said.

"Your Earth Base? What is that for?" David ask.

"It's from here that we help the people on Earth."

"So, why can't we see it—except after having gone through those bright lights?"

"We wanted to keep it a secret, so we built it in another dimension."

"Why?"

"Because we don't want anyone who is not Atlantean to know that our portal is here, especially not the VARS."

"And why are there so many planes here?" Jimmy asked.

"Because of the Prophecy."

"And you want me to talk to Aunt Maryka to find out what this Prophecy is all about."

"That's right."

"But those planes of yours have no wings or propellers, and I don't see any engines." Mirah said. "So what makes 'em fly?"

"Anti-gravity," Happy said. "They've got anti-gravity engines that let you go straight up. And after you fly around, they'll let you come straight back down again."

"That's amazing. I can't wait to see 'em take off."

"I can't either," David said. "But who will be doing all the flying? You'll need hundreds of Atlantean pilots for that. They must all be soundly asleep in one of your buildings over here."

"Actually, we have only a few Atlantean pilots on our Earth Base," Sam said, "and they are here to train people from Earth to fly those planes for their own defense—but we've not yet started any training."

"I'd love to learn to fly one of these planes," David said. "I can just imagine how much fun I'll have zooming around in one of 'em without having to worry about running out of fuel."

"You're right," Sam said, with a serious face. "It's a lot of fun to fly one of our planes, except when the enemy shoots at you; and the VARS have many spaceships capable of doing just that."

"Thanks for reminding us," Jimmy said, with a shudder. "Perhaps, we should get going to Atlantis now."

"Yes, let's do that," Sam said. Then, he hesitated. "On second thought, your aunt may frown upon us for bringing you and your two friends to Atlantis without letting her know beforehand."

"Oh, don't be afraid, Sam," Jimmy said. "She's my only aunt, and she'll love to see me. And these are my closest friends, so there is really nothing to worry about."

His words swayed Sam and Happy to accompany the three youngsters to Atlantis. "Okay, come with us," Sam said, opening the small hangar door and stepping inside.

The others followed him into the large structure. What they saw in the back of it left the three kids open-mouthed yet again. A huge curtain of streaming lights—similar to the one they passed through earlier, except nearly ten times as high and more than twenty times as wide—took up the full height and width of the back of the hangar. It shone so brightly, it lit up the whole area inside of it.

"Is that it…the portal?" Jimmy asked, using one hand to shield his eyes from the bright lights.

"Yes, that's it," Happy said. "Welcome aboard."

From what John had told him, Jimmy knew the Atlanteans had used this space portal for thousands of years to travel back and forth between Atlantis and Earth instantaneously. He felt excited about the prospect of using this ancient means of intra-galactic transportation and couldn't wait to meet Aunt Maryka and the rest of his father's family.

Interestingly enough, when he and his friends followed Sam and Happy into the portal, he was the topic of conversation between two high-ranking officers of the Atlantean Civil Service Corps. This conversation took place at their Headquarters building on a base at the outskirts of Poseidon.

"Yesterday, I kept an eye on our boy late at night from my office at Piedmont through the surveillance systems I had installed around his dorm," a Colonel told the Commander of the Corps. "I noticed the two cowboys, who gave us all that useful information about the VARS, hanging around his dorm for over an hour."

"What were they doing?"

"I'm not sure. Then, I noticed one of our people keeping an eye on them, too."

"Who was that?"

"Our music teacher at Piedmont, Becksbury; he was hiding in the bushes alongside another dormitory, but I could see him clearly on one of our surveillance screens."

"Why was he keeping track of 'em?"

"I'm not sure."

"So, what did you do?"

"I walked over to Jimmy's dorm to talk to the teacher."

"What did he say?"

"I did not have a chance to talk to him. Before I got there, I saw the two men cross the street and go into the water tower. Shortly thereafter, Becksbury crossed the street and also went into the tower."

"Did you follow 'em to see where they went?" the Commanding General asked.

"Yes, I also went into the water tower and noticed all three of 'em went through our portal."

"And, where did they go?"

"I don't know. I didn't follow 'em here. I went back to my office through the underground passageway and ordered two of my people to watch Jimmy's dorm while I went back to Atlantis."

"We need to know who these men are and why Becksbury was checking up on 'em," the General said, thoughtfully. "Have our people keep all three under close surveillance. Please, let me know right away if they come up with anything suspicious."

"Yes, General."

"Needless to say, I want the boy protected at all costs."

"Be assured, protecting the boy is my number one priority. I should also tell you, I believe that, for whatever reason, while I was in my office, one of our people was in our training room in the admin building. Whoever it was left the lights on."

"Just be very careful, Colonel; we're entering a dangerous time period. There are traitors among the highest levels of our Leadership, who want to hurt the boy and keep him from becoming our Leader. I hope to have all the pieces in place soon to deal with this predicament, but until that time we have to tread lightly when it comes to getting things ready both here on Atlantis and on Earth for the coming confrontation with the VARS."

"Yes, General; and for your information, we have everything ready at Piedmont to acquaint the boy with our planes and spaceships, and other weapon systems at our disposal for countering any Varsian plans to invade Earth."

"That's great, Colonel," the General said, thanking him for the briefing, and excusing himself to attend to Civil Service affairs.

Chapter 17: Planet Atlantis

Maryka was in a tizzy; she had just taken a call on her home communication device from her butler, who had arrived at the Atlantis Space Center, and she could hardly believe what he told her. He and Happy had come back from Earth with three guests in tow—one of whom was her young nephew, Jimmy Starlight.

"Oh, my goodness, how can you two do this to me—my house is not ready for guests!" was all she could say.

Sam explained to her, privately, that Jimmy and his friends had discovered the location of the space portal by themselves and insisted on coming to Atlantis to visit her. Even though she was very excited about finally meeting her late brother's son, she mostly worried about his safety. Maryka had her reasons and knew he would be in harm's way if certain individuals in Poseidon learned of his presence on Atlantis. She couldn't help but think about the warning contained in the Prophecy, *"But beware of your own, for they will try to harm him and keep him from realizing his destiny."*

"Do you want us to teleport over?" Sam asked her, in a low voice. "Or should we take a FlyAway taxi home, so they can take in some of the scenery on the way to your house?"

"No, no…no taxis," she said. "The driver might recognize Jimmy and, then, the news of him being in town will be all over the city in no time. And I don't want the 'Exaggerazzi' camping on our doorsteps."

While the leadership of Atlantis had been mostly silent about the Prophecy, over the past few months a lot of attention had been given to it by the Exaggerazzi—the Atlantean equivalent of the Paparazzi on Earth. Even though

331

they were not nearly as aggressive as their earthly counterparts in getting the latest tell-all pictures of celebrities and other prominent Atlanteans, if a really big story broke, like the fulfillment of an ancient prophecy, they would do their utmost to search it out and snap a few pictures of the story's major partakers. Recently, they had been able to link Jimmy's name specifically to the Prophecy. To Maryka's surprise, her nephew's picture had appeared all over the on-line tabloids and gossip columns. Accompanied by headlines of a soon-to-be Atlantean victory under his leadership over their arch enemy—the VARS—his picture had also graced the outdoor TV news-screens embedded in the outside walls of almost all commercial and office buildings in downtown Poseidon.

"So, you want us to teleport over then," Sam said. "Anytime soon, or do you want us to take it slow, so you can have Elizabeth tidy up a bit?"

The Elizabeth he was referring to was Maryka's housekeeper, who had been with the family for the past three years. Just like Sam and Happy, Elizabeth had worked for Maryka's father, Marcus Starlight, for a few years before his death. After he passed away, she remained in the service of the Starlight family when Maryka employed her—along with Sam and Happy.

"Better come over right away," Maryka said. "And, please, try to keep Jimmy from being recognized by anyone."

Maryka, her three children, and her mother lived in the center of Poseidon, about twenty-five miles from the Space Center. Her husband died tragically about three years ago in a FlyAway accident—not too long after Marcus Starlight passed away. Her house was situated directly behind the Starlight Mansion where Regent Traitus Deliritus resided. When her father, as the Leader of Atlantis, occupied the

Mansion, he had purchased the private residence behind it for Maryka, so he and his wife could be close to her and their grandchildren.

The large Space Center, situated in a suburb of Poseidon on the same airbase as the Headquarters of the Atlantean Civil Service Corps, contained the Atlantean side of the space portal. This was where Jimmy and the others arrived less than a second after they stepped into the portal on Earth and zoomed through spacetime to Atlantis—without the kids having had an inkling they traveled faster than the speed of light. Sam had called Maryka right after they walked through the streaming lights of the portal into the back of a well-lit hangar on the bottom floor of the two-story Space Center. In addition to housing the space portal, the hangar was filled to the brim with shiny planes just like the ones they had seen earlier on the Atlantean Earth Base.

"Are we on Atlantis?" Jimmy asked Sam, when the tall man finished talking to Maryka.

"Yes, we are," he said, "We're at the Atlantean Space Center. Your Aunt wants us to come to her house as soon as possible, so let's hurry outside."

"Just a minute, please," Jimmy said, looking around the large hangar. "How come these planes look exactly like the ones we saw at Piedmont?"

"Because the ones at Piedmont came from here," Happy replied. "We brought them to Earth through this portal."

"Why are they just sitting around here?"

"So we can quickly take 'em to Earth, in case they need more of 'em over there."

"But I don't see any mechanics in here making sure they're ready to go." David said.

"No need to," Sam said. "Just like our FlyAways, these planes constantly check themselves, and if something is wrong, the onboard computer will send a message to whomever needs to know about it—and they will send someone over to quickly fix it."

"What's a FlyAway?" Mirah asked.

"FlyAways are cars that can also fly," Happy replied. "You can drive 'em around, or take 'em into the air and fly to wherever you need to go."

"Isn't it a little dangerous to have all these cars flying around? What if they bump into each other?"

"That won't happen. When our FlyAways take to the air, they're under control of our traffic-management system, which keeps 'em from having accidents."

"I can't wait to ride in one of those," she said.

"Me neither," Jimmy added.

Knowing Maryka wanted him to bring Jimmy over right away, Sam felt impatient. "We really must go, right now," he insisted. "Please, follow us." With the Center's sliding doors closed, Sam and Happy led them outside through the small side door in the front of the building.

When he stepped outside into the bright sunlight, it finally hit Jimmy he had arrived on Atlantis.

Wow, I'm really here on my dad's planet, he thought, *and I got here just the way Tooku said I would. I made friends with Mirah, she helped me find the passageway, it led us to Atlantis, and I found out why Sam and Happy were trying to get a hold of me. Now, all I have to do is to find the Prophecy, and I will learn why I had my strange dreams.*

He made two fists and raised his arms straight up in the air, just like Rocky Balboa did in the movies after he climbed the steps of the Art Museum in Philadelphia. *"We're here, on Atlantis!"* he said to David, lowering his arms and shaking him by the shoulders. *"We're really here!"*

"Yes, we are," David said. "Look at all the stuff around here. What kind of a place is this anyway?"

They stood on a concourse that, except for being much larger, looked just like the one on the Atlantean Earth Base at Piedmont; and it appeared to have been made out of the same rubbery material as well. Around them, dozens of airplanes, shaped like the ones parked inside the Space Center, sat at the edge of the concourse. Several airplanes crossed overhead, while others were in the process of either taking off or landing vertically in their designated areas in the center of the concourse. Having landed, quite a few airplanes taxied slowly towards the large cargo terminals situated just outside the concourse, across from where Jimmy and the others stood.

"We're on Airbase Jupiter," Sam said. "This belongs to our Civil Service Corps; it's the largest airbase on our planet."

"For a large airbase, it's sure quiet around here." David said. Almost every day, he could hear the roar of the jets taking off or landing at Ronald Reagan Airport, not too far from his home in Alexandria.

"You're right; it is quiet. But that's true of all of our airbases; we only fly anti-gravity planes, which don't make any noise at all."

Sam led them along a pedestrian path on the side of the concourse. Before too long, they passed by several buildings similar in shape to the one they just walked out of, but with a few more levels and an outer facade made completely of glass. The translucent glass allowed light to come into the buildings but kept anyone from looking inside.

335

They did not see the person watching them from the top floor of one of the buildings, curious about the children that came out of the Space Center.

"What are those for?" Mirah asked, nodding towards the glass buildings.

"Civil Service," Happy said. "These buildings serve as the offices of our Civil Service Corps."

"And what do they do—this Civil Service Corps?" she also wanted to know.

"They're kind of like your National Guard," Sam said. "On Atlantis, the Corps makes sure our people have their needs taken care of, no matter what. And they also help the people of your planet by sharing our technologies with you and working to keep the peace on Earth, and undo the chaos created by the VARS."

Jimmy noticed Mirah thinking about what Sam said. She started to say something, but then changed her mind and kept quiet.

"So, where are we going?" Jimmy asked, as they continued walking down the path.

"To the main entrance of the base," Sam said. "We have to go there because…"

Jimmy interrupted him before he had a chance to finish his sentence.

"Hey, that looks just like our science building at Piedmont," he said, staring at a Space Needle, towering over the airbase from where it sat in a field a few hundred yards from the concourse.

"That's our control tower," Sam said. "It regulates all the traffic on the base. And the shiny thing on top is a crystal that provides the airbase with all of its electricity."

336

He started to explain once more why they had to walk over to the base's main entrance, but he was again interrupted—this time by David.

"What's that over there?" he said, pointing to his right at the skyline of a large city, glittering on the horizon about twenty-five miles from the airbase.

"That's Poseidon," Happy replied. "That's where Jimmy's aunt lives."

"How are we going to get over there?" Jimmy asked.

"Your aunt wants us to teleport over," Sam replied.

"Tele-what?" Mirah queried.

"Teleport," Sam said.

"What's that?"

"That's when you go from one place to another without moving your feet," David said.

"Yep, that's how we mostly get around here," Happy piped in.

"You guys are confusing me," Mirah said.

Sam quietly explained that on Atlantis, when you need to go somewhere, all you have to do is mentally depict having arrived at your destination and, "voila," you will be there.

"Nah—you're kidding us," Mirah said, laughing.

"No, we're not," Happy said. "That's how we do it."

"How can that be?" Jimmy asked, also finding it hard to believe what he heard.

"We have learned to use our minds to make certain things happen," Sam replied.

"So, you just think about where you want to go, and—'poof'—you're there?"

"That's right, except you have to first visualize having already arrived at your destination and, then, you will instantly go there."

"And how are the three of us going to do that?" David wondered out loud. "How can we visualize something when we don't know where it is we're supposed to go?"

"Don't worry,' Happy said. "We'll all hold hands and travel together."

"But before we do that we must, first, go to the base's main entrance," Sam said, pleased he could finally explain why they had to go there. "We have to go outside the gate," he told them, "because we're not allowed to teleport on or off a public facility—like this airbase—except with special permission of the base commander."

"Why is that?" Mirah asked.

"Because it would be like a nest full of flying ants around here if people pop up all over the place," Sam replied, "and it would be the same inside our office buildings. You can imagine the havoc this would create, and how difficult it would be to keep your mind on your work."

While walking towards the entrance to the airbase, they occasionally came across Atlanteans going in the opposite direction. Almost all of them were dressed in colorful tailored flight suits with the insignia of the Civil Service Corps—two hands reaching for each other— prominently displayed on their chests. A few of the higher- level civil servants wore colorful double-breasted jackets and matching pleated pants. The jackets had stand-up collars and jetted pockets and were also properly adorned with the Civil Service insignia. When the Atlanteans got close, Sam sprang into action, wanting to comply with Maryka's wish not to have anyone recognize her nephew. He quickly moved between Jimmy and the passersby and, after grabbing Happy by the arm, forcefully pulled the chubby man next to him, completely shielding Jimmy from the passersby's view.

As they went by, the Atlanteans always smiled and bowed their heads slightly in their direction.

"Wow, these people are sure friendly," David said, politely nodding his head at them and smiling broadly. "Why are these guys being so nice to us?"

"They're demonstrating appreciation and respect," Sam said, "because they think we've been on special assignment to Earth."

He explained that, because all five of them wore Earth clothing, the Atlanteans believed they just returned from a special mission for the Civil Service Corps to help the people from Earth.

"And because all special missions entail going up against our archenemy, the VARS," he said, "all Atlanteans greatly admire us for doing such work—hence their smiles and gentle bows."

Since kids were normally not involved in special assignments to Earth, Jimmy and his two friends were a real curiosity to the Atlanteans and drew many wondering stares. Sam and Happy, however, kept anyone from getting a good look at Jimmy and making the connection between him and the face on the many posters plastered all around town. But their frantic actions to shield him from view did not go unnoticed by the man who had been watching them from the top floor of one of the office buildings ever since they left the Space Center. And he was determined to find out who these people were and where they came from.

Having arrived at the entrance way to Jupiter Airbase, the three kids couldn't believe what happened right before their eyes on the fifty-foot, covered platform on the side of the road leading into the base. Some of the people standing there, all of sudden, vanished from view—like a bursting soap bubble. Others suddenly materialized out of nowhere and, after stepping off the platform, casually walked onto the base.

"Look, they're teleporting!" Jimmy said, in amazement.

"You're right," Happy said, "And that's what *we're* going to do."

As he watched the people walk onto the airbase, Jimmy realized there were no security guards at the entrance. Recalling the same was true of both Earth's and Atlantis' entrances to the space portal, he was curious as to why the Atlanteans didn't safeguard their all-important facilities.

"Why doesn't anyone keep track of who goes on or off the base?" he asked.

"No need for that," Happy informed him.

"Why not?" Jimmy asked. "Don't you need to safeguard important places?"

"Safeguard from whom?"

"From people—who will take things."

"We don't do that."

"Why not?"

"Because we're not supposed to."

"Atlanteans don't take something just because they're not supposed to?"

"That's right," Happy said, with a cheerful voice. "We don't take anything we didn't pay for."

"You sound just like my uncle," Jimmy said, as he and his friends followed Sam and Happy onto the platform.

"Now we're going to teleport to Aunt Maryka's house," Sam said, as he gathered everyone around him. "Let's all hold hands while the three of you stand right here in between the two of us."

With bated breath, all three kids followed his instructions.

"Please, close your eyes and let your mind go blank," he continued.

Sam took a deep breath and focused his mind on only one thought—all of them having just arrived at the front door to Maryka's house.

A second later, Happy said, jubilantly, "You can open your eyes now—*we are at our destination.*"

At about the same time Jimmy arrived at his aunt's house, Traitus Deliritus received a call from his contact at Airbase Jupiter.

"You're not going to believe who just showed up on Atlantis," an officer in the Atlantean Civil Service Corps told the Regent.

"So why don't you just tell me," Traitus said.

"Jimmy Starlight."

"*No!*"

"Yes, he came here through our space portal with two other kids and two adults I don't know."

"Don't kid me or I'll have your hide!"

"I'm not kidding you; he's here on Atlantis. I saw him from the window of my office building."

"Where exactly is he now?"

"I don't know, they all teleported somewhere from the base entrance."

"Find him; and when you do, let me know immediately. We'll get rid of the little imposter right here, for once and for all!"

"Yes, sir, I'll do that," the officer said before he hung up.

The End

Story Continues In:

Jimmy Starlight and the Galactic Crystal
Book 2: Wander World

In Book 2, Jimmy meets the relatives of his deceased father on Planet Atlantis, and his cousin helps him locate the Sacred Book of History. He sees for himself what the Atlantean Prophecy predicts for his future, and he gets in a struggle for his life with the Regent's assassin. He also finds out why there was a Wander World video in the training room of the admin building of the Piedmont International Academy—a video of the assassination attempt on his life while he was sailing the Chesapeake with his parents.

About the Author

A one-time associate professor of business, A. W. van Rest has traveled the world promoting sustainable economic development and the use of clean energy technologies. He spent time in Tibet working to electrify villages, schools, and clinics using solar energy, and collaborated with local governments in other Chinese regions to implement sustainable energy projects. He advised government agencies in Europe and the Asia-Pacific region in developing clean energy policies and programs. In the United States, he directed national programs to promote the use of energy efficiency and renewable energy technologies. He also headed up an east-coast clean energy center and served as chairman of a mid-Atlantic hydrogen and fuel cell coalition.

This book is his first entry into the science fiction/fantasy world.

www.ingramcontent.com/pod-product-compliance
Lightning Source LLC
Chambersburg PA
CBHW061321170626
46817CB00001B/255